I0708699

THE GREAT SHOUT

SERIES NAME: THE DECEIVED

SERIES NO: 2

BY

TOMM A. BOYER

RELATED TO:

THE GREAT SHOUT (SOUNDTRACK)

AN EP ALBUM

THE GREAT SHOUT

TOMM A. BOYER

PUBLISHED BY

LIGHTHOUSE MANUSCRIPTS LLC

COPYRIGHT © 2024 BY TOMM A. BOYER

Lighthouse Manuscripts™

The Great Shout

Series Name: The Deceived
Series No: 2

Published by Lighthouse Manuscripts LLC
3060 Williams Drive
Suite 300 PMB #1012
Fairfax, VA 22031-4648

All rights reserved. No part of this book may be used in any manner whatsoever, reproduced or transmitted in any form or by any means, electronic or mechanical, including photocopying and recording, or by any information storage and retrieval system, without the express written permission of Lighthouse Manuscripts and/or the author.

Scriptures are the King James Version – Public domain.

This is a work of fiction. Names, places, characters and incidents used or referenced in any manner in this work are either the product of the author's imagination or are used fictitiously, and any resemblance to any actual persons, living or dead, businesses, companies, organizations, entities, events or locales is entirely coincidental.

Warning: The unauthorized reproduction or distribution of this copyrighted work is illegal. Criminal copyright infringement, including infringement without monetary gain, is investigated by the FBI and is punishable up to maximum prison term and maximum fines.

ISBN: 978-1-7358723-3-9
Library of Congress Control Number: 2025924984

Copyright © 2024 by Tomm A. Boyer

Printed in the United States of America

For more information, email: info@lighthousemanuscripts.com

Acknowledgements

◊◊◊

Frank & Sharlene.
Your ministry focused on a group of kids that forced leadership roles, pushed for bold independent thoughts and voices, and showed how to build long meaningful relationships. Also, it was the depth of your teachings that helped unlock my desire to constantly evolve my beliefs and growth.
You both made a difference.

Thank you.

◊◊◊

Charlotte.
When I was young, you spoke a message that said when we operate with full belief and faith, "...we are unstoppable and become WMDs or Weapons of Mass Destruction against the enemy." That message was so powerful that from that point on, I never lacked confidence or felt I didn't belong in a room. While writing this story of Joshua, I'm constantly reminded of this message.
Thank you.

◊◊◊

To
the alien
who helped me reach this level.

Also, when my mother could not walk and was in so much pain, and when our closest just sat back and from a distance told me what I needed to do, you showed up out of nowhere and did what was needed without us even asking. Complete healing was found in your faith and actions.
The world needs that person.

Thank you.

◊◊◊

N.M. aka MASE.
*To **My All Seeing Eye**, I look forward to the heights and elevations we are climbing with this new journey.*

Thank you.

◊◊◊

A Message & Dedication from the Author

Tomm A. Boyer

After I released The Deceived, an atheist who read this book mentioned to me that it was "…an enjoyable read and made [him] question [his] belief." He'd always believed in being a good person but said the events in the novel were very similar to a life experience of his own where he was also accused of something serious that no one that knew him should have believed. But they did anyway. He didn't see any spiritual connections of good versus evil until he read Joshua going through the same. The Deceived, and the novel series are adaptations of many traditional biblical stories combined with my own real life experiences of two opposite forces that no one can deny exists, even if labeled differently (e.g., positive vs. negative). For example, a personal goal can be to reach an elevated mindset. To achieve this, you must avoid people, places, and situations that could distract or preclude you from reaching this goal, so that you can get to a place where you can't be tempted, manipulated, or deceived. But when you reach this place or mindset, your enemy, or evil, will target the minds and emotions of those close to you, such as how they view you or getting them to believe a lie, just like this man I spoke to experienced. One Saturday night before a Sunday service at a new church that I was attending in Pittsburgh, PA, I had a long night of unwise eating and drinking choices. Waking up late and immediately rushing to this service would eventually reveal the consequences of the previous night's decisions. Traditionally, Pentecostal churches request no unnecessary talking, walking, or leaving the sanctuary during the altar call segment of the service or praying for individuals of the congregation. However, this part of the service took longer than typical. After an unbearable forty-five minutes of my stomach churning in agony and pain, I could no longer hold off going to the bathroom. Before I got up to leave, one of the deacons, who was watching me the entire time, incorrectly perceived my visible discomfort, perspiration, and occasional grimace as I was struggling against God's spirit pushing me to go up to the altar for prayer, instead of the truth that I had to go to the bathroom and bad! He came over to my pew, leaned in front of others and loudly said, "Stop quenching and fighting God's spirit boy and go up to the altar for prayer!" I thought, *Dude, if there was ever a time for you not to be wrong in church, it was now.* Being respectful, but also not taking his direction to go up to the altar and risk an accidental consequence within my slacks, I did not respond and endured the pain much longer. When the altar call was finally over, I ran to the exit door of the sanctuary to head straight for the bathroom. But this same deacon jumped in front of me on the way out and yelled for everyone to hear, "See, the devil was upon you and made you miss God's blessing!" I pushed through him just like Lauren did to the police officers in the first novel. When I went back the following Sunday, everyone appeared uncomfortable around me, and no one wanted to sit next to me. From the deacon's misunderstanding and voiced perspective, I was now the boy that had the devil upon him during last Sunday's service. So, even though it was not the truth, it became their reality or their "perceived truth." This was because the perspective that they heard and witnessed was from someone that they knew, trusted, and liked. Now, relate this same principle to a historic event. Hundreds of years ago, did villagers in Honduras live next to an evil or cursed cave because people they knew got sick or died from being in it, or was the cave just filled with harmful radioactive material? Without knowing God's truth, these villagers may have been deceived, even unintentionally. I learned later that some church members, even a few that knew me, months later continued to talk about how I possibly had the devil on me that day, and only one of them asked me about it. Why is that? This was because the deacon's loud words both comforted their own logic of God and gave them an opportunity to apply their despise for the devil. So, there was no need to speak to me. In other words, we rather be deceived by a lie from someone we like or trust that comforts our own logic or desire, than hear the truth from someone else, even from the source. For people in love, life-long friends, or powerful and purposeful organizations, this tool of deception has been used many times by the enemy to cause chaos and destruction.

Joshua faces the same in The Great Shout. A series of lies, ulterior motives, and secrets from organizations and the people he loves. But are they from a dark evil entity, a set of family curses, or simply misunderstood situations? For Joshua, far more is at stake, and the fate of the world is at hand…his. So, what visions are real? What perspectives are true? It is my hope that The Great Shout challenges your own belief no matter what it is, and you desire to know the truth, that you are greater than you think. Below are two narratives to keep in mind while reading this story:

Perspective #1 – Person to Person: *So, you believe some mythical being no one can prove exists, called God? He is all around us, created us, has all knowledge, speaks to us, and provides for us? And you think this is a loving God yet allows pain, suffering, and death, and if we don't do what He wants based on the rules He made up on his own, or if we don't ask for forgiveness, then He's going to punish us or even condemn us to burn in hell fire for eternity? Please explain how this is logical or even love.*

Perspective #2 - Unborn Twin to Unborn Twin: *So, you believe some mythical being that you can't prove exists, called Mother? She is all around us, created us, has way more knowledge than us, speaks to us, and feeds us? And you think that there is this after birth life where we will finally meet Her and she will love us in this new earthly heaven as you call it. Not only that, in this earthly heaven, we will be able to move freely and do unimaginable things that we can't do here in this womb, and Mother will have rules that we must follow that she made up, and will punish us if we don't listen, and even though She's powerful, She will allow injury, pain, and suffering, instead of keeping us in here protected? Please explain how this is logical or even love.*

The truth is not always logical my good friends. If you believe so, then you may be living in a cursed cave. I hope you enjoy The Great Shout.

◊◊◊

This book is dedicated to Isabella Williams Sterling, who died in the Fourth Month on the 15th day, 1864 in Trenton, New Jersey at the age of thirteen.

Chapters

Prologue

Protocol-11

Right after The Great Depression, citing past and horrific pandemics, such as Mt. Toba, the Ice Age, and other past colossal events that could have wiped out mankind forever, a few prominent futurists argued that, as a global society, we must have specific and defined protocols in place to deal with potential world threats and catastrophic events to ensure the survival of the human race. It wasn't until 1949, after the Hiroshima and Nagasaki nuclear bombings, that almost every nation finally agreed with these futurists that, in the event of a global threat to human existence, the whole world must have measures in place to mitigate such possible devastating events. Coincidentally, this was the same year that NATO and other unknown ancillary groups were formed. From either a rogue nation releasing a destructive biological weapon, or a massive meteor impact that wipes out two-thirds of our planet's life and radically changes our climate and atmosphere; or even an alien invasion of life more intelligent than our own, there are now twenty-one strictly classified and defined procedures with agreed upon world diplomatic laws called Global Survival Protocols ("GSPs"), also referred to simply as "Protocols 1 - 21". These twenty-one protocols have been designed, and tested, albeit without your knowledge (e.g., unproven vaccinations, fake terrorist bombings, UFO and counter air-craft tests), and are currently on hold waiting to be activated for such events to occur. With this, all major government leaders, top military officials, and even prominent secret society leaders are debriefed on these Protocols immediately upon inauguration or appointment.

Out of the many protocols created, the least likely or believed to be needed, Protocol-11, was recently initiated. Protocol-11 is the strategic implementation of certain measures to maintain survival during and after the Biblical apocalypse. One of the world's oldest secret societies and religious futurists, called The Circle, has prophesied that this type of event is going to occur soon, resulting in the end of the world. When all the members of this religious order had the exact same vision, that vision has always come true. In almost two thousand years of existence and hundreds of predictions, they have never been wrong. More importantly, they have never predicted the end of the world until now. From trusting The Circle and protecting its anonymity, each major nation's leader has agreed to initiate Protocol-11, and no one knows it. However, with the design of Protocol-11, it is understood that initiating it alone may cause the loss of hundreds of thousands of lives, if not millions, even if it turns out that The Circle's prediction is wrong. Why? Because even though Protocol-11 is designed for the world's protection, it promotes military positioning, weapon mobilization, and power grabs that by default could escalate and bring nations to the brink of a global war.

In "The Great Shout" Joshua finds out why, at the recommendation of world leaders, top secret societies, and major religious organizations, except the Catholic Church, Protocol-11 was initiated. He also finds out that the past week's string of church fires along the Boulevard in Philadelphia, including his mother's previous lengthy disappearances and death, is somehow related to the end of the world prediction and Protocol-11. Therefore, he and Lauren, who is his newfound love, maybe the only ones able to stop it.

Or perhaps, they are the very cause of it.

* * *

The Deceived

From an incredibly young age, Joshua—also called 'Josh' by his family and friends—played the organ and piano at his uncle's church, New

Lighthouse Temple. This church was located along the Boulevard in Northeast Philadelphia, Pennsylvania, and was one of the most active and involved community churches in Philadelphia. His uncle, Jerome 'Jerry' Williams, or simply called 'Pastor Williams' by everyone, was the brother of Joshua's mother, Denise, and pastor of New Lighthouse Temple. No other pastor cared more about the neighborhood and its residents than Pastor Williams. But a month after Joshua's eighteenth birthday, his mother, Denise, died in his very arms at this church. The medical report claimed it was from a heart attack she'd experienced while shouting in praise during a Sunday service.

After Denise's death, Pastor Williams and his wife Angela took Joshua into their home and looked after him. In addition, Bishop Hines, the pastor and bishop of the globally recognized International Covenant Ministries, looked after Joshua as well. This was natural as Bishop Hines was a family friend and former mentor of Pastor Williams. His son, Mike, who was older than Joshua, grew up with Joshua and Joshua's best friend, Monty. The three were inseparable until Mike left for college. After that, Joshua and Monty became even closer friends.

Joshua did not know of his father, nor did he ever care to find out. His mother, Denise, was very attractive, independent, and always out of town chasing some big opportunity, at least that's what she told him. Whenever she went away, she would ask her brother Pastor Williams to watch Joshua. He did not mind. Joshua needed a father figure, and he felt a deep involvement in his church would have a positive influence on him. But Pastor Williams had the same thoughts about Denise as others in their family and neighborhood; because she was secretive about her travels and disappeared frequently, she must be very promiscuous and was not a good mother. From experiencing his mother's death, meeting and falling in love with the very pretty and intelligent Lauren Alexander, who was coincidentally Mike's ex-fiancé, and then being in the wrong place at the wrong time to become the primary suspect of the string of church fires along the Boulevard, Joshua's life would change forever.

In "The Great Shout" Joshua is about to find out the true reason for his mother's repeated disappearances and death; the true reason and evil behind the string of church fires; why he met Lauren and why they may have a connection with distinct abilities, a thousand year old religious secret and conspiracy, and an ancient theory to obtain boundless power. But this knowledge and revelation will come at a great cost, greater than Joshua, local officer Reese, the ATF, their churches, or anyone else could have ever imagined. Who knew that his mother's secret would lead him across the Atlantic Ocean to Rome, Italy with past and present events connected to his mother, Archbishop Bennett, who is Bishop Hines' close friend, the Roman Catholic Church, the religious secret society called The Circle, and an evil so great that nothing like it has been seen in over seventeen hundred years. The string of church fires along the Boulevard in Philadelphia was just the beginning.

The Circle has had a shared vision and recently prophesied the end of the world; and from knowing their hundreds of predictions in their two thousand year existence have never been wrong, all major world leaders agreed to secretly initiate Protocol-11.

"…Woe to the bloody city! I will even make the pile for the fire great!"
-Ezekiel 24:9

1

Remembrance

Philadelphia, PA – The morning after the community revival.
Three days before Hands Across the World.

It was chaos. The church's large, beautiful cathedral ceiling and the colorful pane-glass windows along the high walls only amplified the sounds of the screams, the yelling, and the noise of objects falling to the ground. The heavy dark smoke was visible in the air. They used their clothes and hands to cover their mouths as they attempted to escape. The large and previously accommodating sanctuary now appeared to be too small for the filled church, way above capacity. Joshua stood in the middle aisle of the church focused on the evil enemy that held strong in front of the altar with his tight grip on Lauren.

Lauren screamed, "Joshua!" He ran toward the altar to save her, but the crowd was too thick. The more he pushed his way through the crowd, the more people appeared running against him. As more people got in his way pushing to get out, Lauren and the evil enemy appeared further and further away. Greater frustration raged within Joshua. Then, the evil enemy's position, with Lauren in its grasp, became a faint small image too far away. As Joshua grabbed toward their direction amongst the crowd and the monstrous heavy smoke, he painfully gave up the chase. His spirit dwindled and agony set deep into his bones. Then, when he saw someone else, standing behind the altar, watching them the whole time, he became very weak and fell to the ground, vision dark.

Joshua's eyes slowly reopened to a hazy overcast. He awakened confused, lying on the ground of a cemetery. He thought, *It was only a dream.* Once his eyes focused, he propped himself up with his hands. He noticed an upright headstone situated directly in front of him. It read, 'Lauren Ann Alexander – *A Gift to This World, Now A Gift to Heaven.*' He felt his heart collapsed like a bridge with too much weight. He violently pounded the ground as he cried. When he heard a noise in the distance, he regained his composure, and then whispered to Lauren's headstone, "My soul loves your soul, Lauren. My soul still loves you." Then, a tall slender man with boots that had been steadily used, overalls, and a shovel in his hand walked to the side of Joshua. Joshua knew it was one of the cemetery workers.

"I will be gone in a few minutes," said Joshua, not looking up.

'Take your time, Joshua. But why do you keep weeping for the living among the dead?" asked the man.

Joshua quickly looked up at him in amazement. The man's face was dark and distorted, out of focus. Then, the man looked down at Joshua, and said, "Joshua, have you checked on your mother? She's been trying to give you a message."

Joshua closed his eyes and then quickly reopened them to focus, but the man was gone. He then thought, *My mother. I need to check on her.* He got up from the grave and ran out of the cemetery all the way to his mother's place of work, the Penn Fresh grocery store. The distance seemed too short. It only took him less than a minute to approach the automatic entrance doors. Right before he entered the store, he slowed down, but not to a complete stop, as he remembered that his mother, Denise, was dead. He'd remembered that she died in his arms in his uncle's church, New Lighthouse Temple. So, why would he be running to check on her at work? His momentum and curiosity forced him through the entrance anyway. He softly greeted the front-end workers and a few customers with a smile, and kept the same slow pace until he got back to the deli department. To his surprise, there she was, his mother in her work uniform and name tag just like he remembered. She was squatted down close to the ground placing pre-made hoagies in one of the low refrigerated cases.

"Mom?" said Joshua, hesitantly as he could not believe it was her, alive. She turned toward Joshua and smiled but then kept working. He controlled the tears, wiped his nose and face with his sleeve. He was nervous, but spoke again. "How are you here? I thought you were…"

She immediately cut him off by turning her head to him again, put her finger over her lips, and said, "Shhhh…It's almost time Joshua. Remember to stack them side by side, soldier-course style, Joshua. *That will make them all strong and on one accord.* Be strong and of good courage, only be thou strong and of good courage." Then, she went back to stacking the hoagies in the case.

Not focused on his mother's words, Joshua spoke again, but louder, "I missed you so much. We all miss you."

She then looked up at the ceiling and said, "Stack them all side by side before it's too late, Joshua. The dark angel is free. I held it back, as long as I could, but the dark angel is free."

Suddenly, a deafening thunder occurred so loud and strong that it vibrated throughout the grocery store building and within Joshua's entire upper body. He looked up at the ceiling with caution at the noise and the rumble. When he looked back down to his mother, she was gone. Then, the store building began to violently shake. It was an earthquake. Joshua pointlessly grabbed closely onto the case and squatted down to the ground with his head down. Food and other products fell from the gondolas and shelves. Parts of the ceiling broke apart and fell to the floor. Then, Joshua heard a piercing scream.

* * *

With the piercing scream, Joshua jumped up from the hospital bed. It was another dream. This time a dream within a dream. He was currently in his hospital bed. The same bed and room that he stayed in overnight after the New Lighthouse Temple church fire that he and Lauren tried to prevent during the community revival. Unfortunately, his uncle's church was lit up in flames, but the evil enemy was finally stopped and revealed. So, he'd thought. Joshua turned to his right side facing the large wall window with his head on the pillow as he reminisced about the past and recent events. *How he used to play the organ for his uncle, Pastor Williams. But now their church, New Lighthouse Temple, victim of the evil enemy's power and destroyed by the fire, just like a few other churches along the Boulevard. How he loved playing backup accompanying his uncle while he preached. Most likely the only time they ever had a connection. How Bishop Hines, who was their family's closest friend and Pastor Williams' former mentor, was always there for him and his mother. And even though he was the great bishop of International Covenant Ministries, world-renowned and respected all over the world, he always had time to help out Pastor Williams with his church. More sincerely, Bishop Hines was extensively there for Joshua when his mother, Denise, died. And then most unexpectedly, through Bishop Hines, Joshua met Lauren, Lauren Alexander. She was the only person that Joshua ever loved other than his family. When they were next to each other, he could feel his soul loving her soul. He thought, Lauren, so fiery, yet so stubborn. So forceful, yet so intelligent.* Joshua laughed quietly at the thought of what person, other than Lauren, could anger his meek uncle so much, but also gain the respect of Bishop Hines even over his own. He realized that Bishop Hines was like a father to Lauren. But Bishop Hines was also like a father to Joshua. He connected more with Bishop Hines than his uncle. His mother disappeared for weeks at a time for what she always excused as "a big opportunity." Joshua then remembered *how Lauren stayed by his side in the underground tunnel. How she then ran along the Boulevard with him above ground, while he ran underground. They ran step by step, parallel to each other to each church. How she then fought for him against anyone that stood in their way, including the evil enemy, which was not what he thought, not what anyone thought--not even the police and ATF. She saved Joshua in so many ways, and he saved* her in the end. But not without a cost. Her eyes were damaged in the fight and Joshua had no idea if she would ever see again. Additionally, he still wasn't sure if he saved her from the fire with some type of supernatural power or was it from the help of spirits or angels; or perhaps, it was all just hallucinations, and he saved her from pure fear and his dramatically increased strength from endorphins. Either way, he unfortunately could not save her eyes from harm, now blind and bandaged up from their fight against the evil enemy. Joshua then thought, *"Oh, Lauren! Are you okay? Will you be able to see again?' Where are you?* He missed her greatly and would give anything to embrace her right now. He whispered to himself, *"I should've ridden in the ambulance with her. I should've never let her out of my sight, not for one moment!"* After the fight with the evil enemy, Lauren was taken to the same hospital and put in separate ambulances and separate hospital rooms. Just a few hours ago, she was taken from the hospital without his knowledge by Bishop Hines' colleague and close friend, Archbishop Bennett of the Catholic Church. But he doesn't know where or why. He regretted falling asleep or wished he'd stayed in the room with her. That way, he could have prevented her from being taken or at least know where she was. At that moment, Joshua noticed a small piece of paper on the meal tray next to his bed. He reached over and grabbed it. He wondered why he didn't notice it before, or maybe someone placed it there while he slept. He opened it up. It was a note from Lauren. But he could tell someone else wrote it for her. It read:

'The day may change, but never the plan.
No matter what happens, for you and by you,
I will forever stand.'
-Your twin soul, Lauren.

Even though he saved her life, the guilt of not doing everything he could to protect her from injury, he quietly wept, and said out loud, "I will never let that happen again!"

Then, Joshua's best friend, Monty, walked in and joked, "Wow, Josh. I never knew a Philadelphian hero could be such a crybaby!" Now, everyone in Philadelphia called Joshua "Josh" except for Bishop Hines and Lauren. Joshua didn't like the sound of his full name. But for some reason, when Bishop Hines or Lauren said it, it sounded genuine.

Joshua quickly put the note under his covers, wiped the tears from his eyes with his hands, and then responded, "Monty, you're such an ass! No wonder you have no friends."

"Well, I think I got at least one, sitting right here in this hospital. Seriously, Josh. You can cry all you want. Just don't expect to use my sleeve to blow your nose." Joshua did not acknowledge his joke.

"You know, you and that girl Lauren are the talk of the neighborhood," said Monty. "After the fire, everyone stayed in the streets all night sharing different stories about how you two solved the mystery and saved our neighborhood. Of course, there are some embellishments, admittedly some from me, of how you two stole police files, conducted your own detailed investigations, and then knew when, where, and the exact time the next fire was going to strike!" exclaimed Monty, proud of himself for having a connection with the two heroes.

"Umm…it was not quite like that," responded Joshua as he pondered the hundreds of other story variations that would be told.

"It doesn't matter. Your story will go down in Philadelphian history."

"If you say so,"

"What, you're not going to call me an idgit? Speaking of nicknames, where *is* Wonder Woman? Is she okay? I heard that her eyes got burned by the fire," said Monty referring to Lauren.

Joshua did not want to respond. "I don't know," he said, hesitantly.

"What do you mean you don't know?" yelled Monty.

"Keep it down you idgit! We're in a hospital."

Monty relentlessly continued. "You mean you don't know what floor she is on, what room she is in…if she went home…if she…"

Joshua interrupted, "Enough with the twenty questions. I just don't know," said Joshua with a forceful tone. He paused, then took a deep breath, and continued with desperation in his voice, "She was here last night; and when I went to go see her in her hospital room, she was gone." Monty wanted to interrupt with more questions, but he refrained as he finally saw the pain and frustration Joshua was experiencing. Joshua continued, "All I know is that Bishop Hines' friend Archbishop Bennett was in her room when I went in there, and he said they took her to wherever Bishop Hines was. Then I got this weird call from Bishop, and he just said be ready and he will pick me up soon."

Monty's remaining questions left his body. He was speechless. He then sat in the chair beside Joshua's bed and grabbed the television remote, turning it on. As he flipped through the channels, Joshua noticed something on one of the channels. "Wait go back!" said Joshua with a raised voice. Monty flipped back one channel to Live News 10. Both Joshua and Monty's eyes widened as they watched the channel. The news cameras were filming outside on a familiar street with a house on fire. Fire trucks, ambulances, and police were all on the scene in view of the camera as well. "Turn it up!" exclaimed Joshua.

They caught the audio in the middle of the dialogue.

"…like you said Talia, it's hard to believe that these fires are not over. We are standing a block away from the 700 Block of Prout Avenue where there's a house on fire and could possibly set fire to its adjoining homes as well. Witnesses and residents of this small Philadelphia neighborhood section say they heard a loud explosion and when they came outside, the home was on fire," said Calvin Leech, field reporter for Live News 10.

"Do they know if anyone was inside at the time of the explosion?" asked Talia Jones, Live 10 News anchor.

"No, and the police are keeping everyone away and not answering any questions. But witnesses say the explosion was very loud, and part of the home was immediately destroyed and set on fire. If anyone was in there, it is highly unlikely that they survived."

Joshua wondered if this explosion occurred around the same time that he heard one in his dream.

"Calvin. I'm getting reports confirming that this is Jerome Williams' house, pastor of New Lighthouse Temple, whose church was set on fire last night during the community revival. And that this is the same uncle of Joshua Williams, who was the center of investigation of the string of church fires," said Talia Jones.

"That is correct, Talia. Our research, Through the app LandGlide, we confirmed that this is Pastor Williams' home. Prayers are going up all over this community with the hope that no one was inside. I would also like to add that it looks like the entire police force is out here in full force. That may be because there's a police car in front of the home taped off and looks like it's being investigated as well. We're too far away to see or confirm anything, but one of the neighbors told us that an officer was found dead in that car..."

Joshua's hospital room was empty. Before field reporter Calvin Leech finished his sentence, Joshua had already ripped the monitoring wires off his arm, put on his pants, placed Lauren's note in his pocket, then grabbed his shirt, and quickly ran out of the room with Monty. They were long gone when the floor doctor, nurse, and a police officer arrived at Joshua's room. Then, Joshua and Monty made it down the stairwell steps out to the hospital parking lot.

"Give me the keys!" yelled Joshua, as he put on his shirt following Monty running to his car. Monty was still in possession of Joshua's car, ever since he dropped Lauren off at Joshua's former job, the Penn Fresh grocery store, the same place of employment where his mother Denise worked before she passed away. Without hesitation, Monty threw Joshua the keys. Joshua caught them, unlocked the doors and they quickly jumped inside as Joshua then sped off to his uncle's house.

"Slow down Josh," said Monty calmly, but he was not calm at all. Not only was he scared of getting into an accident, but he feared what they would find out once they got to Joshua's uncle's house. He couldn't imagine Joshua going through more unfortunate events, especially more death. After a few minutes, they arrived at the scene but a few blocks away from the house, as fireman crews had pushed the area back for fear of another explosion. Monty's heart sank into the pit of his stomach as he saw the enormous amount of police officers and EMTs on the street. Joshua put the car in park, immediately jumped out, and ran toward the house. He could see the dark smoke rising from the home filling the air. Smoke but no flames. When Joshua reached the police barrier, he was grabbed forcefully by two police officers.

"Hey! Stop, young man! You can't get in there!" yelled one of the officers. Joshua fought their hold and attempted to break through.

"That's my uncle's house! I live there!" yelled Joshua.

One of the officers, who knew Joshua and his uncle, finally realized that it was him. "Josh!" said the officer. "Listen to me. Please calm down. You can't go in there, right now. There might be another explosion, any minute. Just hold on…let the experts handle this." Joshua stopped fighting but still held his anger.

"Officer Reese!" yelled the officer holding Joshua, calling for more assistance. Officer Reese was one of Pastor Williams' close friends. Unfortunately, he was one of many who did not believe Joshua's innocence regarding the string of church fires. When Officer Reese heard his name, he was talking to another officer and turned towards the voice. He saw Joshua being held back by the two officers. Just like many of the officers on the scene, Officer Reese's eyes were red and slightly swollen. They'd been crying over the loss of one of their own, along with a community leader that they worked with and loved. Their split emotions of sadness and anger filled the air.

Officer Reese walked over to Joshua and the officers, and said, "I'll take it from here gentlemen." The officers let Joshua go and walked away. When Joshua saw Officer Reese's sullen face, he knew his worst fear had happened.

"I'm sorry Josh. They're both gone," Officer Reese was referring to Joshua's uncle and aunt, Pastor Williams and his wife Angela. He continued, "They were great community members and activists who helped save so many in the neighborhood. Just like you, Josh." A few years ago, Joshua felt the pain of losing his mother, losing her in his very arms. But the pain that he felt in his heart at that moment was now multiplied to the tenth power. Joshua cried. Officer Reese embraced him. Then, after only a few seconds, Joshua looked at his uncle's house and remembered that before he was rescued from his uncle's church during the fire, he had turned around and thought he saw the image of a person or something worse behind the altar of the church watching them amid the fire and flames. It was not Lauren or the arsonist. He remembered how he thought it was staring at him with pure hate and evil through the flames, and with no concern for the fire around it. Pastor Williams told Joshua that he saw the very same thing when he looked through the church window to check on Joshua and Lauren. So, Joshua knew that this mystery was not over. More importantly, something was after him and killing everyone that he loved. Joshua then broke Officer Reese's embrace and screamed, "Agghhhhhhh!"

2

Dark Action

A few hours earlier.

Pastor Williams walked into his Philadelphia row home, situated just a few blocks off the Boulevard. His dog Rocky, a young Sprollie, eagerly waited to greet him before he put the key in the door. "Hello, Rocky," said Pastor Williams, unenthusiastically as he gave Rocky a quick pet. Even though he was emotionally drained from the horrific events of the evening; the community revival, his church being set ablaze, and Joshua and Lauren ending up in the hospital, he knew Rocky would not leave him alone unless he received immediate attention. Right after Rocky greeted him, his wife, Angela, got up from the sofa and did the same, but with a soft hug and a kiss on his cheek. She'd been sitting in the living room reading to pass the time and take her mind off her worry until he got home.

"You were at the hospital all that time?" asked Angela.

"Yes," responded Pastor Williams.

"Shary and Franklin just left," said Angela, referring to their next-door neighbors, who were also ministers.

"Were they there tonight?" asked Pastor Wiliams.

"No. Thankfully, they were working a revival at a church in Mt. Airy Are you okay, honey?"

Pastor Williams did not immediately respond. He thought, "*Thank goodness they were not part of the community revival. They would have been working in the church assisting and no doubt been caught up in the aftermath too.* He then went over to his office desk which was also in the living room and sat down. He'd remembered Lauren sitting there for the very first time. He could not think of anyone else who came into his home and sat at his desk. He thought, *Lauren's first time here and she sits at my desk.* Apparent to him now, he smiled at her free will and how far it had gotten her in life. But then, that thought turned to grief and guilt on how he now thought he was wrong about her. He communicated this to Angela.

"I was so focused on Lauren and how her beliefs and opinions were so different than mine; I automatically considered her as the culprit. I didn't see the real enemy. The enemy who I let into our church, who I fed, who I thought was my friend." He paused for a few seconds and then continued, "I used to be able to discern everyone and everything around me, even felt like I could see things coming a mile away, a bit of prophecy. It's one of the things that I thought made me a good Pastor and a great community leader. Am I getting old? Have I lost it?"

Angela walked over to Pastor Williams and sat on his lap and kissed him on his forehead. "Don't be so hard on yourself. You've been an outstanding leader. Even the ATF and the mighty Officer Reese got it wrong too."

"Well, you didn't think Josh or Lauren was involved and treat them like criminals, like I did," he said, feeling guilt.

Angela smiled. "I guess the motherly instinct in me would not let me think of those two as suspects. Also, Josh has always been a good kid, and love always wins, right?"

Pastor Williams smiled and nodded in agreement. But then he pulled away with a concerned look on his face. Angela clearly noticed, "Okay, what's wrong?" He did not immediately respond. "Jerry...that neighborhood evil is dead or locked up, right?" asked Angela, arms folded.

"Well, after I spoke to Josh, Reese showed up at the hospital, and we sat in the cafeteria and he got me up to speed on all the events, from the very first fire until now."

"And."

"And, I am still having a hard time wrapping my mind around everything and what he said."

She vocalized her impatience. "For instance, for example, such as..."

"First, all the church fires. How could that evil thing do all of that? Think about it. Reese said there were satanic rituals and a bunch of other crap involved, right in our own neighborhood, under our own neighborhood; and no one knew..."

Angela chimed in before he finished his thought. "You won't always know why honey. With a hard life and Satan in their ear, sometimes the only options they see are never the right ones. Something else?"

"I hate to bring this up, but all I keep hearing is Josh's voice."

"Josh's voice?" she repeated, perplexed.

"Remember when Denise died, and Josh was there holding her in his arms on the floor of our church, yelling at me to do something?"

"How could I forget? His voice pierced straight through my heart. Nothing worse than hearing a child cry in grief like that, especially over his mother."

"Do you remember what he said?" When she did not promptly respond, he continued, "He looked at me with that pain and tears in his eyes and yelled, 'Where's God now? Where's all the faith you talk about?' I froze unable to help him." Angela looked away as tears formed in her eyes. Pastor Williams continued. "Just a few hours ago,

Josh yelled that same cry for help in my church, within the same walls. But this time, instead of a cry for help for his mother, it was a cry for Lauren, as they were stuck in my church. It pierced my heart and soul just the same. And again, there was nothing I could do. I prayed for Denise, but she still died. I prayed for the fires to stop, but they didn't. I prayed for everyone's safety, but people that I know and love, even within my own congregation— and they still got injured, a few even died. Maybe, I don't have enough godly power or faith anymore. Am I no longer strong enough to overcome evil? What's the point if my faith can't overpower someone else's free will?"

"Everyone has unfettered free will, honey."

"But what's the point of my faith if someone else's free will wins?"

"That's an interesting thought, my wise and intelligent Pastor Jerome Jerry Williams," said Angela jokingly. "I hear a new sermon coming your way. Why don't you seek God on that very thought? You know He always reveals some magical things when you do."

"Ain't that the truth. What would I ever do without you?"

"Maybe live a miserable life of loneliness and regret, that's what!"

Pastor Williams laughed. Suddenly, the phone on Pastor Williams' desk rang loudly.

"The only person who calls that old archaic landline of yours is Reese. So, you better answer it," said Angela, annoyed.

"He's a good friend because he's the only one who knows I hate talking on that complicated cellular phone."

"It's late, and just now you sounded really old," joked Angela. She got up from his lap and walked upstairs. Pastor Williams smiled at her; and picked up the phone on the fourth ring while he petted Rocky, who went over to him right after Angela left.

"Hey Reese," said Pastor Williams answering the phone.

"Hey Pastor," said Officer Reese.

"I just walked in the door. Do you have our evil arsonist locked up and secure?"

"Well, that's what I am calling you about…"

Pastor Williams interjected. "The last time you called this phone and said those words, things ended up going from bad to worse."

"We now have concrete evidence that there is another person or another thing involved in all of this."

"Person or thing?" Pastor Williams phrased as question, perplexed.

"Trust me, I know how that sounds. But after everything that has happened and how wrong I was about the fires, and what the community is saying about Josh and Lauren and this so-called supernatural power that they had earlier this evening, I'm not ruling anything out. Besides, what we are uncovering doesn't make logical sense for these events to be from one person."

Before Officer Reese finished this sentence, Pastor Williams was already in deep thought. He envisioned how early that evening he stood outside his church while it was on fire, looking through the window and seeing Joshua, Lauren, and the evil that caused the fires. But when he looked further into the church, he saw something else. He could barely see through the flames, but he knew it was the image of another person or being. It stood behind his pulpit unbothered by the fire, watching. Even though Pastor Williams wasn't sure who or what he was seeing, he knew it was nothing but true evil. While Officer Reese was still talking, he thought, *Is this the person or thing that Reese is referring to?*

Since Officer Reese heard nothing but silence from Pastor Williams, he pushed for a response, "You there, Pastor?"

"Yes. I hear you."

"So just as a precaution, we are going to send a cruiser to your street to keep watch."

"You really think that's necessary, Reese?"

"I rather one of our men be there and not needed, than needed and not be there."

"Good point. Well, can you tell me what concrete evidence you have that is causing this belief that someone else is involved?"

"What I can tell you is that more than one person was hanging out in the Underground Tunnels going from church to church. When we asked the suspect about this, he said it was his *dark angel* visiting him and helping him with the fires."

"*Dark angel.* What does that mean?"

"Not sure. So, until we get more information on this, we are under the assumption that this is not over."

"Agreed."

"In any event, you should be very proud of your nephew. Josh saved so many lives, and I also believe that Lauren girl had a lot to do with it too. It looks like Bishop Hines brought her around just at the right time, right?"

"It appears so," said Pastor Williams being forced to remember again about his bad judgment of Lauren thinking she was the culprit.

After a few more questions unanswered, Pastor Williams hung up the phone and turned off the two lamps that Angela had on while she was reading. He grabbed the railing to go up the steps, but he really didn't need its help. It just gave him an excuse to go up slowly enough to prepare his words and thoughts before discussing this new unsettling information with Angela. When he made it up to the top, he let out such a loud sigh that even Rocky barked from downstairs.

"Oh, Lord. What is it?" asked Angela, as Pastor Williams walked into the bedroom.

"You want to take a guess?" he responded while changing his clothes into his typical t-shirt and bottom shorts sleeping gear.

"Why don't you wear pajamas like the rest of the world, Jerry?"

"The day I start wearing pajamas is the day that you can officially call me old." Pastor Williams continued with a demonstration joke, acting like his hand had an imaginary phone in it, and raising it up to his ear. He cleared his throat, then said, "Hold on Officer Reese and distinguished ATF agents while I change out of my PJs into something more professional. Then we can go catch these evil suspects!"

He expected laughter, but she just shook her head, and said, "So corny. What did Officer Reese say, young man?"

"He said, there may have been another person involved in all of this. A *dark angel*."

"A dark what the what?" said Angela, baffled.

"I have no idea what that means, either. With that, they don't think this is over. So, Reese is sending over a police car to sit in front of our house as a precaution."

"Oh great! I feel safer already," she replied, sarcastically.

Through their slightly opened bedroom window, they heard a car pull up on the street. Pastor Williams looked out the window as he pulled up his shorts, now fully dressed for bed. "That's him alright." As the officer parked, he noticed Pastor Williams in the window and waved. Pastor Williams waved back then pushed down the window fully shut and closed the blinds. He pulled back the covers and got in bed with Angela. She leaned over and gave him a kiss. He then said, "I love you. Everything is going to be okay." Angela then smiled and turned over facing away from him.

* * *

After some time had passed, both Pastor Williams and Angela were sound asleep. Pastor Williams was snoring, but being married for so many years, Angela slept right through it. Rocky remained downstairs in the living room, half-awake in his large-cushioned floor bed appearing to fight sleep. Rocky then heard a noise and perked up with his nose pointed to the ceiling. He got up and walked along the wall from the living room to the kitchen to the back door. Then, Rocky started to bark.

* * *

Just moments before this, the patrol officer sat in the police car listening to soft music from his cell phone through his Bluetooth earpiece. He had his driver's side door window all the way down and only one earpiece in the right ear so that he could hear any noise from outside his patrol car. After a few moments, he did hear a noise. He poked his head outside the car window and looked around. Not noticing anything, he quickly pulled his head back in the window and flopped his head hard back onto the headrest. He sighed as he looked at the time on his phone. After one minute passed, he then heard another noise. This time, he took out his earpiece. It sounded like it came from the back of his car. The officer looked in the rearview mirror and saw nothing. He then looked in his side mirror and adjusted the setting to look down at the car's side panel and ground. Again, he saw nothing. The officer felt more apprehension but not enough to get out and check. But suddenly, as he went to flop back on his headrest like before, a knife quickly reached through the open window and cut the officer's throat, right before his head hit the headrest. The quick slashing of his throat caused his body to fall toward the passenger seat without a sound, or at least not loud enough to be heard by anyone in the homes.

* * *

After that moment, Rocky continued to bark. But it wasn't a forceful bark. It was a friendly bark, but loud enough to be annoying and wake up Angela, and maybe a few close neighbors. But Pastor Williams continued to snore like a bagpipe with a rock stuck in it. Angela violently shook him to awaken.

"Jerry. Get up! Rocky's barking!"

Pastor Williams awakened and heard Rocky barking. "What's wrong with that dog, at this hour?" he questioned as he looked at the clock on his nightstand.

"It sounds like he's in the kitchen," said Angela, worried.

Pastor Williams got out of bed and put on his slippers. "Well, it doesn't sound like he's barking at an intruder," referring to how loud and forceful Rocky's bark can get when he feels threatened by another dog or a conspicuous person.

"Maybe it's Franklin and Shary coming back," suggested Angela.

* * *

Since Franklin and Shary Fullerton spent a lot of time with Pastor Williams and Angela in their backyard. They would sometimes knock on their back door when they wanted to say hi or talk. They were both biblical scholars and would talk for hours with Pastor Williams and Angela about God, their church, and seemingly easy solutions to the current-day problems of the world. In addition, they were also members and one of the biggest supporters of Pastor Williams' church. Right before Pastor Williams arrived back from the hospital to check on Joshua, they had already kept Angela company for a few hours. So, Angela thought that they might still be up and knocking wanting an update; especially since her husband just got home, and possibly seeing a police car outside. Within their church's denomination, Franklin and Shary were also considered to have the gift of prophecy, which according to the Bible, they had the ability to foresee the future. They would run church revivals and people would stand in line for their turn to be told their future, or maybe something they needed to do to receive God's blessing or direction. Sometimes, this line of people would get ignored while Franklin and Shary looked through the crowd and selected someone not in the line, that they felt God's spirit leading to them. Before Joshua was born, Pastor Williams was just an associate minister at Bishop Hines church. They were all leading a prophetic night revival when Joshua's mother, Denise, showed up at the service. The church had well over three hundred people in attendance with packed pews. Others were standing against the wall, praising God, or sitting in the back watching the miracles happen, or just listening to musicians while they played shouting music, which this time sounded more like contemporary jazz, just played at a faster beat. That night, Shary noticed Denise sitting in the back of the church, amongst the crowd. She stared at Denise for a few seconds and then looked over at her husband, Franklin. From their connection, he could tell that Shary noticed Denise. He nodded his head yes to her in silent agreement. Shary walked past the line of people to the back of the church and stretched her right hand out to Denise for her to come up. Denise complied, grabbed her hand, and walked up to the front of the church. With one of her hands raised high up in the air and then immediately put down, Shary commanded the musicians to stop playing. The church was silent. Shary then put the microphone to her mouth, and said, "My sister. I can see that God has one of the greatest callings on your life. So, neglect not the gift that is within thee," said Shary referencing, First Timothy Chapter Four Verse Fourteen. Even though Denise had no clue what she meant, Denise stood with her eyes closed, as she thought that's what she was supposed to do to receive the message from God through Shary. Shary continued, "The gift that God has given you is without repentance; but with repentance, it can be one of the greatest gifts that this world has ever seen. You shall also bear a child and that child will have even a greater calling." Then Shary paused for a moment, and said, "The Spirit of God is telling me that this child shall cause this world to experience the full presence and power of God. Your presence, Denise, will be like rain replenishing those around you.

But your child's voice shall be mighty, and like thunder." The intensity and anointing of her words were so great that many people immediately yelled out in praise or passed out. Denise remained silent and calm. Then Shary whispered into Denise's ear, and suddenly, Denise passed out, slain by the Spirit of God. The crowd surrounded her with praise! Pastor Williams was there that night. Still to this moment, he always wondered what Shary quietly said to Denise. But he never asked, nor did Denise ever tell.

* * *

Next door, Shary could hear Rocky barking. "Do you hear that?" asked Shary to Franklin.

"It's just Rocky barking," said Franklin.

"Okay, but do you feel that?"

"Feel what?"

"Feel that presence. Next door. Something is very wrong, Franklin,"

"That dog barks all the time. I'm sure it's nothing." said Franklin, nonchalantly and tired.

* * *

Rocky continued to bark while Pastor Williams made haste to go downstairs. Angela frustrated, said, "Yes, that dog always barks. But, at this hour, Jerry?"

"Maybe he's hungry," he replied as one last attempt to avoid checking.

"I doubt it—and you know very well, I'm not going down there!"

Pastor Williams sighed as he had given up the fight and walked into the hallway. He pierced down the steps in the hope of seeing Rocky at the bottom, and back to normal. But with no success. Just another bark coming from the kitchen near the back door. He then grabbed the rail, and as soon as he took his first step going down, Rocky's barking oddly stopped. Pastor Williams paused his movement.

"What is it?" asked Angela concerned. Pastor Williams did not re-

22

spond. He could hear Rocky now panting in excitement. Pastor Williams wondered if someone had walked in. If someone did, Rocky must have been familiar with this person. There is no way he would have stopped barking over a stranger. Then, Pastor Williams continued cautiously down the steps and hesitantly said, "Hello. Is somebody there?" No one responded. When his feet planted on the main floor, there was a sudden loud crack that came from the kitchen, very similar to the sound of a bone breaking. Rocky then let out a painful whimper. Pastor Williams' face dampened in fear. Angela heard the same.

"Jerry!" yelled Angela in fear.

Either from fear or instinct to protect Angela, Pastor Williams ran up the steps. But it did not matter. The dark angel caught up with him and filled the house with its terror.

3

Ruination

Present Day – Philadelphia, PA.
Three days before Hands Across the World.

Firefighters extinguished the final flames of the house. But smoke still filled the air while a crowd filled the streets all in disbelief of another fire and loss of life. News reporters were on the scene.

"I'm Calvin Leech reporting from Live 10 News on the street of Prout Avenue, located just off the Boulevard. Just last night, these streets were filled with people from the community revival. But continuing the string of church fires, another church, New Lighthouse Temple, was set ablaze. Today, there's another fire, but this time a resident's home. The home of the prominent minister and community activist, Pastor Jerry Williams, where earlier, it appeared that two bodies were pulled from the burning blaze. The bodies are believed to be those of Pastor Jerry Williams and his wife Angela Williams. We also believe that an officer was watching the home last night in his patrol car and was also killed. But be advised, the police have not confirmed any of this to us." Calvin Leech and other news reporters continued their stories to the cameras while Joshua sat in the back of an ambulance next to Monty, silent. Monty had no clue what to say, nor did he want to. Every time he thought of something, he foresaw it coming out wrong. Nearby, Officer Reese stood on the sidewalk talking to the other police officers and plotting how they were going to make the unknown criminal eventually pay for killing one of their own and a key leader of their community and his wife. Shary and Franklin walked up to him.

"Hello, Officer Reese," said Shary.

"Hello," he replied, acknowledging them both while Franklin nodded. "Thank you for your statement and cooperation earlier."

"Is Josh in there?" asked Shary, as she tried to look in the ambulance.

"Yes. But I don't think it's a good time for you to talk to him right now," replied Officer Reese, forcefully.

"Please," said Shary. This time with a soft tone, as she placed her hand on his shoulder. "I'll just be a few minutes. He needs some motherly comfort, right now. Don't you think?" Officer Reese paused with reserve. "Just for one minute, Reese," she pleaded, convincingly.

"Okay. But be quick. I don't need any reporters seeing him getting upset and then they start filming that shi…oh sorry." Officer Reese remembered that they were both ministers. He continued, "…and then it goes viral. You know how things can get out of hand."

"I do. Thank you, Reese."

Shary then hopped up into the back of the ambulance truck to speak to Joshua. Franklin did his job as her partner and reengaged Officer Reese and the officers in small talk taking their attention off his wife and her discussion with Joshua. Joshua noticed it was her and immediately greeted her with a half-smile.

"Monty. Can you give us a moment?" asked Shary.

"Sure. I need to stretch my legs anyway," said Monty. "Do you want anything when I come back Josh, like water or a snack or something?"

"No thanks," said Joshua.

Monty got up and jumped out of the ambulance. Shary then immediately sat next to Joshua. She leaned over and gave him a big hug. He felt her warmth.

"You know, I watched you grow up so fast living at your uncle's house, especially after your mother died. God, I miss her," said Shary, softly. Joshua just listened as he looked away. She continued, "Some nights, I'd look out my window and see you and Monty right down this street, smoking who knows what." Joshua looked up in surprise waiting for her to scold him for smoking weed on the streets. But she didn't. She said, "Don't worry. Franklin and I were once young, too." Shary then smiled, and Joshua returned the same. With that, Joshua paid more attention to what she'd say next. "Other than that, you were always a good kid. I'm so sorry your mother didn't get to see the man that you have become, helping your uncle; getting a secure job at the Penn Fresh…assistant manager, right?" Joshua nodded in agreement. She then gave him an affectionate bump against his shoulder. "The same store that your mother worked, and now all grown up, the Northeast Philly neighborhood hero. Your mother would be very proud."

Joshua finally spoke. "Well, I didn't save everyone," referring to his uncle and aunt that just died in their home.

"Evil never sleeps, Joshua. When you go against it, it can be a life-long battle. Unfortunately, it's the balance of life." She then paused, and said, "You know your mother was something very special, fighting evil." Joshua perked up in curiosity. Shary confirmed, "Yes, I knew your mother very well. I got to watch her do some amazing things."

"Amazing things?" asked Joshua needing further explanation.

"Oh Josh, your mom was a very powerful woman. But not many knew it. Not the kind that they talk about today, not at all. I'd seen her do some miracles that would make the prophet Elijah's head spin." Joshua's eyes widened, which revealed his lack of knowledge about his mother. "You didn't know? You mean to tell me that you never saw any of this?" asked Shary, dumbfounded.

"Saw any of what?"

"Well, I'm not surprised. She was always a very private and humble person; never wanted to take credit for anything. But your uncle or Bishop Hines never said anything to you as well?"

"No," replied Joshua, disappointed to find out there was a secret about his mother he didn't know. He continued, "Uncle Jerry always helped us out and showed her love. But every now and then, I got the feeling that he hated and despised her, especially when she would be gone for so long and would not give him an explanation."

"Denise and your uncle's relationship was complicated. I would say it was a love-slash-hate relationship between those two. But more love than hate. And when it was about you, Josh, they always put you first."

"What do you mean by miracles that my mother did?" asked Joshua.

Shary perked up with excitement. "Oh lord, I can't even begin! Most things she did outside of the city and even outside the country."

Joshua interrupted, "Outside the country?"

"Oh yes, my dear. Bishop Hines would take her to all his international ministry events where she would use her gifts to encourage, speak life, and many times heal."

"Heal?"

"Listen. Before she started running off here and there, we used to run these night revivals with Bishop Hines. One night, your mother attended one and even came up for prayer. I gave her a direct message that she was going to do great things. But I didn't see her again until the following year at the same annual night revival. I was at the front of the church praying for people, and I saw Denise in the back. I waved for her to come up front and she did. This time, I asked her to help me pray for the crowd. Oh Lord, there were so many people at the altar that night. We would have been there all night if we didn't have help" Joshua anxiously wanted her to continue to the part about his mother. She noticed and intentionally skipped a few parts. "I could feel everyone looking at me wondering why I chose your mother, who was not known for being active in the church. Shoot…she wasn't even a member. But as she walked up, I just felt the spirit of peace and healing flowing through her. Franklin said he felt it as well. When she got up to the altar, she immediately set eyes on a little girl in a wheelchair, who was in the middle aisle just a few pews back from the front. She walked up to her, took a deep breath, then slowly exhaled, and then whispered something in the girl's ear."

Joshua couldn't believe what he was hearing. He always took a deep breath and exhaled before he played the piano or sang a solo. Then with Lauren, it helped him solve the string of church fires' mystery.

Shary continued, "Your mother then grabbed that little girl's hands as if for her to walk out of her wheelchair. The crowd was so thick, I think that only I and a few others could see this child's legs and feet. And as the girl tried to stand up, I thought my eyes were playing tricks on me. I saw both her feet levitate equally about two inches off the ground. But then she fell hard and started to cry. The girl's mother reacted by going into a slight rage and pushing Denise off her. The mother and others didn't see what I saw. She didn't walk but she floated in the air. But they looked at your mother in disgust, and then they looked at me like I lost my spiritual discernment gift, and it was unwise to choose your mother to assist me. Your uncle was there and immediately changed the direction of the service, blatantly shunned Denise. Denise then walked away, grabbed her stuff, and left the church like nothing happened. I thought she'd never step foot in another church again."

"So, she didn't heal her?" asked Joshua.

"But she did. I knew it and that little girl knew it too. Before Denise tried to get the girl to stand, she whispered in her ear, '*God has already healed you to walk my child, so let's try it. But if it doesn't work, then go home and pour seven buckets of water on your legs before you go to bed, and when you wake up you will be healed.*' So that little girl went home that night and asked her mother to help her with the buckets of water. But when her mother found out why, she refused. So, this little girl, God bless her, rolled herself into their bathroom, climbed out of her wheelchair, and with her limp legs crawled herself into the bathtub. She didn't have a bucket, so she filled the bathtub up and used a plastic cup to dip in the bathtub and poured water over her legs. She did it seventy times as she estimated that ten cups would be the equivalent of one bucket. Just like your mother instructed her to do."

"Wow. And did it work?" asked Joshua.

"Did it ever. But not immediately. Each day she got better at walking until she was fully able to run. Her muscles just needed the time to learn how to walk. She was healed, just like your mother said. She grew up and even joined the track team and became a great distance runner. But unfortunately, everyone just assumed that she grew out of her condition or specialist doctors had something to do with it, not your mother. But I tell you, when I saw her levitate from that wheelchair, I knew your mother's words were true. Glory be to God!"

"So, why didn't it work the first time?"

"Let me ask you, Josh. Why did Jesus put mud over the blind man's eyes, when he could have just said your healed? Why did God give Moses a wooden staff, basically a stick, to raise with each miracle and plague, when he could have told Moses to just point his finger?"

"I never really thought about that. Why?"

"God can do anything at any time without any prop or gadget. But it's man…or us humans…that is limited. We have an innate or human condition where *faith without works is dead*. So even though someone might think they have faith, most times they need to see a work, their own work to obtain the faith they need of no fear or doubt. Would you believe a magician if they didn't wave a magic wand? Your mother's true gift was more than just healing. She had a gift of discernment knowing exactly what action, work, or even a placebo a person needed to activate their own faith, not hers. Since her method was not always immediate, not everyone saw her ability. And because it didn't come in the form of shouting, television recording, or social media viral hits as everyone expects, she never received any large praise or recognition for her gift. But she did great healing work, more than anyone I know. And without a doubt, you're even a greater weapon for God against evil, a weapon of mass destruction for the Kingdom. I know this because someone or something with the most darkest and evilest power I ever felt is trying to deceive and eliminate all those you love and maybe you as well. Maybe, it's trying to prevent you from finding out the truth about yourself or your mother."

"But, why?" asked Joshua.

"You're the only one that can find out, Josh. I'm sorry for all your losses and at such a young age. These fires and deaths are too great to only be a coincidence. Evil has shown up on your doorstep and is forcing itself in every aspect of your life; and the question is why now?"

"Why me?" replied Joshua, perplexed.

"That's another good question, Josh. Until you said that, I almost forgot one more thing. When I was prophesying to Denise for the first time, I whispered something in her ear that only God wanted to Denise know." Joshua perked up. "After I told her that she was going to have a gifted child. A child who would have a voice like thunder and..."

Joshua interrupted, "What? You never told me that."

Shary knew Joshua was correct, but she acted perplexed, and said, "I didn't...Are you sure? Well still, look at you know." Joshua shook his head, slightly disappointed. She continued, "I told her that your voice would be like thunder. Then, I whispered in her ear that God shall give her child help that shall have a touch like lighting."

"Wow." said Joshua.

"For so long, I had clue what God meant when he told me to whisper that to Denise...until now. Your help that has a touch like lighting is Lauren! Before the explosion, I sat with Angela in the house and she was raving about you and Lauren. What you two did together for this community was nothing but extraordinary." She paused, and said, "Since I didn't tell you before, I will tell you now, Josh. Your voice is like thunder, and Lauren's touch is like lightning. You two are the greatest power couple on this planet, literally. You are greater together than apart. So, evil will do everything to deceive and separate you two. No matter what, don't let that happen!"

At that moment, Monty arrived back with two waters in one hand and two lemon-lime Gatorades in the other. "Thirsty?" asked Monty.

Joshua and Shary looked at Monty and smiled. "Be strong and of good courage, Josh, and be careful," said Shary.

Joshua remembered that a few days prior during the string of church fires, a sphere of light spoke to him and said almost the same things as Shary. He still doesn't know if it was a dream or was he really transported to the spiritual realm or *True Realm* as Lauren would have called it. Joshua thought, *This is so much to take in, hearing about my mother... my uncle and aunt killed in another fire. I can't even mourn because I can only think about Lauren...where is she?*

4

An Explosive Relation

Present Day – Rome, Italy – Three days before Hands Across the World.

Lauren woke up. But when she attempted to open her eyes, it failed. She could see nothing but complete darkness. Her eyes and head were still bandaged up from the attack during the infamous fight. The fight that she and Joshua had against the evil that was responsible for the string of church fires along the Boulevard. She remembered them. She remembered breaking into New Lighthouse Temple to go after Joshua. She remembered her eyes being set on fire. She remembered the pain. Then, she remembered feeling Joshua's anger and rage as he held her. But after that, she did not remember anything at all. First, she saved Joshua's life. Then, Joshua saved her life, but not before her eyes were intentionally set on fire by their enemy.

She felt a vehicle moving through the streets with her inside. It was a black Mercedes Sprinter van. The inside of the van had been retrofitted to carry many things, but none such as a young female with a cushioned head immobilizer on a spine board and a paramedic's stretcher. In addition, she was strapped down just beneath her chest and lower legs, making sure she was secure during the transport to prevent any further injury. When she reached up to her eyes to feel what was creating the blockage, she became frustrated when she realized that they were still covered in bandages. She lifted one of the edges of the bandages in hopes of seeing, even getting a glimmer of light to know that her eyesight was not as bad, but she could not. Even with the bandage lifted, she only saw darkness. She was still blind with no recovery. She thought, *Will I be blind forever?* She then wondered about her surroundings, and thought, *Who is in this vehicle with me and where are we going?* "Hello! Where am I?" yelled Lauren.

"It's okay Lauren," said Bishop Hines as he sat on a ledge in the back of the van next to Lauren and a hired EMT worker.

"Bishop?" asked Lauren, confirming it was him.

"Yes, my dear. I'm here. I've been with you this whole time. I knew you needed to hear my voice as soon as you woke up. If not, I imagined that you would have immediately broken out of those straps and flipped this van over wondering what was happening." The driver looked back at Bishop Hines wondering if she truly had that ability. The EMT looked at him the same, but Bishop Hines gave them both a look back, with eyes alert and wide, suggesting that he was serious.

"Bishop," said Lauren, as she felt the bandages over her eyes again.

"Yes, my dear. Everything is going to be okay."

"What the he…" She stopped herself from cursing. "…heck is going on?" she asked. This time with great inflection.

"Your eyes are still damaged from the fire. We are taking you somewhere safe, and where you can be properly treated."

Lauren ignored Bishop Hines' reference that she still may be in danger, and that she is going somewhere unknown.

"Where's Joshua?"

"He's still in Philadelphia. But he will be with us soon."

Ignoring the comment that suggested that she was no longer in Philadelphia, Lauren pursued more, "Where's my phone? I want to talk to him, now!" exclaimed Lauren.

"You will my dear. But right now, you need tending to; and he is dealing with another major issue right now."

"Another major issue! What are you talking about?" asked Lauren. She tried to sit up with the restraints, but the EMT gently pushed her back down, and said, "Signorina. We don't want you to injure yourself."

Bishop Hines responded. "I hate to tell you this, but even though you and Joshua did a miraculous job of saving yourselves and everyone at the community revival—it's not over."

"What do you mean? So, that evil villain got away?" yelled Lauren.

"Peace be still," said Bishop Hines firmly. "No. There is someone else or something else involved. Last night, I received word from Officer Reese and…" Bishop Hines then immediately stopped talking, hesitant to how Lauren would respond if she knew the full truth about Joshua's uncle and aunt and their recent home explosion.

"…and!" said Lauren impatiently.

Bishop Hines then played out in his mind what would happen if he finished that statement and visualized her breaking her straps and flipping over the van just like he suggested earlier. She did somewhat the same when she forced herself into New Lighthouse Temple to save Joshua by breaking through two large police officers who were standing in her way. With her strength and determination, she put them both flat on their butts. Either with that thought or with Holy Spirit discernment warning, he decided against it. He thought, *The EMT and I would not stand a chance against her.* Then he smiled. He continued with a vague alternate. "I don't know my dear, but Officer Reese said he will contact me when he finds out more."

Lauren knew Bishop Hines was not being completely truthful. But she was more concerned about Joshua. "As soon as we get to our destination. I want to call Joshua. Okay, Bishop?"

"Understood, my dear," confirmed Bishop Hines.

Lauren reached up to her face again to feel the bandages. Bishop Hines sat up and corrected his posture, preparing for another question from Lauren regarding her eyesight. But she said nothing. She rested her arms back in place by her side. She drifted deep into thought about Joshua. First, how the very first time she saw him at his mother's funeral. Even though, at the time, she'd just started dating Bishop Hines' son Mike, she felt a connection towards Joshua. She remembered how she couldn't believe this young fellow was going to play and sing at his own mother's funeral. How he sat at the large electronic piano, took a deep breath, then exhaled, and then went off script from the funeral's program and sang a different song that got the whole church in worship and praise. It was the first time she felt the Holy Spirit; and knew exactly what it was.

She thought, *Joshua was so young, but so calm and in control. His voice was so powerful and the way he played the piano was something she never witnessed, not even at Bishop Hines' church, International Covenant Ministries. And then the chance to see him again, after she broke off the wedding with Mike, right before the string of church fires. Sitting in his uncle's house, Pastor Williams, with his family, but feeling like Joshua and she were the only ones in the room. Then talking outside afterwards, with butterflies in her stomach like a little schoolgirl with her first crush. Without thought, wiping dripping snot from Joshua's nose like they had known each other for a few lifetimes. Sitting in the library in Camden, New Jersey, investigating the fires together. How Joshua punched Mike out, defending her honor.*

Together, walking the aftermath of Ebenezer AME, the first church set on fire along the Boulevard. Finding the hidden tunnel together and the Enochian letters written in blood, making a breakthrough in the church fire mystery, something even Officer Reese and the ATF could not do. Then, running parallel together to save everyone during the community revival, Joshua in the Underground tunnels underneath Philadelphia's Boulevard constructed by the one and only Harriet Tubman and her allies; and Lauren running on top of the Boulevard in sync with Joshua from church to church that was affected by the church fires to finally get to New Lighthouse Temple, the final destination of the evil arsonist trying to kill as many people as possible attending the Community Revival. But together, Joshua and Lauren saved so many lives. With Joshua, she felt unconditional love and unlimited spiritual power. Then for some reason, she thought about Mike and their past relationship. She mentioned this last thought to Bishop Hines.

"Why did you let us go so far…let it go so far?" asked Lauren.

"Excuse me, dear," he replied, not clear what she was referencing.

"Mike and me. Besides him being your son, why did you continue to let us date, get engaged, and almost get married?"

"Oh, that."

"With all of your wisdom and experience, couldn't you see that we were not meant to be together?"

For anyone else, Bishop Hines would have taken that tone as an insult or disrespect. Other than high-level clergy, security, or even his wife Sarah, no one is ever this close to Bishop Hines, except Lauren.

He responded, "Candidly, I believe I was blinded by hope. Your demanding personality, presence, intelligence, and logic made me question my own level on the spiritual ladder. You gave me the desire to be a better bishop, a better leader. You were the daughter I never had. Also, I thought you would influence him the same way that you influenced me. At least that's what I hoped."

"Me influence Mike, the Ivy League ministering golden child? Yeah, right," said Lauren.

"Yes. Mike has accomplished so much, but something is missing about him, especially lately."

Lauren interjected with her own thought, "Other than wanting to be the center of attention and loving the limelight?"

Bishop Hines grimaced. "He has so much potential and always said the right and most political things at the right time, but I just felt there was something different about him."

"Really," said Lauren surprised.

"He wasn't always the rude, self-centered man that you know of him today. He used to be a good kid with a kind heart. I remember when he and Joshua were close friends. But one day, that all changed. One day I came home and just felt he was different. He was my son, said the same things, and even acted the same, but it just felt different. As months passed, he started becoming increasingly unlike me, not like the child or person that I knew I raised. I thought things would get better. But it didn't."

"Why didn't you tell me this before, especially when he and I started the *testing process* with Archbishop Bennett and the..."

"Hush!" yelled Bishop Hines.

The EMT, who was half paying attention, jumped back in fear of Bishop Hines from his loud deep, and intimidating voice. He also realized that Lauren was obviously going to let out a secret that he and the driver were not supposed to hear. Then the van stopped.

"We are here," said the driver, as they pulled up to a three-story stone building with a narrow front door made of oak.

"Where is here?" asked Lauren reaching back up to the bandages over her eyes.

"We're back in Rome," said Bishop Hines.

"Italy!" exclaimed Lauren. "How did we get here? Was I unconscious that whole time? What day is it?"

Bishop Hines ignored every question. He opened the rear door to get out. He hurdled out the back of the van and then looked down at the old cobblestone alley. It was an empty view—only a few cars and no people. All the buildings looked gorgeously the same, antiquated structures with dull yellow and pinkish colored large stone structures. If it wasn't for the flowers and fresh greenery skirted along the window frames and small balconies, one would have thought the buildings had been vacant for many years. Bishop Hines then turned to the left and walked along the sidewalk adjacent to the van. He then walked up to a distinct building, which appeared commercial but had no signage. It had one word carved into the bottom stone to the right of the door, which read, '*Asclepieia*.' An asclepieia was known to be an ancient Greek healing temple or hospital where doctors were known to cure the sick and even raise the dead. Then, the door opened and a lady in a pinafore apron and cap came out to greet them.

"Buongiorno, Bishop Hines," said the nurse.

"Buongiorno," he replied.

"Signorina Lauren?" asked the nurse as she looked in the van.

"Si," confirmed Bishop Hines.

The driver and EMT lifted Lauren's stretcher out of the van and rolled her toward the small hospital entrance door. Then, suddenly, Lauren felt deep within her soul that something was wrong. She immediately reached back up to her eyes as if that would help her see what she was feeling. Thinking of Joshua, and what he would do, she took a deep breath and slowly exhaled. Her spirit and senses became even more alarmed. She could not contain it.

"Bishop! Something is wrong! We need to get back in the van, right now!" yelled Lauren, frantic.

They all looked at Lauren, confused. Bishop Hines attempted to calm her down. "Lauren, it's okay. We're safe here…"

Lauren interrupted him. "No Bishop. I feel it. Behind the building!" yelled Lauren. Even though she was blind, she could somehow envision what was around her as cloudy gray haze shadows, like the buildings, the van, and the people. Taking heed, Bishop Hines turned toward the building, and then Lauren said again, "Behind the…"

Before Lauren finished her sentence, Bishop Hines saw someone wearing all black, running away from behind the building. Then, almost immediately, the building exploded. The force of the explosion was so great that Bishop Hines, the driver, the EMT, and the nurse all fell to the ground, back towards the van. Lauren's stretcher was flipped on its side to the ground, close to the van, facing away from the building. The nurse screamed in horror as she looked at flames coming from the back of the building and with knowledge of those inside. The EMT worked to get Lauren and her stretcher back upright.

"Bishop! Bishop!" yelled Lauren as she was still strapped to the stretcher now upright, corrected by the EMT.

"He's hit!" yelled the driver hovering over top of Bishop Hines who was lying on the ground from the impact. "He's alive, but it looks like he was hit in the head by a fragment or something from the explosion," providing more detail to Lauren. Bishop Hines laid flat on his back conscious but dazed, but his head was bleeding badly.

"Bishop!" yelled Lauren again as she attempted to turn her head back towards him.

But he did not respond. The EMT ran over to Bishop Hines and pulled out a gauze package from his jacket to tend to his wound.

Injured and half unconscious, Bishop Hines whispered, "Not again… Denise. Not again…we die daily."

Lauren, still blind and disoriented, just barely heard his mumble. She replayed it in her mind to decipher what he said. She thought, *What does Bishop mean this is happening again, and what name did he just mumble? Oh, my goodness! Did Bishop Hines just mumble the name Denise? Is he talking about Joshua's mother...but why?*

At that moment, the earth began to violently shake, an earthquake.

5

AGO I or II

21 years ago – Rome, Italy.
The day before the Carnevale di Venezia (Carnival of Venice).

Denise is awakened by an accidental bump by the stewardess who carried a clear plastic bag, gathering trash before the plane landed. Denise felt the plane slowing down, as the Italian pilot made an announcement over the speaker system, *"Gentili passeggeri, stiamo effettuando l'avvicinamento finale all'aeroporto di Rome-Fiumicino International Airport, noto anche come aeroporto Leonardo da Vinci. L'atterraggio è previsto tra circa quindici minuti, Vi preghiamo di riportare lo schienale del sedile in posizione verticale, riporre i tavolini e spegnere tutti i dispositivi elettronici di grandi dimensioni. Grazie per aver volato con noi."* The announcement was repeated. But this time, translated in English, "Hello passengers. We are in our final approach to Rome–Fiumicino International, also known as the Leonardo da Vinci airport. Our landing will be in approximately fifteen minutes. Make sure your seat is upright and your trays are stored away with all large electronics turned off. Thank you for flying with us." Denise stretched and yawned as she attempted to look out the window from

41

the aisle seat. "Would you like to switch seats to look out the window before we land? You slept most of the trip and saw nothing," said the lady in the window seat next to her.

"No thank you. But I appreciate the offer," said Denise as she looked away with the hope that ended the conversation.

The lady put her head down, disappointed that their interaction may have come to a quick end. She looked back up at Denise and stared as she'd pondered what she could say next to keep the conversation going. Denise felt her stare and intentionally avoided it. But that would not work for long.

"First time in Rome?" asked the lady.

"Yes, very first," replied Denise.

"Oh, my goodness! You're going to love it!" Denise smiled. The lady continued the conversation. "I come out every year for the Carnival."

"Carnival?" asked Denise. Denise's response confirmed that she was unfamiliar with the popular event.

"Yes, the Carnival of Venice. I always pronounce wrong in Italian. So, my dear, you traveled out way out here during this time, and you have no idea what the Carnival is?" Denise shrugged her shoulders. "The Carnival of Venice is one of the most celebrated festivals here each year, maybe even around the world. From the decorations to the culture, from the music to the dancing, and the large celebration in Saint Mark's Square…" She then paused to catch her breath from her own excitement. "Oh, and the lovely costumes and masks! It's a great event."

"No, food?" asked Denise with a smile.

"And oh darling, in Italy, the food is amazing everywhere!"

"Sounds fun."

"It is. Everyone takes off for this event and will be out in celebration. The costumes and masks are so creative and mysterious. You get to hide your identity…and maybe even get a little lucky, if you know what

I mean," she said as she raised her eyebrows repeatedly. Denise decided not to take the bait and did not respond to that comment. The lady then said, "Every hotel is already booked up or extremely expensive during this time. If you don't mind me asking, if you're not traveling here for the Carnival, why are you traveling all the way here, my dear?"

"Frankly, I was invited."

"Invited. By whom? Are you a singer or something?"

"No," laughed Denise.

She then looked at Denise's left hand and seeking clarity asked, "Do you have children or married?"

"Definitely a no!" exclaimed Denise. Before the lady could dive deeper into Denise's personal life with more presumptuous questions, Denise said, "I'm here for some big Christian event. I was invited by some of the local clergy."

"Really, interesting. Are you a female minister?"

"No, not at all."

"Oh, that's good. I don't believe in female ministers or priests. So, what's your purpose then darling?"

"That's what I've been trying to figure out my whole life."

Denise's statement ended the conversation as the plane came to a full landing. She looked at her watch and realized their plane had arrived late. In forty minutes, she was supposed to meet up with Bishop Hines and Archbishop Bennett near Vatican City. She had no idea how far that was from the airport, and she still had to get her luggage from baggage claim. She walked off the airplane into the gate area and was surprised to see the signage and directional wayfinding hints in both Italian and English. But everyone getting off the plane was guided toward security for customs, passport verification, and stamping. The security officer only asked Denise one question, "Is your visit to Rome for business or pleasure?" To keep things simple, she deferred to pleasure as her response. The officer flipped to a page on her passport and stamped it. Denise's first international passport stamp. She looked at the stamp like it was a first-place gold medal, just like one of the ones she received when she ran track in high school. As she made her way toward baggage claim, she noticed a currency exchange booth. She remembered Bishop Hines' advice to exchange her money from dollar to euro when she arrived at the airport. But she forgot that he'd specifically instructed her to take money out of the ATM instead of going to an exchange booth to save money on the conversion rate fee. As Denise walked up to the currency exchange booth, she reached into her small purse to get her wallet. Before getting in line, she noticed everyone in the airport staring up at the television monitors. The news was on, but it was in Italian. She could not understand what they were saying, but she could interpret the banner headline across the top of the screen, 'Notizie Urgenti' which she instinctively interpreted to mean Breaking News. The news showed images of the aftermath of a terrorist attack bomb hitting some building, which left part of the building fully exposed showing the interior floors with concrete debris, rubble, and iron rebar all revealing the massive destruction.

Denise walked up to the counter, and said, "Buongiorno." It was the only other word in Italian besides Ciao that she confidently knew.

"Hello. Exchanging dollar to euro, Miss?" asked the booth attendant responding to her in English.

Prior to her trip, Denise heard that many Europeans spoke English fluently and they would most likely want to forego the stress of an American attempting to speak their language, especially when most Americans decide to learn their language from just a few hours on the plane with a language app. "Is it that obvious I'm from the U.S.?"

The booth attendant smiled. "How much will you be exchanging?"

Before Denise replied, she inquired about the events on the television. "What's all the news about?"

He responded with more energy. "A terrorist group that took respon-sibility for setting of that bomb that hit in France about a week ago just detonated another in the U.K. about an hour ago. That's what you're seeing on the monitor."

"I do remember the one that hit in France, but I didn't think anything of it," confirmed Denise, now more alarmed than ever being in Europe.

"Terrorists make threats all the time. No one took them seriously, until now. Then, today they announced that they will be setting more off in Europe, America, and other parts of the world. The Italian State Police say they have credible information that next may hit somewhere here in Italy. They recently issued a high alert for flights in and out of the country, and airlines have begun putting all flights on hold. Guess you made it here just in time, or just at the wrong time," he joked.

Denise did not think it was funny. "Seventy-five dollars. I want to exchange seventy-five U.S. dollars for Euros," said Denise.

He looked down at his computer. "You will get a better rate if you exchange at least one hundred dollars or more."

"No, thank you."

"Are you sure?"

"Yes, and can you hurry? I'm in a rush," said Denise, impatiently.

After the exchange was completed, Denise rushed to baggage claim. Finding her luggage turned out to be more difficult than she expected. After searching seven different baggage carousels, and a few of them twice with the assistance of an airport worker, she finally found her set of four various-sized bags and then a cart to push them. She walked outside into the taxi line that was longer than a roller coaster line at a theme park. It was chilly, 54° Fahrenheit or 12° Celsius, just below the average temperature for February in Rome. Denise opened one of her bags and pulled out a jacket. After she put it on, she pulled out the e-mailed itinerary from Bishop Hines that she printed out before she left for the Philadelphia airport. She went through each listed event again and again until it was her turn in the taxi line. The taxicab driver placed all her bags in the trunk as Denise got into the cab. When he got back into the driver's seat, Denise immediately showed him her destination from the itinerary, '*Meet at AGO & LILLO restaurant, Vatican City.*' "Grazie," he said. Then pulled off with confidence.

Denise reached into her purse and pulled out her new Blackberry phone that she received from Bishop Hines. Knowing her little flip phone may not be reliable, he wanted to make sure he was able to communicate with her while she was in Italy. So, before she left for the trip, he sent her a package that, among other things, included this Blackberry phone with activated international service. When she looked at the phone, she noticed that she received an email from Bishop Hines while she was in the air.

[Bishop Hines]: *Did you land?*

Denise then immediately.

[Denise]: *Yes. Just got into the taxi. Heading to that AGO place now.*

She waited for his response. It did not take long.

[Bishop Hines]: *Glory to God. I'm here already, but no rush. It should take you 35 minutes or so. It's right next to Vatican City.*

[Denise]: *I'll tell him to step on it. Look forward to seeing you again and the event this evening.*

[Bishop Hines]: *Likewise. No rush.*

Denise put the phone away and looked out the car window. She couldn't believe the amount of traffic in Rome. She thought, '*It's so much traffic but it's still moving so fast. If this amount of traffic was on the Boulevard or the Schuylkill Expressway, it would be like a parking lot, cars not moving at all.*' She watched the small motorcycles and scooters weave in and out of lanes and between cars, barely fitting, with no hesitation or remorse. And more importantly, no one aggressively honked at them to stay in the lanes. The cab driver looked in his rearview mirror and noticed the concern on Denise's face.

"No apologies. This is normal," said the driver. Due to his strong accent, Denise assumed his English may not be as good as others and knew he meant no worries instead of no apologies.

"How about the graffiti?" asked Denise referring to the excessive amount of spray paint markings she saw on all the buildings. She felt like she was driving up a section of Broad Street. However, the apartments and buildings looked completely different. They were much older, with faded light and pastel colors. Repainting was definitely needed, but it would have taken away from the buildings' comforting aesthetic appearance. With the number of decorative plants, vines, and furniture on the balconies and porches, it was evident that outdoor living was common. Coming from America, one might think that not having a landscaped or greenery-dressed balcony would most certainly be a violation of their homeowner's association. In the distance, Denise could see a large serene, and landscaped mountain area with perfectly trimmed high-topped Broccoli trees that sat on top of a very high wall. The trees got closer and closer, and when she could no longer see their top, the taxicab stopped.

"We are here. Ago restaurant is right there," as he pointed to one of the set of restaurants next to them.

Denise looked over in nodded. She then looked across the street and noticed the large, structured walls.

"Vatican City is just over that wall," he stated.

"The wall surrounds the whole place?" asked Denise.

"All around. They say to keep people out. But I say to keep something in, you know," laughed the driver. Then, he said, "Eighty Euros."

"Eighty!" exclaimed Denise. "I heard the trip would only be between thirty and fifty Euros."

"*Sì!* But lots of traffic and I get her quickly for you! Eighty Euros now," demanded the taxi driver.

"I'm not giving you eighty Euros. I will give you fifty but that's it!"

"Eighty Euros. Pay me now or no bags!"

With his last comment, Denise now realized that he had the leverage on her with her bags stuck in the trunk of his taxicab. But her stubbornness would not let her accept it. She then put fifty Euros on his console, jumped out of the cab, banged on the trunk, and demanded that he open it up to get her bags. "Give me my bags now!"

A waiter from the restaurant saw Denise banging on the trunk and knew exactly what was going on. He rushed to stand in between Denise and the taxicab driver. He was tall, skinny, and wore small eyeglasses on the edge of his nose. "*Perché stai sfruttando di nuovo i turisti, Aldo!*" exclaimed the waiter. He firmly yelled at the taxicab driver by name for repeatedly taking advantage of tourists. The taxicab driver looked at him and smiled with partial embarrassment. The waiter continued to reprimand him in English so Denise could also understand. "You're going to make so much money this week during the Carnivale. Get her bags out of the trunk!"

With extreme confidence from the waiter having her back, Denise extended her arm and hand toward the trunk for the driver to open it, and gave him a strong grin that unmistakenly reflected her thought, *What are you going to do now, mister?* As he looked at Denise, then back at the waiter, and the few patrons sitting outside, now quiet and watching the spectacle and waiting for his response, he realized that all his leverage was gone. So, he grinned back at Denise, laughed, and opened the trunk. He took out her four bags and placed them on the curb. "I just play prank with you, Signora. Welcome to Rome, ciao!" he said, as he quickly got back into the cab.

"Thank you," said Denise to the waiter, relieved to get her bags.

"No problem. You must be very careful with certain cab drivers. Also, you never want to put anything important in the trunk, like your passport, money, or keys, ever."

"Got it. Good advice."

"Where are you staying?" asked the waiter, as he wondered here to put all her bags.

"I don't know yet," replied Denise. "I'm meeting someone here at this restaurant."

"Okay, I will put your bags against the wall over there, so you can see them. I can also sit you right here at this empty table. Is that okay?" said the waiter as he guided her to the table. Denise nodded in agreement. He sat her at a small two-seated table close to the sidewalk. The restaurant had a section of outdoor seating with a good view of *Piazza del Risorgimento Square*, which is adjacent to one of the main entrances to Vatican City. Speeding around the square was a police car promoting a very loud piercing siren alarm that repeated again and again, which reminded Denise of some of the foreign films she used to watch. She thought, *This is definitely not Philadelphia.*

"Would you like some water while you wait?" asked the waiter as he looked down at Denise with his glasses falling off his nose.

"Please."

"Naturale o gassata?"

"Excuse me."

"Oh sorry, habit. Still or sparkling water?"

"Still water, please. I noticed you don't have an accent. Frankly, you sound pretty American. Where are you from?

"I'm from Minnesota. Been living in Italy since I was twelve."

"Wow. How did that happen?"

"My dad is American, and my mom is Italian. They met here before

I was born. She tried living in the States, but she hated it. My father always said, 'Miserable wife, miserable life.' So, we moved back here."

"That's an interesting. We usually say, 'Happy wife, happy life.'

"Do you want to look at the menu?" asked the waiter.

"Not right now. I am just going to wait for my other party." With that statement, Denise remembered when she arrived at the airport, Bishop Hines said he was already at the restaurant waiting for her. "But he should be here already. Is there another section to this restaurant," asked Denise, now concerned.

"No. This is it. The inside is small and only a few of my regulars are in there right now. Are you here for the Carnivale?"

Denise remembered the Carnivale from her conversation with the lady on the airplane. "No. I'm actually here on religious business."

"Really. What type of religious business?"

"There's an interdenominational organization that is hosting a church summit; I think I am one of the special guests…I guess."

"You don't sound too confident about that."

"I know. I just have no idea what to expect or how things will go."

"Are you a singer?"

Denise laughed. "I haven't been in Rome for a whole day yet, and that's the second time I was asked that."

The waiter looked around. "Give me a minute. I forgot that I was still working." He then left to tend to a couple waiting to be seated.

Denise looked around and could see the Vatican City wall and the infamous Square. It reminded her of Washington Square in Center City Philadelphia but with more people. She was excited imagining what was behind the wall. But still wondered, *where was Bishop Hines*?

The waiter came back with her glass of water. "Sorry about the singer question. But you do have this presence about you," he said with the hope that he did not offend her.

"No worries. What's your name?" asked Denise.

"My name is Angelo." He then looked down at his apron and said, "I know, I forgot my name tag again. One more time and they said I will be in big trouble," as he patted where his name tag should have been.

"You said your mother is Italian and your father is American, right?"

"My mother was born here in Rome; and my father is an Italian American born in Fairfield, New Jersey, but moved out to Minnesota after he graduated college."

"Oh, North Jersey. I'm from Philadelphia," said Denise.

"I love Philly,"

"No one from Philadelphia ever says, Philly. It's just Philadelphia," said Denise with a little swag.

"Got it. Well, welcome to Rome, and it's just called Rome, no matter who you are," he joked.

"Thank you. And thank you again for saving me and my bags earlier."

"My pleasure. Angelo's always at your service, madam."

"I like the name. May I ask who named you, your mother or father?"

"Both. My full name is Angelo Joshua Fazio. Both my parents are very religious, and my mother loved the name Angelo, meaning angel or messenger. But my father wanted my name to be Yehoshua or Joshua."

"Joshua or Yehoshua," repeated Denise him asking for it's meaning.

He understood her. "Translated, both mean, *Jehovah is salvation*. Of course, my mother liked Joshua better than Yehoshua and convinced my dad to go with Joshua for my middle name."

"I'm sort of confused. But I do like all your names, especially the name Joshua. It sounds so powerful and strong. They sound like good people. I bet they are great parents."

"They are. But it's tough because I am taking care of them both."

"Are they in their old age?"

"Yes, and with complications."

"How so?'

"My mother needs hip and knee surgery, and I think my father is in the early stages of Parkinson's disease. He has tremors and issues with his hands, and he shakes a lot, especially when he walks. Recently, I noticed his speech is starting to slur too. But every time I try to get him to go to the doctor, he throws a fit and goes crazy. It looks like I am trying to kidnap him. So, I just give up."

"Sorry to hear that."

"It's okay but thank you."

Denise assumed the introductory conversation would be over, so she sipped from the glass of water and again looked at her surroundings. But Angelo continued, "Again, what's this religious business and how are you a part of it?"

"Well. Some believe I have a gift. A gift of healing."

"Are you just saying that because of what I just told you?"

"No, not at all. It's true, really. I find it hard to believe it myself and was just thinking that this is a crazy coincidence to sit at your restaurant and hear about your parents."

"So, you just raise your hands or say something like, 'Abracadabra!' and the person is healed?" asked Angelo, joking and skeptical.

"For me, it doesn't work like that. It's more complicated. And be careful with that 'A' word. It is a lot of meaning behind it most people don't realize." Denise looked at her watch and noticed even more time had passed. She vocalized her thoughts to Angelo. "It's not like my friend to be late. If there is anyone that is ever on time, it is him."

"I bet he's across the street," said Angelo with a quick giggle.

"What do you mean?"

"This restaurant is *Historia AGO & LILLO*. Across the street, right over there is our sister restaurant *AGO & LILLO Bistro*," emphasized the waiter as he pointed to another restaurant within view.

"You're joking, right," said Denise, feeling like she was part of a prank.

"People get them confused all the time. I can call over if you want."

"No. I will send him a message."

When Angelo went to tend to the couple he seated earlier, Denise took the Blackberry out of her purse and sent Bishop Hines a message.

[Denise]: Your message said to meet at AGO & LILLO.

Bishop Hines responded immediately.

[Bishop Hines]: Yes. Do you need to give the taxi directions? You should have been here by now.

[Denise]: No because I am here.

Bishop Hines did not respond. She knew he was confused and looking around, and that made her chuckle.

[Denise:] I guess you didn't know that there are two AGO & LILLO restaurants.

[Bishop Hines]: Two, can't be. Where are you?

[Denise]: Look across the street.

Bishop Hines got up from his table inside the AGO & LILLO Bistro and walked out the entrance door to the edge of the sidewalk and then looked across the square. He saw Denise as she waved her hand and jumped up and down to get his attention. He then carefully walked across the busy streets to get to her restaurant. Upon arrival, he sat down at her table still confused, looking at the name of the restaurant on the door. Bishop Hines in this state of confusion was a rarity, and Denise gladly used it as an opportunity to tease him.

"Hello, Mr. International Traveler. This is Historia AGO-LILLO the sister restaurant to the Bistro across the street," stated Denise proudly. For once, she felt higher in stature above him.

Because he rarely makes any mistakes, Bishop Hines was embarrassed and apologized to Denise and himself. "Shame on me. I had no idea that there were two. I'm sorry Denise. I feel like a donkey walking away from town with everyone watching."

"It's okay, Bishop. None of us are perfect." She knew that statement would get under his skin even more. It worked, but he ignored it.

"How was the flight?" he asked pushing off the topic.

"Long. And should we be worried about these terrorist attacks? At the airport I saw the news and they're saying Rome is on high alert."

"We die daily," said Bishop Hines.

"What's that supposed to mean?"

"It means to get closer to Christ and be more like him, our own natural will and desire must die, even our life when required. Therefore, we should not be afraid of death or persecution."

"We die daily, huh? Well, you can have that one, Bishop. I am afraid of death, and I am definitely afraid of persecution," she replied.

"Indeed. We have a long evening ahead of us. Are you ready?"

Denise realized that he was still frustrated at himself for the location mistake. But fear started to set in again. "Ready, meaning in general, or ready like, right now, let's go?"

"Right now. The service starts in an about hour and we have a bit of a drive to get there." His voice deepened and with an angry tone, he said, "The taxi should have dropped you off at the right restaurant. Since it did not, we're running late because of him." Denise thought he was serious and did not know what to say. He then smiled and started to laugh, and exclaimed, "Got you!" Denise released her breath and smiled with relief.

Still amused by his prank, Bishop Hines unhooked his phone from his belt clip and called his driver. "We're ready to go. But I am now across the street, but still in the square." He then stood up, opened his wallet, and put twenty Euros on the table. "Are those your bags?" he asked pointing to them against the exterior wall of the restaurant.

Bishop Hines' driver pulled up in a black Mercedes S500 and got out and helped with the bags.

Angelo, the waiter, came out and was surprised they were leaving so soon. "Leaving already?" he asked.

Denise replied. "Yes, sorry. You should come out tonight. Bring your mother and father, as well." She then turned to Bishop Hines, and asked, "Where is the event tonight, again Bishop?"

"There's a church right up the street from *Fountain of the Frogs*, in the district of…"

"*Quartiere Coppedè*," interrupted the waiter. "I know where it is."

"Great! So, you will come?" asked Denise.

"I will see. My parents really don't like to go anywhere, but they might, especially if I tell them it's to meet a special lady."

"Please do, Angelo, And I won't forget how you saved me and my bags. I guess you're living up to that name of yours!" she exclaimed and smiled. Angelo smiled back.

Bishop Hines and Denise got in the vehicle and drove off. "Frog of the what? Where are we headed?" asked Denise.

"There is a little section of Rome called Quartiere Coppedè, famous for the architect Gino Coppedè. Our interdenominational organization owns a few homes in the area. Among other things, we use them for special guests just like you. And the area is so beautiful. It has a fountain with statue frogs in the center of the village that attracts lots of attention from both tourists and locals," said Bishop Hines.

"Wow. I feel special."

"You should. Not everyone gets this treatment. But you caught the attention of so many clergy officials with our last event in Lancaster, Pennsylvania. That progressive Amish group can't stop singing your praises. You healed so many of their children. We haven't seen healing like that since Smith Wigglesworth."

"Wiggle who?"

"Smith Wigglesworth. An early British minister that was part of the early Pentecostalism movement. He was known to heal the sick and even raised the dead. There was also Saint Padre Pio who healed through prayer and bared stigmata or the wounds of Christ. But the earliest, maybe even one of the founding members of The Circle was Apollonius of Tyana. A Greek philosopher known for his repeated demonstration of different types of miracles and healing."

"What about this guy I saw on T.V.? I think he lives in Brazil. It was like hundreds or thousands of people go to see him throughout the year to be healed?" She wanted to share more but could not remember.

"Oh, you're referring to João de Deus or John of God. I met him when I was a lot younger. For decades, not thousands, but tens of thousands of people, maybe even more, visited his small village to either be healed or witness his healings. He received much global press and television coverage, many mesmerized by his healings. But there have been reports of him engaging in inappropriate and ungodly activities. Whether true or untrue, The Circle decided to not associate with him."

"How can someone do miracles if they are ungodly, Bishop?"

"Good question. Only God knows. But you must remember three things. Number one, God has all power can give it to whoever He wills. Number two, the Bible tells us that the gifts of God are without repentance. This means you don't have to be saved or holy to perform the gifts of God."

"...and what's number three?"

"Unlike any other religion or cultural belief at the time, Jesus preached a message that if you believe on him and had faith, you shall be able to do even greater miracles and works than him, and it didn't matter what nation or culture you were from. Before Christ, there was no prophet, people's god, or divine being that spoke like that to people.

That is why his message was so popular and spread across nations The whole world wondered who is this that performs miracles like a god, but also saying we can and shall be like him if we believe."

"So do you think my gift is the same, like all these other healers?"

"No. I believe there is something different about yours."

"Really? What?"

"Not sure. But that's what I am waiting to find out."

Denise did not respond. She decided to turn away and looked out the car window and her eyes widened at what she saw as they drove past Rome's historical scenery--Basilica Papale di San Pietro in Citta di Vaticano or St. Peter's Basilica, Castel Sant'Angelo, the Colosseum, and the Altar of the Fatherland and the view of many unique architectural structures and churches during the short trip to Quartiere Coppedè. Upon arrival, the driver drove around the circle of the Fountain of Frogs to give Denise a good view of the entire area. She was pleased. The driver slowed down as he parked against the curb. "You're staying right up there," said Bishop Hines as he pointed to one of the windowed balconies above a decorated building with angelic statues. Then suddenly, they felt and heard a large explosion that shook the ground and the buildings around them. Bishop Hines automatically jumped across the seat to cover Denise from any impact. The driver fell over flat on the front seat and covered his head. The people in the circle, taking pictures of the fountain, ran for cover as loose and unsecured items, like plants and hanging signs, fell from the buildings. Another bomb had hit just like the terrorist group said it would. It hit somewhere in Rome, but close enough for them to experience the impact.

We die daily.

6

Express Ways

Present Day – Philadelphia, PA.
Three days before Hands Across the World.

Joshua jumped out of the ambulance, then helped Shary out as well. She gave him a big, long hug, and said, "Just so you know, we were up late last night. I had a bad feeling when I heard Rocky barking. When I got out the bed and looked out the window, I saw somebody running down the street, possibly away from the back of your house. At first, I thought it was you or your uncle, but that didn't make any sense. Why would either of you be running out this late and through the back? And then a few minutes later, the explosion went off." She then paused, and said, "There is something else I think you should know, and I'm sure Officer Reese won't tell you this."

"What?" asked Joshua, alarmed.

"The explosion was very small, in the bedroom. I think targeted specifically to kill anyone that was in that room. The rest of the home, like the lower level, didn't ablaze until after the explosion. I believe that's why none of the other homes experienced as much damage. Whoever did this is extremely smart and knew exactly what they were doing."

"Thank you for sharing that, Miss Shary," said Joshua now more concerned than ever, and thought, *Who could it be?*

"Be strong Joshua," said Shary walking away.

"I will. Thank you."

Then suddenly, a black Mercedes Sprinter van quickly pulled up to the police barrier right in front of the ambulances and came to a screeching halt. A young male and young female, both wearing long black priest cassocks but missing the white collars, jumped out of the side door of the van. Clearly out of place, they still walked with confidence and in sync toward Joshua, almost like they'd walked the streets of Philadelphia all the time. Maybe from instinct, Joshua knew they were coming for him. But he was unaware of why and the news they would eventually provide.

The female spoke first. "Joshua. My name is Ezra and this is Jacob," said the female.

"Hello, Joshua," said Jacob.

"We are Archbishop Bennett's assistants. We're here to take you to Lauren and Bishop Hines," she said.

Without a thought, Joshua walked past them and towards the van. Ezra and Jacob looked at each other puzzled. They assumed he would have a bunch of questions, maybe even grab a bag or some personal items if he'd agreed.

"Are you two coming, or am I going by myself," said Joshua as he opened the van door.

"That was easy," said Ezra.

"Pretty much," replied Jacob with a chuckle and smile.

Officer Reese and Monty saw Joshua getting in the van. "Where's Josh going?" asked Monty.

"I'm not sure. Hold on." Officer Reese then sprinted toward the van. He made it just in time to stop the door from closing with his hand.

He forcefully opened it back up. "Where do think you're going, Josh? And who are these people?" he firmly asked looking primarily at Jacob. Jacob smiled and waved hello.

"I'll be back. They're taking me to Lauren and Bishop," responded Joshua, just as firm.

"Not right now they're not! There are three deaths and an open investigation into the attack on your house and on one of our officers. With all these police officers out here, no one is going anywhere. And what about your aunt and uncle? Who's going to handle the bod…" Before he could finish, referring to Angela and Pastor Williams, Ezra interrupted him.

"Officer Reese. There will be another van just like this one that will be here within the hour. The people inside it will help you with whatever you need, they are very resourceful and will be able to handle it with you," said Ezra convincingly. He paused, surprised that she knew his name, and he didn't know what to say next.

Joshua then leaned toward him, placed his hand on the door, and said, "These two are with Archbishop Bennett. It will be okay. I will be okay. I must go right now. You know this right?"

Officer Reese looked at Joshua's face full of sadness and determination. He realized that—especially with all that he had been through, including the police and ATF belief that he was the primary suspect of the previous string of church fires—he had no choice but to let Joshua go. "Alright. But you better call me in a few hours to let me know you're okay and how things are going with Bishop." Joshua nodded in agreement. "And this so-called help you speak of young lady, better be here within the hour," he said, as he looked and pointed at Ezra and Jacob.

"It will be, Officer Reese. On behalf of The Church, you have my word," said Ezra.

"Be careful, Joshua," said Officer Reese.

"Thank you." Joshua shut the door and the van driver pulled away. From the distance, Monty looked at Officer Reese perturbed, and Officer Reese gave him no comforting reaction. Joshua squeezed his way to the back row, as the basic model Sprinter van had bench row seats like his uncle's church van.

* * *

Ten minutes went by and Joshua still had not said a word. Jacob could not take the silence.

"Joshua. Aren't you going to ask where we are going?" asked Jacob.

"You already told me."

"But you don't know where exactly."

"Does it matter? If Lauren is there, that's where I want to be."

Ezra interjected, "There is something I must tell you, Joshua."

Joshua looked at her in frustration, potentially hearing more bad news. He thought, *Things could not get worse.* But they did.

"There was an accident. The hospital where Bishop Hines was taking Lauren had a bomb go off inside," said Ezra. She immediately continued before Joshua assumed the worst. "Lauren and Bishop Hines are both okay. Well, Lauren is fine, but Bishop Hines was hit in the head by debris from the explosion. It exploded as their van pulled up to the entrance. Luckily, they were not inside the building. But unfortunately, a few others that were inside were not as fortunate."

"Just get me there quickly!" demanded Joshua.

"Yes, of course. We're getting there as fast as humanly possible," said Ezra with an excited and urgent tone.

Joshua had a million other questions, but now he only really cared about one, especially with Ezra's last comment. "What do you mean? How long is it going to take us to get to them?" he asked.

"And there's the question. Ever been to Italy?" asked Jacob.

"Italy! You're kidding, right?" Joshua thought Jacob was joking.

"Not kidding, Joshua. We have a private plane ready to go and our driver is taking us there right now."

"Private plane," said Joshua questioning him even more.

"Yes. Most commercial flights are delayed, so we're flying out of a small regional airport in Coatesville, Chester County. It's about forty minutes outside of Philadelphia, and with the Church's private jet, we should be able to get there easily within eight to nine hours," said Ezra, as the driver sped down the Schuylkill Expressway.

"I don't even have a passport."

"No worries, Joshua. We already have it for you," said Ezra, as she handed Joshua his passport.

Joshua opened it up and he saw a picture of himself with the name *'Joshua Alexander Williams.'*

"This seems legit," he said, as he rubbed his fingers along the exterior.

"It is, Joshua. That's your real passport," said Ezra.

He flipped through the passport and noticed that it already had a stamp on one of the pages. "Umm…this is saying I've been to Italy before. How?"

Ezra and Jacob looked at each other and wondered if the other was going to explain.

Jacob responded without any detail, "Not sure, Bro. I think you better ask Bishop Hines regarding that one."

Joshua decided not to pry any further, as nothing seemed weird anymore. Then, he looked at their attire again, both wearing long black cassocks. "Are you both priests?" asked Joshua.

"Deacons," said Ezra.

Jacob jumped in immediately to correct. "You're not a deacon! She's not a deacon! Being female, she can't be a priest or a deacon in the Catholic Church. Plus, she has a hard enough time being a female with the name Ezra," said Jacob, frantically.

Ezra countered, "You're not a priest or deacon either, Jacob!" She then continued but with a lower tone. "Well, I like the name Ezra. My father swore I was going to be a boy and didn't want to change the name he'd already given me."

Jacob looked back at Joshua, and said, "Well, I'm a deacon in training. So, I will be one very soon."

"And I will be too, just watch. The Pope will reinstate the ability of females to become deacons again, you just wait and see. And I will be the reason," said Ezra confidently.

"You. The first female deacon since the Middle Ages? Good luck waiting on that," responded Jacob.

"The Middle Ages?" stated Joshua, as a question.

Ezra responded, "The Catholic Church allowed women to serve as deacons up until the 12th century. Then, they abolished this role for men in the late 1500s as well. It wasn't reinstated for men until the 1960s. And, my turn will be soon," said Ezra.

"That's interesting. In my faith, deacons and even deaconesses are common, and have been for quite some time," commented Joshua.

"Really? How long of a servantship do they have to do?" asked Ezra.

"For our church, I don't think it's that complicated. I think they just tell the pastor or elders that's what they want to do, and if the Pastor likes you, then you're in," said Joshua. Ezra looked at him in shock. Joshua continued, "Maybe it's a bit more to it than that; especially if you're ordained as one. But from what I can remember, I don't think it's as complicated as with the Catholic Church."

"Ezra, you already know everything with the Catholic Church is way more difficult or complex than with others," said Jacob. Done with the conversation, she turned to look out the window.

"Even though you're not priests or deacons, you still get to wear those clothes?" asked Joshua.

"We are direct assistants, well more like servants, to Archbishop Bennett. Because he is so highly respected in the Church, Ezra and I have more flexibility and power than most our age or in our positions," said Jacob.

"Actually, most of them hate us," said Ezra with a faint desire to join back in the conversation.

"True. But if Archbishop Bennett tells everyone we can remain in a meeting room or a certain section of the Church, no one argues," explained Jacob.

"Are you two brother and sister?" asked Joshua.

"No!" Ezra and Jacob exclaimed said at the exact same time!"

"Do you two know Bishop Hines?" asked Joshua.

"Yes, for quite some time," said Ezra.

"She knows him better than I do. Why don't you explain to Joshua the other reason why we are able to do what we do, Ezra?" said Jacob, urging Ezra to reveal more to Joshua.

Ezra looked at Jacob in frustration. She turned back to the window before she spoke. Her voice degraded just barely audible, but more intimate. "Archbishop Bennett is my father. My dad and Bishop Hines have been friends for a very long time."

"How long?" asked Joshua.

"As long as I can remember. Your mom…" Joshua's eyes perked. "…well, I was among the first group of people healed by your mom. She healed me the first time she went to Rome," said Ezra.

"What are you talking about?" exclaimed Joshua. He thought, *These two are more people who knew about my mother. Why did I not know?*

"It's true. Your mother saved me and my father," said Ezra. Joshua turned his body toward Ezra to listen more attentively. She continued, "When I was a child, I had a condition where I could not control myself, my words, or even my body. One moment I would be playing with my toys, like my doll baby, and the next moment, I would be scream-ing, going into convulsions, and my eyes even rolled into the back of my head. Whether at dinner or during mass, it would just happen, randomly. Growing up in the Church and in Vatican City, many clergy officials assumed that I was a wild child or possessed by demons. After many doctor visits with no diagnosis, hundreds of prayers of priests laying hands on me whenever they had the chance; and then a horrible exorcism ceremony, it turned out that I just had severe seizures and other issues from a condition that would take too long to explain."

"Wow. Sorry to hear that," said Joshua.

"It's okay. But during all that, it was a few priests, not all, who felt my father did some bad sin to have this demon daughter as they called me. But my father kept bringing me around despite their concerns. He loved me no differently than any other normal child. Two or three of them threatened my father all the time and even lobbied to have him *excommunicated* if he did not restrict me from the Church."

"Excommunicated. What does that mean?" asked Joshua.

Jacob answered, "It means that he would never be able to receive sacraments, communion, or even have a catholic church funeral."

Ezra continued, "It's the worst thing that could happen to a priest. My father loves me and the Church too much, so he didn't listen."

"Are you serious? So, what happened?" asked Joshua.

"Bishop Hines brought your mom to Rome. He told my dad that she could help," said Ezra, emotional.

"Did she?"

"More than you will ever know, Joshua. That day, your mom changed my life and the Church, forever. And I am so grateful and proof of it."

[*ring-ring ring-ring*]

Joshua's phone rang. It was Lauren's phone calling him.

7

Spiritual Reunion

Present Day – Chester County G.O. Carson Airport.
Three days before Hands Across the World.

Joshua looked at his phone and could not believe that it was Lauren calling. Since they took her from the hospital in Philadelphia after the fires, he called her over three hundred times and sent about just as many text messages. He held back the tears as he saw her name on the display screen of his phone glad that she was at least alive. However, Joshua did not realize how drained and emotional he was from not hearing from her, not knowing if she was okay, where she was, or if she was permanently blind. The fire at his uncle's church ended with Lauren being blinded by the vicious attack of their evil enemy. Joshua remembered that event and re-envisioned her lying on the church floor, knocked down and unconscious. A wood beam fully on fire that fell from the ceiling and lay just over the top of her with the rest of the church engulfed in flames. During that moment, he lost all hope. He thought he lost the fight, and most importantly, he thought he'd lost Lauren. But then, whether reality or just in his imagination, spheres of light appeared and surrounded him, giving him back hope and courage to save her life. He still doesn't know if those images were real or just his imagination. But he does know that the one of the last things his uncle, Pastor Williams, spoke to him before he died were real and no imagination, 'No greater love than a person lay down his life for another,' and how he witnessed Lauren risking her life for his. How his uncle then uncharacteristically said, 'Adam and Eve were the first twin flames, so imagine what unlimited power a couple can have together that both love God, have His power, and possess unconditional love together…where two or three are gathered in His name nothing shall be impossible to them; especially for a couple like that.' Joshua smiled thinking his extremely conservative uncle finally had a progressive thought. His uncle was a great man. But did Lauren challenging his beliefs make him even better?

Joshua answered the phone, nervous, "Lauren?"

But it was not Lauren. "Ciao, Joshua?" asked the Italian nurse who was with Lauren and used Lauren's phone to call him. She spoke a little bit of English, but not a lot, and with a heavy Italian accent.

"Yes," said Joshua, concerned. He thought, *Who was this lady with this accent and why does she have Lauren's phone?*

The nurse responded. "Lauren is here. She can talk to you."

"Okay," said Joshua, excited and anxious to hear her voice.

Ezra was anxious to know who called. "Is that Lauren?" she asked.

"Yes," said Joshua.

Then, Ezra looked over at Jacob and placed her pointing finger over her lips to instruct Jacob to remain quiet. He whispered back with a slight brotherly attitude, "I know!"

The nurse handed Lauren the phone. "Joshua!" exclaimed Lauren, as she held the phone against her ear. She laid down in a bed with bandages still over her eyes.

"Oh my god, Lauren! Are you okay? Where are you!" yelled Joshua.

His breath was short and his heartbeat was fast paced.

"Stop yelling, you cornball. I'm fine. But I still got these mummy bandages over my eyes, so I guess that's not good. Other than that, I'm doing okay. How are you, my strong Joshua?"

"Stronger now that I hear your voice." He paused, then said, "My soul loves your soul." He said it with so much emotion that everyone felt it. Ezra and Jacob looked at each other with emotion and appreciation of bringing them together again.

"My soul loves your soul too, Joshua," said Lauren with tears filling up behind the bandages.

Joshua lifted his phone and put it against his forehead to feel her presence, closer to him. He could still hear her, but not as loud.

"I have bad news, Joshua," said Lauren.

"Unfortunately, I have really bad news too," he replied. Lauren continued before him.

"There was an explosion and Bishop Hines was hurt pretty bad. He's in the hospital. Then we experienced a minor earthquake right after that," said Lauren.

"I didn't hear about the earthquake, but I heard about Bishop Hines…I pray he is okay. There was an explosion here as well. Well in Philadelphia. My uncle and aunt…" Joshua paused, and he briefly cried. "My Uncle and Aunt Angela are both dead." Joshua wept.

Lauren was silent as she remembered the arguments she had with Pastor Williams, but she would have never wished death upon him, or this loss upon Joshua.

"Oh heavens, Joshua! I am so so sorry! No one told me that! Oh my goodness, I am so sorry! I love you so much. I love you."

Ezra and Jacob could overhear Lauren speaking and weeping over the phone. They felt their pain and their connection.

Out of habit, Lauren tried to wipe the tears coming from her eyes through the bandages. Joshua could tell that she was doing this. So, Joshua brought the phone back to his ear to speak. "Stop trying to wipe away your tears through your bandages, silly?" joked Joshua.

"Shut up!" said Lauren as she laughed and wondered how he knew. "Was it the same evil enemy?" asked Lauren.

"No. Apparently, there is someone else or something else involved, as Officer Reese put it. They found more evidence about the string of church fires. So, it's not over."

"Apparently not," replied Lauren.

Joshua wiped the last tears away from his eyes with his sleeve, now more composed. "What about your eyesight? Did the doctors say anything about it?"

For a moment, Lauren ignored Joshua's question, remembering the night of the fire. "We sure made a good team that night, didn't we, Joshua?" asked Lauren.

"We sure did," said Joshua as he smiled.

"We figured out the mystery and saved the day. We are like major superheroes, you know!" joked Lauren.

"Well, don't get it twisted. I'm the superhero and you're my trusty sidekick," joked Joshua.

Lauren joked back, "Sidekick. Don't get kicked in the side, Joshua. Do you remember how we found that secret tunnel together in Ebenezer AME?" asked Lauren.

"Umm…we searched," said Joshua without any real thought about it.

"We did more than that, silly. You used your breathing technique to tap into your spiritual gift, right?" Lauren then thought about how Joshua used it during his mother's funeral before he played the piano and sang the solo to usher in the presence of God during the service. But she realized, now would not be a good time to also bring up the death of his mother.

"I do remember," said Joshua.

"You were led to that large stone in the wall that was loose and took us underneath the churches along the Boulevard," said Lauren.

"Wow. I forgot all about that."

"How could you forget about that?"

Joshua paused as he thought about the many times that he took a deep breath and slowly exhaled as his own personal way to remove anxiety and tap into God's presence and power prior to performing. Suddenly, the Holy Spirit fell upon Joshua. He then, said, "Lauren, do you trust me?" asked Joshua.

"Yes, of course, Joshua," she replied.

"Do you trust God?"

"Do you even have to ask?"

With more intensity in his voice, Joshua said, "Listen. This is very important right now." With that command, Ezra and Jacob felt a spiritual shift in the van. Their driver felt it as well and looked on from the rearview mirror.

Joshua then put the phone on speaker, so he could easily speak into the phone without holding it up to his face. He took a deep breath, exhaled, and said, "Everything I say, do. Will you do that, Lauren?"

Lauren responded without hesitation, as she still lay on the bed with the bandages over her eyes, "Okay, Joshua."

"Take a deep breath and hold it."

Lauren took a deep breath.

"Now, I want you to slowly release your breath while I count to the number seven." Lauren did not say anything, but Joshua knew her silence was her acknowledgment and acceptance. Joshua continued, "One…Two…Three."

Lauren slowly exhaled as Joshua instructed. While she exhaled, Joshua reached up over the seat and grabbed Ezra's hand, and without hesitation or thought Ezra reached up and grabbed Jacob's hand as well. Then, being on one accord, the driver automatically took one hand off the wheel and reached back to grab Jacob's hand. Joshua continued, "Four…Five…Six…Seven" Lauren finished the slow exhale. "Now, Lauren, put your hands over the bandages over your eyes." Just like Joshua instructed, Lauren slowly reached up and covered the bandages over her eyes. Then, Joshua tightly gripped Ezra's hand, and then Ezra, Jacob, and the driver gripped each other's hands strongly the same.

"Lauren, repeat after me," said Joshua, as he looked at everyone and the van, and they all knew to do the same.

Joshua: "She was blind."

Everyone repeated: "She was blind."

Joshua: "Not of sin."

Everyone repeated: "Not of sin,"

Joshua: "But so the miracle works of God be manifested in her, today."

Everyone repeated: "But so the miracle works of God be manifested in her, today."

Joshua: "We speak life, light, and sight in Lauren, right now, in the name of Jesus Christ."

Everyone repeated: "We speak life, light and sight, in Lauren, right now, in the name of Jesus Christ."

Joshua: "Amen."

Everyone repeated: "Amen."

At that instant, Lauren's eyes painfully burned as if they were set on fire! She immediately sat up from the bed and screamed violently, pressing her hands on her eyes to stop the pain.

"It burns! It burns!" screamed Lauren, as she shook her head left to right, and attempted to rip the bandages off.

Then, large amounts of puss and mucus fluids excreted from her eyes, which soaked through and out of the sides of her bandages. Everyone in the van could hear her screaming and were alarmed, but not Joshua. He remained calm, patiently waiting for the final result. The nurse who was in the room with Lauren was scared and immediately grabbed Lauren's hands away and quickly ripped off the bandages over her eyes. She looked around the room and grabbed a pitcher of water that was situated on the mini table next to Lauren's bed, and began pouring it over Lauren's eyes, while forcefully wiping away the puss and water down and away from her eyes. As soon as the pitcher was completely emptied, the burning stopped and so did Lauren's screaming. The nurse then noticed a small hand towel that was at the foot of the bed, grabbed it, and put it over Lauren's eyes and face. Lauren grabbed it and slowly wiped her eyes and face dry. Wondering what happened, Jacob opened his mouth to speak, but Joshua quickly hushed him by placing his finger in front of his mouth and shaking his head for Jacob not to speak. The nurse then told Lauren to blink her eyes repeatedly again and again as that would help clean her eyes out. Drenched with the water and while she attempted to catch her breath, Lauren slowly opened her eyes. At first, it was dark, then it turned blurry, then she could see a dark skewed, and distorted view of the nurse, and then, in the next moment, it fully focused to clear. Her sight fully returned and was clearer than ever before. She could see the nurse and the room all around her, clearly. The nurse could tell from the way Lauren looked around the room back and forth that she could finally see. The nurse was so excited.

"Hallelujah! *La tua vista è guarita!*" yelled the Italian nurse, which in English translated, 'Your vision is healed!'

Back in the van, Ezra understood the nurse, and said hesitantly, "Did it work? Is she really healed?"

Lauren heard Ezra's question over the phone. "Joshua! I can see! I can really see!" exclaimed Lauren in joy.

Ignoring the miraculous healing for a moment, Joshua looked at Ezra and Jacob and asked, "Is Hallelujah the same in Italian as it is in English?" referring to the nurse's proclamation.

"Yes. I believe it's one of the few, if not only, word that is spoken and means the same in every language across the world," replied Jacob.

Lauren interjected, "Really, Joshua! I can see now and all you're worried about is spoken languages?" Everyone laughed.

"Sorry. Yes, I heard you. Praise God! I love you," said Joshua.

"I love you too! Thank you!" said Lauren.

"Well, Jacob. It looks like Bishop Hines might be right about these two," said Ezra, joyful.

"Truth!" Jacob replied.

"Right, about what?" asked Joshua, referring to their comments.

"We're here," said Jacob as the van turned into the entrance of the small airport.

"We'll get situated on the plane. You take your time on the phone with Lauren. So, no rush, Joshua," said Ezra.

Joshua smiled showing thanks. Ezra and Jacob got out of the van. The driver got out as well but kept the van running. Now that she could see, Lauren hit the Facetime button on her phone to video chat with Joshua. Joshua clicked on this alert notification and the screen showed Lauren with her face and nose close to the camera in anticipation of seeing Joshua's face. Joshua laughed as he saw her face extremely close to the phone.

"Hello, my Lauren."

"Hello, my Joshua."

Joshua did a quick exhale, "Wow. It's so good to finally see you."

"I missed you," Lauren replied.

"And I was so worried about you...I should have gotten in the ambulance with you. I should have stayed with you at the hospital in Philadelphia, I should have never let you out of my sight. I'm sorry."

"It's okay, Joshua. So much was going on the day and night of the fire. We both could have done things differently. But we are both okay, and it worked out."

"At least for now."

"Don't think like that, Joshua. Haven't you learned anything?"

"Well. I'm about to get on the plane to come see you," said Joshua as he smiled showing most of his teeth.

"Oh, my goodness, those teeth," said Lauren as she chuckled. Joshua then smiled even harder. "So, you're getting on a plane right now?" asked Lauren for confirmation.

"Yes, right now."

Lauren smiled back into the phone's camera, showing most of her teeth as well. The nurse was still in the room standing near Lauren and laughed hysterically and then said, "*Sembrate due cavalli stupidi che si sorridono a vicenda*," as she walked away. Lauren did not understand her Italian, but it translated, 'You both look like two dumb horses smiling at each other.' At that moment, the driver knocked on the van for Joshua.

"I can't wait to see you," said Joshua.

"I can't wait to see you," said Lauren.

"I will call you as soon as we land. Until then, check on Bishop Hines, and see what you can find out about what's really going on."

"Okay."

"My soul loves your soul, Lauren."

"My soul loves your soul, Joshua."

8

The Light of Life

Present Day – Rome, Italy – Three days before Hands Across the World.

After speaking with Joshua, Lauren hung up the phone and used her hand to slowly glide the phone down her body with comfort, after finally able to speak to him. She looked around the room and saw the bandages that had previously wrapped her face and eyes and then smiled from being able to see again. But with that thought, also came the realization that her clothes and bed were soaked from the nurse drowning her eyes out with the pitcher of water when they started to burn. That thought lasted for a moment, then she went back to the thought of finally reconnecting with Joshua. She decided to get out of bed and change her clothes. She went over to the tall, elegant dresser and pulled out a pair of jeans and then a flowery yellow and blue blouse, which were clothes left from her last visit. She'd been in this room, this house, many times before with Bishop Hines. It was the same room that Joshua's mother stayed in when she visited Rome many years before she died. The room was approximately eight hundred square feet. It followed the same Baroque interior design as the rest of the home. It had an eighteen-foot-high ceiling decorated with intricate paintings and bronze patterned molding, and you could see the *Fountain of the Frogs* from the room's balcony.

Lauren went into the bathroom, grabbed a hand towel to completely dry herself off, and then changed her clothes. When she walked out of the bathroom, she noticed something shiny underneath the bed. It looked like a small silver box. Lauren got on the floor and reached under the bed. After a few attempts, she was able to grab it and then sat on the bed to admire it. It was an aluminum jewelry box, handcrafted with a tree-embossed emblem. She thought, *How come I'd never seen this box before? Was it always there underneath the bed?* Once she got past that, she thought it was gorgeous and slowly opened the lid to peek inside. In it was a silver birth flower band ring. She took it out of the box, placed the box on the bed, and then put the ring on her ring finger. It fit perfectly, as she raised her hand admiring its beauty. She realized that it must have been Denise's, and then quickly took it off. But she had the compulsion to not put it back and keep it. She placed the empty box back under the bed, then she put the ring in a handkerchief that she found on the dresser, folded the ring in it, and placed it in her pocket. Then, she cheerfully walked out of the room, and down the long dark wood floor hallway.

The light reddish walls featured large-sized tapestry antique Israeli Marbediah hung rugs with detailed images telling various historic religious stories. The ceiling staggered with 17th-century tapered candlelight chandeliers now retrofitted for modern electricity. She walked down the steps swiping her hand across the base of a *Roma* statue situated on the mid-way platform halfway down to the ground level. She wandered cheerfully as she looked for the nurse to get an update on Bishop Hines' injuries, most likely still at a hospital recovering. But when Lauren walked past the home's library study, she noticed Bishop Hines in her periphery. She came to an abrupt stop, walked a few steps backward, and leaned her head into the doorway. There Bishop Hines was, sitting at his desk. He held a book in one hand reading, and with the other, he held an ice pack over a large gauze pad bandage stained with blood. It was placed on his forehead where he sustained injury from the impact of debris from the explosion.

"Hello, my dear," said Bishop Hines, not looking up with his reading glasses on the tip of his nose.

"What are you doing here? You're supposed to be at the hospital," said Lauren, more concerned about his injury than his presence. From spending so much time with Bishop Hines, she should have known his stubbornness would not allow him to be held in a hospital too long, let alone answer her question.

"You have your eyesight back?" asked Bishop Hines, nonchalantly.

"Yes! I spoke to Joshua and he healed my eyesight! Right over the phone!" said Lauren excitedly. "But you don't seem surprised."

"From all the miracles that I have seen, I'm rarely surprised, my dear."

"Are you referring to Joshua's mother?"

He paused for a moment, then answered. "Yes, among others. Denise was one of the many vessels that I've seen do God's healing work. So, when I heard your screams from upstairs, I had a pretty good feeling and confidence in what had happened. Nothing is impossible with God, especially when two or three people are on one accord."

"Bishop. After the explosion at that little hospital, why would you call her name?" she asked, referring to when he whispered Denise's name after the explosion at the asclepieia.

"Why would I call whose name?" he replied, not remembering.

"So, you don't remember? After you got hit and lying on the ground, you said, 'Not again, Denise.' Then something about *dying daily.*"

"I did?" questioned Bishop Hines, perplexed.

"Yes you did," said Lauren with the expectation of a definitive answer.

Bishop Hines took the ice pack off his forehead and lowered his head without giving her a response.

"Bishop, what does that mean?"

"Before we get to that, when we arrived at the asclepieia, you felt something, something right before the building exploded, correct?"

"Yes, Bishop. Even though I could not see and had the bandages over my eyes, for some reason, I was able to visualize the building, and then right before the explosion, I saw the image of a shadow of a person running away from it."

"A person?"

"A person. But they had a presence, and evil presence. The same feeling we had during the last fire at Joshua's uncle's church."

"I believe that whatever we're dealing with, your ability, along with Joshua, will come in handy very soon."

"Did you know that Joshua has this technique to tap into his spiritual…" He interrupted Lauren before she finished her sentence.

"Did you ever tell Joshua or anyone else I brought you and Mike to here to Rome, and why?" referring to his son, Mike, who was previously engaged to Lauren before she met Joshua.

"No, of course not. Why would I tell Joshua specific details about Mike and me, and everything that we did here? It was bad enough how he found out about us through his friend Monty before I had a chance to tell him first. I hate social media!"

Bishop Hines got up from the desk and walked over to shut the door. He wanted to make sure that no one heard about their secret activities in the past. Then he sat back down on a sofa in the center of the room. His hand gestured for Lauren to join him in the adjacent chair. She obliged, then sat quietly waiting for him to speak.

"So again, you've told no one about the rituals that you both had to go through?" Bishop Hines was referring to a series of spiritual tests and events that Archbishop Bennett and he had Lauren and Mike go through during their engagement, just right before Lauren and Mike called off their wedding. However, Lauren and Mike were unaware of the true reasons for these tests, and still unaware at this moment.

"Rituals! What do you mean rituals?" asked Lauren, now alarmed. "I thought you said Mike and I were doing all those tests and insane physical challenges just to test our faith in God and trust in each other, maybe become part of some elite spiritual group if we passed."

"Well, my dear, that is partially true," said Bishop Hines reluctantly.

"What do you mean, partially true?"

Bishop Hines put the icepack back on his head. "I apologize for not providing you with the truth sooner, Lauren. But with recent, I have no choice now." Lauren waited with a surprised look on her face realizing that Bishop Hines and Archbishop Bennett may have deceived her. He continued, "Archbishop Bennett and I are a part of this very old secret religious group called *The Circle*. He and I mostly are agents to help their cause, but we are still technically members."

"A religious secret society?" interjected Lauren.

"Well, we don't like to look at it that way. It started from a few members after the death and resurrection of Christ. Then it continued and developed because of many failed or unproductive secret societies. The structure and accuracy of it was formed from a few *Mystery Schools*."

"You mean, the ancient Mystery Schools? I read all about them. They were small exclusive schools that taught the elite of elite from Greece to around the world, right? Some taught theories of time travel, artificial intelligence, and technology beyond imagination hundreds of years ago which may have paved the way for what we have today."

"Correct. Some schools still exist today, and a few prominent and productive secret societies were created from within them. The Circle was formed in the effort to foresee and possibly prevent disasters or world-ending wars being started by a rogue nation, or to foresee a new plague and disease that could wipe out half the earth, or even demonic forces coming back to this realm active again."

"What do you mean by demonic forces coming back again?"

"That's a separate lengthy discussion we don't have time for my dear. But briefly, do you ever wonder why, we do not see or hear about demons possessing people, violently, like we did centuries ago?"

"Now that you mention it, no. Why not?" she asked, perplexed.

"You don't for two reasons. Number one, a lot of true diseases and illnesses, like seizures and other conditions centuries ago, were misinterpreted as being possessed by demons. This same thing happened to Archbishop Bennett's daughter, Ezra, when she was very young."

"Really? I didn't know that."

"The second is that earth, the universe, and God's creation is all part of distinct mathematical equations in some way shape or form that needs to be balanced. And without good or God being a priority in everyone's life, then the devil and evil don't have to be either. It's the balance of life on earth. For example, a structural engineer calculates how much weight of earth needs to be held up by a retaining wall, and then the wall is designed mathematically accordingly to hold it. To travel in space, we need to calculate the earth's rotation, its revolution, distance from takeoff, wind resistance, and hundreds of other variables to plan a trip. An unbalanced equation means the rocket ship doesn't fly, or fully reaches its destination, or explodes on its way. Whether Christians believe it or not, or even understand it, God's creation and everything that it does, and what we do, from weather seasons changing to rotating automobile car tires, are all based on mathematical equations." He paused before he uttered a related memory, "What's funny is that, in the past, people used to attempt to debate me about God or religion by using general theology, past doctrine, and other ideas all created and defined by man. But I would tell them, if you don't have a deep knowledge of physics and math and can relate them to biblical principles, then you are outmatched to debate me about the Bible and God." He then looked away selfishly happy with that thought.

"Study up on my physics and calculus…got it," joked Lauren.

Bishop Hines ignored her joke, "As a result, the equation between good and evil must always be balanced on earth, that is until the apocalypse and the end of the world, when the good, our Heavenly Father will destroy evil forever."

"So, following your math equation based thinking, Bishop. In past centuries, God, or the concept of God, was a primary focus on earth and in people's life, so evil equated the same."

"You're saying that Evil matched God's energy?" Lauren chuckled.

"Say, what?" he asked, not getting the reference.

"Never mind, continue." Lauren continued to giggle a bit more.

"But now, since God is no longer a priority in our lives, in schools, work, or even in our hearts, evil and demons don't appear like they used to because…they don't have to?" asked Lauren.

"As always, you pick up things very quickly. The Bible says, the devil is as a roaring lion seeking whom he may devour, and lions are lazy and don't do any work—unless they must. Most of humankind no longer feels the need for God or His power. They believe he exists, even acknowledge him as the creator and judge between good and evil. But God is not worshipped or feared like in the past. Thus, making the devil's job much easier than ever. Interestingly, people still blame the devil for many things, but he's been on a quiet vacation."

Lauren interrupted. "So, he's just sitting in some day spa somewhere scrolling through social media watching us send ourselves to hell?"

Bishop Hines did not find this joke funny, either. He continued, "But the primary goal of The Circle was always to reach what a few historic

Christian philosophers call, *The Light of Life.*"

"The Light of Life. What is that? I never heard of it" It was a rarity for Bishop Hines or anyone to hear those words from Lauren.

"The Light of Life is mentioned three times in the Bible. Jesus mentions it in John 8 verse 12, saying, '…he that followeth me shall not walk in darkness, but shall have the light of life.' This was amazing coming from Jesus, as the Light of Life was also mentioned by King David in Psalm 56, and in the book of Job chapter 33. But what's interesting is that when it's mentioned in the book of Job, it's very specific, it says in verse 29, 'Behold, God does all these things, twice, three times, with a man, *to bring back his soul from the pit, that he may be lighted with the light of life.'* Then Jesus goes on later to say in John 14 verse 12, '…he that believeth on me, the works that I do shall he do also; and greater works than these shall he do…' Then, Jesus, who had already done so many wonderful things and great miracles, before he was crucified on the cross and died, said, we are able to do even greater works than him."

"Are you saying the Light of Life is some kind of power?"

"The Holy Spirit is power. But The Circle, and many other past cultures, secretly believed that the Light of Life is the actual *key* to God's power, as described by Job, King David, and Jesus. This is one of the reasons why you see so many different cultures around the world thousands of miles and hundreds of centuries apart from each other use the key or keyhole as a symbol for doors, landmarks, and ritual sites."

"Really?"

"Search what cultures and when used keyholes as symbols in the design of their cities. You be surprised how many are right under your nose, all in hopes of obtaining the Light of Life first before others."

"But how?" asked Lauren.

"First, think about it in the natural. What is the common denominator for all the greatest accomplishments?"

"Hard work, intelligence, perseverance," responded Lauren.

"No. All those things can help toward success but the most common denominator in one's greatest accomplishments is failure, adversity, or even death. A colleague of mine, who is a real estate developer and a writer, said that some of his greatest successes came after failure. So, instead of ROI or return on investment, he called it ROF, return on failure. Think about it, my dear. The greatest love songs ever written are created by artists who went through the worst breakups. The best paintings are created during the worst and broke time of a painter's life, sometimes becoming famous only until after death. The best inventions were made after much ridicule and failure, like the Wright Brother's and the airplane. The best athletes typically went through the most adversity to get to their level of accomplishment. Even scripturally, the Bible says, '...*the trying of your faith worketh patience and patience worketh that you may be perfect, lacking nothing.*' Loss of a loved one, loss of a relationship that meant everything, loss of a job, a horrible accident that one barely survived, and having to overcome mountains of trials and tribulations, all give a person a portion of the Light of Life. Suffering for a moment with faith always yields God's glory and perfection as Peter mentions in his letter to the pilgrims of Anatolia aka Asia Minor..."

Lauren interrupted, as only she could with Bishop Hines, "Way too much detail, Bishop. I got it. The best success stories have the most struggle behind them. But if that's the natural, then what about the spiritual?"

"We die daily," said Bishop Hines.

"Okay, we die daily," repeated Lauren. "But what does that really mean, Bishop?"

"It's the code of The Circle, based on Paul's statement in his letter to the church of Corinth. The Circle and many others believe that Jesus and others in the Bible showed the key to God's power and that was found through suffering, long-suffering to the brink of death, and even death itself. Our Lord and Savior, Jesus Christ came to the earth, dwelled amongst us, and most importantly, experienced all three."

"Wait. Let me get this straight. The Circle believes that the key to God's power is to suffer and die, or almost die...or even die?"

"With all you know, is it that so hard to grasp? Think of how many scriptures, prophets, and biblical stories show us this concept. Jesus said, 'Whosoever will save his life shall lose it, whosoever will lose his life for my sake shall find it,' or how about Abraham raising his knife bringing his son to the brink of death only to have God stop him right before the killing strike and making Isaac the producer of a great and blessed nation still to this day.; or even his brother and the persecution that he and his mother experienced to produce another great nation. I could go on and on."

Hearing his theory and explanation, Lauren thought about possible actions that Bishop Hines engaged in to acquire the Light of Life. She became angered and did not hold back with her next words, "So what are you saying, Bishop? Please don't tell me you go around killing people or almost killing them to see if God's power rises up within them!"

"Watch your tone, young lady," he countered with the same raised tone. "I'm still the bishop, and you're still a guest in this house."

Lauren did not apologize but she replied in a softer tone, "Are you going to answer the question, Bishop?"

"In the past, yes. The Circle would engage in what some may feel are nefarious actions to help selected individuals obtain the Light of Life. But I assure you, it's not like that now."

"Hold on. When you and Archbishop Bennett had Mike and me in those large water tank pods in the basement of the asclepieia, you said we were there training to see how in sync we were together. But then the lids on our tanks got jammed and it forced us to hold our breaths longer than we ever could. Was that part of you trying to find out if we could obtain the Light of Life!" exclaimed Lauren. Bishop Hines did not respond confirming her truth. She continued, "I wondered why you and everyone just stood around so calmly while only the trainers acted frantic to get us out."

He interjected, "My dear, Lauren. What you don't realize is that the world has changed. In the past, all we had to do was preach about how God was omniscient, omnipotent, and omnipresent, or preach about hell and burning for all eternity if you did not give your life to Christ, and that alone caused people to believe and want to change their ways. That old messaging is only working on backsliders who were raised up in the church. Now, it's not that simple. Even you, my dear, I heard arguing with my son Mike through technology, we would be considered gods by people who lived thousands of years ago. With technology, we have a lot of the same powers and abilities that we used to say only God possessed. We can argue the correctness of scriptures with non-believers or Calvinism versus Lutheranism with so-called Christians all day long. But unless the body and followers of Christ start showing true love, sacrifice, character, and wonderous miracles as they did in the past to confirm God's existence and power, why else would anyone believe? Where's our Elijahs sending fire down from heaven? Where's our Peters going into hospitals healing the crippled?

"With all due respect Bishop, those are the questions you should be asking God, not yourself! The problem doesn't justify your actions! You are playing with God or want to play God. What you're doing may very well be the cause of the wrong end of that equation opening a door that we don't want opened," exclaimed Lauren, fiercely.

"Time is running out Lauren. The real end of the world is near, and closer than you think. The explosion and the earthquake were just the beginning—and it's going to get worse."

"You don't know that," said Lauren, frustrated.

"Actually, we do. All the biblical signs have fallen into order, and The Circle members have had a joint prophetic vision, and all our nations leaders have enacted Protocol-11. It's only a matter of moments now,"

"Protocol-11. What do you mean by Protocol-11?"

"Lauren. Protocol-11 means the possible end of the world."

"Respectfully Bishop. Can you quit being vague? I'm thirty seconds away from being over with this conversation."

"Very well. Protocol-11 is one of twenty-one Global Survival Protocols that are a series of new global laws, allowable actions, and measures that countries are allowed to take which may violate existing treaties or agreements."

"Why would this be allowed and why know?"

"They are defined exactly as they are titled—to help maintain mankind's existence after a global catastrophic event. These protocols are to ensure a certain level of safety for a few, but they also open the possibility of war and destruction for most of the world. Each Protocol correlates to a possible disaster, like a dramatic climate change, alien invasion, and even a biblical apocalypse. We believe the world is about to end, and now so do all the world leaders. Confidentially, they're taking measures in conjunction with Protocol-11 and to ensure their safety. This is not just about a string of church fires in Philadelphia anymore. It is the entire world and millions of souls that could be lost. You think you and Joshua can save the entire world? With what we know, and through the teachings of Jesus and others in the Bible, if we can just demonstrate God's power and miracles through just a few people, we can save many who would believe," said Bishop Hines.

"All of this sounds to me like nonsense. Even if true, the God we serve, Bishop, has the power to overcome any catastrophic event."

Suddenly, the earth and house began to ominously shake. The house staff ran down the hallway taking cover. It was an earthquake; another small earthquake of many that had occurred in various countries during the past two weeks. Bishop Hines got up and flipped over the sofa and told Lauren to get underneath it. She complied. Then he ran back to his desk and got under it right before books started falling off the shelves. The vibration and shaking occurred for about thirty more seconds. When it was over, they both got up from their coverings and looked at each other. They were glad that they were both safe.

"Evidence again that it has begun, my dear," said Bishop Hines. Malcontented, Lauren abruptly walked out of the room. Bishop Hines yelled after her presence, "Don't go too far! Remember, we are the primary facilitators and sponsors of this 'Hands Across the World' charity event. Earthquakes or not, it's still happening in just a few days!" He sighed, as he knew she was intentionally ignoring him.

[*ring-ring ring-ring*]

Bishop Hines' cell phone rang. It was Archbishop Bennett calling.

"Hello," answered Bishop Hines.

"Did you feel that way over there?" asked Archbishop Bennett as he was much further away in Venice.

"Of course. Lauren and I were here in the library when it hit."

"How did that go?"

"Not good," Bishop Hines replied.

"We are running out of time, Bishop."

"You're preaching to the choir."

"Well, the choir is running out of songs to sing. I wanted to ask you, again. Even with The Circle's prediction and Protocol-11 being enacted, we should continue with the Hands Across the World event, correct?" he asked, desiring Bishop Hines confirmation of support to proceed with the event.

Bishop Hines avoided directly answering, "So, it's official, Protocol-11 will not be withdrawn by any nation? Couldn't The Church and his excellency do anything about it?"

"Our Holy Father, the Pope himself has sent a personalized written letter with an embossed seal from drops of his own blood to all the major nations imploring them to withdraw from Protocol-11. That hasn't been done since Pope Urban II in 1095, and they have all rejected his request," said Archbishop Bennett, frustrated.

"Twenty-one years ago, we were dealing with terrorist bombs. Now, we are dealing with fires, bombs, earthquakes, and Protocol-11. Can things get any worse?" said Bishop Hines, even more frustrated.

"What about the recent explosion in Philadelphia, killing Pastor Williams at his home? Does Officer Reese have any leads?"

"Not yet. Do you think they're all related?"

"It must be, right Bishop? We haven't been this close to an apocalypse since *1888*." Then, Archbishop Bennett quietly said, "Does Lauren know that she and Joshua may be the cause of this?"

Bishop Hines cleared his throat, "Honestly, for some reason I get the feeling that it started with Denise. But if you say, Joshua and Lauren are the last seal, one more time, I'm going to…"

Archbishop Bennett interrupted before he'd finished, "I hope you're right because we are about to find out. See you in The Chamber, Bishop. The Light of Life or Denise's Hands Across the World event seems to be our only hope now." Archbishop Bennett hung up the phone.

With a doleful thought, Bishop Hines said quietly to himself, "We still don't even know what your idea of the Hands Across the World meant in all of this, Denise. If only you could have figured it out before you died. Hopefully, Joshua knows. God, I hope he knows."

9

A Soulless Solace

Present Evening – Rome, Italy.
Three days before Hands Across the World.

Joshua got up from the grave and ran out of the cemetery all the way to his mother's place of work, the Penn Fresh grocery store. The distance seemed too short. It only took him less than a minute to approach the automatic entrance doors. Right before he entered the store, he slowed down, but not to a complete stop, as he remembered that his mother was dead. He'd remembered that she died in his arms in his uncle's church, So, why would he be running to check on her at work? His momentum and curiosity forced him through the entrance anyway. He softly greeted the front-end workers and a few customers with a smile, and kept the same slow pace until he got back to the deli department. To his surprise, there she was, his mother in her work uniform and name tag just like he remembered. She was squatted down close to the ground placing pre-made hoagies in one of the low refrigerated cases.

"Mom?" said Joshua, hesitantly as he could not believe it was her, alive. She turned toward Joshua and smiled but then kept working. He controlled the tears, wiped his nose and face with his sleeve. He was nervous, but spoke again. "How are you here? I thought you were…"

She immediately cut him off by turning her head to him again, put her finger over her lips, and said, "Shhhh…It's almost time Joshua. Remember to stack them side by side, soldier-course style, Joshua. *That will make them all strong and on one accord.* Be strong and of good courage, only be thou strong and of good courage." Then, she went back to stacking the hoagies in the case.

Not focused on his mother's words, Joshua spoke again, but louder, "I missed you so much. We all miss you."

She then looked up at the ceiling and said, "Stack them all side by side before it's too late, Joshua. The dark angel is free. I held it back, as long as I could, but the dark angel is free."

Suddenly, a deafening thunder occurred so loud and strong that it vibrated throughout the grocery store building and within Joshua's entire upper body. He looked up at the ceiling with caution at the noise and the rumble. When he looked back down to his mother, she was gone. Then, the store building began to violently shake. It was an earthquake. Joshua pointlessly grabbed closely onto the case and squatted down to the ground with his head down. Food and other products fell from the gondolas and shelves. Parts of the ceiling broke apart and fell to the floor. Then, Joshua heard a piercing scream.

* * *

Joshua was awakened by a bump from the private plane's stewardess. She accidentally hit him as she walked up the aisle checking to make sure everything was in order for the landing, no unsecured bags within the aisle or in empty seats, everyone with their seat belts buckled. It was just a dream. The same dream he had while in the hospital. It scared him, and he felt that fear within his heart as he remembered that his dreams carried some reality or future events with them. Joshua felt the plane slow down. The Italian pilot made an announcement over the speaker system. "*Signore e signori, stiamo iniziando la fase di avvicinamento alla Base Aerea di Guidonia, nei pressi di Roma. L'atterraggio av-*

verrà tra circa dieci minuti. Vi preghiamo di tenere le cinture di sicurezza allacciate." The announcement was repeated. But this time, translated in English, "Ladies and gentlemen, we are beginning our approach to Guidonia Air Base, near Rome. Landing will take place in approximately ten minutes. Please keep your seatbelts fastened." Joshua looked out the window, and his eyes consumed the intricate and historic buildings from on high, all the way down until the landing. From having cellular reception again, his cell phone's alert notifications began to pop up. He received a few messages and missed calls from Officer Reese and Monty, and numerous text messages from Lauren. Of course, he only focused on Lauren's messages and texted her back.

[Joshua]: Just landed.

Lauren immediately responded.

[Lauren]: Hooray! Omg that took forever! I can't wait to see you.

[Joshua]: My legs hurt so bad.

[Lauren]: You better exhale and heal them like you did my eyes. We have so much to see when you get here. First time in Rome right?

[Joshua]: Yup. I think lol.

[Lauren]: What does that mean?

Joshua wondered if he should tell Lauren about his passport or new dream. He then concluded, *'Now is not the time."*

[Joshua]: Tell you later but I'm okay. My soul loves your soul.

[Lauren]: My soul loves your soul!

Ezra was asleep, but Jacob was awake and saw Joshua texting Lauren decided to speak to Joshua. "Except for that weird passport thing, you ever been in Rome," asked Jacob.

"Funny. Lauren just asked the same thing," he replied.

"You're going to love it."

"That's what I've been told."

After a few minutes, the plane came to a stop and Ezra awakened.

Once they got off the plane, Joshua saw another black Mercedes Sprinter van on the tarmac waiting for them. Unlike the one that took them from Philadelphia to the regional airport, this one was luxurious. It had captain's chairs, a television monitor, and a minibar filled with snacks and drinks. Jacob went straight for the snacks, opened a small bag of chips, and stuck about half of the contents in his mouth all at once. Ezra shook her head, and said, "You're such an embarrassment."

"You envy me," countered Jacob with his mouth full.

"Are you sure you two aren't brother and sister?" asked Joshua with a chuckle. Jacob stopped chewing, but just for moment.

"Are there any barf bags in here?" replied Lauren, as she jokingly looked around. Jacob continued to chomp on his chips even louder.

The driver drove them from the airbase into the heart of Rome. Joshua loved seeing both the beautiful architectural buildings and the excessive amount of graffiti that covered their walls. It reminded him of a section of Broad Street, but with more historic buildings. Even at night, the traffic was the same. It was heavy but with many mini-vehicles and motor scooters that just weaved in and out of lanes, and in between cars, without care or a horn that followed. *This is definitely not Philadelphia*, thought Joshua.

Like always, Jacob broke the silence, as he opened his third bag of chips. "This is the life.

"Does the clergy of the Catholic Church travel like this all the time?" asked Joshua.

"Most of the time, they fly commercial, even the Pope," said Jacob.

"The Church is not about doing anything in excess of our basic needs. However, every now and then, we do get a taste of the good life, especially when time or safety is a necessity," said Ezra.

"With the recent earthquakes and the high threat level we are on, we have special permission and access from Ezra's father," said Jacob.

"Earthquakes?" asked Joshua, also remembering the earthquakes that's been part of his dream.

"Yes. You probably haven't been paying attention during the past week or two, dealing with your string of church fires. But there were quite a few recently, all over the globe. Another one just hit here in Rome not too long ago while we were in the air," said Ezra.

Joshua knew that this was a bad sign. His dream; the explosion at the house that killed his uncle and aunt; and the explosion that injured his mentor and father figure, Bishop Hines. It all had to be related.

"All occurring right before Hands Across the World," said Jacob.

"Hands Across the World, what is that?" asked Joshua.

"Seriously, Joshua. You don't know about Hands Across the World, either?" Ezra asked in unbelief.

Understandably, Joshua became extremely frustrated and with a raised tone addressed Ezra's question. "Umm…let's see Ezra! About two years ago, my mother died. Then, just this past week was the primary suspect of a string of church fires in my own neighbor; was running from the police; I lost my job; found out my aunt and uncle were killed by an explosion; was strapped to a wooden table under the city, almost died a few times, and I keep running into people that claim they knew my mother more than me. Oh yeah, and I lost my job, my girlfriend is blind now, and just got on a damn plane with you, who I don't know, to somewhere I never been with a passport that says I've been here! I just can't wait to see what God has in store for me next week! So, forgive me if I'm a little behind on damn current events!" exclaimed Joshua now extremely angry and almost with no control. Jacob and the driver were frightened as Joshua's voice was just deeper than usual and vibrated through the van.

"You're right. I'm sorry, Joshua," said Ezra composed and apologetically, with the hope of calming him down. She continued with empathy and said, "I remember the first time your mother came up with this event, Hands Across the Word. It even got my father excited. She felt it was going to change the world. Have the world look at us Christians differently, respected, maybe even be the solution to Protocol-11." Joshua let go of his anger and listened for more. "If you didn't know, Hands Across America was a fundraising event in the mid-80s that over five million people participated in, including many well-known celebrities and politicians."

Jacob chimed in, "I think it raised over fifteen million dollars."

Now calm and back to normal, Joshua responded, "Okay. I do remember my mother telling me about that and how she participated in it when she was younger. She would talk about it all the time."

"Really, Joshua. What did she say?" asked Ezra, desperate.

For some unknown reason, Joshua now realized that Ezra and Jacob are calling him Joshua, instead of Josh, just like Lauren and Bishop Hines. And for some reason, this does not bother him. But he responded to Ezra's question. "I remember she said many people of different religions and races came together for a good cause. She also mentioned how angry she was, even as a kid, when she found out that there were so many gaps in the human chain link."

"Well, Hands Across the World is your mother's idea of basically the same thing, Joshua. It has been in the works for over two years now. Your mother and my father started planning it together, right before she died," said Ezra.

Jacob decided to provide more details. "When your mother died, that put a long hold on the planning. No one was really motivated after that. That was until Archbishop Bennett decided to keep the plans going. It's been his passion ever since," said Jacob.

"So, if it's across the world, how are they thinking of linking across the oceans and seas?" asked Joshua.

"Your mother's idea was that no link can be broken, not like it happened before. Therefore, if a line of people cannot fully connect, they must create a circle, even if it is a small one at the end of a line. She always emphasized that no line should be broken," said Ezra.

"Across the whole world. No line broken at all. How is that even possible?" said Joshua.

"She said it could be done and would be done, and my father believed her," said Ezra.

"Why was it so important?" asked Joshua.

"That's what we're hoping you can tell us, Joshua. The Circle believed that the end of the world is approaching and approaching soon. Your mother and now my father believe this event is the only thing that may be able to stop the end of the world," said Ezra.

"The Circle. What's The Circle?" asked Joshua.

"It's the oldest religious secret society of prophets and healers, people with the gift of prophecy and healing. But Joshua, Bishop Hines and my father should be the ones to give you more details on that. Just know that because of The Circle's prophecy and what's now occurring around the world, things seen and unseen, many countries are taking precautions to endure and/or protect themselves, just in case it's true. And the Circle has never been wrong," said Ezra.

"What are they doing to take precautions?" asked Joshua, concerned and in unbelief.

"Protocol-11," said Ezra.

"What's Protocol-11," said Joshua.

"Like I just she said, Bishop Hines and Archbishop Bennett should explain later in more detail. Hold off on your questions until then. But for now, let's just say it's the world's response to The Circle's prediction that the world is about to end. Therefore, people are building underground bunkers again; and stocking up on weapons, dry food, and canned goods supplies," said Jacob.

Ezra added, "More importantly, Joshua, countries are fighting for adjacent lands for new military bases or protective barriers and buffers. Other countries and localities are even setting fires to their own land and building up walls or creating underground self-sufficient cities to sustain themselves and their people against possible missile or nuclear attacks, or even evil enemies."

"Evil enemies?" asked Joshua, perplexed.

"Zombies...the undead rising...people possessed by demons...all of the above," joked Jacob as he laughed.

"Don't listen to him, Joshua," said Ezra. "No one knows what will really happen, so they're taking precautions for anything. But the preparation will raise the level of potential threats and may bring us to an all-out war," said Ezra.

"Our weapons today have unimaginable power, Joshua," said Jacob.

Joshua clarified, "Just so I understand, the end of the world is approaching, and my mother was convinced that Hands Across the World was the key to stopping it—or at least saving most of it."

"Yes. But she could not explain how," Jacob interjected.

Ezra continued, "My father believed her, or believed in her, especially after what she had done for us...for me. But as Jacob said, without an explanation on how, Bishop Hines and The Circle felt it necessary to pursue another course. An undesirable one."

"What course?" asked Joshua, again.

"The Light of Life," said Ezra. Ezra then looked at Jacob, and Jacob turned toward the window.

"God! Not another thing that I don't know about. Okay, what in the world is the Light of Life?" asked Joshua.

10

Tunnel Vision

Present Evening – Rome, Italy.
Three days before Hands Across the World.

After they drove for about twenty minutes, their van slowed down and came to a stop and without pulling over to the side. As a result, the traffic behind them had also come to a complete halt.

"He's not going to park the van here in the middle of the street is he?" asked Joshua, concerned for their safety.

"He's just letting us out. It would take him longer to park. It's easier for us to just jump out and keep going," said Jacob.

As they exited the van, Joshua looked at the amount of traffic behind them and realized not one vehicle honked at them to keep moving or get out of the way. He thought, *This is definitely, definitely not Philadelphia.* However, he did hear a very loud piercing alarm noise that repeated over and over, which reminded him of the old foreign movies his mother used to watch.

"So, that loud siren is real and still being used today?" asked Joshua loudly, annoyed.

"You mean, the polizia?" asked Jacob.

"Police! Yes. That noise is so annoying," explained Joshua.

"Are you telling me that the police alarms in the States sound nice and pleasant?" countered Jacob.

"Okay, good point," said Joshua as he grimaced.

Ezra led the way southward, down the road known as the *Lungote-vere* which runs parallel with the river named Tiber.

"Where are we headed?" asked Joshua.

"You see that building over to the southwest," said Ezra, referring to a large castle structure that was approximately six blocks away. It was easily seen through the trees and behind a bridge with Vatican City just right behind it.

"Wow. That sucker is huge! Is that a real castle?" asked Joshua.

"It is. Castel Sant'Angelo. It's a museum now," said Jacob.

"Underneath and surrounding it, there are underground tunnels under that go to Vatican City and the inner parts of Rome. Some are known, some are not," said Ezra.

Joshua thought about the secret Harriet Tubman underground tunnels that Lauren and he discovered in Philadelphia that connected the churches along the Boulevard.

Ezra continued, "One of the secret tunnels lead to The Chamber. That's where we're headed," said Ezra.

"What's The Chamber?" asked Joshua.

"It's where the members of The Circle meet...or met. We will be meeting my father and Bishop Hines there. I assume Lauren will be there as well," Ezra replied.

Joshua realized that he had forgotten to text Lauren and inform her that they had gotten out of the van and were near Vatican City. He grabbed his phone.

[Joshua]: Just got out van. Walking toward this castle.

Lauren responded immediately.

[Lauren]: I figured I'd let you enjoy the views of Rome from the airport to here. I'm with Bishop. Headed to the same place to meet up.

[Joshua]: Rome's views are gorgeous. But I only care about the view of seeing you asap.

[Lauren]: So corny, but I love it and same. Guess where I am.

[Joshua]: Where?

[Lauren]: We're walking in an underground tunnel. Reminds me of being in Philadelphia with you.

[Joshua]: I just found that out! Sounds like you are a few minutes ahead of us. I guess secret underground tunnels are just part of our date nights lol.

[Lauren]: Haha! Ever since I told you I wasn't a movie and dinner type of girl, you haven't disappointed with our dates.

[Joshua]: The day may change...

[Lauren]: ...but never the plan.

[Joshua]: No matter what happens, for you and by you...

[Lauren]: I will forever stand. You got my note! I gave it to the nurse when they said I had to leave right away. She seemed busy so I wasn't sure if she would give it to you.

[Joshua]: It worked out. See you soon.

Joshua and Lauren felt connected more than ever. He then looked up from his phone and noticed Ezra and Jacob were way ahead of him, and walked down some steps adjacent to the street next to the Tiber River. He followed and rushed to catch up. The steps led down to a door with a full-sized iron gate attached to it, which also possessed a chain and padlock. Ezra looked up the steps behind Jacob and Joshua to make sure no one was behind them or at the top of the steps watching. She turned back toward the door, squatted down, and pulled out a stone from the side retaining wall. Behind the stone was a black round button that she quickly pressed and then immediately put the stone back. After a few seconds, they heard a buzz tone and then a loud click that came from the door that signified that the door was unlocked.

Ezra pulled the door open revealing that the attached iron gate, chain, and padlock were bogus and deceitful just to keep people away. Ezra and Jacob walked through first. Joshua took a brief moment to inspect the iron gate and door, and said, "The deceived."

"What?" asked Jacob.

"Never mind," said Joshua. He knew Lauren would have gotten that stated inside joke. He decided to text her one more time.

[Joshua]: Looks like we are close. See you soon.

[Lauren]: Okay. Pay attention in the tunnels. It's not like under the Boulevard.

[Joshua]: Of course.

As soon as Joshua hit send on that last text to Lauren and walked into the tunnel, he hit his head on a large rusty water pipe going across the top of the tunnel. The impact made a large bong noise which caused Joshua to grab his head and bend towards the ground in pain. He remembered Lauren's text to pay attention. Ezra and Jacob stopped and looked back to see if he was okay. "I'm good!" yelled Joshua, and waved for them to continue forward.

"Sorry. I forgot to tell you to pay attention and keep your head down. Since we are next to the river and the castle, there are lots of drainage pipes in these tunnels," said Ezra.

Lauren was right. It was not like the Underground Tunnel they found in Philadelphia. This tunnel was dimly lit by small electrical fixtures; and depending on the section, its walls and ceiling composition were either the old original stone or replaced brick where the stone may have eroded or faltered. After a few minutes, the passageway turned toward the right or in a westwardly direction. Joshua knew that this meant that the tunnel's path was going under the river. His assumption was confirmed when they encountered more pipes, water dripping from the ceiling and walls, and large drains built into the ground. Jacob could tell Joshua looked concerned.

"No worries bro. The tunnel is designed to have some leakage to relieve pressure. We're totally safe down here," said Jacob.

"So, none of these tunnels ever collapsed?" countered Joshua.

"Good point. Not sure," replied Jacob.

After walking for quite some time and down numerous levels of steps taking them deep underground, the area finally opened to a large well-lit cavern known as The Chamber. Joshua immediately looked up and the ceiling went from seven feet from in the tunnel to over thirty feet high in the cavern. It had massive carvings on the walls showing the historic Roman empire, from religious figures to warriors in mighty chariot battles. Enormous large statues of the twelve disciples were seated deep within concave portions of the walls, positioned just below the top of the domed ceiling, which had a Christian cross hanging from the center. It was larger than any cross Joshua had seen in any church in America. He then looked down along the lower portion of the cavern and noticed a row of chains with thick iron wrist cuffs bolted into the wall, which had more significance regarding his mother than he knew. But he was about to find out. He was in awe of the architecture, the detail, and more importantly, the significance this secret meeting placed used for centuries, strategic against demonic or enemy threats against the world.

"Joshua!" yelled Lauren, as she ran into his arms. They embraced like two kindergartners meeting for the first time outside of school for a play date.

11

The Circle

Present Evening – Rome, Italy.
Three days before Hands Across the World.

After Joshua and Lauren embraced and kissed each other for quite some time, Bishop Hines had cleared his throat loudly to get them to stop and focus on their mission and reason for being there.

"Why don't they get a tunnel," said Jacob, as he looked as Ezra joking.

"You're not funny," Ezra replied.

Joshua finally looked up from Lauren, and his gaze focused on the massive ceiling of the underground cavern.

"Joshua. Welcome to The Chamber," said Bishop Hines. This finally broke up their lengthy hold. "Over the past two thousand years or less, only about three hundred people have ever stepped foot inside this place, and you're now one of them."

"Two hundred and eighty-seven people to be exact," said Archbishop Bennett as he walked into The Chamber. He lagged the group by just over two minutes.

"*Padre Giovanni!*" exclaimed Ezra and Jacob collectively as they did a quick kneel, calling him Father Giovanni or *Father John* in respect and reverence of his presence. Ezra then ran up to him and hugged him tightly, and said, "*Padre.*"

For the benefit of the group, they spoke in English. "Glad you made it back safely, my lovely daughter," said Archbishop Bennett.

"The mighty Joshua kept us safe, and in his spare time he decided to heal Lauren," joked Ezra.

"That does not surprise me. He is just like his mother," he replied.

"Indeed, he is," said Bishop Hines.

"Why are we here?" asked Joshua and Lauren at the exact same time. They looked at each other and smiled, then looked back at the group with deep intention.

"Please take a seat," said Archbishop Bennett.

In the center of The Chamber was a gigantic circular table with a diameter of exactly seven meters, or approximately twenty-three feet. It was made of travertine, a hard white limestone also referred to as the Stone of Rome.

As they sat down in the large priest chairs at the table, Lauren said, "This table is amazing. I wonder how long it took to carve and smooth out this stone."

"…and how did it get down here in the first place?" asked Joshua.

Before Archbishop Bennett could respond to their questions, Ezra and Jacob went to sit down in the large priest chairs with everyone. Archbishop Bennett immediately yelled at them, "Not you two! *Voi entrambi sapete che se non fate parte del Circolo, non vi è permesso sedervi a questo tavolo!*"

Jacob laughed at their failed attempt to sit at the table, and said, "It was worth a shot. Better than sitting out in the tunnel like usual."

Joshua leaned over and whispered to Lauren, "What do you think he said to them?" He didn't expect her to answer. But she did.

She quickly whispered back, "Bennett said that they are not part of The Circle and should know not to sit at this table."

"So, you speak Italian too?" asked Joshua, partially surprised.

"A little. I did come out here a bit with Bishop Hines," she replied with an automatic response, and without thinking.

Joshua's spidey sense went off. "...with Mike?" he asked, referring to Bishop Hines' son.

Lauren realized she should've been more careful with her response and just activated an undesirable curiosity within Joshua. She decided to ignore him and deflected the situation. "Archbishop Bennett. Joshua and I are not members of The Circle. What is so special about this table; and why are we allowed at it, and not them?" asked Lauren.

Feeling left out from having little to no knowledge of The Circle, Joshua followed and asked, "...and does this confirm that you and Bishop Hines are members of this so-called, Circle?" His tone was as if he was a police interrogator who already knew the answer.

Archbishop Bennett, replied, "Do you two always ask questions in twos, together? I feel like I'm part of some Noah's Ark game show. How about I answer the first; and Bishop, can answer the second?"

"Agreed," concurred Bishop Hines.

"This cavern was discovered a few decades before the crucifixion of Jesus Christ, most likely around the time of his birth. It only had to be partially excavated, suggesting that it was built out many years prior. When they got down to this level, this stone table was found primarily in its existing shape and condition. Therefore, we have no knowledge on how it got down here or made. From then on and centuries later, it was used by Roman Emperors, the Church, and eventually, The Circle for many different purposes, like war planning, settling internal disputes, and even exorcisms," said Archbishop Bennett.

Joshua looked at Ezra and remembered the story she told him in the van about how some priests believed she was possessed as a child.

Ezra looked back at Joshua and could tell what he was thinking. She interrupted, and said, "Yes, Joshua. I was laid down on this very table as a child as they attempted to perform an exorcism on me. It was the scariest moment of my life. Yelling at me in Latin, throwing holy water at me, pushing me back on the table when I tried to escape. Any child would be scared, screaming, and appear to be violent in that situation. But to them, my fear and behavior only confirmed their belief that I was possessed." She then stopped the story and held back her tears.

Her father continued, "The exorcism was not sanctioned by the Church. Another member of The Circle, and some priests that hated me, brought me down here on false pretense. That's when I saw they already had my daughter in those very chains along the wall that I am sure all of you saw when you entered this place. They told me that they would kill her if I didn't let them put me in the chains too. But when they did, they unchained Ezra and threw her on the table to perform the exorcism. There was nothing I could do. They said if they were successful, we would live. If not, they would kill us both."

Lauren interjected, "How did you get free?"

Expectedly, Joshua followed, "...and why are you still a member of this organization?"

He replied, "I love the church and I spent my whole life committed to its mission. When the priests felt the exorcism was unsuccessful, one of them pulled out a gun and pointed it at Ezra. She was so scared. We were both scared. But that's when Bishop Hines walked in with your mother, Denise." Joshua and Lauren looked at Archbishop Bennett astonished. He continued, "She immediately pleaded with him to put the gun down. When that didn't work, she looked directly at Ezra for moment, regained her composure, then boldly asked permission to speak. Seeing Bishop Hines behind her, whom they knew and respected, they reluctantly agreed. Then I watched her take a deep breath, slowly exhale, and say, 'This child suffers from a horrible illness. Because of your lack of knowledge, I will show you by revealing the sins of all those who are against her.' She then looked at each priest, went to them one by one, and whispered in their ear the biggest sin that they ever committed. Some of the priests had unexpected minor sins while others engaged in some very heinous and egregious crimes that you could have never imagined. But just like she said she would, and only with the power of God, she revealed the truth about each one of them, and that was the first time that she had met them. They knew that she spoke with God's power and knowledge. It dwelt within her, so they had no choice but to leave my daughter alone. They unlocked my chains and left this cavern without saying a word."

"The very next month, your mother was officially installed as a member of The Circle," said Bishop Hines, as he looked at Joshua.

"Are you serious?" commented Lauren.

"That's reminiscent of Jesus telling the Pharisees men that whoever is without sin let him cast the first stone?" said Joshua.

"Yes. I owed your mother my life and my daughter's as well," he said.

"So that's what you meant in the van, huh Ezra?" asked Joshua. Ezra half smiled at him, still with tears in her eyes.

Then Lauren had an interesting question. "Bishop Hines. Would Joshua's mother always take a deep breath and exhale before she did something miraculous?" asked Lauren.

"She would." he replied.

"Joshua does the same thing!" exclaimed Lauren.

"He does?" asked Archbishop Bennett, surprised.

"Every time," confirmed Lauren, spoken for Joshua.

Joshua then remembered when his neighbor, Shary, was telling him the story about his mother's first healing at one of Bishop Hines' church revivals, she mentioned that his mother took a deep breath and slowly exhaled, right before she whispered into the girl's ear.

"I will take the story from here, Bennett," said Bishop Hines. "There are many stories in various cultures about a virgin birthing a deity and resurrection, way before the story of Jesus. Knowing that, why do you think the life of Jesus became the only one that was eventually accepted by so many nations across the world? What is known today as the Middle East, Africa, and even parts of Asia accepted and believed Jesus as the Christ, or at least a type of deity higher than others. This acceptance occurred well before it was widely accepted in parts of Europe and even much later in the States.

Archbishop Bennett, interjected, "My Egyptian friend, Hany, laughs every time he hears someone say Christianity is the white man's religion. He says, outside of the States Jesus is just a Middle Eastern phenomenon. While the race of Christianity is mostly debated in America, the rest of the world typically debate his true divinity. But even with that, you'd be surprised what other religions, that's not Christianity, believe, such as Jesus is still alive with God and will judge mankind with God on Judgement Day."

Bishop Hines continued, "In any event, Jesus came into this world and preached an entirely different message than what was previously taught or heard in thousands of years."

"Really, what was that?" asked Joshua.

Bishop Hines replied, "First, Jesus said what most cultures thought but few said out loud for fear of being tortured or killed, and that was that the Israelites or Jews did worship the one true God..."

"But that was not uncommon, right? From the miracles that God did for them in the Old Testament, it was hard to make a claim against that," said Lauren before he finished his sentence.

"Yes. But second, and even more importantly, Jesus said, the God of the Jews is your God too. He is my Father and your Father; and I am His Son. You are all His children, and He and I are one. Our love, forgiveness, power, and Kingdom belong to everyone in every country.

Whether you're a great sinner or a great saint, you will be accepted into heaven through repentance and faith alone. Now, just this message by itself would have sounded surprising and good, but people would have doubted it. But because Jesus also performed miracles on the spot, unlike their gods, and just like the "god of the Hebrews" they said, this man must be the true Messiah and what he says must be true."

Then Archbishop Bennett said, "Now imagine someone is a parent praying to their civilization's god to heal their child of a disease, and it's hasn't been working. When he or she tells their leaders, who are the only ones allowed in the temple, they say, he or she must sacrifice more of your money and possessions to this god to be heard, and because the parent is low and unworthy, they must pray to it on their behalf. Also, imagine someone's elderly parent is dying; and depending on your culture, they endlessly searched for two gold coins or spent time helping their elderly parent do as many good deeds as possible in their old feeble age just so their heart could weigh less than a feather on the *Scales of Ma'at* to get into the afterlife. Then, these same people here about Jesus, and that he said, they can obtain healing and the gift of heaven from only faith and his death sacrifice, not yours. This would undoubtedly make a good portion of the world reconsider their practices and beliefs, especially those being unfairly, taxed, oppressed, or enslaved."

"This message and acceptance spread like wildfire. So, in two millennia, no other phenomenon has influenced the entire world like Jesus, his collectively his teachings and life," said Bishop Hines.

"Other than Michael Jackson or Hip-Hop," said Ezra.

"Excuse me," said Bishop Hines, both offended and requiring clarity.

"Bishop Hines. You said, no other phenomenon has influenced the entire world more than Jesus. So, I said, other than Michael Jackson or Hip-Hop. Their very close," said Ezra, confidently.

Jacob joined, and said, "I never thought about it, but I think Ezra is correct. You must think about it for a moment, but it's kind of true."

Lauren did the same, and said, "Both influenced so many things across the world from music, dance, clothing, style, fads, even language. You see it on television, music videos, and even weddings of traditional cultures now."

Bishop Hines and Archbishop Bennett looked at each feeling that they were losing control of the conversation and reluctantly to concede to Ezra's point. Then, Archbishop Bennett said, "Come back to me in two thousand years and argue that point if it still holds true."

Frustrated, Joshua forced the conversation back on track. He said, "Interesting point, Ezra. But respectfully to you and others, I didn't travel all this way to talk about music culture or even listen to the history of religion, like this is some study abroad theology class! Can we get back to the point on why we are here? Please!"

"You are correct, Joshua. We got off track," said Bishop Hines, apologetically. "After the death and resurrection of Jesus Christ, the disciples had to adhere to Jesus' commandment to go out and preach his gospel to all the nations of the world. But from fear of kings, emperors, and leaders losing control of their subjugated people and dealing with a rebellion, just like the Pharoah of Egypt experienced with the Hebrews, most nations made a decree that "followers of Christ" were outlawed and to be imprisoned or killed, if found.

Archbishop Bennett then added, "Andrew went to what is now parts of Russia, Asia Minor, and Türkiye, and was eventually crucified in Greece. Thomas went to India and was killed by soldiers. Bartholomew preached in Ethiopia and was eventually killed. James preached in Syria and eventually stoned and clubbed to death…"

"*Papà, penso che capiscano...Joshua*," exclaimed Ezra, asking her father to remember what Joshua said earlier and to get to the point.

He responded, "My apologies. I can get overzealous. Please read up on what happened to the disciples after they left to spread the gospel. I ask unbelievers would you leave your home to go to another country, risk starving to death, getting locked up in prison without today's accommodations, or violently mocked and killed just to promote a message about a man that you knew didn't exist or was a lie? Then find eleven to hundreds more people willing to do the same that you just met. After saying that, most acknowledge that would only happen if it wasn't a lie."

"With that, The Circle's original order and duty was to help spread the gospel through their gifts. Therefore, we believe it might have been the man Apollonius of Tyana that started The Circle, a first century healer. Then possibly restructured and continued by Constantine who, despite what people think, went against tradition and the majority of the Roman Empire by supporting Christianity, as Romans were previously enemy number one against Christians. They hated and killed so many. So, a good question is, why did that change? For the most part of history, The Circle was made up of twelve members, all from different nations, and possessed great spiritual abilities, such as healing, but mostly prophecy." said Bishop Hines.

"Who sat in that fancy chair behind this table?" he asked, referring to the large cathedra chair behind them that you typically see in a Roman Catholic church reserved for a bishop.

Archbishop Bennett looked at the chair and then up to the ceiling, and said, "That would be for a physical thirteenth member, such as the Pope himself or some other nation's top leader, like the President of the United States. But again, only if that leader could demonstrate supernatural abilities like the other members. If not, the thirteenth member was Jesus, represented by the large cross hanging over our heads. Now, the reason why we are all here. The Circle's second duty was to watch for signs of the end times and Jesus Christ's return."

"You mean the Apocalypse?" asked Lauren.

"Correct. Before Joshua's mother died, every member of The Circle had the exact same vision on how the world was going to end, and soon," said Archbishop Bennett.

"When all members had the same vision, their prophetic predictions have never been wrong. From the death of kings, fallen empires, great weather disasters, wars, and the Great Depression was all predicted by The Circle," said Bishop Hines.

"In 1940, The Circle had the collective vision that Ronald Reagan, a semi-known actor at the time, was going to become a U.S. President. Leaders laughed, and said, 'The Circle finally got a prediction wrong.' But, as we all know, it did happen, eventually. And with many other seemingly impossible predictions that came true, no nation leader ever doubted them again," said Archbishop Bennett.

"So true. Every nation's leader, and even the leaders of the few secret societies that remain, have taken heed to The Circle's predictions, including this newest one," said Bishop Hines.

Archbishop Bennett then said, "A more extraordinary example of The Circle's prediction is when the United States dropped the atomic bomb on Hiroshima in 1945. Everyone knows about that, right?"

Jacob jokingly put his hand up halfway before it was slapped back down by Ezra.

"Of course we do," replied Lauren.

"In 1933, The Circle members had a collective vision that a small sun fell from the sky and landed on Japan, then exploded and burned all its people. One year later, it was well known that scientists began promoting theories about a type of bomb that could have power equal to that of the sun. Then in 1945, the U.S. dropped the bomb on Hiroshima and Nagasaki," he said.

"And...," expressed Joshua, not yet convinced.

"After the horrible destruction to Japan's land, people, and entire socio-economic condition, every country thought Japan would never recover, and maybe no longer exist. But in 1946, only one year after that occurred..."

Lauren interrupted him, "...Japan had their country and economy up and running again, and in just a few years had already developed their own nuclear bomb," said Lauren still deep in thought. Then an epiphany struck her. She exclaimed, 'There's no way Japan could have recovered so quickly and created a similar bomb so soon, unless they believed and understood The Circle's prediction and implemented measures and stocked piled resources years in advance of the war!"

"Exactly, Lauren. You're still as intelligent as ever," said Archbishop Bennett as he smiled. "While every country was working to create a nuclear bomb, Japan was the only country that was preparing to recover from one. They believed and took heed of The Circle's prediction. This became the primary catalyst for a few prominent futurists calling for the need for the GSPs, or Global Survival Protocols, and them eventually being ratified by the world. From the release of a destructive biological weapon, or a massive meteor impact, or even an alien invasion, the initiation of one of these protocols, among other things, implements and allows new global laws, war crime and land acquisition by force flexibility, and full nuclear weaponry authorization, even if it violates a current treaty or agreement. We are all here because GSP-11 or Protocol-11 has recently been initiated. It was initiated because The Circle had a collective vision that the end of the world was going to happen and happen soon...a global apocalypse, similar to that found in the Book of Revelation. Our world leaders are taking heed, just like Japan did. No one wants to be on the wrong of end of this one."

"Countries are now beefing up their stash of weapons of mass destruction, destroying parts of their own land, even if occupied by residents, and commandeering nearby weaker countries all to have better positioned military bases, protective buffers, or future farming grounds for when this is all over," said Bishop Hines.

After quietly listening, Joshua said, "Let me get this straight. After my mother died, The Circle prophesied the end of the world and soon, and leaders all around the world believe this to be true, and now, they're secretly taking proactive measures to protect themselves, meaning we could be on the brink of a global war, and no one knows it?"

"Yes, Joshua. Nation leaders, top generals, and a few secret organizations are aware of this and are not disclosing this to the masses. Their actions are not confidential, just their reasoning. Larger nations are building new barrier walls along their borders and constructing above ground and underground self-contained cities for defense and protection. These are mostly for their elite and stretch for miles. They are also changing their travel restrictions and requiring new identifications or new types of visas to enter their country. This will make it easier to restrict undesirables' when things get worse," said Archbishop Bennett.

"It's going to be every person and country for itself; and because of that, smaller nations are also making secret pacts with larger ones to increase their chance of survival. For example, one country has already agreed to be taken over by another in exchange for their safety and protection. But since this is confidential and they do not want to receive backlash from its own people or the world for this deal, they're in a real war right now sacrificing so many lives just to make claim that their country is being taken by force, when it's not," said Bishop Hines.

"Wars and rumor of wars," said Ezra, referencing biblical signs.

"Are all the member of The Circle known to each country's leader?" asked Joshua.

Bishop Hines answered, "No. Nation leaders only know of their own respective representative member of The Circle. All prophecies are then communicated their member with an official letter that has The Circle's official embossed seal."

"Well, Bishop. It's higher tech than that now, with special key devices and authentication codes to open its electronic communication. But the same premise exists," said Archbishop Bennett.

Lauren had a thought, and asked, "What if The Circle is wrong? Just like Joshua mentioned earlier, if each country is preparing to protect its own country and vying for greater position, won't this create a nuclear or apocalyptic war by default?"

"Right. If everyone is allowed to be fully armed with their nuclear weapons, allowed to take over other countries, and destroy their own occupied land all without recourse, this will create total chaos and wars with other countries and even inside countries. We could have a global war in addition to a bunch of civil wars!" exclaimed Joshua.

"Lauren and Joshua, you are correct. Once this gets out publicly, which it eventually will, there will be an unstoppable chaos of events: crime, abuse, murder, rape, theft, and most likely with little to no police or security presence. Even the most secure buildings and locations would not be secure. Lawless and unprotected cities would exist like never before," added Ezra.

For some odd reason, hearing that the most secure buildings and locations would not be secure anymore vibrated into Joshua's chest. It was like out of everything that he heard, he feared that the most.

Jacob then said, "Do you remember the movie, *The Purge* or any recent zombie movie? It would be like that, but no defined end or no cure." Ezra looked down at him in disappointment. He stared back at her, and said, "What?"

"Don't keep us in suspense. When did The Circle predict the end of the world occurring? Doesn't the Bible say that no man knows the day or the hour of the world's end?" asked Joshua.

"That is still debated, Joshua. Some believe that the biblical prophecy has already occurred. But most disagree with this belief. With the signs mentioned in the Bible, and now from technology and algorithms, the recent and random earthquakes where they shouldn't occur, and even the string of church fires in Philadelphia, all must be related and point to the end of the world approaching. Therefore, The Circle needed to come up with a plan to either prevent it or save as many souls as possible before it occurred," said Archbishop Bennett.

"Where are The Circle's members now? How come they are not here?" asked Lauren.

Ezra answered, "Since they could not come up with a plan, and the end of the world would be happening soon, all the members quit. They felt there was no need for The Circle anymore. My father and Bishop Hines are the only two that remain."

"So, what can we do?" asked Joshua.

Lauren wondered if Bishop Hines was going to bring up the Light of Life. But he did not, not yet. "Before we get to that Joshua, something else is going on too. Your mother, Denise, my beloved friend and Circle member, who according to witnesses said she died of a heart attack. But that may not have been the case," said Bishop Hines.

"We believe that her death was intentional and a message to us. So, we're requesting, more like requiring, that you and Lauren become the newest members of The Circle. You both demonstrated your supernatural gifts and ability to solve the mystery in Philadelphia, which must be related to all of this," said Archbishop Bennett.

"Together, there is no greater weapon that we can have against what we are facing than you two. Plus, we're confident that you both have not tapped into your full abilities yet," said Bishop Hines.

"*Quindi, diventano membri dell'organizzazione Circle così, senza nulla?*" Jacob whispered to Ezra, which translated in English, "So they get to be Circle members just like that?"

"Shh!" replied Ezra, immediately.

Joshua then remembered what Shary said about Lauren and him.

"Even with supernatural abilities, how do we help? What can we do to stop a bunch of wars from happening?" asked Lauren.

"All we know is that Joshua's mother had a vision that the key to stopping this was the Hands Across the World event, which is already in motion. In two days, over one hundred nations will be participating in joining hands across the world to raise money for child poverty and starvation," said Archbishop Bennett.

"And how will this event help?" asked Joshua.

"We were hoping you tell us, Joshua. She kept having visions about this event and was certain it was the key to stopping Protocol-11 and the wars. But she was unable to fully decipher it," said Bishop Hines.

"From what your mother did that day long ago for Ezra and me, I'm in full support of her visions and have been working for the past few years to make sure Hands Across the World comes to fruition, even more now since she passed away," said Archbishop Bennett.

Ezra felt the need to contribute to the conversation, as she was close to Denise as well. She said, "The majority of The Circle was against Hands Across the World. None of them had the same vision as Denise relating to it. So, they refused to see any benefit in it. However, they all agreed that churches and Christians needed to show the world unity and leadership, and possibly the power and gifts, as seen in past Biblical times to cause unbelievers to believe. Therefore, they were not opposed to Denise's event and us somehow having a global altar call where priests, ministers, and elders could lay hands on the sick, afflicted, and disabled to show the world that God's power still exists."

"But there are very few Christians and Christian churches demonstrating the miracles of God as commanded by Jesus that we shall do greater works than him," said Bishop Hines.

Joshua and Lauren were already talking amongst themselves making plans. Bishop Hines incorrectly thought they weren't paying any attention and got angered. He yelled, "Listen, love birds…!"

But Lauren interrupted him by speaking faster than a kid on a sugar high, "Yes. There are two strategic plans. Joshua and I agreed to work on the first one, which is working with Bennett with Hands Across the World. Oops…I meant Archbishop Bennett, sorry. We'll do some digging, praying, and inquiring to figure out the meaning of Denise's visions for that event. Simultaneously, Ezra and Jacob could work on the second plan, which is finding people with extraordinary spiritual gifts that they can demonstrate to the world, while also spreading the gospel, preaching repentance, and warning of the potential end of the world. With social media, that should be easy right?" stated Lauren.

"For forty plus years, it has been extremely difficult to find individuals, let alone qualified ones, with true spiritual gifts. Despite their claims or high self-given titles, other than Joshua's mother, most turn out to be phonies," said Bishop Hines.

At that moment, Joshua turned his head toward the entrance of The Chamber and saw a dark shadow looking in. Joshua pierced harder in this direction to confirm. He could clearly tell it was a shadow of a large man. When Joshua did a doubletake, the shadow immediately disappeared going back into the tunnels.

"Someone" here! I just saw a shadow!" exclaimed Joshua looking toward the entrance. He wondered, *Is this be the dark angel that his mother spoke about in his dream?*

Jacob responded carelessly, "It's a dark cave. You can't trust every shadow you see."

Suddenly, a bomb went off and exploded near the entrance. The blast was great, collapsing brick and stone in front of the entrance to The

Chamber. The force of the explosion plunged everyone away from the stone table. Because of where Ezra and Jacob were positioned, they both were flung against the wall behind them. The smoke and dust filled The Chamber causing visibility to be almost zero.

After a few minutes, Lauren got up slowly coughing with her inner arm over her mouth. For some reason, Lauren could miraculously see through it all. She could see through the smoke and dust. She could see everyone where they lay. She wondered, if maybe, the almost-death experience and the healing of her eyesight caused her to have even greater vision than before, supernatural. She thought, *How am I able to see? Am I getting more of the Light of Life like Bishop Hines said?* Then, she looked over to see the entrance, which was supposed to be their exit, now completely blocked, barricaded by the large fallen stones and bricks. There was no way out. Then Lauren yelled, "The river!" as she heard water rushing into The Chamber.

<h1 align="center">12</h1>

<h1 align="center">The Healer</h1>

21 years ago – Rome, Italy.
The day before the Carnevale di Venezia (Carnival of Venice).

Even though the explosion was quite a distance away, its large impact shook the ground, the car, and the buildings surrounding them. Thankfully, Bishop Hines, Denise, and their driver had no injuries, and the buildings around them did not sustain any significant damage. However, that was not the case for those closer to the blast. With emergency vehicles and news reporters rushing to the scene that area would soon replicate what Denise saw on the television monitor at the airport, few dead and hundreds injured. They were unaware.

"Are you okay?" asked Bishop Hines, as he removed himself from hovering over Denise. He had instinctively used his body to protect her when they felt the blast.

"I'm okay. Thanks for the cover, I guess," said Denise, appreciative, but mildly uncomfortable from him over top of her.

"How about you, up there?" asked Bishop Hines speaking up towards the driver.

"I'm fine, Bishop Hines. Thank you. I think you two better get inside quickly. I will get the bags and bring them inside," he replied.

"Grazie," said Bishop Hines. He then got out of the vehicle and assist-

119

ed Denise out as well.

"Aren't you afraid that there may be another bomb, Bishop? Maybe, this time even closer to us?" asked Denise, concerned.

"I die daily," said Bishop Hines.

"Oh yeah. That's right. I forgot about that," said Denise.

They walked up a short set of steps into a gorgeous Baroque-style home. She was awe-struck by red and bronze-pattern theme, the high ceilings, the deep color paintings, and the large tapestry-imprinted rugs hung along the walls, Gothic-style bifora windows, and Corinthian columns typically found in temples, a mix of architecture she'd never seen. Even though she tried, Denise was unable express the excitement she felt or provide Bishop Hines with the appropriate words of compliment, which made her even more elated. She then noticed a large stairway directly in front of her. Her eyes followed them to a tall female statue on the mid-way platform that further continued to the home's upper level. Denise smiled with excitement and ran halfway up the steps to the platform to greet her.

"Who is this?" asked Denise.

"That is *Roma*. The female deity of Rome," replied Bishop Hines, vibrantly and struck by her enthusiasm.

"Roma not Roman?

"Correct, Roma. No letter n at the end."

Denise then reached out to the statue with her hand and felt its texture. She happily envied its physique and admired its workmanship.

"She's gorgeous. Is she a goddess?"

"No. Well, not in the manner you think. She was created to be the embodiment of all of Rome, its values, history, and character."

"Are most statues in Rome white?" said Denise in admiration.

Bishop Hines continued, "I think so, but don't hold me to that. I don't want you taking some guided tour and they contradict me, and you come back with some to hang over my head."

"As I should," she joked.

"I do know that their white statues used to be made from white marble, and they represented notions of purity and clarity. They were seen as set apart from others, strong and godlike. But most of the white statues that you see today have real color or paint associated with them. Over time, the colors fade or disappear completely turning them white. These colors have been greatly debated among artists and scholars for over a thousand years."

"As I get older, Bishop, I realize that everything is debated, and nothing is ever truly known."

"I'm surprised by your appreciation for all of this. Now I may be biased, but particularly when they're not well traveled outside of the country, most Christian-Americans that I encounter don't appreciate, let alone respect, other cultures' history or religion that possess what they consider as pagan beliefs."

Shocked, Denise immediately replied, "What do religious beliefs have to do with appreciation or respect? Their creativity and meticulous attention to detail are a work of art and significant no matter what they believe." She continued her thoughts while she walked backed down the steps. "Look at this house for example. The amount of planning, time, and discipline that had to go into each section of this house by both the artists and workers is unfathomable to me. You rarely see anything newly built like this in America. Even in Las Vegas, most of that creative design is fake, like EIFS or other synthetic materials used to mimic designs like this. But there're no comparison to what I see in this house alone."

"EIFS?" said Bishop Hines with one eyebrow raised, now attracted to her knowledge.

"Let's just say I worked on a couple of construction sites."

"I see. This is all bronze, and in the kitchen, the pots and pans are made of copper and date back many years. A good bit of furniture and fixtures were either created specifically for this house or brought in from other countries."

"That reminds me of what I heard when I toured the Biltmore Estate in Asheville, North Carolina. I would still choose this over that one."

"That is a beautiful home and estate. I've been there a few times."

At that moment, the driver brought in Denise's bags. At the same time, Marco, the male caretaker of the home walked into the room. He was in the kitchen waiting for the door to open as he knew their driver would bring in their bags.

"Buonasera, Bishop Hines," said Marco.

"Buonasera, Marco," said Bishop Hines. "Please meet Denise Williams, from Philadelphia."

"Buonasera, Denise. I heard so much about you. It is an honor to have you stay with us."

"Why thank you…I mean, Grazie," said Denise.

"English is perfectly fine. I will take your bags to your room. It's up the stairs, then down the long hallway, and the only door on your left. If you need anything at all, I am at your service," said Marco.

"Will do, Marco. Thank you," said Denise. She turned to Bishop Hines and continued, "He seems very nice."

"Yes, he is. He has been working for us as caretaker for a few years. He used to be in the military."

"Why would you hire a person that used to be in the military as your housekeeper?" asked Denise.

Bishop Hines chuckled. "His military experience was quite some time ago and he loves keeping things in order. Plus, it's like I have an undercover bodyguard in the home."

"Interesting," said Denise, as she still felt it was odd.

"When he's off the clock, he spends a lot of time with little Mike," said Bishop Hines referring to his young son.

"Little Mikey! How old is he now?"

"He's two, and the smartest two-year-old you will ever meet. Be aware that he hates being called Mikey."

"Got it. I'm surprised at that young age."

"Sarah tries to call him that all the time and he immediately gives her this mean look, and she's his mother," he replied, referring to his wife.

"Got it. Mike, it is."

"Speaking of children. Have you given any thought to our request?" asked Bishop Hines as he placed both of his hands gently on the sides of her arms.

"So, you and Sarah really are serious," she said as she brushed him off and then walked a few paces back.

"We are Denise. We prayed about it for quite some time now. We're confident that we want you to carry and birth our next child," said Bishop Hines, confidently.

"Bishop. I do feel honored. But I'm still trying to wrap my head around all of this. This is a big decision, and I don't want anyone to regret doing this."

"Like I told you before, Sarah and I always talked about having two or more children. And you already know that, with the complications that came with the birth of little Mike, Sarah can no longer have any children."

"But, why me?"

"Frankly, Denise, there is no other person that we would consider as a surrogate mother. After the complications Sarah experienced with little Mike, we accepted the possibility that God did not want us to have another child. That was until we started spending more time with us through this healing ministry. You had such an influence on our life and relationship," said Bishop Hines, convincingly.

"I love my friendship with Sarah. We connect and that's rare for me. I don't want to do anything that could damage that."

He paid no attention to her last statement. "Is it the money?" he asked knowing that this would cause tension.

"No, Bishop! I hate it when you bring that up. You know I never cared about money. I'm only considering it out of my respect for you and my love for Sarah. I just need more time to think about it."

"Fair enough. I won't bring it up again until you're ready. Right now, we are already late for tonight's event," he said as he locked at his watch. "Feel free to go upstairs to freshen up and change, and then we will walk over to the church."

"Walk?" asked Denise.

"Yes. The church is right up the road."

"I know I keep bring this up, but will it be safe? We just had a bomb go off not too far from us."

"In this part of the world, nothing stops us from going to church."

"If you say so, Bishop. Give me ten minutes."

"All right. We will meet back down here in ten minutes," confirmed Bishop Hines.

Denise slowly walked back up the steps, admiring the Roma statue once again, only to be even more amazed as she reached the top of the steps that revealed the bronze molding, the 17th-century tapered candlelight chandeliers, and the Marbediah rugs. As she walked into the bedroom, she heard the voice of Bishop Hines speaking with someone else downstairs. She had an itch to eavesdrop, but since they were already running late she decided against it and walked into her prepared room to get ready for the evening.

Bishop Hines was still downstairs on his Blackberry phone with Archbishop Bennett. "Yes, she's here. We are heading over to the church in a few minutes," said Bishop Hines.

"Great. Unfortunately, I can't make it tonight. After the church service, make sure you come by The Chamber. A few members asked that I meet them there for a special meeting," said Archbishop Bennett.

"Are these the same members that have been trying to get you excommunicated and have Ezra put away?"

"Yes, Bishop. But they sounded positive. I have hope that we are meeting because my prayers have been answered, and they have come to their senses."

"Well, be careful Bennett. I don't trust them."

"It will be fine."

"Denise and I will be there as soon as we're done here. Are you certain they're going to be okay with me bringing her to The Chamber?"

"She demonstrated her gift of healing on demand; and with my written commission on her, it should not be a problem."

"Okay, we will be there tonight. See you then."

He hung up just as Denise walked back down the steps.

"That was quicker than ten minutes" he said, surprised.

"I quickly washed my face and brushed my teeth. Is everything okay?" asked Denise, referring to his phone call.

"That was Archbishop Bennett. We will meet him after church this evening. You, my dear, have a special invitation to The Chamber."

"The Chamber. Sounds exciting and dangerous." she said, playfully.

He looked around to make sure no one could hear them, then said, "It's The Circle's meeting headquarters," said Bishop Hines, softly.

"You keep talking about this Circle. If I didn't know you any better, I'd think you're making all of this up."

He then looked at his watch, and said, "Let's go now, I hate…"

She interrupted him, and said, "Being late. Yes. Everyone knows that you hate being late, Bishop."

Bishop Hines led Denise out and made a right onto the sidewalk, then they walked past the Fountain of Frogs and a few other homes, and then after a few left and right turns, they appeared at the edge of the church. Denise looked at the church and was amazed at this building as well. It had many windows. But the largest rose window featured all twelve apostles. The front porch had six large columns made of *Baveno* pink granite, three large doors made of Lebanon cedar, and three mosaics with symbols of the *Holy Eucharist*. She then noticed the aluminum dome with embellished edges and the two angels adored the '*Holy Face of Christ*' on one of the large high windows. In the early 1940s, this church, and a few others like it, would drop food and aid supplies from this window during the night to help Jewish refugees, which at the time was risking severe punishment.

"Oh, my goodness, Bishop! The churches here are amazing!" exclaimed Denise, again in awe of the architecture.

"It's just not here in Rome, my dear. But in many other parts of Italy, Spain, France, Russia, and even parts of Africa and China have some of the most gorgeous churches," he replied.

"You, out of all people would know that wouldn't you, thee Bishop Hines of International Covenant Ministries?" said Denise, sarcastically, and with a smile.

"It's one of the reasons why I took my ministry international. In many aspects, American Christianity is good, but it is clearly missing both the full and historic message of Christ."

At that moment, Denise's thoughts focused on the open church doors and the number of people that could be in there. Her breath shortened and her heart pounded as she became nervous and anxious. She thought, *What if they ask me questions in Italian?' What if I can't heal tonight?* She looked ahead and noticed Bishop Hines did not go up the steps. He had walked past the front porch to the corner of the church and then stopped.

"Are you coming?" he asked and wondered why she stopped.

Denise moved forward and followed him around the corner of the church, through the side courtyard that led to a rear parking field with a recently constructed temporary tent placed on the parking lot asphalt. The tent was just large enough to fit about twenty-five to thirty people. Inside, it had chairs, a few lights, and just one microphone on a stand connected to a floor speaker by a cord. From her expectations, Denise was baffled.

"This is where you will be working tonight," said Bishop Hines, accomplished reaching in their destination.

"In this tent?" asked Denise, confused expecting to be in the church.

"Were you expecting something less luxurious? We set up this accommodation and all these amenities just for you," joked Bishop Hines.

Denise smiled and unconsciously let out sigh. "So, we will not be in the church this evening?"

"No. The clergy does knows you're here. But your commission or order has yet to be officially authorized. Therefore, tonight isn't exactly sanctioned by the Church. But thankfully, we're able to use this parking lot, and if all goes well tonight, and maybe a few more times, then you could be widely accepted by the Church and even The Circle."

"A few more times?"

"You didn't think being accepted was going to be that easy, did you?"

Annoyed at his tone, she replied, "Listen, Bishop. I don't care about being accepted, fitting in, or even being part of your circle group. All I care about is doing what God tells me to do; and if it's to heal someone here in Rome, in Amish Country, or even in the alley behind the Liacouras Center that's all that concerns me. Do you understand that?"

Taken back by her response, Bishop Hines conceded, and said, "Yes, understood. There should be about ten to twelve people who will be coming over from the church into this tent who need healing. They have been pre-selected and with illnesses or injuries that have been officially verified. We instructed them to come over to this tent when service is over. Feel free to pray, sing, shout, or do whatever you feel to get ready until they arrive."

"Thank you, Bishop. I think just praying would be best.."

"Okay. I'm going over to the church just to show my face. It should be over soon. So be ready. Neglect not the gift that is within thee, and God will bless you above all that you can ask or even think." She smiled as he walked away.

Denise closed her eyes and envisioned a large crowd running into the tent taking seats. Some felt some would be there to be healed, but most would be there in hopes of witnessing a spectacle that they could laugh about. With that vision, fear overwhelmed her. After she took time to calm her nerves, she whispered to herself, "*God has not given me the spirit of fear but of love, power, and a sound mind. I have no fear, but a sound mind. I have no fear, but a sound mind.*" She then walked to the front of the tent area, closed her eyes, and took a deep breath and exhaled. She then had a new vision, a vision of only three people walking into the tent, and not a large crowd. She envisioned the three approaching her; and as they got closer, she felt their sadness, their loss of hope and despair. She then prayed:

Dear awesome and gracious God. I am available to you. I pray that you will use my heart, body, mind, and soul to meet the needs of the people here in Rome. Be my help, so that I can be theirs. I am your instrument, play your wonderful song and music through me. Give me the right spiritual frequency to give hope, strength, and healing to the broken, the weak, and those needing a miracle. In the mighty name of Jesus, I pray, Amen.

When Denise finished her prayer, Bishop Hines and three people walked into the tent just as she had envisioned. A mother, father, and their eleven-year-old son. They walked past all the empty chairs and sat in the very front facing Denise. Bishop Hines stood in the back and gestured that no one else was going to show up. But Denise smiled with appreciation for those three.

"Ciao, fellow Saints of God," said Denise, still with a smile.

"Ciao," responded the mother and son, collectively.

"Buonasera," said the father.

"Buonasera," replied Denise directly to the father.

"They did not tell us that you were American," said the father.

"Is that a problem?" asked Denise.

He did not answer. He then looked back at the tent's entrance as he expected others, or at least a priest or two to join them. Observing his focus on himself and not on the mother or son, Denise concluded he was the one who was ill.

She took another deep breath, exhaled, and with compassion said, "Sir, I stand before you and your family not as an American, and not even as Miss Denise Williams given name, but as a vessel of God, standing on behalf of the Spirit of God, asking you, what would you have God, the same great and almighty God that you and I both serve together, do for you this evening?"

Before the man could respond, his son answered for him, "*Mio padre ha il cancro!*" exclaimed the boy, who spoke just a little English.

"He has cancer, pancreatic," said the mother.

Hearing his brave son speak and his caring wife follow, the father then remembered what was important. He felt obligated to apologize. "I'm sorry, Signorina. For a moment, I lost focus. Please forgive me. Thank you for being here. This must be *importante* for you being far away from your country."

Denise felt relieved by his words, and she longer had any fear. That's when Denise and Bishop Hines looked up at the entrance of the tent, as three more people just walked in. It was Angelo, the waiter from the restaurant earlier. He also brought his mother, who he pushed into the tent in a wheelchair, and his father, by his side, holding onto Angelo's shoulder trembling as they entered the tent. She grinned cheerfully and Angelo smiled back feeling the same. Denise waved instructing them to come up to the front. As they complied, she took another deep breath, exhaled, and said, "Can I have both families up at the front of this tent facing each other? Father facing father, mother facing mother, and son facing son?" Once they figured out exactly what she meant and faced each other, with Angelo's mother in the wheelchair facing the other mother, the fathers facing each other, and Angelo facing down to the young boy and the young boy looking back up with his neck stretched since Angelo was so tall. Bishop Hines walked behind Denise to show her lead and his support.

Denise said, "Thus saith the Lord, no greater love than a man lay down his life for another. And I also say, no greater faith than someone forgetting about their own need to help someone else. If can pray and believe for the healing of the family facing you, and not of your own, then our God will be gracious and not only heal their need but heal your own needs as well. But let each of you ask in faith, in caring, and in love for your brother and sister across from you, who you do not know for their healing. If you do, then Lord will be in the midst of us and heal every illness and need in all of us."

Feeling the emotion and Spirit of God within Denise's words, they all nodded in agreement, except for the young boy. Then, the boy raised his hand. Denise looked down at him and smiled and said, "Yes sir. You have something to say?"

"*Non capisco,*" said the boy.

"He said, he doesn't understand," said his mother.

Denise walked over to the side of him in between him and his mother and squatted down so that she could look into his eyes. Suddenly, she remembered a few words in Italian that she learned while preparing for her trip.

In a soft voice, she asked, "*Amare dio?*" *He heard, 'Do you love God?'*

"*Sì,*" he replied.

"*Amare il padre?*" asked Denise. *He heard, 'Do you love your father?'*

"*Sì!*" he replied, much louder and with greater confidence.

Denise then said, "You are such a brave and smart young man. Last question, *Dio guarisca il padre?*" *He heard, 'Do you want God to heal your father?'*

"*Sì,*" he said, now crying and wiping his tears with his arm.

As Denise got up and patted him on his shoulder, she realized that she never learned the word heal. But somehow, it just came out of her mouth. She never said it before; nor did she even know what it looked like in Italian. But when she said it, she understood what it meant. Bishop Hines looked on amazed and proud. Denise then stood straight up, looked down at the boy, and with a voice that was higher pitched, she said, "God is saying, as much as you love your father, and as much as you want God to heal your father, then you must love this other family too. God wants you to pray for them instead of your own family. Because they are sick too. And if your love is sincere and faith is true, then God will not only heal them, but He will also heal your father as well. Do you understand, young Matteo?"

The young boy joyfully answered, "*La Capisco! La Capisco!*"

Everyone wondered how Denise knew the little boy's name and how could the boy fully understand Denise. Later, they would say her voice sounded like an angel when she spoke this day.

She continued, "Please begin to pray and have faith for one another. But do it in way that you feel comfortable or led to do. May your love and faith heal one another."

Surprisingly, Angelo's father took the first step, literally. With his tremors, he took a few steps closer to the father with cancer, and said with a slight stutter, "You…you…are my…my brother, and I love… you. I pray that God…gi…gi…gives you a…long life so that you continue to be a…gre…great father and husband that I…kn…know you are." He then embraced him with a big hug. The younger father never felt so much unconditional and brotherly love in an embrace, so much that he'd burst into tears with an uncontrollable cry. His wife and son were amazed. Years of pain and emotional hurt were released out of him like a flood. From seeing this, Matteo immediately ran up to Angelo and gave him a hug. Angelo never felt the embrace of a child. He felt like he became a big brother in an instant. He warmly embraced him back as a big brother would. Both mothers were in tears seeing the compassion for each other. So much so that Angelo's mother attempted to get out of her wheelchair. However, she still desperately struggled. But the other mother with confidence and faith, stretched out her hand and said, "Take up they bed and walk! For your family's faith for my husband's healing has made your whole!" Angelo's mother reached up from the wheelchair and grabbed her hand and easily stood up from the wheelchair. She slowly walked confidently over to her with no struggle and no pain. They embraced like two young, displaced sisters that hadn't seen each other in thirty years. Everyone was healed physically and emotionally from all their troubles, and they knew it.

Matteo ran over to Denise and gave her a big hug, and said, "*Ce l'hai fatta. Hai guarito mio padre. Lo so. Dio è veramente con te.*" Denise fully understood and heard, '*You did it. You healed my dad. I know it. God is truly with you.*' She then looked back at Bishop Hines. He whispered, "Well done. Well done."

Bishop Hines and Denise ended up back near Vatican City walking along the boulevard known as the *Lungotevere* which runs parallel with the river named Tiber. The same road that her son, Joshua, yet to be conceived and born, would walk twenty-one years from now, following in the same footsteps to The Chamber.

"You did extraordinary this evening. I can't repeat it enough, Denise. We literally experienced the speaking and understanding of different tongues. In all my years, I never experienced anything like that," said Bishop Hines, zestfully.

"I just took a deep breath, exhaled, waited a moment, and listened to what God wanted; and it happened," said Denise.

"I just wished more people were there to witness it," said Bishop Hines, concerned.

"No, Bishop. Whoever was there was meant to be there, and the same for those who were not."

"You are correct, my dear. Just like the waiter from the restaurant that showed up with his family."

"Bishop! If we didn't get the two restaurants mixed up, then I would have never met him, and never invited him!"

"Look at God! Even when we make mistakes, it can all be part of God's great and mighty plan that we do not see."

"Amen to that!" exclaimed Denise.

"Thank God you listened to the Holy Spirit and invited him. What was his name again?" asked Bishop Hines.

"Angelo," said Denise happily. "I can't believe he came. And honestly, at the time, it was just a simple invitation and not necessarily a command that I felt from God."

"I could tell he's a good young man."

"He is. Oh lord, he saved me from this horrible taxicab driver, right before you arrived."

"He did?"

"Yes, and his middle name is Joshua."

"Oh yes, meaning God is salvation and deliverance."

"Of course, you know that too."

"Joshua *is* one of the most preached about biblical prophets. His faith and obedience tore down walls."

"Joshua. I do like that name."

"Well, not to bring it up again, but if you do finally agree to surrogate Sarah and our second child, maybe we can all name him that, Joshua."

"And, what if it's a girl, Bishop?"

Bishop Hines paused for a moment. "Well, then we could call her Josheena," joked Bishop Hines.

"Oh no! You lost your mind, Bishop," said Denise. They both laughed.

"But if it's a boy, then it's Joshua. Agreed?" asked Bishop Hines wanting confirmation and stopped walking for an immediate answer. He even stretched out his hand for them to shake on it.

"I haven't agreed to do it yet," said Denise as she continued to walk and ignore his hand towards her. "But seeing Angelo tonight and hearing the name Joshua, does make me feel more comfortable about it. How would your family and all your dignitary friends feel about this?" she asked, concerned about his reputation.

"They don't know and wouldn't know. And as part of our agreement, you would sign a confidentiality agreement with strict punishment if ever violated. You could never let anyone know that Joshua is your child, or Josheena."

"Understood. I guess I already knew that. But you're only giving me leverage to negotiate a higher payment amount," joked Denise.

He countered, "I thought you said it wasn't about the money."

Denise acted like she didn't hear him. "Bishop. We have been walking for quite some time and it's so late. Can you please tell me, where we are going?" she asked, feeling restless.

Bishop Hines sighed. "We are going to meet Archbishop Bennett."

"This late?"

"Yes. He would have been at the tent with us this evening, but he has been dealing with a few hardened priests from the Church who have it out for him and his young daughter."

"Why?"

"They never liked him and hated that he worked more on interdenominational relationships and events than within their own church. Also, his daughter is very special and has some type of disability that causes her to randomly speak or act violently. Because of this, a few priests believe that she is possessed by a demon."

"C'mon, seriously?"

"Seriously. But I believe that you can help his daughter and heal her from her true condition whatever that is. After this evening, I am more confident than ever."

"What's her name?"

"Ezra. Logic tells you that the Church won't take this type of accusation lightly. Possessed or not, her behavior has been disruptive to their Mass and other services; and those that have been against him for years are now using her as leverage to get him *excommunicated* or even dismissed from the clerical state."

"Dismissed from what?" asked Denise.

"…the clerical state, meaning kicked out from the clergy." Bishop Hines had led them to steps that went down to a dark gated door.

"Really. We are going down there?" asked Denise.

"It's a tunnel that leads to our meeting place," said Bishop Hines as he walked down the steps and pulled out a key to open the gate in front of the door, which would be subsequently retrofitted for a remote buzzer to let in those qualified.

After Denise walked through the door, Bishop Hines worked to lock it behind them. Denise then asked, "Is this tunnel the meeting place for The Circle?"

"The tunnel leads to a place we call The Chamber, the primary meeting place of our society called, The Circle."

"A religious secret society. I don't know how I feel about that."

As they got further into the tunnel and closer to The Chamber, they heard faint sounds of a child screaming. They picked up the pace and walked faster to find out what was happening. As the screaming continued louder, they also heard a few men yelling in Latin. Bishop Hines deciphered. "They're performing an exorcism!" he exclaimed. They quickly ran toward the entrance of The Chamber. Denise got there first, prepared for the worst. Bishop Hines lagged slightly behind but arrived with the same concern. They saw Ezra, Archbishop Bennett's daughter, on The Circle's meeting table, scared and screaming, as a few priests surrounded her. Some had crucifixes pointed toward her in their attempt to cast out a demon that they believed possessed her. Denise scanned to see if anything else was happening. When she slowly turned to her left, she saw Archbishop Bennett in tears, kneeling on the ground and restrained in chains attached to the stone wall. He looked on in fear and horror unable to do anything as the priests surrounded his helpless daughter. Then, to Denise's surprise, she saw one of the priests had a gun pointed directly at Ezra, about to fire.

Denise fully stepped into The Chamber, stretched out her hand toward the priests, with her palm facing them, and yelled, "In the name of God, stop!"

13

Family Chains

Present Evening – Rome, Italy.
Three days before Hands Across the World.

Joshua, Bishop Hines, Archbishop Bennett, Ezra, and Jacob were disoriented from the blast, but not Lauren. She was covered in dust and dirt just like them, but she was alert and focused, her wits about her and eyesight strong. She heard water rushing into The Chamber like a loud waterfall that came from the tunnel. The large explosion ruptured one of the main water pipes and caused a breach in the wall barrier to the river. The cavern was no longer lit and extremely dark. For anyone else, the visibility would have been zero. However, when Lauren looked around, for some reason she could easily see. She saw through the darkness and through the heavy smoke that resulted from the blast, collapsed stone, and clouds of dirt. Amid her investigation of the area with her gifted eyesight, she couldn't help remembering how she was blinded by the evil enemy during the fire and fight in New Lighthouse Temple back in Philadelphia, and then her recent healing and recovery from the prayer and faith of Joshua. She wondered if both events caused this change, a sample of the Light of Life as Bishop Hines mentioned. She then thought, *I cannot believe I can see perfectly through all of this! It's like I have night vision and smoke vision combined.* Amid her visible search, she saw the destruction of the blast and the rest of the group still on the ground. She immediately ran over to Joshua.

"Joshua!" yelled Lauren as she sat down on the ground and pulled his upper body against hers. "Joshua!" she yelled again.

He slowly opened his eyes with dirt and dust all over them both, and said, "Lauren. You and I gotta stop having dates like this!"

She laughed, and said, "Dinner and movies from now on I promise! Are you okay?"

"I'm fine," he said. He then pushed himself up and then fully stood up with the help of Lauren. The others rose up as well, still disoriented.

Lauren then remembered the urgency of the water rushing into the cavern, and yelled, "We need to get out now!"

"Is that water I hear?" voiced Bishop Hines, strong and concerned.

"Yes. That's why we need to hurry up. The explosion caused something to break tied to the river like a wall or water pipe," said Lauren.

"But I can't see," said Jacob, as he coughed.

"Neither can I. I can't tell whether it's just dark or the smoke and dust are too thick," said Ezra, coughing too.

"With hardly any ventilation down here, the smoke and dust are not clearing. Is anyone able to see the entrance?" asked Bishop Hines.

Lauren responded, "I can. But it's completely blocked. The collapse of the entrance barricaded us in, and water is coming in fast."

"Most of these tunnels were built with a drainage system, except for this section. This area is old and unstable. The water will rise in here fast," said Bishop Hines.

"How can you see the entrance, Lauren? I can't see anything at all," said Joshua covering his mouth with his shirt.

"I'll explain later. Archbishop Bennett is there another way out?"

asked Lauren, desperately.

Like Joshua, Archbishop Bennett used the top of his shirt to cover his mouth. He removed it and answered, "Yes. Behind the cathedra is an old emergency exit door that leads to a pathway up to the public tunnels. But I can't see anything or tell how to get back there." He then recovered his mouth with this shirt.

"No worries. I got this!" exclaimed Lauren, confident. Lauren then grabbed Joshua's hand and led him over to both Ezra and Jacob that were next to each other. She then got them all to hold hands. Then, as Joshua, Ezra, and Jacob held hands, she led them over to Bishop Hines and Archbishop Bennett and connected their hands to the group as well. When they were all linked, she led Joshua and them to the area hidden behind the large cathedra chair. Just like Archbishop Bennett directed, they saw the emergency exit door, a possible way out. It was an antiquated wooden door constructed into the stone wall that possessed a wooden plank board as a barrier lock which prevented anyone from opening it from the other side. Archbishop Bennett approached the door. Then he lifted and removed the plank board from its large door hooks and threw it to its side. He then grabbed the door's iron handle to open the door, but it wouldn't budge. He attempted again and got the same result. With time not on their side, they all looked down towards their feet as the water was now covering their shoes and up to their ankles.

"Let me try," said Bishop Hines. He pulled on the door three times and still no movement.

"It must be bolted shut from the other side of this door," said Archbishop Bennett.

"But how," countered Bishop Hines.

Joshua remembered seeing a glimpse of the person's shadow at the entrance before the bomb went off. He then said, "If I had to guess,

I think whoever set that bomb off, knew what they were doing, and bolted this door from the other side. They did not want us to escape."

"But why, and who would do that?" asked Jacob.

"It must be someone that knows this place intimately. Maybe your enemy back in the States is here too," said Ezra as she looked at Joshua and Lauren. They did not respond.

Jacob looked down and noticed the water again, and said, "It's now up to our shins, that quickly. There must be another way out."

"This is the only other way out, right Bennett?" asked Bishop Hines.

"Not necessarily, I think," said Archbishop Bennett.

"What do you mean," said Bishop Hines.

"Old documents showed that previous Circle members talked about another way out, hidden to the eye," said Archbishop Bennett.

"Where is it?" asked Jacob.

He replied, "I don't know. Since we never found it, we thought it was a myth or part of The Chamber's many mysterious stories."

After a long pause of disappointment and no new ideas, Bishop Hines eventually added, "Even if it is true, it could take us hours to find, especially with Lauren being the only one able to see."

"We don't have hours," said Ezra as she looked at the water that had risen to most of their waists.

Jacob looked at the water level and then the tall height of Bishop Hines and said, "Looks like Bishop Hines is going to live just a few minutes longer than the rest of us. Can I stand on your shoulders, Bishop?" Bishop Hines ignored him.

"Maybe, we are just meant to die here," said Ezra.

Instantaneously, Joshua and Lauren then looked at each other and at the exact same time, yelled, "Ebenezer!"

The group looked at them like they just went crazy.

"What do you two mean by 'Ebenezer'?" asked Bishop Hines.

"Ebenezer AME!" said Joshua, excited.

"It's where we found the Underground Tunnel in Philadelphia!" said Lauren, even more excited than Joshua.

"Tunnels connected to other places!" said Joshua as he faced Lauren.

"Secret passages hidden by stone!" exclaimed Lauren, as she smiled and looked back at Joshua.

"What are you both talking about?" asked Jacob.

"Don't worry. We've been in this situation before. We got this!" exclaimed Lauren.

"Yes. We got this!" exclaimed Joshua as he patted Jacob's shoulder.

Archbishop Bennett looked at Bishop Hines surprised, and asked for confirmation, "They've been in this situation before?" Bishop Hines shrugged his shoulders, surprised himself.

Amid the level of water quickly rising higher, the two gifted individuals stood face to face.

"Let's do this," said Joshua as he grabbed Lauren's hands.

"Let's do this," repeated Lauren.

They held hands and closed their eyes. Then they took a deep breath, slowly exhaled, and were silent and without movement. The others looked at each other and then back at Lauren and Joshua and wondered what might happen. Joshua and Lauren knew what they were doing. They were both envisioning The Chamber or the cavern, in its entirety, waiting for the Spirit of God to reveal their possible way out, just like they did in Ebenezer AME, the first of the church fires along the Boulevard set by their evil enemy. Then, simultaneously they both saw it. Just like The Circle members with their predictions, Joshua and Lauren had a vision, and in this vision their focus was drawn to the chains attached to the stone wall near the entrance. The same chains that bound many people over many centuries for various right or wrong reasons, including Archbishop Bennett by rogue priests during their attempt to perform an exorcism on his daughter, Ezra.

"The chains!" exclaimed Joshua and Lauren together. Archbishop Bennett and Ezra knew exactly what they meant.

"The chains attached to the wall near the entrance?" asked Ezra.

"Yes," said Lauren. She continued, "Everyone. Hold hands and let's go over to the chains."

They complied and slowly traversed through the water and around the table and fallen stones. A lot of the smoke had cleared, so visibility had significantly improved. When they got over to that area of the wall with the chains, the chains were fully underwater and about halfway down from the top. Jacob looked down and noticed something odd.

"Bubbles! I see bubbles!" yelled Jacob. This confirmed that Joshua and Lauren's vision was correct.

"That's a sign air is on the other side and water is leaking through," said Lauren.

"At Ebenezer AME, the stone was moveable and led to a tunnel on the other side," said Joshua.

"Joshua and Lauren, I think you're right. Through the other side of this deep wall may be another passageway that leads back up to one of the public tunnels," said Archbishop Bennett, as he looked up and down the wall and its set location.

"So, what do we do now? I can't hold my breath long," asked Jacob while he looked at the chains now well below the water.

Then Lauren's eyes pierced into the water and saw the outline of the individual stone that was connected to the chains, and said, "I can see through the water. The chains are both attached to one large stone block. If we pull the chains, it may pull the stone out of place."

"She also sees through water. Okay, Aquagirl," joked Jacob.

"Shut up," said Ezra. She then said to Lauren, "That's assuming the chains don't break. They're pretty old."

"And, with the water level so high, whoever pulls them must go fully under the water and looks like you have to grab them awkwardly to pull the chains and stone out," said Bishop Hines.

"I can grab the right chain and use my foot on the other stones as leverage," said Archbishop Bennett.

"I can hold my breath for a very long time and will grab the left chain," added Ezra. She then looked at Joshua and Lauren and said, "You two aren't the only ones who know how to take a deep breath."

"No way. I'm the tallest. I will do it," said Bishop Hines.

Archbishop Bennett immediately responded. "Respectfully no, Bishop. It will be me and my daughter. We have a history with these chains. Over twenty years ago, they bound me while I was forced to watch an attack on Ezra, my lovely daughter. Now they will be used to free us."

"Yes. We got this," said Ezra.

Everyone smiled in agreement. Archbishop Bennett and his daughter Ezra then got into position against the wall, and with their hands, felt below the water for the chains. Once they got the chains in their grasp, they looked at each other, counted to three, took a deep breath, and plunged under the water. As Archbishop Bennett suggested, he placed his right foot on the right side of the stone and Ezra put her left foot on the left side of the stone, and they pulled with all their might. But the stone did not budge. At this moment, the water level had risen to everyone's chin, except Bishop Hines.

"I sure could use that shoulder right now, Bishop," said Jacob, standing on his tiptoes.

"They got this," said Lauren as she lifted her head to keep her mouth above the water.

"Yes, they got this," said Joshua doing the same.

Archbishop Bennett and Ezra continued to pull as hard as they could and struggled to get the stone to move, let alone budge. Bishop Hines became extremely frustrated and fearful of the possibility of seeing everyone die, including himself. He then yelled, "In the name of Jesus, stone be thou moved!" At that instant, the stone became loose. Archbishop Bennett and Ezra felt the stone move and pulled even harder as they struggled for air with bubbles now seeping from their mouths. Then, with one last hard collective pull from the two, the stone was pulled completely out from the wall and fell to the ground. The water rapidly escaped The Chamber, quickly lowering the water level and giving relief to the group. It flowed into an adjacent tunnel that possessed large drains built into the floor to prevent flooding. Archbishop Bennett and Ezra popped out of the water simultaneously catching their breath. They all randomly hugged, grabbed hands, and cheered in their accomplishment.

"They did it!" yelled Jacob.

"Yes they did," said Bishop Hines.

One by one, they climbed through the large opening, freely into the adjacent tunnel. As everyone walked down the tunnel and continued to celebrate their escape from the near-death experience, Joshua and Lauren kept looking at each other concerned.

"Who did this, Joshua?" whispered Lauren.

"Obviously somebody that wanted us dead, just like in Philadelphia," whispered Joshua. They continued whispering as they slowed down to let the group get further ahead of them.

"So, we have a potential apocalypse at hand, and what, someone trying to kill us as well?" asked Lauren.

"Whoever it is, it's clear they want us dead. But back in The Chamber, they wanted us to suffer. This must be about vengeance," said Joshua.

"Just because we foiled their big plot in Philadelphia, they're now after us here in Rome? That doesn't make any sense," she replied.

"Depending on who or what it is, maybe it does."

Lauren stopped walking. Joshua did the same. She had an idea, then spoke it in a rush.

"Quick. Who is behind this? Close your eyes and take a deep breath on…one…two…three!"

Being on the same accord as Lauren, Joshua immediately took a deep breath and shut his eyes. They both envisioned the same person.

"No! It can't be!" exclaimed Lauren, as they opened their eyes together and looked at each other in disbelief. They saw the same person. Lauren's heart pounded like thunder and Joshua's did the same.

"We're going to trust that shadow in our vision is the evil we are dealing with," said Lauren.

"Without a doubt," Joshua confirmed.

"What about…?"

Joshua interrupted, "Don't say it. Together, we have all we need."

14

Distrust

Present Day – Rome, Italy – Two days before Hands Across the World.

"Mom?" said Joshua, hesitantly as he could not believe it was her, his mother alive. She turned toward Joshua and smiled but then kept working. He controlled the tears, wiped his nose and face with his sleeve. He was nervous, but spoke again. "How are you here? I thought you were…"

She immediately cut him off by turning her head to him again, put her finger over her lips, and said, "Shhhh…It's almost time Joshua. Remember to stack them side by side, soldier-course style, Joshua. *That will make them all strong and on one accord.* Be strong and of good courage, only be thou strong and of good courage." Then, she went back to stacking the hoagies in the case.

Not focused on his mother's words, Joshua spoke again, but louder, "I missed you so much. We all miss you."

She then looked up at the ceiling and said, "Stack them all side by side before it's too late, Joshua. The dark angel is free. I held it back, as long as I could, but the dark angel is free."

Suddenly, a deafening thunder occurred so loud and strong that it vibrated throughout the grocery store building and within Joshua's entire upper body. He looked up at the ceiling with caution at the noise and the rumble. When he looked back down to his mother, she was gone. Then, the store building began to violently shake. It was an earthquake. Joshua pointlessly grabbed closely onto the case and squatted down to the ground with his head down. Food and other products fell from the gondolas and shelves. Parts of the ceiling broke apart and fell to the floor. Then, Joshua heard a piercing scream.

* * *

Joshua awakened from the dream and thought, *Not this dream again!* But this time he remembered two things that his mother said, which were hoagies side by side and the dark angel was free. As he looked around the room, he realized that he was in the same house that his mother stayed in twenty-one years ago that was near the Fountain of the Frogs. This time, Lauren stayed in the room just across the hall. After they left The Chamber, they had to stop at a store to go clothing and supply shopping for Joshua since he left Philadelphia in such a hurry and decided not to pack a bag. When they got to the house, Joshua and Lauren desperately wanted to hang out on the porch together, alone. This was to reconnect and recap events while no one was around. However, Bishop Hines asked everyone to go directly to their rooms. With all that had happened, he felt a good rest and a reset was necessary and encouraged them to get as much sleep as possible. Adhering to his request, Joshua and Lauren went to their rooms as directed, albeit disappointed. That didn't stop them from sending text messages as soon as they got into their bedrooms. More tired than they realized, both fell asleep within minutes. With his eyes wide open and attentive, Joshua looked at his phone to see if Lauren texted him while he slept. There were no new text messages. He looked at the previous messages at the top, which read,

[Joshua]: Are you sleeping-beauty, or awake-ugly lol.

[Lauren]: Awake beautiful duh!

[Joshua]: Don't you mean crazy week?

[Lauren]: Yes. So, we both saw the same person in our vision. Right?

[Joshua]: Yes. But part of me says maybe it was just a coincidence.

[Lauren]: But Bennett and Bishop said The Circle's members prophecies happened when they had the same vision. That was us tonight. And…

[Joshua]: And what?

[Lauren]: And we're official members of The Circle lol.

[Joshua]: Pretty convincing. But there may be something else to this. I keep having another dream.

Lauren did not respond as quickly, so Joshua waited patiently for over a minute for her response.

[Lauren]: You and your dreams Joshua. Tell me about it after I had a few dreams of my own. I just got very sleepy.

[Joshua]: Same here. My soul loves your soul. Gn.

[Lauren]: My soul loves your soul. Gn.

Not long after, Joshua walked out of the room showered and wearing a new set of clothes. His mother would have been proud that he didn't have to grab a shirt or a set of socks off the floor and do a sniff test to see what was clean enough to wear. He walked across the hall to Lauren's door and raised his fist to knock. Inexplicably, he refrained and decided to put his ear to the door first, maybe to hear if she was awake or just out of curiosity. He listened. There was no sound coming from the room. But he did hear someone speaking at the end of the hall. Joshua's ear was still against the door when he glanced down the hallway to see who it was. It was Marco, the caretaker, standing at the very end of the long hallway with his back facing Joshua. Joshua could only tell that he held something in his hands while he eerily looked up at the corner of the ceiling and quietly repeated the same thing. Being puzzled, Joshua wondered, who is this man and what is he doing. He then carefully took his ear off the door to watch and listen. It sounded like a chant and reminded him of the same satanic chant he heard just a few days ago in Philadelphia while strapped to a wooden table by their evil enemy for a sacrifice ritual. Feeling someone's presence behind him, Marco lowered his head, slowly turned around, and saw Joshua staring at him. Joshua immediately jumped away from the door, startled.

"Bonjourno," said Marco, graciously and revealing that he was holding a set of bath towels. He then walked towards Joshua, rigid. Joshua's feet remained planted, and body uneasy. When Marco reached him, he said, "If you're looking for Lauren, she's downstairs with Bishop Hines." With the wind gone from him, Joshua could only nod his head. "These towels are for you," Marco said, and tried to hand them to him.

"There was set was in my room," Joshua replied, breaking his discomfort.

"Is that so? They must have been in there for quite some time. My name is Marco. I am the caretaker of this wonderful place, and an old friend of Bishop Hines."

"Please to meet you," said Joshua, now at ease.

"I must say, it is an honor to have you here and to finally meet you. Your mother, Denise, would be very proud to see you here."

"Is that right?" said Joshua frustrated that Marco spoke like he knew a lot about him and his mother.

Marco noticed Joshua's tone, and asked, "Is everything okay?"

"I just keep meeting people that I don't know talking about my mother. She had this entire life that I knew nothing about."

"Precisely," responded Marco with a low ominous tone.

"Come again?" asked Joshua, questioning the intent of his statement.

"That is how The Circle operates. It was for your protection. You can't have gifts like your mother and be part of that organization and not be a target." Joshua did not respond. Marco then said, "You will find the two in the kitchen. If you desire anything, please let me know."

"Thank you."

"Joshua nodded again and walked down the hallway and down the steps past the Roma statue to the ground floor and made his way back to the kitchen where he saw Lauren and Bishop Hines at the large island counter and talking.

"The dead has arisen," said Bishop Hines, as he ate a bowl of raisins.

Joshua looked at the bowl, disgusted. He said, "No amount of money could make me endure the nasty taste and texture of raisins."

"I can't get enough of them," replied Bishop Hines, throwing another set of raisins in his mouth.

"Where's everyone else?" asked Joshua.

"Still in their rooms," replied Bishop Hines.

Lauren felt there was something off about Joshua. "Is everything okay?" she asked, as she ran up to him and kissed him on the cheek.

"Yes. I'm fine," he replied. She then grabbed his hand to sit in one of the tall chairs against the large island. As he sat down, he noticed the cookware hanging and a large open square rack above them. "Wow. Look at these pots and pans," said Joshua.

"They're copper and they look pretty cool, right? Did you sleep well?" asked Lauren.

"Sort of. I kept thinking about my uncle and auntie. With all that has been going on, I haven't had time to think about their death, mourn, or even what to do next. Shouldn't I be getting back on a plane to prepare for their funeral? Are they doing any type of investigation on the home and explosion? Did anyone confirm that the explosion is related to what's going on here?"

Bishop Hines sighed, then responded, "You have many questions, Joshua. We all do. The Church has a team of assistants, like Ezra and

Jacob. They're in Philadelphia taking care of everything for you."

"Like what?" asked Joshua.

"From maintaining the bodies of your uncle and aunt for a proper funeral when we return, and they're working with Officer Reese investigating what happened at the home and why," replied Bishop Hines.

"When do you expect us to return?" asked Lauren.

"If the world does not end anytime soon, we should be returning to the States right after the Hands Across the World. It's imperative that we participate in this event," answered Bishop Hines.

"Joshua, it must be very difficult for you to be here. Your uncle and aunt were amazing people. I'm so sorry you are going through another loss," said Lauren, concerned for him.

"I echo the same, Joshua. Jerry was like a brother to me, and he was truly a righteous man of God. No other Pastor did as much for the Philadelphia community than him," said Bishop Hines.

Joshua became angered as Bishop Hines talked, and he expressed it. "Did my uncle know about my mother too, just like everyone else does around here?" asked Joshua, tempered.

"No, Joshua. He did not," said Bishop Hines.

"How come? Everyone I meet mentions how great my mother was, but my uncle and I knew nothing. Do you know how many times we had to defend my mother from people in church and in our neighborhood? Everyone always questioned her character or thought she was wild and promiscuous. I heard it all and not once did anyone share any of this with me, not even after her death!" exclaimed Joshua, now outraged. Lauren had the urge to put her hand on his shoulder to calm him down. But she refrained, afraid of his potential reaction.

Arrogantly, Bishop Hines thought it was best if he provided an explanation and defense. He said, "Joshua. The way your mother healed, and the miracles she performed weren't exactly how most people expect or even how movies or T.V. portray them. People want glamour, suspense, and an instantaneous flashy reveal just like a magician on a big stage. But with Denise, every healing was different and usually required some subsequent action or faith from the person in need. There was rarely any excitement, publicity, or money for that matter. The people who didn't believe her gift would mock her; and the ones that did could have easily been a threat. Not telling you or your uncle was for your protection." When he was done speaking, he expected his words to soften Joshua's temper. Unfortunately, it did the exact opposite and angered and insulted Joshua even more.

"Bishop. How do you feel about that decision now? My mom, my uncle, and my auntie are all dead! All dead, Bishop! So, what the hell did you protect?" Before Bishop Hines could reprimand Joshua for his tone and cursing at him, Joshua immediately followed up with another thought, and said, "When did secrecy and lies become part of your ministry? Is there anything else you're hiding from me?" He then got up and walked out of the kitchen.

"Joshua!" exclaimed Lauren, as he continued to walk away. They heard the front door open and then slammed shut. Lauren looked back at Bishop Hines and said, "Bishop, I don't think either one of us can relate to how he's feeling, and your speeches don't work for every situation. I can't believe no one told him about his mother or what she could do. Maybe, he's right. What else are you hiding from him?" referring to a previous conversation that she had with Mike while they were engaged, where Lauren inferred from him that Bishop Hines had been hiding secrets. She then left the kitchen to go after Joshua.

Bishop Hines watched her leave the kitchen. He then turned his head and saw Marco staring at him from the kitchen's side entrance. Bishop Hines looked back at him stern. Marco then walked away.

Lauren ran out of the house and caught up to Joshua on the sidewalk.

She was slightly behind him, and called his name, "Joshua." He continued to walk without turning around. "Joshua! I said that I'm sorry."

"For what? You did nothing wrong, so stop apologizing for everyone else's actions. I never apologize," he responded, and continued his pace.

Lauren ran past Joshua, turned around then jumped in front to face him, and skillfully walked backwards at the same pace. She showed the same tenacity that Joshua's uncle also noticed about her and wittingly forced him to speak with her. "Well, unlike you, I do apologize. So much so that it will annoy you. I'm sorry for the loss of your mother. I'm sorry for the loss of your aunt and uncle. I'm sorry for Bishop Hines' actions and lack of transparency. I'm also sorry for your pain and I'm so sorry that there is nothing I can do to take it away. But you know you have a bad knee and stomping hard on this sidewalk at this pace is only going to cause you problems as you get older. Do you knee-ed me to remind you again?" she joked.

Joshua stopped walking and noticed her gentle demeanor and soft eyes which authenticated her sincerity. Lauren always had a way to deflate his anger. "That was so cheesy. You can't ever just let me be miserable, can you?" he said, sarcastically and with a laugh.

"Nope! Deal with it," she responded, happily with her successful effort to make him feel better.

Lauren then stopped walking backward, turned around to face forward, grabbed Joshua's arm, and walked alongside him. They were in Rome, had no idea where they were going, and they did not care. They walked many blocks playing, pushing, and poking fun at each other and laughed like they'd been best friends since elementary school even though they technically met just a few weeks ago. Eventually, they came to a park's large entrance and stopped. The park was part of the grounds for the *Villa Torlonia*, which was the former home of the Torlonia family who generated great wealth by taking care of the Vatican's finances. The home was subsequently rented out by Mussolini and now turned into a public museum.

"Wow, look at this park, Joshua. Let's go in!" exclaimed Lauren.

Joshua looked at the entrance's large iron gate connected to the even larger stone walls. He noticed the gate's door was fully shut. "I think it's closed. Maybe, it's too early."

"Maybe, not," she replied, as she walked further down the sidewalk looking for another entrance.

As Lauren went ahead, a man sitting on the curb, previously unnoticed by them, turned toward Joshua and said, "The young lady's right. It's early, but one of the other entrances should be open."

"Thank you," said Joshua. As Joshua walked away to catch up to Lauren, the man said, "I told you she was among the living. Do you hear thunder yet, Joshua?"

"Excuse me," said Joshua, now alarmed and bewildered.

The man looked up at the sky and said, "With rain, we need thunder, Joshua. The dark angel is free, and this is what it sounds like…"

At that moment, Joshua thought he looked familiar and then he felt a sharp jolt of the ground beneath his feet. The earth then vibrated and shook back and forth causing him to almost lose balance. Lauren was frozen, feet planted hard on the sidewalk, as she felt the earth tremble underneath her. It was another earthquake. Joshua then ran to her, grabbed her hand, and pulled her to get under a nearby bus stop pavilion. It wasn't much of a cover, but it was the best he could find within proximity of them. After a few more seconds, the earthquake stopped. It was strong, but they saw no present damage. Joshua looked back down the street to look at the man again, but he was gone.

"Lord, another earthquake," said Lauren. Joshua was still preoccupied with his focus down the street and wondered who the man was and where did he go. "What are you looking at," she asked looking in the same direction as Joshua.

"Did you see that man I was talking to?"

"No. What man?"

"He was sitting on the curb."

She looked down the street again and saw no one. "I don't remember seeing anyone, and you know I'm quite observant. What about him?"

"He asked me if I heard thunder and then the earthquake happened." For some reason, Joshua decided not to disclose that this man also mentioned that the dark angel was free.

She replied, "I don't remember hearing thunder. Did you?"

"No. I didn't. But it was very eerie and similar to my new recurring dream. He looked like the same man that's in them."

"Does this man warn you about earthquakes?" she asked.

"No. But he warns me to check on my mother; and when I do, that's when the earthquake happens."

More impressed with the park than Joshua's dream or concern for the recent earthquake, Lauren looked down at the nearby corner of the street and noticed another entrance. "I see another way in. C'mon!" She rushed away and left Joshua under the pavilion. Joshua slowly followed her into the park. They would agree later that it was both impressive and unimpressive at the same time. The park and garden area included many historic landmarks not known to most tourists, such as the tall *Obelisco*, or Obelisk made of granite, the *Tempio di Saturno* or Temple of Saturn, and the *Casina delle Civette* or House of the Owls which is a little house with art nouveau design that possessed many different types of aesthetics. Its various brick and stone sections, multi-windows, unique roof design, and a stone road that surrounded the perimeter creatively made it feel like an old small town rather than just one house. But the actual grounds of the park appeared like they had not been cared for in months. The grass was high and weeds were high, and the landscaping was either overgrown, trampled, or dead.

"How can such an amazing and beautiful place be so unamazing and unbeautiful?" asked Lauren.

"Unbeautiful, really?" he questioned.

"I'm allowed to describe it any way I feel," she replied, confidently.

Joshua looked around and saw the park's mini version of the Temple of Saturn and ran over to it. It was a small unique architecturally designed stone building home. Because it did not possess a rear wall, the back house was exposed to nature. Two-thirds of the home was partially destroyed and removed, so only the front section of the home was left standing. The front section was still intact and retained its character with small support columns and historic statues built into the exterior walls. Joshua hopped over an old barrier-wired fence that was semi-protecting it. But instead of landing on his feet as he anticipated, they slipped out from under him as soon as they touched the ground. He landed hard, right on his bum. The loose dirt on the ground rewarded him with a large dust cloud that covered his jeans and flew in his face.

"Trying to impress me with your non-athleticism, Joshua?" asked Lauren, mocking him as she easily entered through a nearby opening in the fence. Joshua got up embarrassed and wiped the dust off himself. He decided to redeem himself by making a running leap over the building's short set of steps onto its platform porch. As he safely landed, he stretched out his arms and hands to the sky in victory. "Well done, Sir Joshua. There's hope for you yet," cheered Lauren.

"If at first you don't succeed, don't waste your time!"

"Interesting philosophy. So, if you didn't succeed with me initially, I would have been a waste of your time?" asked Lauren, half joking.

"Well, I'm not the one who was engaged before we met," said Joshua as a ding back referring to her previous engagement with Mike.

"That was low. Does it still bother you that I was engaged to Bishop Hines' son?"

"You mean, Mike."

"Yeah, That guy."

"I don't like saying his name either. To answer your question, I think it will always bother me."

"Well, grow up, Joshua. That was a long time ago," she argued, as she walked up the steps to the porch to meet him.

He immediately responded, "Did you just tell me to grow up?"

"For god's sake, Joshua. Life happened well before I knew you."

He then shook his head, changed his tone, and said, "Lauren. I think you're misunderstanding me. I'm absolutely okay with any past you may have had and don't care. But we are talking about Mike and that makes a big difference; and I found out about it through Monty and not you. Would you be okay with knowing that I didn't tell you that I had a serious intimate relationship with one of your closest friends?"

"You and Mike weren't close," she countered.

"Where did you get that fake news? My uncle was a minister at Bishop Hines' church before he opened his own church. So, Mike and I grew up together. We went to Vacation Bible school together. We played video games together. We played soccer and basketball together. We rode our bikes together down Cottman Ave to get cheesesteaks every Saturday. We even smoked weed together. We…"

Lauren interrupted, "Lord, enough! I got it. I didn't know all of that."

Joshua then said, "I can easily live with the past, people's mistakes, and even with bad news. That's part of life. But I'm sorry, but just like how I found out things I didn't know from Monty and now the same with Bishop Hines about my mother, it's diabolical for people to expect me to be fine with that. Bishop Hines says he cares about me and that I know everything now, but we both know he's lying to me about something else and feels justified for not telling me. I can just feel it. Now, I find out two years later that they all believe my mother's death was not from a heart attacked and no one told me. Yet, I'm supposed to be fine with that too. Who in this world can heal and move forward when things keep revealing themselves over time and piece by piece? A few months after they promised me that there was nothing else hidden, I found out there was. Then, a year later I found out there were even more things left out. Now, two years later after I'm all over it and in a good place, it's like a box is handed to me from someone I don't know, and when I open it, it's a note that says, here's the rest of the crap that you didn't know. So, in two years, Bishop Hines didn't think it was best to tell me, her only son, that she may not have died of a heart attack! How could he hide something so important to me? After she died, I'm embracing him with love from his support and he's deceiving me by not telling me everything. I would have rather had the entire truth from him than his damn hugs and visits! I can at least respect the truth and him as a person. But now, all that support he thought he was giving me and my uncle means nothing. Because now, my mind can only wonder, what else don't I know, what else did he lie about? How can I have a relationship with him after this? If he cared like he said he did, then just now in the kitchen, he should have said, 'Joshua. I'm sorry. I should have told you everything, especially after your mother died. Here is everything else that I have been hiding from you that you don't know about.' But did he say that? No, he didn't. Instead, he arrogantly justified his lies. But the worst part of it all is that if I had stayed in that kitchen, he would have yelled at me for my tone towards him like he does with everyone, accepting no responsibility for how this has affected me and not doing what I need for him to make this right. That's why I left. So, he does not deserve anything from me that lying sneaky bastard!" Joshua then looked up at the sky, and said, "Hey you up there.

I don't mind taking life's medicine. But for God's sake, why can't you just give it to me all at fucking once!"

"Was that last statement for God or for you, Joshua?" asked Lauren. He shrugged his shoulders. She continued, "Joshua. In Ephesians, the Bible tells us that it's okay to be angry, so long as we don't sin because of it. For some reason, people get so upset when someone gets angry like it's not a perfectly human emotion. God gets angry, so why wouldn't we also? So long as it's not hurtful, disrespectful, or threating, allowing someone close to you voice their anger is a form of therapy and can really help them release their negative emotions and feelings within them. After, they typically see things clearly and are not as upset. So, do you feel better now, Joshua?"

He did feel much better and realized that Lauren was correct. He then remembered that she must have taken some psychology classes during her schooling and handled that situation very well. He replayed everything in his mind and had a completely different outlook. He then conceded and apologized. "Sorry, God and sorry, Lauren. Please forgive me. I can't believe I let my anger get the best of me, and I should have controlled my thoughts better. If you felt I was using you as a venting punching bag, that was not my intention. Let me rewind that whole rant and rephrase it differently." He paused, and then said, "Bishop Hines does not realize that I can get over the truth, but I won't accept or get over being misled with lies or omissions, especially from someone that says they care about me. I'm sorry, I won't ever apologize for being like that. I would rather have the truth than any consoling gifts or support a person thinks they're giving me, which is most likely just their way of dealing with their own guilt. No, thanks. I'm sorry, that is not what I will ever accept." He then stared at Lauren waiting for a response. He then impatiently said, "How was that, much better?"

Lauren looked at Joshua, and said, "Joshua. I thought you said that you never apologize. Oh, my goodness, I just heard a whole slew of 'I'm sorry' in that rant, and you also said, 'I'm sorry, but I won't ever apologize...' How in the world can you apologize for never apologizing!" exclaimed Lauren, now laughing hysterically. Realizing his silly contradictory statement, Joshua joined in laughter with Lauren.

Lauren then said, "I get it now. When a person is lying, hiding the truth, even omitting part of the truth, just so the other person doesn't behave or react in a certain way is not deception, it's actually manipulation. Manipulating the mind and behavior of a person just to protect themselves or their own interests. But manipulation without truth and reconciliation will eventually suck the life, love, and trust out of the relationship. Oh, and I agree with your point that if you stayed in the kitchen Bishop Hines would have undoubtedly reprimanded you for your tone against him, even though he is completely wrong and your anger is justified."

"Thanks for that confirmation. I'm glad we're on the same page."

"If any thing bad ever happens or there is something that I think you can't handle, I promise to tell you, and tell you in its entirety, no half-truths. I just ask that you give me the exact same courtesy. I rather our foundation be strong built on truth, instead of it fall apart because it was built on lies."

Joshua then smiled in appreciation, and said, "Agreed."

At this moment, Lauren knew she had to immediately share something about Mike that up until this point had hidden from Joshua. She always had a feeling of guilt for not sharing this secret, but their open conversation had just caused her to feel even worse and regretted not mentioning it to him sooner. Now was the time. She decided to build up to it first, and asked him, "Does this mean you're not going to be bothered about my past with Mike anymore?"

Joshua pondered for a moment, then said, "Before Mike became the well-known Ivy League graduate and minister extraordinaire, he was like my big brother. I can't believe I punched him in the face just a few days ago back in Philadelphia defending you."

"He deserved it," said Lauren, still upset.

"Maybe. But he wasn't always like how he is now," he said, reminiscing. Lauren remembered hearing Bishop Hines say the same thing when they were in the van on their way to the asclepieia. Joshua then said, "Before my uncle started his church on the Boulevard, he was an associate minister at Bishop Hines' church. It's where I played the organ in public for the very first time. I was so scared. I had extra practices with the choir all month, but nothing ever prepares you for that very first time of playing in front of hundreds of people."

"His church does have a lot of members," she added.

"Yes. But this particular Sunday, Bishop Hines had organized this special fundraising event. So, a bunch of Philadelphia City council members were there, a few local celebrities, and even Live 10 News reporting on the event."

"Live 10 News!" exclaimed Lauren, as she realized the magnitude of this event and Joshua's moment. She then asked, "Why on God's earth did you choose to play on that Sunday?"

"I didn't! No one told me! I only knew that I was going to play with the choir that day. This is exactly one of the reasons why I get triggered when everyone knows something but me."

"So, what happened? Did you take a deep breath and exhale?" asked Lauren in anticipation.

"No, I didn't start doing that yet. The choir lined up and I got on the organ. I played the introduction to the song, and when I did, the choir did not join in on their cue."

"What do you mean, they didn't join in?"

"The choir director wasn't paying any attention. She was focused on digging dirt out of her nails and missed the cue for the choir to sing on their starting chord."

"And?"

Joshua walked to the platform's steps of the house, sat down, and said, "I froze."

"What do you mean, you froze?"

"I froze holding their starting G chord."

She repeated his answer for the third time, "What do you mean, you froze holding the G Chord?"

"Oh my god, please stop repeating everything I say," he joked.

"Oh, sorry," she replied softly, and then with the original tone said, "Why didn't you just replay the introduction all over again?"

"If it was that easy. I tried, but I couldn't move. After about twenty seconds of sustaining that chord, everyone in the church stared at me waiting for me to just play. Seeing their faces locked my muscles and made me freeze even more."

"Joshua. I don't think you can freeze any more than frozen. It's not like there's such a thing as freeze, freezier, and freeziest."

"You mean, like the 'unbeautiful' you said earlier?"

"Finish your story, young man."

"Then, Mike appeared out of nowhere, ran up onto our church's electronic piano, and started playing the introduction to the song. He gestured his hands to me and to the congregation and patted himself on the chest just to make it appear that it was all his fault, and I was holding the chord waiting for him to join."

"Did you continue to play with him?"

"Yes. I was unfrozen. Thawed out…melted. I went from being ice to directly being evaporated. I skipped the water phase altogether."

"Really, Joshua. You went through sublimation?"

"Okay. That is where my brain neurons end and yours begins."

"You mean dendrites."

"Stop it! Seriously, Mike saved me that day and we had a blast playing together. After church, he came up to me and said, whenever I feel nervous in front of people, just take a deep breath to allow in God's presence, and then slowly exhale to release anything in me that's not like Him, like fear. Since then, I have had no problems playing or singing in front of anyone ever since."

"So, wait. If you got that from Mike, then where did your mom get it from?" said Lauren, loud and surprised.

"Exactly. That's why I was so surprised to hear that she did the same thing, and that's how I know there is something else that Bishop Hines and Bennett are not telling us. That can't just be a coincidence, right?"

"Wow. It's always those loose ends of the lies, which the liar never sees or knows about, that gives their lies away."

"Yes. But I told you that story to let you know I care about Mike; and I definitely care about you. So, unless there is something else I don't know, I am not bothered about the past and have no worries anymore."

"Good," she replied, relieved.

Just as she was about to share with Joshua the secret about Mike, he redirected their discussion about him, and said, "This brings us to a more significant issue. We haven't officially said it out loud yet, but we both saw Mike in our collective vision in the tunnel, correct?"

"Yes. Mike is the one behind all of this, the fires, the bombs, and has been deceiving everyone. Maybe, Bishop Hines is protecting him," she said, as it led up to what she needed to tell Joshua.

Joshua got up and walked to the edge of the porch. He looked out into the garden, and said, "There is something else very troubling that has been bothering me today."

Lauren was now shocked and afraid. She immediately thought that he knew that she hadn't been entirely truthful and was hiding another thing about Mike. She said to herself, *I need to tell him now!*

Before she could get it out, he said, "You know that caretaker guy?"

"You mean, Marco?" she replied, now confused and thought to herself, *Why is he now talking about Marco?*

"Yes, Marco. This morning, when I mentioned to him that I did not know a lot of things about my mother, he responded like I didn't even know half of it, almost like he was throwing shade or something."

"Really? Marco is such a nice guy," she responded, not aware of anything dubious with Marco.

"So, you know him?" asked Joshua.

"Mike said that Marco would look after him when he was a child. He also said that he viewed Marco more like an uncle than just the house caretaker. I always got the feeling that Mike appreciated Marco more than he did Bishop Hines, maybe because Marco spent way more time with him as a child."

Joshua then walked over to her and grabbed the sides of her body and boldly pulled her against his frame. He then said, "You know what, I don't want to talk about Mike anymore. I finally have you back and I'm not going to waste any moment." He then kissed her lips, and she kissed back. "I could kiss them forever," said Joshua. "Why don't you try?" asked Lauren smiling as she raised her hand and wiggled her ring finger. Joshua led Lauren through an opening of the structure where the front door no longer existed, to the other side of the partially standing home. Joshua positioned the two of them in a shaded corner where they could not be seen. A soft breeze entered their area as they continued their kiss, more passionately. With everything Joshua just said, Lauren was remorseful and felt that at this moment, there was no way she could mention to Joshua what she knew. She thought, '*God. Please forgive me for not telling Joshua sooner. But now is not the right time.*

15

Distress in This Dress

21 years ago – Rome, Italy.
The day of the Carnevale di Venezia (Carnival of Venice).

Denise looked around and then above her head and admired the large church. Even though it was located a few blocks north of Vatican City, it was very similar to the Sistine Chapel. It had no windows, a decorated granite floor, and a twenty-meter, or sixty-six-foot, high ceiling. The side walls were twice as long and possessed old paintings and statues that depicted the twelve apostles and many biblical events from the Old Testament, such as Elijah setting fire from heaven to a stone and Moses leading the Hebrews out of Egypt. Some of these events, Denise could decipher, like the depiction of the life of Moses. Others she could not. She wondered if Michelangelo painted this church too. She then noticed a depiction of Mary and baby Jesus on the front wall. But it wasn't like any of the pictures or paintings of the two that she had previously seen in America. They both appeared very dark-skinned and with dark hair.

She leaned over on her chair to Bishop Hines and quietly whispered, "Is that a black Madonna on the wall?"

Bishop Hines waited a moment to respond. He did not want to draw any attention to them. He then leaned over to Denise and whispered back in her ear, "Maybe."

Denise whispered back, "Here in Italy?"

Bishop Hines did not want to respond again as Denise, Archbishop Bennett, and he was sitting in three chairs in the front of this church, and in front of a panel of a private group of high-ranking clergy priests, called the *Concilium Iustitiae*, which is Latin for the Council of Justice. Their purpose was to discreetly, and sometimes nefariously, handle threats within the Church. They gathered to discuss the event that occurred the previous night in which a few rogue priests attempted an exorcism on Ezra, Archbishop Bennett's daughter. During this fact-finding session, any side conversation or whispering would be considered inappropriate, or even a sign of disrespect. But Bishop Hines was wise enough to know that if he did not respond to Denise quickly, she would ask again; and this time it would be a louder broadcast instead of a whisper. He then whispered, "Yes. Europe churches alone have over four hundred depictions of a *Black Madonna*, many of which can be found here in Italy."

"How long ago were they…" Denise attempted to ask the age of their creations, but Bishop Hines quickly answered before she could finish.

"13th Century," whispered Bishop Hines out of the side of his mouth in hopes of being unnoticed.

Cardinal Arancio, who led the council, heard the two and loudly interjected, "What about the 13th Century, Bishop Hines? Would you like to indulge us with the same gallery chatter that must have a priority greater than the one that we are conducting?"

"My sincere apologies, your Eminence," responded Bishop Hines, as he looked down at Denise, embarrassed and in correction.

Since Bishop Hines' response was immediate and adequate, Cardinal

Arancio continued, "For the benefit of Bishop Hines and Signora Denise Williams, I will convey our final collective comments in English." Up until this point, the entire discussion was in Italian, while Denise sat quietly not understanding any of it. Cardinal Arancio then said, forcefully, "Last night's exorcism attempt on the child was not sanctioned by the Church. And to hear that my good amico and friend, Bennett, was chained to a wall, while his child was held at gunpoint and feared for her life, is unfathomable. We apologize for the evil that has occurred within our walls." Cardinal Arancio then looked directly at Denise and said, "Signora Denise Williams. Your gift of healing, actions of grace, sacrifice, and humbleness are sincerely appreciated and accepted by the Church. From the miracles that you performed in the United States, also in the tent yesterday, and how you handled yourself in the face of danger, there is no doubt that the Spirit of God dwells within you. For obvious reasons, we cannot grant you official recognition from the Church. Albeit the panel before you vow that the Church's resources will forever be at your disposal. May you continue to do the work of Christ and may God's light forever be in you."

"Thank you so much," said Denise.

"Yes, thank you," added Bishop Hines.

As the Council members were getting up to adjourn, Archbishop Bennett stood up from his chair and signaled that he wanted to speak. Cardinal Arancio nodded to show his approval. He said, "Your Eminence. Again, thank you for your great wisdom and consideration in this matter. May I ask what will happen to the priests involved in the incident last night, and more importantly, what will become of my daughter, Ezra, in the eyes of the Church?"

Cardinal Arancio looked at the other members for confirmation, then back at Archbishop Bennett. "The priests involved in the incident last night will be dealt with severely. Regarding Ezra, she is a daughter of the Church and is always welcome. We presume that Signora Denise Williams will work with her. We are confident that whatever your daughter needs, this gifted lady will be the one to figure it out."

With tears of joy in his eyes, Archbishop Bennett clasped his hands together in appreciation. Denise got up from her chair and hugged him. He ecstatically voiced his appreciation. "Thank you, Denise! Thank you! I am forever in your debt."

"I think this is the first time that I ever witnessed you truly happy, Bennett," said Bishop Hines.

"With Ezra's issues, the past few years have been very difficult. But now with Denise, I have hope. For the first time in years, I have hope!" he exclaimed.

"She does have that effect," confirmed Bishop Hines.

Then, Archbishop Bennett turned to face Denise intently. "If you are willing to work with my daughter, Ezra, I promise that I will dedicate my life to assisting you with your gifts."

"I would be honored, Archbishop Bennett," said Denise smiling.

The council members exited out of the back of the church, while Denise, Archbishop Bennett, and Bishop Hines walked out of the front of it. When they got to the entrance steps, Archbishop Bennett stopped and said, "I must go check on Ezra. Thank you again, Denise."

"No problem," she replied.

"So, what are you two kids about to do, another tent healing revival?" joked Archbishop Bennett.

"No. After all that Denise has done already, I think she deserves a break, maybe even some fun time," answered Bishop Hines, already with a plan.

"What does that mean?" asked Denise.

"It means tonight, I'm taking you to the Carnevale di Venezia," said Bishop Hines, as he smiled.

"The what?" asked Denise, forgetting that the lady next to her on the plane, and Angelo the waiter, both mentioned it to her.

"The Carnival of Venice, Venice's annual festival," said Bishop Hines.

Concerned, Archbishop Bennett cautioned and added, "A festival that attracts millions of visitors; and remember, it was previously banned from 1797 to 1979."

Denise chimed in when she finally remembered the previous conversations she'd had about it. "Now, I remember. It sounds fun. But with the terrorist activity, is that a good idea?"

"We die daily," said Bishop Hines.

"I guess we do," said Denise, still apprehensive.

"We cannot let the evil of this world ever stop us from living our normal lives, Denise. No matter what," said Bishop Hines in defense.

"I will let you two figure it out. You're adults, so I will not persuade you either way. Plus, my daughter is my focus today. I wish you a good day and enjoy yourselves and be safe this evening. Just stay away from any tunnels," said Archbishop Bennett as he smiled and walked away.

"Take care, Archbishop Bennett," said Denise.

"Take care, Bennett," said Bishop Hines.

Denise looked up at Bishop Hines. "So do many churchgoers and bishops go to this banned festival?"

"It's no longer banned, and I'm not forcing you to go. I thought it would be a good and fun experience while you're out here."

"You know my brother would be totally against us going to this festival," said Denise, hesitant about going.

"Your brother, Jerry is a good and ethical man. None of my ministers live by the book like him. So, I do not doubt that he would be against us going, and so would many other Christians for that matter. But I don't judge them when they put on their favorite sports jersey and worship their team or favorite player as a god. When their team loses, they let it ruin their whole day and walk around sad, depressed, or with unremovable angered emotions," argued Bishop Hines.

"That's an interesting way of thinking of it, Bishop."

"Christians will sit in the cold and in all types of weather for hours for their favorite sports team or a concert, yet will complain about church service lasting too long or the…"

Denise interrupted, "…and with good HVAC conditions."

"I was going to say temperature, but exactly. If it's raining or if they're tired, they don't even come out to help our homeless, food drive, or prison ministry. It takes willing and able bodies to feed the hungry, pass out tracts, or come to the jail or hospital with me. Yet, these same people will judge unbelievers, and even other Christians, for what they feel or see is wrong; even if it's not biblical," said Bishop Hines, frustrated.

"Now that sounds exactly like my brother," said Denise.

"Jerry will make a good pastor one day. Out of all my ministers, he's the one that I know cares the most about humanity's well-being and soul."

"So, it doesn't have anything to do with the fact that when you ordained him as a minister in your church, you incorrectly kept calling him Pastor Williams, instead of Minister Williams?" asked Denise, with a giggle.

Bishop Hines laughed so loud that Denise felt the base in his deep voice. "He told you that?" asked Bishop Hines, as he continued to laugh.

"One day, Angela and I were chatting. He came up to us and asked us for advice. He said that you kept calling him Pastor Williams and sometimes you didn't even realize it. So, he wondered if he should correct you or not."

"He's a good man. I have the utmost respect for his compassion for others and strive for true holiness. The world would view Christianity, or followers of Christ, so much differently if there were more men and ministers like him. As much as I hate to eventually let him go, I will do everything I can to support him leaving International Covenant Ministries and building his own church. His calling is to be a pastor, no doubt."

"Well, you have the opportunity to raise a minister of your own from scratch with little Mikey. I mean Mike."

"I would never force the ministry on little Mike. But I sure would love to see that day. He's smart, energetic, and the professionalism he portrays at such a young age is astounding."

"Well, look at who his father is, he has a good example to watch."

"Thank you. But I think Marco, with his military-style training and living, also has a lot to do with it."

"I don't have any kids, yet. But I always felt that children need love, education, discipline, and structure. With you, your wife Sarah, and Marco, sounds like he has all four covered."

"I believe so," confirmed Bishop Hines. "Are you good to go for the festival this evening?"

"I guess so. What do I need to do to get ready?"

"I have a meeting I must attend in about an hour. But the driver will take you back to the house to get ready. Your attire for this evening is being delivered, and then you will take our private plane out to Venice. I will meet you there later this evening," said Bishop Hines.

"Private plane? We are not driving?" she asked.

"It's a five to six-hour drive, and with event traffic it's most likely double that. But it's only an hour on the plane," he explained.

"I'm going way out to Venice, alone?"

"Don't tell me you're afraid to go by yourself?"

"What if I am?" she said, playfully.

"I find that hard to believe. You know how to handle yourself in all environments. I witnessed it."

"Well, maybe I'm afraid you will stand me up."

"You know I adhere to all my commitments. The Bible says, '*Don't let your mouth cause your flesh to sin.*'

"In Philadelphia, Bishop, we say that in another way."

"Really. What way is that, Denise?" asked Bishop Hines, intrigued.

"Don't let your mouth write a check that your butt can't cash!"

They both laughed hysterically, then slightly touching each other.

Bishop Hines walked over to the car waiting for them. "Take Signora Denise back to the house," said Bishop Hines to the driver.

"Sì," said the driver.

Bishop Hines opened the car door to let Denise in the backseat. "I will see you in Venice later this evening. I promise you will have an enjoyable evening."

"I'm looking forward to it," she said, excited.

Bishop Hines smiled and shut the car door. The driver drove off to take Denise back to the house to get ready. As Denise sat in the back seat, she reflected on the recent events since she'd been in Rome. Met with high-level clergy members and gained their respect and support for her works; helped to save Archbishop Bennett and his daughter the night before; healed two families in the tent service and how that was meant by God since one of the families was only there because she or Biship Hines went to the wrong restaurant, and met the waiter Angelo, who brought his mother and father to the tent to be healed. She thought about how kind and grateful Angelo was and how she loved the sound of his middle name Joshua. She felt that name commanded a sense of power and peace at the same time. Knowing that she was nowhere close to being married or even ready for kids, Denise thought, *Why wouldn't I help Bishop Hines and his wife Sarah with an-*

other child? Without them, I would not be here in Italy. Without Bishop Hines, I wouldn't be in the position to heal so many people in America and abroad. Maybe, I will let Bishop Hines know this evening that I agree to surrogate their next child. If so, maybe I will include in the agreement that it is required that we name him Joshua if it is a boy.

When she arrived back at the house and walked through the front door, she noticed a large gray box sitting up against the wall. A large white tag placed on the box had her name, *Denise Williams*, written on it. As soon as she picked it up, the caretaker, Marco came out from the kitchen, and said, "Bishop Hines told me that he had to attend a meeting and to look out for a delivery for you."

"Yes. He told me the same," replied Denise.

As Denise continued to admire the box, Marco gazed upon her in the hope of gaining her attention. "If Bishop Hines is tied up today. I'd be more than happy to show you around, Signora Denise." He smiled waiting for her response, as he already thought of places that he could take her. Unfortunately, Denise did not hear Marco as she sat on the floor in excitement like a kid on Christmas morning and wondered what was in the box. "What is it?" asked Marco seeing the surprise on Denise's face when she opened it. Denise pulled the item out of the box. It was an elegant red dress with thick black lining, artfully decorated with embroidery and sheer accents, most definitely very expensive.

"Oh my god! This dress is gorgeous!" exclaimed Denise. Marco looked surprised. Denise looked back in the box and noticed another item. It was a matching red and black Venetian mask that would cover just the top part of her face. "What is this, a mask?" asked Denise, as she turned toward Marco and finally re-acknowledged his presence.

"That type of mask is used for masquerading, such as a party or formal event where slight anonymity is encouraged. Is Bishop Hines taking you somewhere?" he asked, seemingly disturbed.

"We are going to a carnival in Venice," said Denise, focused back on the dress and mask.

"The Carnevale di Venezia," said Marco, surprised and disappointed.

"Yes. That thing."

"Elaborate costumes and masquerades are common attire for the Carnivale," said Marco, reserved and back in his hired role.

Denise looked up at the clock on the wall and exclaimed, "Oh, Lord, I must hurry! But I already know what I'm wearing!"

"Indeed," said Marco in a softer tone, and appeared that he'd rather be back in the kitchen.

"I'm sorry, Marco. What was your question earlier?" asked Denise, referring to when she did not hear him asking to take her out.

"Never mind. Is there anything else you desire, Signora Denise?"

"No, and thank you, Marco!" She then ran upstairs to try on her dress and paused for a second near the platform and excitedly showed the beauty of her dress to the Roma statue and then ran up the rest of the way like she was in high school getting ready for the prom.

Marco fiercely watched her go up the stairs. His disposition appeared angered. He then clinched his fist tightly, walked out of the house, and slammed the door.

16

Code Red

Present Day – Rome, Italy – Two days before Hands Across the World.

Bishop Hines received a call from Officer Reese. He answered, "Good Morning, Officer Reese."

"Good morning, Bishop Hines," he replied.

"How are things going?"

"They're going. I'm here in Bala Cynwyd."

"Oh, in one of our regional homes. Are The Church's assistants being of any help to you, Officer?"

"They are very helpful. Thank you. Hey. I don't have much time, so I want to say this quickly before somebody comes around," he said, as he looked around to make sure no one was near him. "First, is Josh with you and is he okay?" he asked.

"Yes, he is with me and he is okay."

Officer Reese was relieved, then said, "We uncovered new evidence at Pastor Williams house."

"That's great news. Right, Officer Reese?"

"That depends. Is your son, Mike with you?"

"No. He's not. Why?" he asked, now concerned.

Before he answered Bishop Hines, he asked him one more question. "Where are you now, Bishop?"

"We are in Rome."

"As in Rome, Italy?" he asked, loud and surprised.

"Can you just tell me what you found, Officer?" he said, impatient.

"The evidence is pointing too*****or it could belong to*****person." His reception was spotty, going in and out.

"Can you repeat that, Officer Reese? Your signal broke up."

Officer Reese tried to communicate again. "Before I share this with the other officers, I need you to confirm for me if…"

The call dropped. The cause—another bomb explosion at The Church's regional house in Bala Cynwyd, Pennsylvania, which was located on the west border of Philadelphia, and it was a couple of the Church's assistants, Officer Reese, a few other policemen, and two ATF agents. Now all dead.

* * *

Later, despite experiencing another earthquake and Joshua possibly seeing the man in his recurring dream, Joshua and Lauren came back into the house laughing, teasing each other about their adventure in the park. They walked toward the kitchen to get something to eat but they stopped when they saw Bishop Hines, Archbishop Bennett, Ezra, and Jacob sitting in the library study, and quiet.

"Whose dog died?" joked Joshua as he saw their somber faces.

No one responded. Lauren knew this meant that something serious had happened. "What is it?" she asked.

"There was another explosion," said Bishop Hines.

"You mean the earthquake we just felt?" asked Lauren.

"No. Another bomb just went" said Bishop Hines.

"Where?" asked Joshua, as they'd both sat down on one of the sofas.

"In one of our homes in Bala Cynwyd," said Archbishop Bennett.

"A home," questioned Lauren.

"The Church owns many homes all over the world just like this one. The one hit was being used by the Church's assistants helping Officer Reese with the investigation into the explosion that hit Joshua's uncle's house. Unfortunately, I was on the phone with Officer Reese when the bomb went off," said Bishop Hines.

"Is he dead," asked Joshua, fearful of more death.

"We were talking and the phone just went blank," said Bishop Hines.

Archbishop Bennett added, "I called a nearby parish of ours. Everyone in the house, including our assistants, Officer Reese, and three ATF agents were purportedly in the house at the time of the explosion."

"Certainly, with the previous church fires along the Boulevard, and now this incident that may have taken the lives of a few ATF agents, you can bet that the FBI and every single governmental task force agency will be clawing their way into this matter," said Bishop Hines.

"That's exactly what we don't need, especially with the Hands Across the World event tomorrow," said Archbishop Bennett.

Joshua sat silently and attempted not to let his emotions get out of control like they did earlier.

Jacob was scrolling on his phone when he saw numerous news alerts. "Holy socks! Turn on the TV!" he exclaimed.

Bishop Hines grabbed the remote and turned on the television positioned over the fireplace. The news headline read, '*NOTIZIE URGENT*' with three separate split screens that showed three different regions across the world. Two of the sections showed military groups with guns fighting, and the third showed the aftermath of another bomb explosion in the Middle East—police and emergency workers rushing to help rescue victims injured and bloodied by the impact. Then the screens switched and flashed back and forth to many other areas around the world showing massive uncontrollable fires set to communities and cities all over the world.

Since the news' narration was in Italian, Joshua said, "What's going on? I can't understand a thing!"

"They're reporting that explosions, small wars, and fires are breaking out all over the world," said Archbishop Bennett. Joshua grabbed Lauren's hand. He continued, "As we suspected would happen, neighboring countries are fighting over adjoining land, natural resources, and pocket areas for new strategically placed popup military bases." He then paused to listen to the reports and communicated the same, "They're reporting skirmishes in parts of Africa have intensified on the border of many countries…others have joined in the war against Israel and…Russia has started to expand its war beyond the Ukraine heading west, attempting to take over parts of Estonia and Latvia…the U.S. and Mexican border is now a war zone…and both Spain and France are sending troops to its border to expedite the building of their new walls. And…." He then paused in unbelief.

"And…" said Lauren.

"And…Back in the U.S., Homeland Security, with *Presidential Directive-3*, has raised the *Threat Condition Level* to red, and many other countries have raised their threat levels to the highest level as well."

"What does that mean?" asked Jacob.

Bishop Hines replied, "That means troops, naval ships, missiles, and bombs are active and ready to be deployed at a moment's notice."

"It looks bad. Protocol-11 is starting and they're taking actions just as anticipated, right?" asked Joshua, expecting confirmation.

"Yes. But much earlier than we thought," said Archbishop Bennett.

"I was just thinking the same thing. Why is this happening all at once? I thought it would spread over weeks or months," said Lauren. Hearing Lauren's question, Joshua then remembered that he yelled at God earlier to give him life's medicine all at once. He sunk in the sofa now regretting yelling at God even more. He wondered, *Is this God saying, 'Okay, Joshua. Here's your medicine all at once like you asked!'*

"Other than humans, land, including its resources, has always been the most important commodity to a nation; and it's second, only to religion as being the most cause for wars," said Archbishop Bennett.

"Even next-door neighbors will fight over the smallest piece of land that they want as their property," contributed Ezra.

"Now imagine that everyone believes it's the end of the world. Complete chaos, killings, and no law and order in place for protection or to stop any violence would all be expected," said Archbishop Bennett.

"That's why countries would destroy parts of their own country where they saw fit for buffers or military bases!" stated Jacob, with belief that he contributed something new.

"Jacob. Where have you been this whole time? We already mentioned that a few times!" yelled Ezra. She then said, "Never mind. That was the smartest thing you said all year."

"Are you sure you're not brother and sister?" asked Joshua again, laughing with Lauren. Bishop Hines and Archbishop Bennett kept their composure as they were used to their banter.

Lauren stopped laughing and voiced a new thought, "At some point these countries will be ready for anything, and once they do, we will have antsy world leaders with itchy trigger finger generals that will most likely start a global nuclear war before any Apocalypse could begin. So, instead of Protocol-11 being the protection from the world ending, it may very well be the reason it ends," said Lauren.

Excited to redeem himself, Jacob said, "Just like if you go back in time in the movies to prevent an event, but your actions in the past actually causes that event to happen."

"Good points, Lauren and Jacob," said Archbishop Bennett. Jacob then made two shaped letter Ls with his hands and threw them in Ezra's face to identify her as a loser, but she ignored him.

Bishop Hines added, "You don't want to be the nation that pushed a button too early and caused the destruction of half the world. However, you don't want to be remembered as the nation that didn't push a button at all and let others be the cause of your destruction."

"It will be a while before all these new barrier walls and those so-called self-contained cities are built, correct?" asked Joshua.

"No, Joshua. In China, they construct thirty to fifty-story buildings in just one week. The U.S. and other countries can replicate by using the same technology and getting rid of all the permit and inspection hindrances. Now imagine the urgency is the end of the world. I bet this activity will wind down within a day or two, maybe sooner," said Bishop Hines.

Archbishop Bennett then got up from his chair, walked over to Joshua still sitting on the sofa next to Lauren. He put his hands in his pockets, and said, "Joshua. Your mother was certain that this Hands Across the World event was the solution to all of this. Even though she could not explain how or why, deep within my soul, I trusted and believed her. But since her death, we have nothing." He paused, and then asked, "Can you think of anything that she may have mentioned to you? Anything at all about this event that could help us?"

Joshua quickly replied, frustrated and without thought, "No. Nothing. She never talked about any of this with me. Everyone in this room knows more about her than me. The only thing she ever talked about was about church or her working at the grocery store."

Bishop Hines attempted to pull more from him. "Joshua. There must be something you can remember. Maybe you can..."

Joshua interrupted Bishop Hines, abruptly, and said, "I just said she told me nothing!" yelled Joshua. He then got up and left the room.

"Not again," said Lauren as she looked at Bishop Hines, disappointed.

She then got up and followed Joshua. Ezra then followed Lauren. Then being the only young adult left in the room, Jacob looked at Archbishop Bennett and Bishop Hines with a grimace, and said, "Awkwaaard," and followed the bunch out of the room.

Lauren ran out of the house after Joshua, but he was on the porch waiting for her. He said, "I'm good. I just wanted to get away from Bishop Hines and get some fresh air. You thought you were going to run after me again, didn't you?" joked Joshua. Lauren then gave him a playful hit against his arm. When Ezra and Jacob walked out the front door and met the two on the porch, they all decided to take a walk. Ezra walked faster than everyone. She eventually led the pack down the street known as *Via Basento* and kept going until she came to a church that was undergoing construction renovation. She walked up its steps, opened its large door, peeked into the church, and then said to the group, "It's open!" She then walked inside. They reluctantly followed her up the steps into the church. Lauren grabbed Joshua's hand and held it tightly as they looked around in amazement. There was scaffolding, paint, bags of cement, and tools all throughout the church.

"I just love how you can just go into these churches freely and get to pray or walk around adoring the architecture," said Lauren.

"Yes. But with all this construction, I'm pretty sure we should not be in here right now," said Jacob.

"The workers must be on break," said Ezra.

They separated from each other admiring the different parts of the church. The massively high ceiling; the stenciled design of stars that appeared to glow in the dark; the statues and apostle memorials; and the polished floor with historic intricate designs.

"Come, here!" yelled Ezra.

The three walked to the front to meet her, turned to the left, and noticed a narrow passageway of steps that went to a lower level.

"Let's see what's down there," said Ezra as she ran down the steps.

"Vite, vite," said Lauren as she hurried down the steps after Ezra.

Jacob, as he looked at Joshua and wondered what she meant.

"She says it a lot. I think it means hurry in French," said Joshua.

"Got it. Well, let's Vite it…Vite it…We better get down there and vite it…" sung Jacob, and snapped his fingers to the tune and melody of Michael Jackson's song 'Beat It'.

Joshua did not laugh. "You remind me of someone," said Joshua referring to his annoying friend, Monty, back in Philadelphia.

"I get the feeling that was not a compliment," said Jacob.

Joshua then walked down the steps and Jacob followed. When they reached the lower level, Lauren and Ezra were standing in front of a roped-off memorial built into the wall. Joshua noticed that it was for a female. But he could not tell who, as the inscription was in Latin.

"Am I reading this right? Someone is buried here?" asked Joshua as he looked at the memorial.

"That's very common for the Roman Catholic Church and others. You'd be surprised at what else you can find at the bottom of these churches," said Ezra.

"We know," said Joshua and Lauren at the same exact time, referring to their experiences back in Philadelphia.

Ezra then said, "She's probably someone special that did something important. But look what I found." Ezra pointed to a small hidden door built into the wall that was slightly cracked. They were surprised and anxious to find out what was behind it. They entered the room and saw many artifacts of the Church, from old Bibles to antique crosses to paintings that were hundreds of years old. In the center of the room, there was a small table carved from stone, just like the one in The Chamber, but much smaller. They sat down at it as if they were all the new members of The Circle and gave random and funny predictions.

Then, Lauren said, "This room is extraordinary."

"The stuff in here has to be worth millions," said Joshua.

"Well, if it's the end of the world, we can't spend any of it," said Jacob.

Wanting to make up for her father and Bishop Hines pushing Joshua's emotions, Ezra felt the need to talk to him. "Joshua. I'm sorry for how my father and Bishop Hines spoke to you back at the house. I know my father would never want to upset or offend you," said Ezra.

"I know, Ezra. Thank you," said Joshua.

"Can I ask you the same thing, but a little differently?" she asked.

"Go ahead," said Joshua.

She asked, "Did you ever overhear your mother talking about anything to anyone over the phone or at church about anything that feels remotely close to all this?"

Out of respect for Ezra, Joshua took a moment to think before he responded, and said, "No. Other than knowing that she attended Hands Across America in the U.S. when she was younger, she never mentioned anything to me, and I never heard her discuss it anyone."

Lauren felt that she might be able to connect better with him, and asked, "What about, what you didn't hear?"

"What do you mean, what I didn't hear?" asked Joshua.

Lauren clarified, "Instead of thinking of what she may have said, what about what she didn't say? Was there ever a time that you think she was hiding something or speaking in code to someone?"

"Not that I can remember," Joshua replied, quickly. Then he said, "Wait. You said, 'in code'. I keep having a dream about her and it's like she is talking to me in code."

"What dream?" asked Ezra, extremely interested.

"In this dream, I need to check on her to make sure she is okay. I know she is dead, but I look for her anyway," said Joshua.

"Do you find her?" asked Lauren.

"Yes," said Joshua.

"What does she say?" asked Ezra, intensely.

"She's at her job at the grocery store, and then she gives me advice on how to fill up one of the refrigerated cases. Once that happens, I hear thunder and there's an earthquake," said Joshua.

Lauren decided to provide a little more color and clarity to Ezra and Jacob about Joshua's dreams. "In Philadelphia, Joshua had a recurring dream that helped us stop the string of church fires along the Boulevard. It sounds like this is another one," said Lauren.

Joshua then closed his eyes, took a deep breath, and slowly exhaled.

"So, he's like Daniel in the Bible, foretelling the future with his dreams? How long has he been able to do this?" asked Ezra.

"I think ever since we had to deal with the string of church fires not too long ago," said Lauren.

Ezra then reached over to Joshua and before she touched him, he opened his eyes and exclaimed, "I got it!" He abruptly stood up from the table and exclaimed, "She was talking about hoagies and Hands Across the World! That's what her vision meant. The hoagies, that's it!" They looked at Joshua and then at each other baffled by his statements. "We must get back to the house right away. I think I know what to do!" exclaimed Joshua with urgency.

"You do?" asked Lauren.

"What are you talking about, Joshua," asked Ezra.

He replied, "You always set up hoagies soldier-course style!"

"What in the world are hoagies?" asked Jacob.

At that moment, Lauren's cell phone rang. She pulled it out of her pocket and looked to see who was calling. It was Mike, Bishop Hines' son...her ex-fiancée. He wanted to meet Lauren without anyone else. After quietly speaking with Joshua and the group, so Mike could not hear them, she agreed.

17

The Masquerade

21 years ago – Venice, Italy.
The Carnevale di Venezia (Carnival of Venice).

The private jet provided by Bishop Hines came to a stop. It transported Denise to the *Venezia Tessera Marco Polo Airport* in Venice. The airstair of the aircraft lowered from the plane and extended to the ground. Denise emerged at its peak, captivating with her effortless grace. She was draped in her elegant red and black dress with its matching Venetian mask and eager to experience *The Carnevale*. The groundworkers, and a few people in the airport who stood near large glass windows, viewed her in awe and wonder. *She must be some well-known foreign singer here to perform for The Carnevale,* they thought. Centered in Saint Mark's Square, the Carnival of Venice brings in about three million visitors making it one of the largest festivals in the world. The pilot assisted Denise as she glided down the steps and enjoyed the view of the twilight in the distance, slightly dark as the night approached and the wind soft. Ready on the ground was a black Mercedes Sprinter van ordered to take her to the carnival. The moment she sat down in the van the Blackberry phone rang that was given to her by Bishop Hines.

"Hello, Bishop," she answered.

"Hello, my gifted Denise," replied Bishop Hines. "I take it that your accommodations to Venice were satisfactory."

"Umm…yes. You sure do know how to make a girl feel special."

"If you don't realize how special you are to us by now, then you probably should just go back to Philadelphia," he joked.

"No way, Jose!"

He laughed, then said, "Honestly, with the number of visitors to this festival, our private jet was the only way to make it there at a reasonable hour. So, a matter of logistics, nothing more."

"Private jets and luxury vans equal logistics…got it, Bishop," she responded, sarcastically.

He chuckled, then provided more information about the evening. "The driver is taking you to *Parco San Giuliano*. It's a large park with lots of trails and a gorgeous lagoon and a lake view of Venice."

"So, we're only viewing Venice this evening from a distance?"

"No way, Jose. There's a port at the edge of the park. I have a boat reserved to take you across. With traffic and the crowd, a reserved boat is the only way we can make it over to Saint Mark's Square before the evening's end."

"Reserved boats, huh. There goes those logistics again," she joked.

"Wait until you see for yourself. The captain will attempt to get you as close to Saint Mark's Square as possible—and that's where I will meet you."

"The Saint Mark of the Bible has a square in Venice?" she asked.

"Correct. Also, I have another surprise to show you in *Basilica di San Marco*, Saint Mark's Basilica.

"You're just full of surprises."

"So, I will meet you in the Square, soon."

"But Bishop, with all the people, how will you find me?"

"Logistics."

"Right," chuckled Denise.

She hung up the phone and enjoyed the traveling view all the way to San Giuliano Park. From there, a shuttle cart drove her from the entrance of the park to the ports. It was chilly, but Denise loved the cold and the cool breeze felt good against her face. When she arrived at the port, she couldn't believe her eyes. First, the multitude of various boats, from ferries to traghettos to speedboats, that swarmed the river and lake to capacity, all filled with people celebrating the annual festival. Second, the gorgeous view of Venice from across the Venetian Lagoon lake took Denise's breath away. And last, even with being a little over two kilometers away from the small islands of Venice, she could easily see the bright lights, hear the loud music, and feel the celebration of The Carnevale.

A man walked up to her and asked, "Signora Denise Williams?"

"Yes. That's me," Denise answered.

"My name is Tommaso. I am the captain of your transport across the waters to Venice. Follow me," as he led her to his *motoscafo* which is a unique type of speedboat. As he held her hand to help her onboard, he admired her in her dress and mask. "Quite stunning and beautiful, Signora Denise. This evening, you will be the sun of Venice!" said Tommaso with pleasure and a much stronger Italian accent than previous.

"Thank you," said Denise, elated. She then looked back at the park for any sign of Bishop Hines approaching.

"No worries. My brother, Riccardo, runs a second boat. He will bring Bishop Hines. He is a good man. Well respected."

She then sat down and couldn't believe the number of boats in front of them and with very little gaps in between them. "How are we going to get through that congregation of boats?" she asked, worried.

"I've been boating these waters for many years. You are in good hands, Signora."

Seeing even more boats in the distance, Denise thought, *This is like I-95 going through Fredericksburg but on water!*

Tommaso then started the engine and sped off into the crowd, fishtailing around the first ferryboat and skidding the water like a drifting car race. Denise held onto the seat tightly and slightly scared as he barely missed the other boats. As they got closer to the beautiful Venice islands, Denise's heart began to race. She couldn't remember the last time that she attended such a more exciting event. After more thought, the closest memory she had of something so electrifying was in 1980. She was much younger, and she and her friends snuck into the Emerald City event center located in Cherry Hill, New Jersey to see the musical artist *Prince* perform. It was the first concert she'd ever been to; the first celebrity she ever saw in person, and the first time she fell in love–at least that's what she would tell all her friends from that moment on. She then smiled at the thought of how all her high school friends would be so jealous; and how just two years ago, who would have ever thought she would be getting off a private jet from Rome to Venice, and then shuttled in a luxurious van to a dock, now on her way in a speed boat to Venice. All while being dressed exquisitely and in masquerade for The Carnivale, one of the largest costume party events in the world. Before Denise knew it, Tommaso had already crossed the lagoon and was carefully steering through the Venice waterways bordered by tall buildings on both sides of the water.

"This is as far as I can take you," said Tommaso.

Denise looked up and saw steps that led to a group of buildings near the famous Ponte di Rialto or Rialto Bridge that crossed over the canal.

He looked at her and said, "Yes. Take the steps to the street, then turn left. That's *San Marco* and will take you all the way to the Square."

"Thank you," said Denise.

"My pleasure, Signora."

He then helped her off the boat. From the steps, Denise turned left as Tommaso had instructed and walked into a narrow tunnel and alley that eventually opened to loud music, a narrow walkway bordered by tall residence buildings, hotels, bars, restaurants, small retail shops, and a wall of groups of people in front of her. *How am I supposed to get through all these people*, she wondered. Before figuring that out, she took a minute to observe and enjoy the crowd's creative, elaborate, and over-the-top costumes with various types of masks. She saw them chatting, profiling, and even dancing. She remembered Tommaso boating skills and acted on the idea of moving through the crowd just like he navigated his boat. She started out slowly, then sped up, and implausibly glided through the crowd, turning and twisting her body to fit through the couples and groups or providing an aggressive look or gentle push to move them out of her way. Her dress and vibrant presence helped. As Denise traversed through the crowd, all looked on admiring her untouchable elegance, just as much as she looked on them adoring their fun filled energy, unique costumes, and masks. She saw a good number of Venetian masks, like her own. Many others were known as a *Bauta,* which were worn mostly by the men and covered their whole face with a squared jaw line and feathery hat. She was also intrigued by the ones that covered their entire face and possessed a long-curved beaked nose, known as the historic *medico della peste* or plague doctor mask. Even those without a mask wore thick makeup applied and designed to give the appearance of a mask. For a moment longer than needed, Denise kept her eyes focused up on the people partying on the second story balconies. As a result, she ran into the back of a tall man, almost knocking him over. Before Denise could say sorry, he'd already turned around to see who hit him in the back with so much force. When he did, he laughed hysterically, which confused Denise until he took off his Bauta mask and hat and revealed his identity. It was Angelo, the waiter from the restaurant, the one who later brought his parents to see Denise for their miracle healing.

"Denise!" yelled Angelo.

It took Denise a few seconds to recognize him. "Oh, my lord, Angelo Joshua Fazio!" she exclaimed, remembering his full name, and embraced him with a hug.

"How did you recognize me?" asked Denise.

"I would recognize your beauty and spirit anywhere. Plus, not too many Black Americans come out for this event. You look fabulous and I love that dress! You might be the best dressed here," he expressed.

"You look amazing yourself, and I just love your hat!" she replied. Part of Angelo's costume was a distinctive colorful iridescent feathered hat that resembled the train of a peacock.

"Denise. These are my friends," he said, as he leaned back to reveal the three other people with him, two females and one male all in full costume. He immediately followed up with, "Everyone! This is the American that I was telling you about, Denise." Angelo told them about how he met Denise at his restaurant and how she healed his family. So, when Angelo's friends saw that it was her, their excitement caused them to let out a great cheer. Then, they each greeted her and gave her a big hug. Denise felt their warmth and love for her, and she didn't even know them.

"I can't believe you're here in Venice," said Angelo.

"I can't believe I ran into you, literally," said Denise.

"Are you wanting to make your way to the square?" he asked.

"Yes, I am," she replied.

"You'll never make it through all of this."

"I won't?" asked Denise, concerned not knowing what to do next.

"Well, not without us!" yelled Angelo. He then raised his hand over his head and yelled, "*Verso la piazza!*" Angelo's friends raised their arms in the same manner and yelled back, "*Verso la piazza!*"

Angelo then repeated it, this time in English, "To the Square!"

Then, he and his friends pushed their way through the crowd as they repeated the chant, "Verso la piazza! Verso la piazza! Verso la piazza!" Not only did it work, but many people joined in with the chant and cheerfully followed behind them, all the way to Saint Mark's Square. Once they arrived, they loudly cheered with their success.

"Thank you, Angelo," said Denise as she gave him one more hug.

"Have fun," said Angelo. He turned away from her and focused back on his friends.

Denise walked a few more steps through the crowd deeper into Saint Mark's Square and then she saw Saint Mark's Basilica, brightly lit up. It was the most gorgeous building that she'd ever seen.

"Breathtaking, isn't it?" said someone directly into her ear who was standing behind her.

Denise turned around and looked up at the tall, massive figure. The man was in full costume as well. A dark black cape with red and grey embroidery; and his face covered with a plague doctor mask with its long-beaked nose. But she knew immediately—it was Bishop Hines.

"Oh my!" said Denise, surprised. "How did you get her so quickly and how did you find me?"

"Logistics," Bishop Hines replied.

Denise looked at him, skeptical. "The cell phone you gave me has a tracker, doesn't it?" she asked, wittingly.

"Yes. But how did you know it was me?" he asked, mystified.

"Bishop, you stand out everywhere you go, mask or no mask; and apparently, not too many of us attend this event." She then grabbed Bishop Hines' hand and showed him his exposed skin.

"Oh, I see." They laughed.

"The captain said you were coming over on another boat much later."

"That's what I told him to say. I arrived just before you did." He paused for a moment, then said, "This place is amazing, isn't it?"

"I can think of a few better words than just amazing. How about extraordinary, electrifying, breathtaking, picturesque? God, I could go on. And this church's exterior detail is incomprehensible. I've done a little construction management and the amount of time and skill needed to complete those intricate designs with that type of material is unthinkable," said Denise, referring to the top of the Basilica.

"Wait until you see the inside. C'mon."

"We're allowed to go inside, now?" she asked, excited.

"Yes. But only a select few. I have a special pass." He then grabbed Denise's hand and held it tightly as he confidently led her through the crowd to the rear side of the church until they got to a gate with four guards. Through his cape, he reached into the collar of his shirt and pulled out a hard plastic card attached to a string around his neck. One of the guards inspected the pass and let them in. This entrance led them down a few steps then into a long tunnel.

"You sure are well connected. Even the guy on the boat had great things to say about you. I can't imagine you accumulated your money and respect from just being a church bishop in Philadelphia."

Bishop Hines chuckled. "It was the international aid and missions that I supported here in Italy, in Africa, and in other parts of the world that helped give me the right connections. Yes. Some of it was funded by my church, International Covenant Ministries, but most of it was through charitable channels from my commercial real estate investments and partners. Donations not only help with taxes, but they also give you access to places and people that appear unattainable."

"So that's how all of this is done. But I can't imagine just a few donations, even very significant ones gave you access to the Catholic Church like this. They must have hundreds of thousands of donors like you."

"You're quite intelligent, Denise. While Archbishop Bennett and I were working on interdenominational missions and aid programs in Africa, my investment group, and with our resources, helped take out a very powerful, unethical, and untouchable national minister. He was funding militant groups responsible for the murders, rapes, and theft of thousands of Africans. The region's jurisdiction and people were so happy that they gave a lot of his property and possessions to us from the seizure. One of his properties had hundreds of verified religious artifacts hidden under a bunker. Things never seen, like biblical tablets and text writings dating back to the same time as the Dead Sea Scrolls, Jewish treasures, statues, paintings, and rugs anywhere from the 13th to 17th century, even never seen epistles or letters appearing to be from the disciples of Jesus Christ or their followers, before they were all stoned, hung, or violently murdered.

"Wow! And what did you do with all that?"

"I donated most of it to the Catholic Church, through Archbishop Bennett of course, a few religious organizations, and various accredited universities and museums across the world."

"Hence, giving you the access."

"Exactly. It opened many doors for my church's international mission efforts and eventually led me to work with the most influential religious secret society, The Circle. I got to work with the truly spiritual and supernaturally gifted. I would have never imagined that one of them would be the sister of one of my very own ministers."

"Did any of those rugs end up back in that house in Rome?"

He laughed, "Among a few other things."

Denise changed the topic to the decision that she made on the way to Venice. "My answer is yes, Bishop."

"Your answer is yes to what?" he asked, as he wanted certainty.

"I will surrogate you and Sarah's next child."

Bishop Hines stopped walking and joined his hands together over his mouth in joy. "Praise God and Hallelujah! Sarah will be so excited to hear this. Thank you, Denise. Whatever you need to make this happen and feel comfortable, we will do."

They continued to walk until the end of the tunnel opened into the gorgeous sanctuary with only a few other people inside. Denise's eyes opened wide in disbelief.

"What word would you use to describe this, Denise?" he asked.

"Paradisical!"

"Interesting choice."

"Bishop. I read on the plane that Saint Peter's Basilica holds the dead body of Saint Peter in an area called the Vatican Necro…Necro…" Denise struggled to remember.

He interjected, "Vatican Necropolis. That's somewhat correct."

"So, what about this church? Does it hold the body of Saint Mark?"

"That question is undefined. Is it the body, remains of the body, or just relics of Mark that's here?"

"I'm the one asking you!"

"Well, let's go see."

When they turned to go towards the Tomb of Saint Mark, a little girl ran out from the tunnel that led to the tomb. She was being chased by a priest and a guard, then ran into the arms of Denise. Denise looked down and noticed it was young Ezra, Archbishop Bennett's daughter.

"My dear, Ezra! What are you doing here?" exclaimed Bishop Hines, perplexed and concerned about how she ended up in Venice and in the church during The Carnivale. She appeared afraid and did not answer.

"What's the meaning of this?" asked Bishop Hines firmly to the priest and guard who finally caught up to Ezra.

"She's not supposed to be here," said the guard, out of breath from running after her.

The priest recognized Bishop Hines and said, "You tell Bennett to keep his daughter on a leash. She's always in these tombs and cutting and talking to herself. She's crazy and needs to be banned!"

"Ezra. I heard you were hanging out with Marco earlier today. How did you get here?" asked Denise. But young Ezra appeared fearful and did not answer. Denise then squatted down and rolled up young Ezra's sleeves and saw that she had fresh cuts on her arm. Denise gasped in horror. "Where's the knife?" Ezra hesitated, but then slowly reached into her jacket pocket and pulled out a small pocket knife. "Give it to me," said Denise. Ezra complied and handed it to her.

"We'll handle this from here," said Bishop Hines. The priest and guard walked away speaking in Italian, visibly furious and frustrated.

Denise grabbed Ezra's face with her hand and turned it so that she could see eye to eye with her, and said firmly, "You and I will have our first therapy session tomorrow."

Young Ezra pleaded, "I'm sorry. I pray to the saints to help me get better with my condition; and I need to change to not be such an embarrassment to my father and the church. When I feel like the saints can't hear me, I get as close as I can to the tombs and I hurt myself to get their attention."

Denise looked at her mad and felt she was lying to avoid punishment.

"Last time. How did you get here? Don't make me ask again, little girl," said Bishop Hines.

"I traveled here to Venice with Sister McCabe and the Daughters of Divine Goodwill. I snuck out, hid on a boat, and hitched a ride here."

Before Bishop Hines could scold her, a large explosion had gone off outside the church. The blast sounded like thunder and violently shook the church. From the proximity of the impact and noise, they had no doubt the bomb went off in Saint Mark's Square while hundreds, if not thousands, of people, were dancing and celebrating.

At that moment, Denise yelled, "Angelo!" She then turned away from Bishop Hines and ran back out of the church.

Bishop Hines led Ezra over to a guard near the exit and said, "Watch her!" He complied with this order but was also torn by his duty to run outside and address whatever had just happened. The terrorists had struck again.

When Denise reached the edge of the square from the church, she came to a complete stop and turned her head away in horror from the view of the massive amount of carnage. The devastation. The broken and dismembered bodies. The heavy amount of blood that covered the square. Bishop Hines caught up to Denise and wrapped his arms around her, then pulled her into his chest hiding her from the monstrosity of evil that had just occurred. Denise turned toward the vicinity of the square where she last saw Angelo. After scanning the crowd back and forth, she saw Angelo's unique colorful hat, with his limp body next to it, greatly damaged and lifeless. Denise's scream in horror was drowned out by the screams of others. "I can heal him!" Denise yelled, as she tried to break free from Bishop Hines' hold and run to Angelo's body.

"No Denise!" Bishop Hines yelled back, holding her and preventing her from leaving their mark to keep her safe.

"Let me go! I can heal him!"

"No. Look at his body, Denise. He's already dead!"

Denise gave up the fight and buried her face into Bishop Hines' chest crying. "I can heal him, Bishop. I can still heal him," said Denise, softly as she realized she could not. To comfort her and himself, Bishop Hines said softy, "We die daily, Denise. We die daily."

18

A Dreamy Idea

Present Day – Rome, Italy – Two days before Hands Across the World.

After Lauren put Mike on hold and muted her cell phone, she and Joshua disclosed to Ezra and Jacob that they had a collective vision that Mike was the person behind the bombs and killings. As a result of that discussion, she unmuted her phone and agreed to meet with Mike, but in a public place. However, she did not inform him that the group also decided that she would not go alone as he requested; and they would confront him together in a public place with lots of people about his possible involvement.

After Lauren ended her call with Mike, Ezra immediately wanted to get back to Joshua's revelation that his recurring dream might be related to the Hands Across the World event. She said, "Joshua. Before Mike called, you said you figured it out. Something about hoagies. What are hoagies?"

"Yeah, Bro. What are hoagies?" repeated Jacob.

Joshua and Lauren looked at each other and laughed. He gladly answered, "Hoagies are subs or submarine sandwiches. In Philadelphia, we call them hoagies."

"What is it about hoagies and your dream, Joshua?" asked Lauren.

"We should get back to the house, quick. I'll explain it there with Bishop Hines and Archbishop Bennett. They're gonna want to hear this too," said Joshua.

* * *

Back at the house, Bishop Hines and Archbishop Bennett were still in the library study having a conversation about recent events. Marco stood behind the wall adjacent to the door but hidden and eavesdropped on their conversation.

"Are you okay with the fact that we did not discuss everything with the kids, Bennett?"

"Like what?" asked Archbishop Bennett.

"For one, The Circle's predictions always came up with a plan to ensure the world went back to normalcy. What's different about this time," asked Bishop Hines.

"This time, not just one country but most of the entire world has nuclear weapons, or access to them, and nothing will preclude anyone from using them in this situation. In the past, empires and kingdoms had to fall to restore world order. After this, there will be nothing left to restore on any continent. So, whether the true Apocalypse is happening or not, it might as well be."

"And what about this other problem we have, Bennett."

"Are you referring to the recent bombs that have been targeting us, like in The Chamber."

"Yes."

"Respectfully Bishop, you're the one that wants to forget that also includes Denise. How long do you think it will be before Joshua puts two and two together?" asked Archbishop Bennett, sternly. Bishop Hines' guilt caused his silence. Archbishop Bennett continued, "I warned you about this before, and now look where we are."

Bishop Hines decided to respond offensively, "Respectfully Bennett, with all of your resources, why haven't you found out who's behind all this, including Denise's death?"

"Evidence from the bomb that hit our regional house in Bala Cynwyd confirms that whoever was behind it is the same person that set off the bomb that went off at Pastor Williams' house."

"Then Joshua holds the key to all the mysteries; his mother's death; the string of church fires; and the recent bombings."

"Yes, Bishop. And not without Lauren."

"Are you suggesting that we start the trials and rituals again to acquire the Light of Life?"

"Do we have any other choice? It didn't work with you and Denise, and it didn't work with Mike and Lauren. Maybe, the third time's a charm with Joshua and Lauren."

"Many people tried before us and failed, Bennett."

"Many people are still trying now, Bishop, and have been for centuries. Whether drinking blood or offering sacrifices, all are trying to be the first to acquire the Light of Life. But from what we uncovered in Africa, we are the only ones that know the exact trials and rituals needed. We just need to find the right couple with a twin soul."

Marco, who was still listening to their conversation, then jumped out from behind the wall and walked into the room and spoke, angered. "You're going to risk getting Denise's son, Joshua killed too!" yelled Marco. Bishop Hines and Archbishop Bennett flinched in surprise and shock that Marco was listening to them. He continued, "All these years, I never said anything. I sat quietly as you two always talked about this Light of Life with no care in the world for the consequences. You don't even feel responsible for Denise's death, or any of the others, do you? Now, you are going to do the same with these children! You used to care about Denise! You used to care about her son...you're..." He then paused. "Don't think I don't know about your dirty little secret Bishop! Others know too and you will pay for your sins. One way or another, you will pay!" He then stormed out of the room.

"Jesus! What is his problem?" exclaimed Archbishop Bennett.

"I never said anything before, but I think he was in love with Denise," Bishop Hines replied.

"Did them two ever…"

"No. She let him down easy and told him she was not interested."

"Well, I can't say, I don't understand or blame him. An amazing, attractive, and friendly woman, like Denise, who wouldn't fall in love with her. You know about that more than any of us, right my good friend? But don't listen to him. Her death was not your fault."

Bishop Hines ignored his statement and had a thought. "He is right about one thing. This time Bennett, we must be completely open with them." But Archbishop Bennett looked away in disagreement. "It's the only way it will work," urged Bishop Hines.

"It's the only way, what will work?" asked Joshua, as the group of him, Lauren, Ezra, and Jacob returned and walked into the room. Without hesitation and fed up with secrets, Joshua pushed his question again onto the two. "What will work, Bishop? We just saw Marco storming out of here like a madman on a mission," said Joshua, more firmly.

"We have an old idea that may help our situation, including stopping Protocol-11 and the inevitable wars," said Bishop Hines, referring to the Light of Life.

"It's not inevitable if we can stop it," said Joshua.

"Joshua said he figured out his mother's vision," said Lauren, excited.

"You have?" asked Archbishop Bennett, anxious. Everyone looked at Joshua with patience, awaiting his big revelation and solution.

"Maybe. Now, what I am about to say is going to sound crazy."

"Just say it, Bro," said Jacob, impatient.

"Before the church fires occurred along the Boulevard, I had a recurring dream that eventually came true and helped Lauren and me stop them and solve the mystery behind them. Well, I have been having another recurring dream. This time about my mother," said Joshua.

"Why didn't you mention that before?" asked Bishop Hines.

"Before, I didn't think it was related. But now, I'm confident it is," said Joshua.

"Explain," said Archbishop Bennett.

"Remember. It's going to sound, crazy," said Joshua, delaying.

"Joshua!" yelled Lauren.

"Okay! Before my mother died, she worked at our neighborhood grocery store, Penn Fresh. After she died, I began working at the store too. I thought it was what she wanted. I kept having this dream that I was with her in the grocery store and she was working in the deli department instructing me how to arrange the premade hoagies in the deli case," said Joshua.

"What are hoagies?' asked Archbishop Bennett.

"Ignore my father, Joshua. Please continue," said Ezra.

"I thought it was her simply telling me how to set up the hoagies in the cases. But now I'm certain it was her in my dream telling me about her vision for Hands Across the World," said Joshua.

"How do you know, Joshua?" asked Bishop Hines.

"When she was alive and started working at the store, she impressed the store manager with her unique presentation of the hoagies in one of the cases. It was the first thing they taught me when I got hired. You stack them side by side, soldier-course style, meaning standing up length top to bottom. This makes the line of them strong and less likely to fall. But the key is to have as many as possible stacked together, just like you do in the military aka soldiers. Having only a few hoagies in the case gives the impression that the product is old and not fresh, so no one wants to buy them. But the more products you have in the case, the greater the strength and presentation. It's a risk, but it is worth it."

Archbishop Bennett interrupted Joshua, "This is good for Supermarket 101, but what does this have to do with your mother's vision for Hands Across the World?"

Suddenly Lauren jumped back into the conversation as she realized what Denise's vision and Joshua's dream meant too. She then exclaimed, "I get it! Your chapter six!"

"Yes, Lauren. My chapter six," said Joshua, now composed and calm.

"What do you mean by his chapter six?" asked Jacob as everyone else remained confused.

"Not me, but Joshua, chapter six in the Bible. God tells Joshua and the people of Israelites to march around the city of Jericho six times in six days without saying a word, and then on the seventh day they are supposed to do this again, but this time the trumpets of ram horns are to play, and when the Israelites *heard this sound*, they were to yell, scream, and shout at the top of their lungs until the walls of Jericho came crumbling down," said Joshua, excited. He continued, "And in my dream, my mother tells me that when I hear this sound, which sounds like thunder, *'it's time'*, and to stack the hoagies as instructed."

"Again, how is all of that connected, Joshua?" asked Bishop Hines.

Ezra immediately responded, and said, "I get it. The Israelites only had about forty thousand people, give or take a thousand. But Denise's Hands Across the World will have millions, maybe tens of millions of people. All standing hand to hand and side by side, across the world, soldier course style and strong just like Denise said in his dream."

Jacob chimed in, "If forty thousand people shouting all at once caused the walls of Jericho to fall, just imagine what millions of people across the world could do giving one loud synchronized shout at the same exact time."

"If we broadcast a spiritual event like this to the entire world, that number may grow to hundreds of millions of people! Like Jacob said, can you imagine all of God's people shouting at once? Do you know how much spiritual impact that would have upon the earth, all on one accord in the name of God for the same purpose?" said Lauren.

Jacob added, excited, "Wow! And if everyone shouts in faith, as loud as they could, for as long as they could. The vibration! The frequency! A great shout and power maybe more than this world have ever experienced or felt, ever!" exclaimed Jacob.

"That's it, Jacob. We will call it, The Great Shout!" exclaimed Lauren.

"The Great Shout!" repeated Joshua.

"I'm still processing this. The good thing is that the Hands Across the World event is already in place to make this, as you call it, Great Shout, happen. Regardless of the result, this is such a great idea. I don't know why we as religious leaders never thought about this before, even if only to demonstrate our belief, faith and unity to the world," said Archbishop Bennett.

"Joshua. Are you expecting this Great Shout will cause some type of supernatural phenomenon like in the Bible were city walls come crashing down?" asked Bishop Hines.

Joshua paused for a moment to think. Then said, "Look, even though my name is Joshua, I am not expecting this great shout to make buildings and walls come crashing down all over the world or have fire reign down on stone from heaven like Elijah did. But what I do believe is a great shout, all at once, at the same time, from millions of people holding hands all around the world, is bound to bring God's spirit down on this earth like never before. If it is the end of the world, or not, that call of God's spirit should immediately fall on tens of thousands of people, if not more. How can the world not feel God's presence and Spirit after that? How could those that do not believe deny His existence?"

"What if nothing happens, Joshua?" asked Bishop Hines.

"Just like my mother told the store manager when he said it was a big risk building a presentation like that, and she responded by saying, 'That's the risk we must take.' Therefore, I say the same to you, Bishop."

Ezra walked up to Archbishop Bennett, quickly and said, "Father. If Joshua is right, this Great Shout would be the exact thing needed to get people to believe again. Restore faith, show love and unity, and maybe even shake down walls, literally and spiritually, and who knows, maybe even influence leaders to avoid potential wars," said Ezra pleading to her father, Archbishop Bennett.

"You may be right, Ezra. But how do we get everyone to shout at the same time, and what are they shouting?" asked Archbishop Bennett.

She answered, "Easy, social media. We have less than twenty-four hours to change the messaging of Hands Across the World and get more people and organizations to participate in this event."

"That's not going to be enough," said Archbishop Bennett. "We need to get to The Circle members again and convince them to push this Great Shout message through to the world leaders, now that we know Denise's vision for the event.

"Do you think they will believe in it?" asked Bishop Hines.

"They don't have to believe in it. We just need them to agree to support and promote it. Believers and non-believers will shout or yell for any reason or no reason at all. If The Circle communicates to their leaders to share and promote it, they all will listen and do as instructed," said Archbishop Bennett.

"You have a point," said Bishop Hines.

"Bishop Hines and I will arrange an immediate conference call with The Circle. We will tell them that The Great Shout is imperative and it was part of Denise's vision. They will go for that. Then we will instruct all religious leaders to communicate that at 15:33 Central European

Standard Time everyone participating in Hands Across the World, will shout, scream, and yell as loud as they can," said Archbishop Bennett.

"Wow, I love it!" exclaimed Lauren.

"That's exactly the collective spiritual power we need. Joshua and Lauren, you must be part of this! We need you both holding hands and shouting with the world. No excuses!" exclaimed Ezra, forcefully.

"Okay. We get it, Ezra," said Joshua, feeling slightly intimidated.

"There is one more thing that we need to do," said Lauren.

"What is that, my dear?" asked Bishop Hines.

"Joshua and I had a joint vision, and we believe we know who may be behind the bombs and attacks on us, back in Philadelphia and now here in Rome," said Lauren.

"You do?" asked Ezra.

"Yes. We believe it's Mike," said Lauren.

"You mean, Bishop Hines' son?" asked Archbishop Bennett.

"Yes. He was in Philadelphia at the time of everything; and not too long ago, I received a call from him asking me to meet him here, alone. So, somehow he made it here in Rome just like us," replied Lauren.

"Also, I'm certain I saw the shadow of a man that fit his height and build outside of The Chamber before that bomb went off and barricaded us in," said Joshua.

"Then, Joshua and I used the breathing and prayer technique to get us on one accord, and we both saw him in our vision as the one behind all this," said Lauren.

Jacob voiced his dissent, "I know we talked about it in the church when he called, but why? Mike is like the Voltron of ministers. What reason would he have to be behind all of this?" Bishop Hines and Archbishop Bennett looked at each other in fear.

Everyone noticed.

19

The Convocation

One year ago – Rome, Italy.
One month before Lauren and Mike's scheduled wedding.

Lauren sat in the chair and looked down at her ring and couldn't believe she was engaged to Mike Hines, a minister and son of Bishop Hines of the infamous International Covenant Ministries, the most prominent church in the City of Philadelphia and one of the most recognized interdenominational charity and missions' partner of the Roman Catholic Church. At this time, they'd been dating for about a year, and he proposed just the prior month. They both wanted a very short engagement, and their wedding was scheduled only five weeks away. Everyone, including Lauren's parents, felt the wedding was too quick after the proposal, but they also felt that she and Mike were meant to be together. Therefore, no one pushed back or made a fuss about the date. For Lauren, she'd never thought about getting married, well not seriously, until she met Mike. From the numerous accolades and praise that his father, Bishop Hines, always gave Lauren in front of him and the other ministers, Mike felt the need to swoop her up before someone else did. However, their first encounter was not magical. They first met at a Church of God in Christ convention at the Valley Forge Convention Center in King of Prussia, Pennsylvania. The Church of God in Christ, also known by the acronym COGIC is a fiery Holiness-Pentecostal Christian denomination primarily within the United States. It has over twelve thousand churches with six and a half million members in many countries all around the world. Mike and Bishop Hines were both guest speakers for two separate biblical seminars. This was quite an honor for them both as they were not members of this church's affiliation. Lauren was also there, along with other students from Bishop Hines' International Covenant Ministries School of Theology. At the request of Bishop Hines, his students attended this convention as he wanted them to get a fiery holiness experience, like only a COGIC convention worship and praise experience could provide; as well as learn from a different church denomination. Lauren smiled with remembrance of the details of this first encounter with Mike, which occurred just over a year prior to this moment, and right before the death of Joshua's mother, Denise. She remembered…

* * *

…the horrendous traffic on the Schuylkill Expressway from Philadelphia, Lauren ran late to one of the seminars being conducted at the COGIC's church convention. Her lateness increased when she mistakenly parked at an entrance of the Valley Forge Hotel & Convention Center that was the furthest away from the seminar's banquet room location. Eventually, she found her way through the many corridors of the building. She arrived at the banquet room forty-five minutes late with only fifteen minutes left in the seminar's allocated time. Mike was leading the seminar. But she'd never met him before. Unlike other students enrolled in the International Covenant Ministries School of Theology, Lauren was not a member of its church, nor did she ever attend a service. She found out about the school while searching online and immediately signed up when she read the school's mission state-ment, charitable endeavors, and reviewed the curriculum descriptions. Before this event, she'd only met Bishop Hines once during orientation where he'd explain his vision for the school. Other than that, she then only saw his name as the author of some of the books and learning ma-terials for her classes. With that, she had no idea that Bishop Hines had a son and he was the speaker and facilitator of the seminar that she was about to join. Slow and quiet, she walked into the large banquet room that had a hundred seats all filled with attentive individuals, mostly of COGIC clergy members.

Mike was speaking to the audience, "With the numerous scriptural references we discussed, can we all agree that social media or even your phone can become a god in your life that we are not supposed to worship? Based on that, we must limit the time that we spend on them. If not, the bad, negativity, and evil that comes along with them can consume us, leading us to discouragement, depression, jealousy, divorce, sin, and many other things that can hinder our relationship with God." Most of the audience nodded in agreement and a few others said, "Amen."

Without needing to get settled or comfortable in the large room, Lauren felt the need to comment and she did. "That's one limited way to think of it," she said, loud from the back of the room. The audience turned back and looked at Lauren in surprise. However, their reaction did not faze her as she was stoic waiting for his response.

"Excuse me," said Mike.

"I thought I was loud enough for you to hear me. Do I need to repeat it?" she responded with no thought if she was out of order with COG-IC seminar and meeting guidelines.

"No. I heard you, and I'm pretty sure everyone in the next banquet room heard you too." The crowd laughed. He continued, "But I would like you to explain, as you put it, my *limited* way of thinking."

"What about the good that cell phones and social media bring to this world?" asked Lauren.

"Such as?" said Mike, as he felt he would play her game, or devil's advocate, and walked a few steps up the aisle to approach her, closer.

"For one, connectivity to family, friends, and businesses across miles that never existed," replied Lauren, confident.

Mike then walked closer to her, and asked, "What is your name?"

"Lauren."

"Lauren. I think you are the one that has limited thinking. The Bible tells us that '*all things that are lawful are not always expedient*' or profitable, found in first Corinthian chapter ten verse twenty-one. The cell phones of today and social media have both good and bad. But is the good worth the bad if the bad causes destruction?"

Lauren decided to return the petty volley, "Well, what is your name, sir?" asked Lauren.

"My name is Mike, and it's on the program."

The crowd laughed again. But Lauren correcting his reference mistake, countered, "Mike. First Corinthian chapter ten verse *twenty-three*, and not twenty-one as you incorrectly said, is exactly what I'm saying."

"Excuse me," said Mike, perplexed.

"Why do you keep saying that? Are the acoustics bad in here?" replied Lauren, sarcastically. A few members of the audience laughed, while others kept quiet in disbelief offended by Lauren's tone and extemporaneous challenges toward him. But she continued, "People love talking about the bad or how bad things are. But very few people talk about how good things can be bad for us and be the very things that hinder our relationship with God."

"Lauren. Maybe it's the acoustics, but did I hear you correctly? You said good is bad. That makes no sense. Would you like time to rethink and restate what you said to the group?" he replied with a chuckle.

Lauren replied, "Let me explain. The Bible says, '*False prophets come in sheep's clothing but inwardly they are ravening wolves,*' found in Matthew chapter seven verse fifteen. It's so common to focus on the bad. But according to the words of Christ, it's really the good of something or someone that should cause us concern."

With that statement, Mike, including the audience, became intrigued. "Go on," he said.

"The enemy, Satan, evil, darkness, or whatever negative force you want to name it, primarily uses two weapons to hold people back from their true gifts, purpose, and destiny. These two things are discouragement and goodness," said Lauren.

"Okay. I preached many times on how discouragement could stop someone from attempting to reach their goals. I also preached a sermon on how being taken for granted or unloved could stop a person from being kind and loving; or how failing again and again could make a person give up or want to end their life; all resulting in a person missing out on their purpose or God's calling for their life, or destiny, as you stated. But the Bible talks about goodness all the time. How could good be bad?" asked Mike.

"One example, Mike, is having lots of friends. We see and feel this as good. But Satan can intentionally give you lots of friends just to give you the wrong impression that you're loved by everyone and provide you with a false sense of value, even if they talk about you behind your back. You could end up lying or withholding information just to keep them around, or overexerting yourself striving to keep them happy, just to cover up your own feelings of low self-worth, forgetting that God is the only one that you should strive to satisfy. A second example is being successful in a specific career. This could distract you from trying another job that is truly your purpose and why God created you, but you are too successful and comfortable to take that risk or even see it as an option. For argument's sake, I will give you one more, Mike. Let's say your good is that you're extremely intelligent. But you're so full of knowledge or full of yourself that you feel no one can teach you anything. You may even look down on those that you think have less knowledge than you," said Lauren.

"Amen to that last one, Miss Lady!" exclaimed a woman near the front row. Mike felt Lauren's comment was a dig at him.

Then, Lauren walked past Mike, stopped in the middle of the aisle of the room, and said, "Let's be honest. We all believe that we could easily recognize a wolf in sheep's clothing. But maybe that's wrong. The devil is way smarter than we think. Don't believe me?" She paused. "I want everyone to close their eyes and imagine a wolf in sheep's clothing that may try to deceive you. Now, what do you see?" She paused, again. "How many of you saw a sheep with a slightly evil face or large canine type teeth?" Almost everyone raised their hand. "Now how many of you saw just a nice kind sheep that looks exactly like a sheep and nothing but a sheep?" No one raised their hand. "Exactly. Satan's sheep or evil will take the form of a sheep and nothing more. We will believe and think it is a sheep. It will look like a sheep, smell like a sheep, feel like a sheep, and sound like a sheep. So, that kind sweet and innocent looking person that everyone sees and loves, that good job that's paying the bills, that one person who keeps going out their way for you no matter what, those friends that you think love you so, could be from God, or they very well could be your distraction, discouragement, or future destruction because you trusted them more than you did God."

Then, one of the deacons seated in the front row, stood up with his Bible and spoke, hitting his Bible with his hand with every spoken syllable like it was a tambourine, and said, "I put all my faith in my wife, my job, my family, and my friends, and they all turned their back on me when I needed them most. As much as I believed they were good, and I sacrificed for them, ignored their faults—they wished for my downfall. I thought that they were the *good* in my life, as Miss Lady just said. But when my life direction changed, so did they. When I had nothing, they rubbed their riches and accomplishments in my face, somehow *accidentally* showing me the amounts in their bank accounts, but I ignored it and loved them the same. They would invite everyone on their vacation trips but me, birthday and anniversary parties the same, or if I did get an invite, it was at the last minute when they already knew my schedule wouldn't allow it. Then, they would tell others that I didn't go because I was anti-social or *too good* for them or the trip, causing others to despise me. The only time I saw or heard from them was when they wanted to gossip about their other friends or had a problem of their own and wanted to vent, or share their scandals, lies, and cheating escapades because they knew I would not tell anyone. Then when I finally became successful myself and put up boundaries of interactions and topics of conversations, and voiced my spiritual expectations, that's when they changed on me, talked bad about me to their family and friends, criticized my every move and decisions, and said *I* was the one showing off when I was just happy to finally be blessed after forty years of no money and struggling almost every day and proclaiming God's blessings. After all my hard work, dedication, and focusing on nothing but God, work, and my children, my wife still repeatedly cheated on me and all those I knew sided with her and didn't even reach out to me to ask what happened. My job screwed me over with my pension after I gave them thirty-five years of commitment. My family made up stories in their heads about me when I finally addressed their lack of help and disrespect. The people I called my best friends and my best loves disappeared and befriended those who they knew were against me. Now, they talk about me like they forgot about my character, loyalty, or unconditional love for them for so many years. I cried with them, cried for them, prayed with them, prayed for them. But they had the nerve and audacity to judge me. Okay, sorry for the rant. But Miss Lady here is correct! The good in my life became evil. I felt my sanity and soul crack and snap in half. My soul broke. I never felt so much hurt and pain in my life and wanted to give up. I was about to give up…but God! God then spoke to me! I finally heard His voice! Really heard His voice, and He said, '*Just as Satan was against Job, so is Satan against you. Just as I was with Job, so am I with you.*' From then on, I lived my life for my own purpose and to make God happy and no one else. I pray and beg that everyone in this room do the same. If not, Satan will deceive you so bad that you will find yourself apologizing to demons and spitting on angels. I thank God I didn't give up! So, don't you give up! Don't give in to deception! Give your life to God and ask God for wisdom! God will bless you with it! If God be for you, then who can be against you! Hallelujah! Hallelujah!" he exclaimed. The audience applauded and many shouted, "Hallelujah!" Others jumped up and down, or swayed side to side with their arms raised high, all praising God in some form or manner.

After the moment of praise, Mike walked over to the deacon and gave him a loving embrace. The deacon rejoiced in joy and appreciation. Lauren smiled at Mike. Mike smiled back. Mike then looked at the audience and said, "Let me paraphrase this moment and Lauren's words and say, the gifts and presents that evil bring us will appear good and may look no different than the gifts of God. However, it is not the gift that we need to consider but the one giving it. So, be not wise in thine own eyes for evil can distract and discourage any of us from the greatness of God if we are not careful! Thank you, Miss Lady Lauren. Praise God for you being obedient and speaking what He placed on your heart to give us all. I think we understand now. Unfortunately, our time is up. May God be with you. You're dismissed from this place, but not from God's presence."

Everyone applauded. Then, a loud deep voice spoke from the entrance of the banquet room as the source walked up to them. "Pretty impressive, young lady. I don't think I've ever witnessed my son without words and to yield a point contrary to his own so easily." It was Bishop Hines as he was done leading his own seminar and wanted to check on Mike. Lauren grimaced from embarrassment. She was now aware that she just challenged the son of the well-known and respected bishop and founder of her theology school.

"Father," said Mike, as he looked at his watch. "We just wrapped up."

Then, Pastor Richardson, a member of the COGIC clergy, who observed the seminar from the very start, walked up to Mike, alongside Bishop Hines. "Good seminar, Mike," said Pastor Richardson.

"Thank you," said Mike.

"So, who's this Lauren lady with all this great insight and unafraid of a large crowd?" asked Pastor Richardson as he turned to her.

She walked up to them, and said, "I'm one of Bishop Hines' students at his School of Theology."

Bishop Hines said, "I thought you looked familiar. Thank you for joining us today. Where are the other students?"

"I think a few of them were here but slipped out quietly after Mike's dismissal. I assume they did not want to get caught in the discussion aftermath when they saw you, Bishop," joked Pastor Richardson.

"Lauren. Good luck in our school; and from your compelling thoughts today, I look forward to eventually reading your graduating thesis," said Bishop Hines.

"Bishop Hines, we need more young Christians like her, unafraid to challenge our traditional thoughts with spirit and truth. That's what will take our church higher," said Pastor Richardson.

"Indeed. Do you agree, Mike?" asked Bishop Hines.

"You mean this lady that was just short of publicly humiliating me," said Mike, offended and impressed.

"Now, Mike. Didn't you say, recently, that you were thinking about becoming a lawyer? Well, it appears Miss Lauren here just gave you your first rebuttal in front of an informal judge and jury. Can you handle it?" said Bishop Hines as he gestured toward Pastor Richardson and the empty chairs.

"I'm still in the room, you know," said Lauren.

Pastor Richardson chuckled and patted Mike on the arm as he and Bishop Hines walked out of the room.

"Do you show up to class late at our school like you do seminars?" questioned Mike.

"Do you perform any research before quoting scriptures, or do you just copy Cliff's Notes from your dad?" rebutted Lauren, immediately.

"Maybe you like showing up late just so you can steal the spotlight and become the center of attention!" exclaimed Mike.

"Maybe you like being the center of attention just so you can be the center of attention!" exclaimed Lauren.

There was a long awkward pause, then Mike exclaimed, "What?" as he unsuccessfully tried to comprehend Lauren's statement and provide retort. They then looked at each other and laughed. Mike continued, "I'm dragging a bit. Do you want to walk with me to get some coffee?"

"Sure," said Lauren, giddy.

* * *

"You'll have to take off the ring," said the male technician, disturbing Lauren's daydream about her first encounter with Mike.

She then, looked at the two tanks in front of them, took a deep breath, and exhaled…

20

No 'Tank' You

One year ago – Rome, Italy.
One month before Lauren and Mike's scheduled wedding.

"You'll have to take off the ring," said the male technician. Lauren was still in a daydream about her first encounter with Mike. The technician tried to get her attention a second time. "Lauren…hello! I need your ring. No jewelry in the tanks, remember." Lauren looked up from her stare at her engagement ring then shook her head to focus back on her environment. She then took the ring off and gave it to him. She was scared. But then, she looked at the two tanks in front of them, took a deep breath, and exhaled just as Mike instructed her to do before they got into the tanks. They were in the lower basement level of a private and historic hospital known as an *asclepieia*, one of the first of its kind established in Italy. The technician running the experiment had two assistants, one female and the other male. They performed safety investigations and checks on two separate floatation tanks for Lauren and Mike. The two tanks were very large and looked like full-sized spaceship sleeping pods, just like in the movies Alien or Passenger.

But they were made entirely of fiberglass and had no view inside. They were situated about twenty feet apart with wide drains built into the floor underneath. The technician's assistants filled the tank pods with just enough water to allow Lauren and Mike to float inside of them on a soft floating board without being completely covered in the water or overflowing the tank.

Mike sat next to her, intrigued by the water hoses and conduit pipes that were attached to the two tanks that led back into the adjacent walls. He then looked at Lauren, and asked, "Are you okay, babe?"

"Yes. Thank you," she replied. She paused, then said, "I assume your father and Bennett are behind that mirrored glass watching us."

The technician heard her and answered, "Yes. They are back there watching. Once the setup is done, I will be back there as well. So, do a quick overview. I'm one of the psychological technicians for The Church and I do a lot of their research studies. In front of you are dual purposed sleeping pods that also act as soundproof floating sensory deprivation tanks. For the purpose of this experiment, I retrofitted them with internal audio speaker earbuds so that I can communicate with you both from that room behind the mirror. For a period of thirty minutes, you will be in the tanks floating without any stimuli. No sound, except the water. No sight, except darkness and we'll cover your eyes just in case; and no smell, as your nose will be plugged. You will only be able to hear me and my voice alone through the earbuds and nothing else, not even each other, especially not each other."

"How will we breathe," said Lauren.

"The water in the pod is only filled up halfway, and that will remain the case even after we close the lids. Also, I will announce the time remaining every ten minutes. During that time pray, meditate, and try to tap into each other's soul or spirit. After that, I will ask you both random questions and we will see if you have the ability to provide the same answers as the other."

"And what if we can't," asked Mike.

"If you can't, then you'll be normal like the rest of the world. But if you can, then we have more tests that we'd like to run with greater difficulty," said the technician.

"While we were waiting upstairs, I overheard one of the hospital staff say to another that we were going down to the *religious underworld* tanks. What does that mean?" asked Lauren.

The technician glanced over at the mirrored glass where he knew Bishop Hines and Archbishop Bennett heard Lauren's question as well.

"She's smart," said Archbishop Bennett, quietly behind the glass.

"Very smart," replied, Bishop Hines.

The technician answered her question, "These tanks, and similar antiquated designed ones, have been used for centuries to help determine if a person had spiritual or supernatural abilities. But it was also used by those who felt sensory deprivation was a way to communicate with the spiritual realm. For that purpose, the water and no sound are extremely important to cross spiritual portals or dimensions."

"The *True Realm*," Lauren, replied.

"Some have called it that. But that's interesting. I haven't heard anyone call it that in a very long time. For religious technicians like me, it is known as entering the *Sound of Silence*. It's a state between our world and the spiritual world or True Realm. It is an area of the mind, a dream, or even actual physical parts of this world, where sound does not exist. Within these silent hallway realms, you can mentally and spiritually see and hear from the other side. Many historic cultures believed mirrors were spiritually frozen water, especially their reflections, and have the same effect. That's why you see them used in rituals, curses, or as portals to another world," said the technician.

"So, people used these tanks to help them enter the Sound of Silence to try to speak to the dead?" asked Lauren, apprehensive.

"Correct. Most Christians believe that, according to the Bible, it is wrong and forbidden to communicate with the dead; and they harshly judge those that have tried. But from what I have witnessed, that is until these same Christians have a loved one possessed by a demon, or they desperately need closure from the death of a loved one that ended horribly wrong or without personal forgiveness. Then, those same people, who previously judged, will go to any lengths and will believe anything that may help them. For example, years ago, I had a minister ask to use these tanks to speak to his wife whom he accidentally killed. He left their stove's gas on when he got distracted by a work phone call arguing with a coworker. He left the house to address the issue at the job site and forgot to turn it off. The house exploded with his wife in it while she was taking a nap, and she was pregnant with their first child. Even though he was a Christian minister, he couldn't sleep or forgive himself. So, he used the pods to communicate with her. Today, these pods are typically used for meditating or relaxing only, unless you come to someone like me," said the technician.

"I'm a minister and our faith is in God, not the dead. Let the dead stay dead," stated Mike.

"Good thought, Mike. But to the contrary, entering the Sound of Silence is exactly what a lot of ministers did, not just psychics and soothsayers. It was and still is more common than you think.

"Why would they do that?" asked Lauren.

"Let's say fifteen hundred years ago you are entering a village spreading the gospel, or even running a community revival today, and you didn't necessarily have any spiritual gifts, like healing or prophecy. Especially if you needed money or wanted to take advantage of people's pain, you could enter the Sound of Silence, or True Realm as Lauren called it, and speak to the dead of that village before showing up. This would allow you to get information about the villagers or attendees of the revival that no outsider or person alive should know. But then, during a ceremony or service, you could portray that this information you previously received from their dead is what you are immediately receiving directly from God. It's the SSS, or Sound of Silence Scam, that's been going on for over a century. The more people you convince that you can hear directly from God, then the more money people are willing to give you, and lots of it.

"Greed," said Mike.

Lauren asked another question. "If it's a portal or hallway to that realm. Then what about…"

The technician finished her sentence, "…Demons," said the technician. Mike's eyes widened. He continued, "That is part of that world too, and it is extremely dangerous if not done properly. For centuries, many cultures believed that you could commune with a demon that possessed a house or person through sensory deprivation and water tanks, even a bathtub full of water. The more silence and water being used, the better the conduit into that realm. It's like going to fight evil on their own turf. Even Socrates believed in the *Daimonion*, a deity, or some say a demon, that he felt warned him from bad decisions."

Lauren then looked concern, then said, "Socrates was a thinking and very smart, yet he listened to a demon regarding the decisions in his life. Is it that easily to be deceived by demons?"

"Absolutely and remember Socrates died by voluntarily drinking poison. Demons have been deceiving humans longer than we've been trying to figure out their deception. They start out by giving you sound advice, pointing out the obvious, so they gain your trust. But eventually, these demons' goal is to push you to the options in life that are the total opposite of what God wants for you. Then, when things don't work out or fail, they are in your ear to help you blame others or yourself," said the technician.

Mike looked over at the mirrored glass, knowingly getting the attention of his father, as he wondered what they got themselves into.

"The tanks are ready," said one of the technician's assistants.

"Good. Lauren, you get in the one on the left, and Mike, you get in the one on the right," said the technician. The technician's assistants helped them get into their respective tanks and placed sensory patches on their body that could be read and analyzed by a computer's control panel in the room behind the mirrored glass.

"Are you sure you are ready to put them through this, Bishop?" asked Archbishop Bennett to Bishop Hines quietly, just in case the others could hear him.

"You didn't ask that when it was Denise and me," said Bishop Hines.

"Then, it wasn't your son and future daughter-in-law. They still look like little children to me," said Archbishop Bennett.

"We are proceeding. We have no choice," said Bishop Hines.

"Alright. But I still think we should have told them the truth. They have no clue what's about to happen," said Archbishop Bennett.

The assistant that helped Lauren get into her tank took slightly longer than the one that helped Mike. This allowed Lauren to watch Mike get fully into the tank and all hooked up and his eyes blindfolded before the assistant covered her own eyes. As a result, Lauren was able to watch the other assistant close Mike's tank's lid and suspiciously push a button on the side of his tank which caused an internal latch to lock and seal his lid tight. Lauren had an uncomfortable feeling about this and wondered why it needed to be locked. As the assistant helping Lauren finished up, she put the earbuds in Lauren's ears and placed the blindfold over her eyes, and laid her back in the tank, Lauren felt the need to say something. She said, "Wait," and stopped the assistant from laying her down in the tank. But then, while blindfolded, she remembered Bishop Hines was there; and thought Mike's father would not be doing this if it wasn't safe. She then said, "Okay. I'm ready." The assistant laid her back, then closed and locked her lid. Lauren's body flinched from the vibration of the lid locking. Then, the technician's assistants remained in the room with Lauren and Mike while the technician left their room and walked into the room behind the mirrored glass. It was a small eight foot by five foot room that had a large, exposed water pipe, a table with a computer control panel, and a microphone that was linked to the tanks in the other room. It also had two small television sets attached to the top of the wall near the ceiling that were recording the event from cameras inside the room.

"The Circle of Life Tank Pods, *take three*!" exclaimed the technician, as he got in front of the control panel and adjusted the microphone that communicated through to their earbuds inside of the tanks. Before he said anything to Lauren and Mike through the microphone, he turned to Bishop Hines and said, "Are you sure you don't want to tell them, Bishop?"

"I asked him the same thing," said Archbishop Bennett.

"Do you two forget that we are under the gun with what The Circle had prophesied? If we don't get a few spiritual warriors to obtain the Light of Life soon, then the end of the world will not be stopped and God's kingdom will lose so many souls damned to Hell," said Bishop Hines, emphatically.

"Respectfully, Bishop. That's if The Circle's prophecy is true. You're willing to risk the lives of those two inside the tanks over a maybe?" asked the technician.

"The Circle's never been wrong," said Bishop Hines.

"There's a first time for everything," said the technician.

"Just do as you're told," commanded Bishop Hines.

"It's your family in there, not mine," said the technician. He then grabbed the microphone, pushed the on button, and said, "Mike and Lauren. The thirty-minute clock of no sensory starts…now."

Lauren meditated and attempted to relax. She focused on nothing but the movement and sound of the water that floated her in the tank. Like the technician said, she could only hear the water moving surrounding her and nothing else, and definitely nothing outside of the tank. Concurrently, Mike was in his tank, and whispered a prayer, *"Dear Gracious and Heavenly Father, I thank you for this wonderful day and for waking Lauren and me up this morning, having movement in our limbs, and allowing us to be together. I pray that Lauren and I have the same love for each other that I've seen and witness with my mother and father. I pray that I will be a great husband to her and a great father to our future children, just like my dad, honest, holy, and a great spiritual leader. Without his example, I don't know what type of man I would be. Speak to my heart and soul, in the name of Jesus, Amen."* Then Mike decided to be quiet and meditated.

After a few minutes, the technician grabbed the microphone, pushed the on button, and said into the tanks, "So far, that's ten minutes. You're both doing great." Both Lauren and Mike tried to remain as still and quiet as possible, focusing only on the sound of the water. Bishop Hines and Archbishop Bennett looked at each other periodically, but all remained silent as more time passed. "That's twenty minutes. Ten more minutes to go," said the technician over the microphone.

Then after ten more minutes, the technician said, "That's thirty minutes. You can relax now." Both Lauren and Mike took deep breaths before the technician continued. "Remember, you can hear me, and I can hear you, but you can't hear each other. Let's start with something simple. Lauren, give me a number between one and ten."

Lauren responded, "Seven."

"Okay, Mike. I have Lauren's number. Try to think of what number

Lauren just gave me. But before you answer, take your time. Attempt to grab it from your soul, and not your mind."

Mike waited a few seconds as he really tried to tap into his soul to see Lauren's number. He then answered, "Seven."

Bishop Hines and Archbishop Bennett looked at each other in excitement, feeling that they may have accomplished something. However, the technician made no reaction.

"Lauren. Give me a word, any word," said the technician.

"Love," said Lauren.

"Mike. What word did Lauren just say? Remember, you both can hear me, but not each other," said the technician.

Mike thought about it and then exclaimed, "Mike!"

"Excuse me. Can you repeat that?" asked the technician.

"I said, Mike. I think she's over there thinking about me." The technician then gave Bishop Hines a look of shame.

"Is he really that arrogant, Bishop?" asked Archbishop Bennett.

"Lauren. Give me another word," said the technician.

"Family," said Lauren.

"Mike. What did she just say? And please don't give me the first thing that pops into your head. Meditate and slowly let it come to you. Take as much time as you need," said the technician.

But Mike immediately responded, and yelled, "Success!"

"Really. What are you teaching this boy?" said the technician, as he looked at Bishop Hines. He then continued with the experiment, "Okay, Lauren. Let's try something different. Give me a quality of Mike that you like,"

She took a moment to think and then said, "Intelligent."

"Mike. What word did Lauren just say?"

"Athletic," said Mike.

The technician and Archbishop Bennett became frustrated. Bishop

Hines was embarrassed.

"Intelligent my ass. Even an *idiota* would know she's not going to say any of those things," said Archbishop Bennett.

"Lauren, give me a color. Any color at all," he said, frustrated.

From the technician's tone, Lauren correctly assumed that they were getting all the questions wrong. So, this time, instead of thinking of a color on her own, she thought of a color that Mike would say. "Yellow…I mean green."

"Which one Lauren? I need you to be sure." said the technician.

"Green," said Lauren.

"Mike, what color did Lauren just say?"

"Yellow," said Mike, without hesitation.

"Interesting," said the technician, thinking Lauren's first thought was correct. "Let's work conversely. Mike, give me one word, any word."

"King," said Mike.

"Lauren. What word do you think Mike said?"

"Crown," said Lauren.

"Say another word, Mike. Any word,"

"Excellence," said Mike.

"Lauren?" asked the technician.

"Perfection," said Lauren.

The technician turned off the microphone, and said to Bishop Hines and Archbishop Bennett, "This is interesting. Are you two seeing what I'm seeing?"

"Yes. It looks like Lauren has a gift that needs developing, but my son Mike has nothing and should take a course in Humbleness 101," said Bishop Hines. With that statement, he noticed a strong smirk on Archbishop Bennett's face.

"You said it, not me," said Archbishop Bennett.

"This is not the result we were hoping for," said the technician.

"Well. We didn't set all of this up for nothing. Proceed with the next phase," said Bishop Hines.

"As you wish, Bishop Hines. May God bless us with the Light of Life," said the technician.

"May God bless us with the Light of Life," collectively said Bishop Hines and Archbishop Bennett at the same time.

The technician then walked over to the back side of the room where an exposed water pipe protruded out the wall. This water pipe led back into the other room with Lauren and Mike and eventually connected to the hoses attached to their tanks. The technician grabbed the pipe's large twist valve and turned it to the left rapidly allowing more water to flow into the tanks. The water in both tanks began to rise. At first, Lauren and Mike didn't pay much attention to the air bubbles and new sound coming from the tank, but then Lauren noticed the level of the water was higher than before and rising.

"Hello. It looks like more water is getting in here. Is this supposed to be happening?" asked Lauren, nervous.

Mike then noticed as well. "Hey! The water is rising in here!" exclaimed Mike. They both banged on the tank lids to not only make noise but also to break the lock. The technician's two assistants stood in their position as they were instructed to do nothing, while the technician, Bishop Hines and Archbishop Bennett stood in the room behind the mirrored glass and watched and listened to their panicked cries for help. The technician did not respond.

When the water level rose to almost covering their entire faces, just below their eyes, nose, and mouth, and with repeated failed attempts to push open the fully secured and locked lids, they both were horrified that nothing was being done and realized that they may die. The technician rapidly turned the water valve shut and stopped the water flow. But the tanks were now filled to the top, covering their bodies and face fully submerged.

Lauren held her breath as she struggled to push open the lid. However, Mike assumed something must be wrong with the equipment, and thought his dad and the others must be outside of the tank doing what they could to fix it. So, when the water covered his face, he remained calm, took a deep breath, held it, and waited patiently as he believed they would open the lid at any moment.

Behind the mirrored glass, Bishop Hines and Archbishop Bennett looked on as the assistants stood patiently for the word. The technician looked at his stopwatch and said, "I will give them a few more seconds. You both look very calm.

"You know this isn't the first time we've been down this road," said Bishop Hines.

"Right," replied the technician. "But I'm sure you remember this is supposed to be the first of many trials to awaken the Light of Life within them."

"After this, we'll see if they improved in their abilities and ask the questions again," said Bishop Hines.

The technician replied, "After this, why would they want to continue? They'll be lucky to be alive; and it will only be because my trained assistants are there to save them just in case. You should have told them what we were doing before they came here. You and Denise knew," said the technician, frustrated.

"We will tell them later," said Bishop Hines.

"Sure. Hey Mike. Hey Lauren. We should have mentioned it to you earlier, but we put you both in a water tank and almost killed you because for centuries it's been known that being pushed to the brink of death awakens your spiritual gifts and greatness. Oh, and in addition to that, for centuries, this secret society called The Circle has been searching for a man and woman that share a oneness to reverse the consequences of *The Fall* bestowed upon us by Adam and Eve. And if they agree to almost die, once or a few times, the Light of Life will awaken within them, allow them to save the world, and bring us back to our true relationship with God. Oh, and by the way, the last time we tried this was with Bishop Hines and Denise Williams and that didn't work out too well either. It put so much strain on Denise's body and heart; it may be the very cause of her heart attack. Yeah, let's see how that works," said the technician.

Bishop Hines responded, "I may be a bishop, but I still know how to throw a heavy punch. Watch it."

The technician continued, "Oh, and Bishop Hines, did you ever tell Mike yet that you're Denise's son's father? What's his name? Joshua. You both are playing with fire, and I'm not going to be the one that gets burned when it blows up in your face." He then paused, and continued, "We all know that if a person weren't aware of the Light of Life, and went through this, they'd go to the police and file charges."

Then, the female technician's assistants pounded on the mirrored glass with her fist in panic that Lauren and Mike had been in the tanks way too long. "Oh, crap!" exclaimed the technician as he looked at his stopwatch. He then hit a large red button that released the water in the tanks into a built in drain that led into the floor and automatically released the lid locks once the water fell below half the tank. When the lids opened, the assistants rushed to help them. Mike strenuously coughed up water and attempted to catch his breath. Lauren was laid on her back in the tank, not moving. The assistant grabbed her out of the tank, placed her on the floor, and immediately performed *CPR*. Bishop Hines, Archbishop Bennett, and the technician ran into the room. They stood and watched as the assistant worked to save Lauren. After a few moments, Lauren jumped up, coughing up water and gasping for air. Mike gave a sigh of relief.

The technician turned to Bishop Hines and Archbishop and whispered, "Looks like you got what you wanted; well, most likely for one of them. But probably the right one. Hope it's worth it." He then walked towards the door and said with a loud voice, "We will pick back up in an hour," and left the room. Then the two assistants helped Lauren up on her feet and put a towel around her from a hanging rack. They led her out of that room and took her to a recovery room down the hall.

Mike grabbed a towel he saw hanging on the same rack, and yelled at his dad, Bishop Hines, and Archbishop Bennett, "What the hell is going on! And do you expect us to continue? For what!"

"Not right now son. We need to make sure Lauren's okay," said Bishop Hines. Bishop Hines and Archbishop Bennett walked out the room and followed Lauren.

After a few moments, Mike dried off his face and wet clothes and wrapped the towel around his neck and slowly walked out of the room. When he was about to walk down the hallway to find the recovery room and Lauren, he took interest in the door that led to the room behind the mirrored glass. He made sure no one was looking, opened the door and walked in. He looked around and saw the control panel, the glass that showed the other room with the tanks, and the tanks that almost cost him his life along with Lauren's. He then noticed the water valve and got suspicious. He wondered if they intentionally controlled more water going into the tanks, and if so, for what purpose. He then looked up and saw the television monitors and noticed they were still recording. He walked back to the control panel and noticed the controls for the video. He hit the *Stop Recording* button and then *Rewind* and then *Play*. He heard the voice of the technician say:

"*...Oh, and in addition to that, for centuries, The Circle has been searching for a man and woman that share a oneness to reverse the consequences of The Fall bestowed upon us by Adam and Eve. And if they* *agree to almost die, once or a few times, the Light of Life will awaken within them, save the world and bring us back to our true relationship with God. Oh, and by the way, the last time we tried this was with Bishop Hines and Denise Williams and that didn't work out too well either. It put so much strain on Denise's body and heart; it may be the very cause of her heart attack. Yeah, let's see how that works…Oh, and Bishop Hines, did you ever tell Mike that you're Denise's son's father? What's his name? Joshua. You both are playing with fire, and I'm not going to be the one that gets burned when it blows up in your face…"*

Mike stopped the video and then clinched his fist as he felt unimaginable anger and rage. His own father, the well-known and respected Bishop Hines, had another son, Joshua. Joshua "Josh" Williams. His best friend growing up; and he had no idea. Mike thought, *How could this happen? Who else knows? Does Josh know? Does mom know?* He then walked over to the door to exit the room, grabbed the doorknob and with such anger and rage flung the door back so hard that it crashed against the wall with a loud bang. Lauren, and the assistant helping her, immediately jumped, as they heard this loud noise from down the hall. She knew it was Mike and could feel his temper, his anger and rage coming towards them. She knew he was different, but why?

21

Protocol-11

Present Evening – Rome, Italy – The night before Hands Across the World.

It was chaos. The dark night and crisp fiery embers only amplified the smoke, randomly set fires and bombs, the shooting, the looting, military skirmishes, and gang like fighting across the world. The words '*LA FINE È VICINA*' in Italian, and '*EL FINAL ESTÁ ACER-CA*' in Spanish, '末日临近' in Chinese and the same in many other countries respective language, translated in English as, 'THE END IS NEAR' or 'DOOMSDAY IS APPROACHING' could be found graffi-tied on buildings and on posted and carried signs everywhere. Those that never believed in guns or supported gun rights were desperate to buy or find one. Those that never believed in God found themselves on their knees praying to Him for protection or salvation, or both. Fear strangled those with good intentions while those with evil intentions had no laws or limitations around their necks, not anymore. The god-ly praised themselves with their hope in salvation, while the ungodly praised themselves with their unfettered right and ability to cause de-struction, and greatly they did. Jacob was right. The results from the rumors, leaks, and then subsequent public acknowledgements of the enactment of Protocol-11 were like a movie. This was unintentionally sped up due to Bishop Hines and Archbishop Bennett's call to The Circle, and then The Circle's call to world leaders relaying Joshua's idea of The Great Shout, originated from Denise's vision. Once nation leaders informed their military leaders and other governmental agencies, the demand for reasoning and answers could no longer be withheld. As a result, the confidentiality of the Global Survival Protocols, including the enactment of Protocol-11, The Circle, and their prophecy of the end of the world were no longer concealed. Those that heard of it spread the details of the same, and the truth continued forward until it was worldwide news. However, the message being communicated was not that an Apocalypse was coming. Even during this time, most people, except for Revelation-loyalists, were still hesitant to make that official claim. Therefore, the main message being interpreted and spread was that Protocol-11 is code for 'The *Governments Are Going to War!*' and survival was necessary, both for your country and for yourself. During small talk, most people said Protocol-11 was because we finally depleted earth's natural resources, which would explain the past decade of major countries' interest in lower industrialized countries rich in natural resources. Others argued that it was because a large meteor or alien invasion threat was eminent. But after the discussions, the only thing that mattered was did you have food, a gun, and safe place to sleep for the night? You could not go down any major street, in any country, without hearing and witnessing repeated gun fire, buildings or homes on fire, bombs going off, children lost or crying, people fighting, or groups searching for a safe habitat. In modernized countries, masses of people swarmed to the disclosed entrances of the newly built self-contained cities and bunkers hoping to gain access. New military bases were set up and fully operational on tracts or acres of land that were formerly residential neighborhoods or owned by another country. Churches, chapels, synagogues, temples, and mosques were filled beyond capacity; and in them, a diversity of beliefs. Christians made room for Jewish families and others. Jews made room for Christian and others. Buddhists made room for the same. Atheists sat next to them all and watched them as they worshipped or prayed and wondered if their non-belief of God was a mistake. They realized that they were inevitably about to find out.

Earlier that day, Joshua, Lauren, Ezra, and Jacob spent the entire day working on the Hands Across the World event. They got caught up on the logistics and strategic plan created by Denise and Archbishop Bennett. Then, they worked diligently to set up relationships with all the event's leaders and put together an organizational list and formal process for the day. When they were done, they decided to play it safe and stay inside the house until they were scheduled to meet Mike. Lauren told Mike that she would meet him that evening in the *Plaza* of Saint Peter's Basilica, which should have occurred about an hour ago. Bishop Hines and Archbishop Bennett were in a small communication room in the basement of the asclepieia located in a separate corridor down from the water tank pod experimental room. Part of the building was barricaded and off limits from the destruction of the bomb that went off just a few days ago. They spent the entire day pleading to the Pope and governmental officials to stop Protocol-11. As a fall back, they also requested that the announcement of global martial law be delayed until after the Hands Across the World event. Both efforts were unsuccessful. At this moment, they were watching a global video conference call with the world's top twelve nation leaders, head military officials, and numerous religious leaders, including The Pope, all safe within their private and protected bunkers. Each spoken word was immediately translated into their earbuds by conference language interpreters.

"Dépêchez-vous, commençons!" said The President of the Republic of France. Translation, "Hurry, let's begin. Quickly!"

"前回と同様に、私たちはこのイベントに備えています" said the Naikaku Sōri-Daijin also known as the head of Japan. Translation, "Similar to previous times, we are prepared for this event."

"Whose great and magnificent idea was Protocol-11, anyway." said The President of the United States, sarcastically.

Due to Bishop Hines' and Archbishop Bennett's low level of authority and recognition, they could only listen in on the global meeting but not speak. Therefore, they conducted their own discussions and plans between each other.

"Everyone believes Protocol-11 is about the world going to war with each other, and not related to an apocalypse," said Archbishop Bennett.

"If you were them, on the outside, would you believe anything else?" asked Bishop Hines.

"Probably not," he replied.

"And even if we don't go to war, things will still get worse."

"Besides war, how could things get any worse?"

Bishop Hines put his hand on his chin. Then said, "As time passes, eventually, the looting and destruction will cause food and necessities to become a scarcity. Then starvation will begin for hundreds of millions of people. The quality of water will decline. All utilities, like electricity, gas, and water will be cut off. And necessary medications will run out and become unavailable, causing unrecoverable illnesses, and rampant diseases to multiply like this world has never seen."

"Interesting. I only thought of the impact of the fires, the random violence, and the potential of another world war. I can't imagine how things will be in a few days, let alone a few months. Once everyone realizes this, we will see more people fighting to get into those bunkers and self-contained cities."

"I'm certain that has already started."

They paused their conversation to listen back to the global conference meeting. The President of the United States was speaking. "…within eighteen hours, America will begin utilizing its own oil reserves, no longer requiring demand from other countries. Our total reserves are much larger than most know, and its use was kept to a minimum for such Global Survival Protocols. It was a lot larger before certain administrations accessed them to drive down gasoline costs, but we can't go back in time can we," he said, sneeringly. He continued, "Okay. Let me get back on track. Global Survival Protocol Article 2-13.1 will be implemented that requires global martial law, including a mandatory curfew at twelve midnight or zero hundred hours, in each respective time zone. And, at the request of *His Holiness…*" he said, referring to The Pope, "…and other prominent religious leaders, this will allow adequate time for the heavily planned and organized charity event, Hands Across the World. May God help us all."

"So, they are holding off on martial law until the Hands Across the World event!" exclaimed Archbishop Bennett, elated as they both heard otherwise.

"Look at God!" exclaimed Bishop Hines.

The U.S. President's next statement was even more of a surprise, and to everyone. "In addition, my good nation neighbors, we calculate that the world has already constructed at least two point one million kilometers of new border walls and structures made of cement blocks, stone, bricks, and other materials with an average height of thirty to forty feet for independent border protection. That's over one hundred times the length of the Great Wall of China. However, what most of the world doesn't know, and maybe even some of you participating in this meeting, is that with Protocol-11, and a few other Protocols, a select group of leaders, including myself, have decided that one-third of the world's population will be going underground in just eight days. This is to ensure the survival of mankind." Those that were not aware, or a part, of this contingency began speaking in their own language going into a frenzy. The U.S. President continued, "From anticipated nuclear attacks, a few of us have a certain quantity of pre-built subterranean cities, already engineered, constructed, and operation ready to handle population and habitability. Be advised that they can withstand nuclear impacts and are sustainable for many months. We will not be affected by what's happening with the outside or world's surface. Therefore, as of this moment, the United States, and other nations in concurrence, are effectively and immediately implementing Global Survival Protocol Article 5-33.7, which states in part that 'Any country, state, or jurisdiction at any time, for any reason, cause, justification or for no reason, may restrict entry into its land or border from another...' So, in other words, if you are not already within our country, you are not allowed in. All international flights both public and private into our nation have been grounded and terminated indefinitely! But there are many military planes fueled and ready to fly you out if you don't belong!" As he continued, many nation's representatives, especially from the smaller countries without these subterranean cities, began yelling and screaming about this newly disclosed information. "You said you were building protected bunkers, not that you had full cities underground already built! How could you hide this from us until now?" asked one with great anger. Another nation's leader said, "So, me and my people are to die slowly, or wait for you to drop a bomb on us with no recourse! This is a mockery of what the creators of the GSPs intended!"

They couldn't believe what they just heard. "Did you know of this?" asked Bishop Hines to Archbishop Bennett.

"I did not," replied Archbishop Bennett, stunned.

"I think, with all of this, it's going to be impossible to get anyone to participate in Hands Across the World tomorrow."

"If it wasn't for my belief and trust in Denise, I would undoubtedly agree with you Bishop. However, she was a miracle to us. There is no way I am not believing in her visions. Plus, it's up to all the local churches, ministers, charity workers, social and community activists now. They have all committed to rounding up people for Hands Across the World, by foot, by van, and spreading the word with mobile traveling microphones and speakers to make sure that as many people as possible stand side by side, or soldier-course style, as Denise said in Joshua's dreams, holding hands, and ready to shout for this great cause. Despite the chaos, many of the faithful Christians and other religious people, see the need for it right now, more than ever. Despite the obstacles and odds, I'm confident that we will have millions and millions of joined hands ready for The Great Shout!"

"I hear you, Bennett. But to me, it still feels like all hope is lost. The Circle's prophecy alone, right or wrong, may be the very cause of the end of the world. Think about it. What if The Circle's prophecy was false, or even falsified? This disaster would still be happening."

"Wait…it would still be happening…" questioned Archbishop Bennett, as he went into deep thought.

"What are you saying, Bennett?" asked Bishop Hines, perplexed.

Archbishop Bennett placed his finger over his mouth and pondered, then said, "If The Circle's prophecy was faked or even falsified, we would still be in this situation, right? So, anyone who wanted Protocol-11 to happen could have easily falsified The Circle's prophecy, right?"

"Well, not easily. But, sure, it's possible," responded Bishop Hines, not yet convinced.

"Not possible, Bishop, but, plausible. Think about it. All of this cannot be a coincidence. From the string of church fires in Philadelphia, the bombings, the deaths, all happened so soon, so quickly."

"Too soon, too quickly, I agree. But why?"

"Exactly. Almost like it was all orchestrated by someone to make sure that Protocol-11 was enacted."

"But who and why? And don't say, Mike, like Joshua and Lauren did earlier. Give me something better than that!"

"You sent them to meet with Mike, right" asked Archbishop Bennett.

"Yes. But you and I both know Mike is not behind this. He can't be."

"I don't believe so either, Bishop. But with all respect to you and your son, one never knows truly, right?"

"Right. That's why I sent Joshua, Ezra, and Jacob to go along with Lauren to see him. I can't believe he's here in Rome."

"If it's not him, then who could it be, Bishop? Who could hate us this much? Who would want Protocol-11 to happen at all costs?"

"…including hating the both of us, The Circle, Joshua and his family, and the entire world; and want to cause this much pain and destruction?" Bishop Hines then had a thought, "Remember earlier today. Do you remember who got so mad earlier when we were talking about the Light of Life?"

At that instant, before Archbishop Bennett could respond, the door to the communication room opened abruptly surprising them both. It was Marco, the caretaker. He yelled, "The dark angel, my master, wanted me to give you both a message! Forget about dying daily. How about you die now!" He then threw a brown square package into the room with them, and then quickly slammed the door shut, leaving them in the room with the package. They both knew it was most likely a bomb and quickly got up from their chairs and ran to the door to exit the room. However, Marco had immediately barricaded the door so that they could not open it. Within a few moments, the small bomb exploded, killing both Bishop Hines and Archbishop Bennett.

* * *

Lauren, along with Joshua, Ezra, and Jacob were waiting to meet

Mike. Earlier, Lauren called him and said she would meet him in the evening, alone in the Plaza in front of Saint Peter's Basilica. Ezra recommended this location and said it would most likely be crowded with saints praying for the world's future and the least likely place of violence. The group agreed. When they first arrived, it was dark and the Plaza was filled with hundreds of people standing, sitting, kneeling, or singing and praying for God to save the world. In the front entrance was a military police van on fire. When they looked over the Vatican City walls, they could see many fires set across Rome and hear gun shots and screaming in the distance. But the location felt safe and they grouped together in more comfort, all leaning up against the *Egyptian Vatican Obelisk* located in the center of the Plaza. They'd been waiting for just over an hour. However, Mike was just like his father, Bishop Hines, never late for anything. So, his tardiness had to be for a reason.

"He's not going to show," said Jacob.

"No. He's never late for anything. He's probably here watching us, wondering why all of us showed up, instead of just Lauren," said Ezra.

"He's here and he's watching from a distance," said Joshua.

Instead of Lauren's attention on the possible appearance of Mike, her attention was on the crowd, the effects of The Circle's prophecy, and Protocol-11. "All of these fires, theft, death, and destruction just from the words of a few people that we think have the gift of prophecy?" asked Lauren.

Joshua added, "Not to mention, the bombings and the killings. I still haven't even mourned the death of my uncle and aunt in Philadelphia," said Joshua. Lauren then pushed herself off the obelisk, turned towards Joshua and rested her body against his. She then placed her head on his chest. He grabbed the back of her head with his hand and kissed her forehead, and then said, "My soul loves your soul."

Lauren looked up at him, and said it right back, "My soul loves your soul, Joshua."

Ezra smiled at them. Suddenly, with Ezra's smile, the earth began to shake. It was another earthquake. The massive crowd ran frantically out of the Plaza or underneath the large colonnades for safety. But Joshua, Lauren, Ezra, and Jacob stayed at the obelisk unbothered by the quake. After a few moments, the minor earthquake stopped.

"I guess after all we have been through, nothing seems to faze us," said Lauren.

"Agreed," said Joshua.

Ezra then looked around the Plaza and said, "C'mon. I think I know where Mike is."

"You do?" asked Lauren.

"Remember. Mike and I spent a lot of time here growing up. Follow me," said Ezra, and they followed.

Ezra took them around to a side alleyway adjacent to Saint Peter's Basilica, which led to a private entrance. The door had a security code lock, which Ezra knew, and inputted the code and opened the door. She held the door open for them as they walked into a long hallway into one of the lower wings of the church.

"Where are all the guards?" asked Jacob.

"With the end of the world and with Protocol-11, would you be more worried about protecting this place or spending your last moments with your family and protecting them?" asked Ezra, rhetorically.

Joshua looked at Ezra and realized that Ezra's words revealed a big clue about The Circle's prophecy and Protocol-11 that they may have missed. He remembered her words in The Cavern that the most secure building and locations would no longer be guarded during Protocol-11. But the focus was finding Mike, so he would have to discuss his thoughts about this later.

"What is this section?" asked Jacob.

"So, you're a deacon in training with the Catholic Church and have never been here before?" asked Joshua to Jacob, as he wondered why Ezra knew about this location, but not him.

"No. Never. This entrance is always heavily guarded."

When they continued into this separate part of the magnificently built church, the area became extremely dark. The corridor led them to a small open area. Then, Ezra stopped. They all stopped as well and looked around. It was extremely dark; they could barely see the three other corridor pathways that led right to this point. Except for Lauren. She could see through the darkness just fine. Then, the temperature dropped dramatically. They shivered from the cold.

"Is it me, or did the temperature just drop?" asked Joshua.

Jacob blew his warm breath into the air causing a visible cloud of condensation. Fear came upon them. Then, they all heard a voice, low-toned, slow and angered.

"It's all your fault, Joshua," said the voice hiding at the edge of one of the other corridor entrances.

"Mike?" asked, Lauren for confirmation as she could see just the edge of his body partially sticking out from the pathway.

When he did not respond, the group all had the same thought, *Mike is the one responsible for the murders, and the bombings, and is he now there to kill them all?*

"Hello, Lauren. It is interesting to see you here in Rome, again. After you dumped me at the altar, I thought I was completely done with your annoying bullshit. Always thought you were better and smarter than everyone else." No one moved or said anything as they were set in fear. He continued, "But no, you just had to get close to my father, like his little pet. He called you the daughter he never had, but you were more like his entertaining circus animal. Then, you just had to dump me only to hook up with one of my best friends and embarrass me and my family. Just like Joshua's whore mother did."

"What! Come out and say that to my face!" yelled Joshua, as he attempted to see through the darkness and move forward towards Mike's voice. But Jacob and Lauren held him back.

"Poor little, Joshua. Don't tell me you didn't know about that dirty little secret about your mother and my father."

"What are you talking about?" shouted Joshua.

"Oh wait, didn't your girlfriend over there tell you?" said Mike, with a heinous chuckle. "I'm sure she hasn't told you many things."

"What is he talking about?" exclaimed Joshua to Lauren.

Lauren looked back at Joshua in fear and guilt. She stuttered to explain. "I…I…Joshua…I wasn't sure if it was true or not. I didn't know. I'm sorry…Joshua," said Lauren as tears dripped from her eyes.

Joshua looked at her in unbelief and broken, knowing something extremely and undoubtedly important was hidden from him. "Didn't tell me what, Lauren?" asked Joshua, forcefully.

Mike's tone then became more dubious, "I guess none of it matters anymore. I just got word that my father and Bennett were killed in an explosion. At first, I thought it was you two in response to everything I've done. But that didn't make sense. Now, I see all of you here. So, I guess that means it could have been only one other person. There's only one person that hated them both as much as I hated you, Joshua. Both of us agreed to serve the dark angel, our master."

Jacob, whispered to himself in unbelief, "Wow. Is he lying? Is Bishop Hines and Archbishop Bennett really dead?"

Lauren continued to cry while Ezra stood stoic ready for Mike's charge, while Jacob found Ezra's composure unnatural. Joshua could not get past this secret about his mother that even Lauren may have known. His anger took control.

"What didn't she tell me, you coward!" yelled Joshua toward him.

Lauren then envisioned Mike pulling out a gun from the back of his waistband and shooting at them. So, she yelled, "He has a gun!"

Mike then jumped out from the corridor with a gun pointed at Joshua, and said calmly, "That my father and your whore mother had a son…and that son was you." He then fired at them with multiple shots.

From the darkness and quick movement of Ezra pushing Joshua out the way, his gunshots missed. Lauren and Jacob escaped running back down the original corridor. But when Joshua ran to follow, Ezra quickly pushed him to the side forcing him down the other corridor next to it. Joshua wanted to go back toward Lauren, but Mike kept firing, and the striking bullets missed them, hitting against the walls. With Ezra at his back and pushing him to keep running forward to escape, she prevented him from going back to Lauren. They kept running down the corridor until they got to an elevator. Ezra pushed a green button on the wall that caused the elevator doors to immediately open. She pushed Joshua inside and then entered a seven digit security code into the elevator's display panel just above the floor buttons. When she did, the doors quickly shut and the elevator went downward.

As the elevator went down, Joshua, heavily breathing, exclaimed, "Why did you do that? We need to go back!" as he remembered his promise to himself to always protect Lauren.

"No. We need to get somewhere safe. Lauren and Jacob can take care of themselves," countered Ezra, calm.

"Where are we going?" asked Joshua, concerned about Ezra's actions and calm behavior. He thought, *She didn't even flinch when she heard that her father and Bishop Hines were dead.*

After a few moments, the door opened to a large archaic stone basement with various crucifixions, and statues of Jesus, Mary, and the twelve disciples all built into concave sections of the walls. In addition, there were writings, religious symbols, and various antiquities on the wall and in the room, arranged in a very specific and noticeable pattern. Even the lights that brightened the basement felt more like spheres of lights or angels, than just light bulbs. Joshua repeatedly pushed the elevator's security code buttons to get back up to the top, but the elevator did not move.

"The doors will remain open, but you can't get back up without the security code, mighty Joshua. And that code changes every day," said Ezra in a wicked manner.

When Joshua slowly walked off the elevator, he finally realized Ezra may not have been what she appeared. He then looked around, looked back at her, and then saw a massive set of doors with an iron gate and an intricate centered lock in front of it, needing another code. It looked like it was the entrance to a high-level sophisticated prison.

"You see it, don't you, Joshua? This is as far as I ever get. Here in St. Peter's Basilica…and in Saint Mark's Basilica…even the same when I went to the Sheshan Basilica in Shanghai, China. Can you believe that Joshua? Even in China, they have the same amount of protection and spiritual warding—like here in Rome. But guess what, Joshua? Today, no guards! Because of The Circle's Prophecy and Protocol-11, finally no guards! Oh, what a glorious day!" Joshua looked confused. "Maybe you don't see it, Joshua? I'm certain if Lauren was here, she could easily see it with her newfound spiritual gift that you helped her unlock." Joshua continued to look at Ezra as he attempted to figure out what was happening. Ezra progressed the one-way conversation. She said, "The pictures, the patterns, the designs, and from this area to the next, just behind those doors, Joshua; and to the ones behind that, down to the pit," said Ezra expecting Joshua to get the references, but he did not. "Hello, Joshua! It's a replica of the *Stations of the Cross*…you see it in some of these very pictures along the wall." Joshua still looked confused. "Really, Joshua. Don't they teach you any of this stuff in Sunday

School? The *Stations of the Cross*…it's the travel of Jesus and his experienced events on the day of his crucifixion…and the *Seal of Solomon*, supposed to be extremely effective in making demons powerless?" said Ezra, expecting Joshua to finally get the references. But he remained silent, as he realized things were worse than he ever imagined.

"For some reason, many people, especially in your country, say Christianity is a Western religion or even the white man's religion. But let me ask you a question, what races and nations were stoning, hanging, and murdering anyone who claimed to be a Christian after the death of Jesus, and why? Wasn't Paul a European Roman, along with many others, who hated Christians and wanted every one of them in prison, beaten to death, or hung? Other than Paul being visited by an angel asking him why he was tormenting God's people, did you ever wonder why that all changed Joshua? All the nations and cultures that hated Christians and wanted them dead weren't all visited by angels like him, you know. So, you ever wonder how and why, especially here in Rome, when they were fighting Christianity, trying to erase the existence of Jesus, and all his miracles, while the rest of the world was embracing him as their new Savior, why did suddenly, after hundreds of years, they had a change of heart? Why did some leaders and some people of Rome and other nations begin this extraordinary push to become the center of a religion that they disbelieved and hated?" At this moment, Joshua listened more carefully and remained quiet, curious but still fearful. She continued to talk as she slowly walked around him. "That very reason is just behind these set of doors and just a few feet below the ground. It is the very reason for the Vatican City walls, and absolute restricted access in certain parts of this religious city and this church, harder to get in and out than your very own White House or a maximum security prison for lawbreakers. Why, Joshua? Why the secrecy and abounding military-style protection? You think all of this is just for the Pope? He can be replaced at any given time with another religious crony. Do you think the thousands of hours of paintings, designs, and intricate patterns and materials, and uncountable renovations that would equate to hundreds of billions of dollars in today's world, all because it just looked pretty?" Ezra then walked over to Joshua and gently leaned against him as she faced the elevators while he faced the opposite direction towards the set of gated locked doors, and said, "Look at it, Joshua. All these centuries, have they been protecting someone from getting in, or something from getting out?"

Joshua then, interjected, "Who are you?"

She sighed. Then said, "Finally, you asked. Unfortunately for me, by the laws of your God, I am obligated and forced to reveal my name and true nature, whenever asked. The only other person that ever asked me who I am was your mother! Joshua Williams, I am Agares! Agares is who I am! I am known by many as The Dark Angel or the great and powerful demonic force that controls earthquakes, among many other things," it said, pridefully. "But please, still call me Ezra. I've grown to become quite fond of it."

Joshua knew it was a demonic name and one that sounded familiar. "I thought that you weren't possessed, and my mother helped you as a child. How is this possible?" said Joshua.

"That's somewhat true, maybe even kind of a lie, from me, of course," she said, as she chuckled. "Your mother did help save Ezra's father and my life, as Ezra, I guess. But believe you me, there was more to the story, including how you just found out that your mother hooked up with the not great and unrespectable Bishop Hines! It must suck finding out about your father that way, huh? Don't worry, she lied to me too once. And now that he's dead, good luck with making up for lost time."

"You didn't answer the question," said Joshua forcefully.

"Okay, Joshua. I see that courageous nature of yours coming through.

Let's just say that when your mother died, her hold on me ceased to exist, and I became free again! That woman was strong! But not strong enough to fully exercise me! She only had the power to…we will save that story for another time. What's more important is why we are here right now. I went through a lot of trouble, lies, deception, and valuable lives to you just to get us in here, Joshua!"

Joshua thought for a second, then said, "I remember now. I know you, don't I? It was your presence I felt back in Philadelphia, in the Underground Tunnel, when my one vision became very dark, during the fires; when I felt and heard nothing, no light, no sound, only darkness. It was you there."

"Finally, using your gifts. Yes, Joshua. You were strapped to the table and put into the *Sound of Silence* by one of my loyal servants. And please don't mention those tunnels again. That Harriet Tubman was surely a worker against our cause and a pain in my…never mind. Let's stay on track. Time is running out," said Ezra as she looked back at the gated doors."

Joshua had another realization, and said, "It was you in my uncle's church, hiding behind the pulpit, watching during the last fire."

"Oh, what a glorious day that was! Seeing those fires, and you and Lauren fight my servant! I longed to get back into action like this! And when I felt your power, Joshua; your true potential of great and mighty courageous supernatural power, saving Lauren and living up to your name, I knew then, that you were the one that was going to help me!"

"Help you do what?" he asked, in disbelief that the demon thought that he would ever help it.

"Help me…free what's back there," Ezra said, as she pointed to the gated door and smiled.

22

The Balanced Equation

Present Evening – Rome, Italy – The night before Hands Across the World.

From the demon's notion that Joshua was going to help free whatever was behind the gated door, the curiosity of it all captured him, even more than the status of Lauren's safety, or the fact that he was calmly speaking to a demon. "So, why *did* the Romans and other people change their tune about Christianity who were originally against it?" asked Joshua as he realized the answer would eventually lead to the reason for the gated doors and what was behind them.

"Oh, goodie, story time!" exclaimed the demon in Ezra. She continued, "Saint Peter was crucified by the order of Pope Nero. Of course, he was crucified upside down. Because who's worthied to die just like Jesus, right?" Joshua listened patiently as she continued the story. "Joshua, ten million people visit this basilica, this church, every year; and everyone has been told that the remains of Saint Peter, lies underneath this church." She paused, then said, "Maybe it's true, maybe not. But there are two undeniable truths here, Joshua."

"And what are those?" asked Joshua, with a chuckle.

"The first is that during the Roman Empire, Vatican City used to be a *necropolis*, a city of the dead. Just one large cemetery that contained the tombs of many Romans and their families. Of all the land in Italy or in Rome, why would Vatican City be built over a cemetery of that great scale. You remember the movie Poltergeist, don't you Joshua? Nothing good can come of that, right?"

"What's the second?" he asked.

"*The second is one of the greatest demonic forces your world has ever seen is hidden, deep underground, locked away underneath this basilica, right through those set of gated doors; buried in a warded tomb, and being contained by this church cemetery and spiritual prison.*"

Joshua replied, "So you're telling me this church in Vatican City is hiding a demon, and it's right behind that door. Do you really expect me to believe that?"

"You should, Joshua."

"Why is that?"

"The balance of Evil and Light of Life called for it."

"Bishop Hines already gave me this biblical lesson."

"I don't think so. Let me explain. The heavens and the earth, good and evil, must always have a balance, until the end of time, or end of this world as you humans believe. It's how your God designed this disgusting universal realm. I believe your well-known philosopher, mathematician, astronomer, and theologian put it simply, '*For every action, there is an equal and opposite reaction.*' It's God's law, one of many that no one can get around, not even us demons. Angels, demons, nature, physics, and anything that God created are bound by this law, so that God can fairly and justly judge all souls on earth on Judgement Day."

"Some say heaven and hell are here on earth, or they're just in the mind," said Joshua.

Then its voice became much deeper, and said with a loud tone, "*No! Heaven and Hell are eternal! Your soul is eternal! But your body is tem-*

poral! How could your weak and pathetic temporal human body and mind reside in one of God's eternals? A deal was made between God and Satan for the souls of the world. But Satan made sure that he had a fair fight and equal chance to win over mankind, and your God agreed! Satan argued that it would be unfair for God to send people to either Heaven or Hell without good and evil being perfectly balanced in their lives and on earth. So, God made it so that Evil and The Light of Life would be perfectly balanced with all things until the end of the world! But before then, I shall reign with death and destruction!" After that, its voice went back to normal, and Ezra's pleasant voice returned, and as she looked at the gated doors said, "Sorry, that wasn't me. Guess somebody beyond those gated doors is listening and wanted to chime in!" suggesting that the demonic force being trapped had just spoke through Ezra.

Joshua responded, hesitantly, "I don't understand."

"Still thinking with your temporal body and mind, instead of your eternal soul, huh, Joshua? I bet Lauren would have gotten it by now? Guess that's why you two make such a great pair...the present-day Adam and Eve. Forgive me if I throw up just thinking about you two."

"Can you please get to the point!" he exclaimed, impatient and no longer fearful.

"C'mon Joshua. I thought you were smarter than this. God and Satan give you humans both crystal clear and subliminal messages of this rule all the time, since the beginning of time. Even from some of your famous authors, in your books, like A Tale of Two Cities, 'It was the best of times, it was the worst of times.' Do you get it now?"

"Maybe," said Joshua as he started to comprehend.

It continued the Balance of Evil and Light of Life explanation, and said, "For every positive, there is a negative. For every superhero, there is an evil villain. Every mathematical equation, God's universal law, must be balanced. The world does not and cannot exist without this law of balance. And for every powerful spiritual human there must be a powerful spiritual demon, and technically vice versa. It will be like that until *Judgement Day*. It started way before today, going back to when God created man in His image and good and so wonderfully in His sight. From God's law of balance, evil had to rise up and use the serpent to balance man back to the level of ordinary, maybe even slightly wicked. But, when man's wickedness and sin became too great, which was a balance too far on the evil side, then God had to send Jesus, his Word, to balance the weight of goodness back on the side of the heavens. The same thing happened with Noah and the flood. It was God balancing the equation, making sure the tally was fair on both sides just as he promised to Satan. The Egyptians were very knowledgeable and close to this with their theory of the underworld, but they missed the interpretation completely. Your despicable sins of violence, rape, genocide, murder, lying, cheating, stealing, against your own kind…how could or should a God love that? At least we demons know who we are and why. How about you and your kind, Joshua?"

"And what happened with the balance of that?"

"With the birth, death, and resurrection of Jesus, all of man's sins, past, present, and future could be easily wiped away with just the belief and salvation of him. Just like that, Joshua, mankind was undeservingly redeemed! But, what God didn't anticipate, or maybe he did, is that the redemptive work on the cross was so great, that when Jesus died and rose from the grave and left this earth, another balance on the weight of evil had to occur. That balance was both the descending of the Holy Spirit for God and the side of the Light of Life, and on the side of Evil, the birth of a new demonic Legion. The Great Legion, Joshua! Oh, what a glorious day!"

"Legion. You mean from the Bible, made of many demons?"

"Yes, but it is not the same Legion. For the proper balance to occur from the work of Jesus and God's Spirit now with mankind, the new Legion had to be greater than ever before, in fact, thirteen times greater. Thirteen demons times thirteen demons, one hundred and sixty-nine in all, possessing one hibernating *Nephilim*, and made in the image of the *Behemoth*. This made it greater than any demon ever known, only second to our Supreme, Satan himself, who right before being enslaved in this dungeon breathed even more power into him. With Satan's breath of death inside of him, we as demons now know him as Satan's son. *Lilith, Abaddon, Mephistopheles*, and even *Bakemono* and many other gods tremble at Satan's son's feet. And he, The Great Legion, my master is lying beyond those doors, in a cell, within a tomb, buried waiting for you and me to release him from this prison. Once you do, he will be stronger than ever before, and he will be known under a different name, *The Wretchedness!* The Wretchedness shall be set free! Oh, what a glorious day!"

"Why would God allow such a thing, a balance? God would never allow that," said Joshua, confident.

"He wouldn't, Joshua? You have examples of this happening directly in your Bible! Didn't God make a similar deal with Satan for Job's soul? Didn't God replace everything Job lost and more to balance what he allowed Satan to do? Also, before that deal was made why was Satan walking and talking with God's heavenly deities in the first place…a balance maybe? Then, what about the story of Adam and Eve? Couldn't God have easily prevented the *Serpent* from entering the Garden of Eden with Eve? Why else would He allow the Serpent to change the perfection of the earth and man through only one act of sin or disobedience? You humans ask all the time, 'Why would a loving God allow so many problems…' and blah…blah…blah! You're so weak and obviously have no idea what is completely at stake for all of eternity! Let me ask you a question. Your God can do anything but what, Joshua?"

"Fail," Joshua replied.

"Wrong! The Bible says, love never fails but isn't every soul that goes to Hell a failure for God? It says clearly in Titus, chapter one verse two of your Bible, that God cannot lie! God was required by his own promise to punish Adam and Eve and bless Job! If He didn't, His deal with Satan would have been a lie! He must keep this balance until the end of the world, Joshua! The only thing God cannot do is lie!"

At this moment, Joshua began to believe in the demons' words and the balance of Evil and Light of Life. He thought, maybe this was the real and true Golden Rule. From getting the demon's question wrong, Joshua silently prayed to God for wisdom, and God immediately gave it to him. Joshua then demonstrated and said, "So, everything on this earth is balanced between good and evil, positive and negative. Like when my mother used to play cards. I remember one time she got so mad from losing that she threw the playing cards in the air from her frustration. If there was no balance of forces, how can there be a gravitational force of disorder to make all her cards fall and scatter everywhere in complete disorder, but there is also a gravitational force of order that keeps our perfectly round planets of massive size to rotate and revolve around the sun in perfect order with each other, so they do not collide? So how can gravity be a force of order and a force of disorder."

"Yes, Joshua, and how can you explain that gravity has both positive and negative forces after a *Big Bang* explosion, be a force of order and also be a force of disorder?"

Joshua continued, as he came up with other examples, "When I was younger, my mother used to be a construction manager. She bought me this bright yellow Tonka truck; and explained to me that the higher you build a building, the deeper you must dig its footings and foundations for the correct balance or the building would fall. God, I loved that Tonka truck!" exclaimed Joshua, as he smiled, nostalgic.

"Have you ever been to the Arctic regions, Joshua? How do you think igloos can have fire in them to keep someone warm yet not melt?" asked the demon in Ezra.

Joshua raised his eyebrows and did a quick shrug of his shoulders acknowledging that he did not know. But then God's wisdom filled him, and he said, "The fire melts a layer of ice of the igloo, but as soon as it does, the negative temperature refreezes it back, creating the perfect balance to maintain the structure and keep whoever is inside warm."

"Astonishing, Joshua! You're finally cultivating your gifts! Being around me is causing that balance for you to grow, see! Even with human love, love isn't given indefinitely unless it is either given back or makes you feel good about yourself. Your God even used love as an excuse to use an evil spirit to cause chaos!"

"I wouldn't have believed that if I didn't read that in the Bible myself."

"Unbelievers use that scripture to say it's a contradiction to God's nature and goodness. But we demons hate that it's in there. It's like a slap in the face to us! We hate to admit it, but your God can do anything He wants at any time, including balancing the universal realm with Evil or the Light of Life. For some reason, when He does, you hate Him and think He's evil or unkind. But, to us demons and angels, we see it differently. Since He can do whatever He wants at any time, and still gives only you disgusting, sinful, forever ungrateful humans, grace and forgiveness, only proves to us that He does love mankind unconditionally, and it's sickening! You're not worth it! Not with the first birth of mankind and definitely not with the last!"

"So, Vatican City, this church, Saint Peter's Basilica is a prison, for this powerful demon, Satan's son?"

"Yes, finally! You get it! But I don't think he's the only one, Joshua. I'm not omniscient or anything, but I think two other basilicas, or more, may contain other prisoned demonic forces too! Imagine the unbalanced scale after just the thought of Jesus Christ being man's savior and king. Jesus claimed that everyone is equal and had access to heaven, regardless of the level of sin, class, money, or political power, and all they had to do was believe in him. That message and thinking could undoubtedly destroy a nation's power and rule over people. To stop this new thinking, and a potential revolt from people that were enslaved or subjugated, *miso-Christians* or anti-Christians as you call them, killed every remaining disciple and anyone that proclaimed Jesus Christ as Lord in hopes of stopping the spread of Christianity. Obviously, that didn't work. So, The Great Legion was made in Satan's image, evil to the core. Don't believe me? Google how many Christians were hung and murdered preaching Jesus Christ and his message. The Great Legion rose with many other demons, including myself. And we caused destruction upon earth like never before, the great fire in Rome; and I, Agares, the demon of earthquakes, caused so many earthquakes that they swallowed up villages into holes and cities into oceans! We possessed millions, made children sick, and created plagues among men with just our touch, made nations fight against each other, tortured, killed, destroyed lands, set fires, and revealed our true selves to every nation around the world. They feared us more than they feared God!" She then started laughing, and said, "The Great Legion was too powerful to stop. But the very ones that were able to cast us out, who walked with Jesus, or had enough faith and had received the power of the Holy Spirit, they killed! Joshua! They stoned, spat on, imprisoned, and then killed the very people that God gave power to save them! You can't make this stuff up, Joshua!" The demon in Ezra laughed hysterically. It then said, "After they killed their potential saviors, no one had enough faith or power to perform an exorcist on The Great Legion! Still to this fucking day, Joshua! No one does! That's why they had to lock him up! Oh, what a glorious day!"

"So, how did they stop it all?" asked Joshua.

"The Great Legion still had limitations being in human form and being bound by God's laws. He couldn't be killed, not with the balance of Evil and Light of Life still in place. But he could be trapped. After over five hundred years of getting it wrong, they finally came up with this church, this prison." Joshua looked around. "That's right, Joshua. Why do you think there are so many various religious items in Vatican City, built into the very essence of this church, and the museum? Antiquities and relics, from all over the world. Even what is considered pagan and other non-Christian artifacts, like the Obelisk in the Plaza, Anubis and the guards of the underworld, statues and paintings of those ugly Jinn who have been rumored to use their powers to help build this church prison. Along with other Chinese, African, and Spanish religious warding symbols. Why Joshua? Even the circle design of the plaza and colonnades in front of this great basilica or prison resembles the shape of the special and powerful *antique keyhole* that your era doesn't use anymore. Do you know what that keyhole symbol represents or why it was found in the designs of so many cultures thousands of kilometers away from each other that never even met?" The demon waited for a response from Joshua. Then said, "Of course you don't. Doesn't your Bible say, your people will perish for a lack of knowledge? Maybe that's why Bishop Hines always said, you all die daily, huh? Guess he doesn't die daily anymore! Oh, what a glorious day!"

"Do all demons love to hear themselves speak?" asked Joshua, who was now just listening to the demon.

"They even used Michelangelo to take over one of its redevelopments to improve the spiritual prison's design and to paint as many heavenly entities as possible here, in the Sistine Chapel, and many other places with such detailed and intricate symbols and angels. Why Joshua? Do you think it was all done just because it looked good? Some of us demons believe that he was put under a spell by a Jinn to create such immense warding. How else could he humanly do all of that?"

Having a bit of revelation, Joshua said, "So, many other societies of different religions gifted things to Rome with anything that they believed could contain an evil so great."

"There you go, Joshua. And The Church happily accepted it, even if its nature went against what they originally believed. Constantine tried the first stab at the prison with his basilica, but it didn't quite work that well. The Great Legion escaped. But over hundreds of years, they finally got it right. Once they captured him, they buried him in lime mortar, the concrete of that time, and immediately sealed it with spiritual warding. But they knew that would only hold The Great Legion for so long. So, that's when they brought him down here within these deep prison cell chambers. But again, the warding, the symbols, and a few priests praying would not be enough, especially now at this point as Satan had breathed directly into him. So, do you want to take a guess of what they needed to keep him contained for over a thousand years, Joshua?"

Joshua now full of wisdom, confident and internally praying, replied "I know. Humankind's greatest weapon against Satan and demons like you, and mankind's best connection to God. Prayer."

"Exactly, Joshua! Who said you needed that girl Lauren? Mike probably killed her by now, anyway. Just joking, Joshua. We all know Mike, one of my loyal servants, doesn't stand a chance against her."

"Can we get to the part where you think I'm going to help you free this other demon?"

"Oh right. Creating the largest church with the remains of Saint Peter, or even just saying they are here, created millions and millions of visitors each year, ten million a year now to be exact, praying to God with faith, all keeping The Wretchedness down to its minimum power and unable to escape."

"So, it's the prayer of the Christians and saints along with all these other items and designs holding him within the prison."

"Yes, Joshua. Millions of daily prayers right over top of him were the last ingredient needed to keep him locked in this prison. Typically, you would have all those millions of people praying above; in addition to twelve high-level priests in this very basement praying all twenty-four hours a day, every seven days without ceasing to help prevent his escape. Now, do you see why Vatican City needed so much military protection? As Jacob said, they would have been locked and loaded with guns at the private entrance, and in the corridor where we saw Mike, at the elevator, and down here when the elevators opened. But not now, Joshua. Where are all the guards? Why are none of them here? Where are all the millions of praying people? Why are none of them above us? Would you like to take a guess?" said Ezra, as she smiled knowing Joshua knew the answer.

"Protocol-11," said Joshua, as he realized Ezra's demon was behind the whole thing, maybe even somehow behind the collective vision of The Circle's prediction of the end of the world.

"Ding! Ding! Absolutely correct, the great and mighty Joshua! There's hope for you yet! Because of The Circle's prophecy and Protocol-11, there are no guards! There aren't thousands of people today over top of us above praying to God in this church! The greatest chance for The Wretchedness to gain his strength and be set free is now! No guards and no prayers! I made it happen! I made it possible! Me, Agares! Oh, what a glorious day!"

"So, you were behind all of this? How?"

"Joshua. Mankind has been weak for centuries. Weak and evil on their own, we had no need to possess people or terrorize them like we used to; again, that balance of life thing. Humans are doing bad all by themselves with technology, being self-centered thinking that life is all about living your best selfish life, instead of banding together strong as families and as one nation under God. I guess because of your own evil hearts and minds, all demons were technically laid off, as you call it. That was until Bishop Hines and Archbishop Bennett made a breakthrough with the balance of Evil and Light of Life. Even though they didn't know it, they opened the door for me to enter your realm with those sensory water tank pods. Since deception was in their methods and hearts, the evil side of the door opened and I was there. From more of their deceptive methods, this allowed me to influence their minds thinking they were on the right track and doing the right things. Their deceptive methods gave me power over their vision and emotions. Then my presence here back on earth forced God to create another balance, which was your mother, Denise. He gifted her with the most amazing healing and discernment ability that equaled my power. We had a little argument and without going into detail, she couldn't exorcise me out of Ezra, but she was powerful enough to lock me in a corner of her without my power. Then when she died, that released her hold on me. Then, I was able to use the anger and hatred that was rooted in Mike and Marco against Bishop Hines, and they willingly decided to be my servants. But apparently that opened the door for the balance of you, Joshua! The equation balancing itself just as God designed and promised Satan! But I am only an instrument, the greater your power becomes Joshua, the greater The Wretchedness' power becomes as well, and vice versa! You see Joshua, you are the only one spiritually strong enough to break the remaining holds within this prison to free him. But you are also the only one strong enough to stop him. It's your destiny!"

"That is not my destiny."

"Yes it is!" she responded with a loud and low vibrating tone that shook the stone walls. "Sorry, about that. The Light of Life has already been fully activated within you, Joshua. You are more powerful now than your mother or any other Christian that has existed besides the great man, Jesus Christ himself. But the design of this basilica, the warding and tomb is too strong for me and The Wretchedness is still too weak, being locked up for hundreds of years and all, and without the fear and death of people to feed on. And I need him free now! So do what you do, and take a deep breath, exhale, and breakthrough that door now, Joshua!"

"I have the Light of Life activated in me right now?" said Joshua, but as a question.

"Yes, all thanks to me, your mother died in your arms, you lost your job, and no one trusts you. I'm the one who recruited a servant in your neighborhood to set the string of church fires along your precious street. I'm the one who convinced Mike to set that bomb off in your uncle's home just right before I picked you up in the van with Jacob. I'm the one who placed the vision of the end of the world into The Circles' minds, knowing it would result in Protocol-11, allowing this rare opportunity that you and I have right now in this place. Actually, at the time, I thought it would be Denise here, but you're even better."

"Why didn't you use any other deception methods? Why did it have to be Protocol-11?"

"Hello, haven't you been listening? Even though I'm a great demon, I still can't go against your God's laws. I don't have the power to fake an alien invasion, not yet anyway. And I can't fake a meteor strike, can I? But I do have the power to give people that have great sin without repentance visions and feelings that they believe are true but are lies. I can direct them to make decisions that are best for me but worse for them. Fortunately for me, all The Circle members had great sins and were unrepentant. Satan was cast into darkness, and if you operate in deception or darkness, then you give Satan and demons like me control over that part of your life, but it will feel as though it is God or truth directing you. I was able to give all The Circle members the same exact collective vision of the end of the world, knowing it would cause all the governments to agree to enact Protocol-11. Who knew that The Circle's perfect prophecy batting average would work in my favor?"

"It hasn't worked in your favor. God still has the last say," said Joshua.

"What worked out is that, if you are a priest or a guard that had been working down here for all your life, and you knew that hundreds of years went by and nothing has happened, are you going to stay here and protect this place, or go be with your family and spend your last moments with them, or even go try to bang that waitress at the diner you go see every week? No one is here, Joshua. It worked!"

Joshua continued to listen, now plotting.

But the demon in Ezra got back on track and taunted Joshua. It said, "Then, you hooking up with Lauren, Mike's ex-fiancé, lordy lordy, I couldn't have planned that if I tried. That had to be God in your favor, but it worked in mine as well, right? Oh, Mike was so easy to influence. I just kept putting in his head that you were the cause of all his problems, and boom. He immediately wanted to kill you and Lauren. Then for you to find out tonight that Bishop Hines was your father, oh that was so glorious. That's right Joshua. Bishop Hines brought Denise here to Rome and took her to many other countries, enjoying each other's company, while his wife Sarah was alone and little Mike was raised mainly by Marco. They both even named you after a waiter that they met in the square just over the entrance wall. He died too, you know, unrest his soul. But, I had nothing to do with that, honestly. That was your kind's doing. The only father figure Mike really knew was Marco, who just so happened to fall in love with Denise as well. But what the vainglorious Bishop Hines wanted, the vainglorious Bishop Hines always got. Marco was easy to influence too. Oh yeah, he's the one that killed your father and Bennett. I guess he killed my father too, right? Joshua, we both lost our dad tonight! Oh, what a glorious day!" She then laughed hysterically at the thought.

Joshua's rage grew, and he showed it. "So, you killed everyone! Everyone I loved!"

"Not everyone. I haven't killed Lauren…well, not yet. I will get to that soon. It's a shame because I believe Bishop Hines loved her, probably more than his own son Mike."

"You will not lay a hand on her!"

"Why? Do you still think her soul loves your soul, too, Joshua? Give me a break. Can't you see by now she never loved you? She was just using you! You and everyone else in her life. She said that my soul loves your soul crap to so many other guys besides you. You meant nothing to her, you will see."

"No way! I made that up for her."

"Okay, Joshua. If you say so. She has more pride than any demon I know and your Bible says, the prideful does not have God in their thoughts. If she did, why are you in this situation right now? Why didn't she share with you what she knew was important to you?" Joshua, listened. "How come she didn't tell you about her past? Why do you think she didn't tell you about Bishop Hines possibly being your father. She *was* engaged to Mike. You think he didn't tell her about it? Why wouldn't she share that information with you, your soulmates, right? What else has she been hiding from you, Joshua?"

"Stop," said Joshua, forcefully.

"You think you were the only one that she hooked up with after Mike? How many guys do you think she slept with and almost died with to attempt to reach the Light of Life before she met up with you, even after she met you, even after she kissed you, even after you two spent that night in the church together along the Boulevard in Philadelphia? Did you know she left you and went to go see Mike right after that intimate moment with you?"

"You're lying," said Joshua, even more angered.

"I saw it all, Joshua. I was around her the whole time. The way she looks at you. The way she kisses you. Everything she tells you. She has done the same to all the many others that came before you and while she's been with you."

"You're lying!"

"Why would I lie, Joshua?"

"Because you're a demon!"

"Okay, besides that. I have nothing to gain by telling you the truth or a lie. My plan worked and you are here. It's going to haunt you all day and night now, isn't it? Thinking about her kissing someone else like she kissed you, opening her legs up for them like she did for you, screaming out in pleasure and in passion for someone else like she did for you. Whispering in your ear…just like I whispered in her ear at your mother's funeral while she watched you play on your uncle's piano. Do you want to know the lie I whispered to her, Joshua. I said, Lauren you will…"

"Stop it!" yelled Joshua interrupting the demon with a loud vibrating tone that it shook the walls and ground with great force.

"There it is, Joshua. Proof that the Light of Life is fully activated now within you. The key to God's power. Centuries of searching by many and you are the only one to finally obtain it." Joshua looked away in regret. "Don't feel bad, Joshua. None of them ever loved you. None of them truly cared about you. Not even your mother. Not your uncle, not your aunt, not the clueless Officer Reese or ATF back in Philadelphia, and definitely not the deceptive Bishop Hines. They just wanted you to grow up to be good, just so they could say they had a part in raising you upright. But they never cared about you. They kept you in the dark about everything, and when you finally voiced your pain and hurt, did they apologize and come out with the truth? No, they just made excuses, said they didn't know, blamed you, or hid it all from you, even your precious girlfriend, Lauren."

Joshua fought hard to hold back his anger and cry, and said in a deep slow voice, "It's not like that. You're a demon and a liar."

"No. I'm the only one being truthful, Joshua. For the first time in your life, I'm the only one telling you the truth and the whole truth and not omitting anything at all. But, just like everybody else, I'm using you right now to get what I want, and I'm a demon. So, what does that say about all of them?"

With using every mental and physical strength to not break down from the demon's words and the hurtful and negative thoughts of Lauren that now consume him and burn deep within his heart and mind, he said in the same deep slow voice, "I'm still not going to help you."

"It's inevitable Joshua. Protocol-11 has left this church, this prison vacant, and people aren't flooding through the doors above us with their prayers like before. You're strong enough to break through this gated door and spiritual warding that restricts me from being able to do it. It's your destiny."

Joshua then looked down at the table next to him and saw a dagger with a silver snake on the handle. It was a *Phurba Dagger*. A Tibetan gift, known for dispelling negative energy and demons, given to the Vatican to help defend against the rising of The Wretchedness. He then softly said, "All that talk, and you're only right about one thing."

"What, Joshua? Do you think your mother's Hands Across the World is going to stop the wars, stop Protocol-11, or stop the rising of our Great Legion, The Wretchedness? Well, it won't! Darkness and light will collide and clash leaving nothing but an aftermath of darkness, chaos, and ash. Hands Across the World will do nothing to stop it!"

"You talk too much. But you're right about one thing. The Light of Life is within me. I can feel it now. I believe your long, drawn-out speech woke it up and it is now *health and strength to my bones and soul.* And if I'm that strong, strong as you say I am, then I also have the power to…"

"…to do what, Joshua?"

"To kill you!" yelled Joshua with his loud vibrating tone. He then quickly grabbed the dagger off the table and stabbed Ezra in the stomach. She hunched over onto his body with a great cry. Then, he twisted the dagger deep into her to make sure that the wound did not heal. After that, he ran into the elevator, slammed his hand on the security panel, and with a green light emitting from his hand on the panel, the elevator magically turned on without the code, closed its doors, and went up to the main level. Agares fell to the ground laughing and Joshua could hear the demon's last words, "It's inevitable Joshua! You will free him. You will free my master, The Wretchedness!" She continued to laugh while holding her wound, lying in her blood. Then it looked back at the gated door, and exclaimed in joy, "Oh, what a glorious day!"

23

Soul Broken

Present Evening – Rome, Italy – The night before Hands Across the World.

When the elevator reached the main level, the doors opened, and Joshua ran down the corridor out to the entrance, the same way the group originally came into the basilica. On his way out, he saw Mike lying on the ground, dead. It looked like he was shot in the face with a gun. He wondered, *Was that from a continued altercation with Lauren and Jacob while I was underground with Ezra?* He then saw them waiting for him outside in the Plaza. They ran up to him.

"Joshua! Are you okay?" exclaimed, Lauren.

"Bro, you should have seen your girlfriend. She stopped Mike…"

Joshua immediately interrupted Jacob, as he looked at Lauren and remembered everything that the demon said to him. He yelled, "Did you know!"

She stuttered not certain how to respond as she knew what he meant and regretted not telling him earlier.

He repeated it and yelled even louder, "I said, did you know! Did you know Bishop Hines was my father?"

"Yes," she said softly and ashamed.

"Stay away from me!" exclaimed Joshua.

"Joshua," Lauren called out, as she reached out to him, apologetically.

"Stay the hell away from me!" he yelled with a vibrating tone that shook the ground of the Plaza and the surrounding colonnades. He then turned away and ran out of the plaza.

"No! Joshua!" she yelled back, as she fell to the ground crying, and watched him disappear.

Once Joshua got past the Vatican City's entrance, and to the street, his run had turned into a slow walk, mainly to catch his breath, but also to decide which way to go. He knew that he didn't want to be around lots of people, or a victim of random violence from the repercussions of Protocol-11. He noticed the hazy fluorescent lights coming from the large castle, Castel Sant'Angelo. It caught his attention, so he gravitated towards it. He walked around to its side, then to the back, away from the street and river. He noticed a skinny, black service door, partially opened. He cautiously looked around. When he confirmed that he was hidden from anyone's direct view, he squeezed through the partially opened door, carefully not to cause any noise or attention. It immediately placed him in front of a long spiral set of stone steps that took him all the way to the top of the castle, overlooking Rome. As soon as he reached the top, he was initially in awe of the view, but then he remembered the terrible events of recent and the past, especially the words and death that came with them.

He envisioned and remembered his mother dying in his very arms during a Sunday service at New Lighthouse Temple, back in Philadelphia; then losing his job right after getting promoted; being accused of the string of church fires by everyone that knew him but should have trusted him; his life turned upside down by being on the run from the local police and ATF; being captured, drugged and almost tortured by Ezra's servant; putting his freedom and safety on the line to stop the fires and then fighting for his life and Lauren's; and only a few hours later, losing his caring uncle, Pastor Williams, and his beautiful and kind aunt, Angela; then flown to Rome by his mentor, Bishop Hines, who turned out to be his father, now dead; along with Bishop Hines' son, Mike, his childhood best friend, and apparent brother, now dead as well, and most of these events within a matter of just a few hours. Despite all this, none of it broke his spirit and his soul greater than the thought of Lauren's possible lies and betrayal. He replayed in his mind, repeatedly, Lauren's reaction of guilt and sadness upon Mike's accusation that confirmed the truth of her hiding the secret of his father. He thought, *If Lauren loved me, how could she not have told me?* If he had a knife, he would have cut out his heart from the unbearable pain he felt within it. He could not control or contain his sanity any longer. At that moment, his hurt and pain broke through his soul like an old and poorly built dam attempting to hold back too much water for way too long. He travailed and cried out loud as he felt and heard his soul within him snap, breaking into pieces. Agares' will had been done in him… all from the deception, lies, and decisions of others, those he loved, and those he trusted. They all paid the ungodly price of giving into sin and allowing themselves to be deceived, and heavy that price was.

* * *

As Joshua felt his broken soul within him, he heard gunshots, and the screams and cries of many possibly going through the same. Either from the thought of an approaching world's end or an inevitable global world war, the freedom of lawless violence and the anticipation of eminent death caused murder and fear, just like Agares plotted and planned. Joshua was then overwhelmed by the feeling of giving up, ending it all. He peeked over the ledge of the castle's brick towers, that purposefully hid his shame and sadness from the world. His silent tears fell down to the empty streets. He saw the shadows as Agares' lies who was the true deceiver, the thief in the night that stole away his hopes and dreams, now out of sight. As he looked all the way to the distant ground, he felt relief in thinking that a simple jump could stop the pain and end his suffering. Then he thought, it may be better to kill those that remained who lied and deceived him or didn't disclose the truth, like Lauren. Then he thought of even killing those that weren't fully responsible but caused him pain in some way, like Monty, Jacob, or his boss, the old store manager back in Philadelphia. Joshua thought, *All my family is dead and all love is gone from me. Agares won. I no longer have purpose. I no longer have a song to play…or a song to sing. I wish I had never been born.* His sadness then turned to anger. He could no longer see light through the gray. He clinched his fist hard as his anger turned into rage. He envisioned how he would kill each, especially Lauren now viewing her intimate with Mike and others as the demon in Ezra revealed to him. He visualized his sweaty hands wrapped around Lauren's neck with a vice-grip strangling life out of her silence and body, strangling the echoes of her deception. His anger and rage then turned into a dark humorous satisfaction. He allowed the evil thoughts to consume his heart, his soul. Then, his eyes blackened as coal. He became stoic, grabbed hold of the ledge, and pulled himself up on it and stood tall. His heart was hardened and the negative thoughts allowed evil to seep into his spirit and take control of him. With his blackened eyes, he looked down towards the ground. He then looked back up and took one more look at the amazing scenery of Rome–the Vatican City, Saint Peter's Basilica, the Sistine Chapel, the Altar of The Fatherland, the Colosseum, the River Tiber. He then closed his eyes, and remembered his mother, Denise; remembered his loving uncle and aunt, Pastor Williams and Angela; remembered his love for Lauren; remembered his mentor and father, Bishop Hines; and even remembered his annoying friend, Monty. He smiled and, said "I die daily." Joshua then closed his eyes, stretched out his arms…and jumped from the ledge.

* * *

Even though she was far away, Lauren's new spiritual gift forced her head up in the air to the sky and allowed her to immediately see through Joshua's eyes. She could see that he had jumped off the building and was falling to the ground. Her heart collapsed into her soul, her twin flame about to die, no longer existing. Right at the point of his impact to the ground, she immediately shouted with thunder, "Nooooooo!" Upon feeling the initial impact on the ground, Joshua came out of this vision of suicide and death. His eyes unblackened and went back to normal. Joshua did not jump; the evil that consumed him only gave him a vision that he did. An evil vision that Lauren was able to see as well. He was still at the top of the castle, peeking over the edge. He was relieved and his body relaxed. But that didn't stop his heart from pounding hard in his chest as if he did jump. He then looked up to the sky and heavens and said, "Lord, forgive me. I refuse to give up. I refuse to let evil win. Unlike others, I will not be deceived. I am your child. I am strong. I am mighty. I am courageous." He then paused, took a deep breath, exhaled, and shouted at the top of his lungs as loud as he could, "I AM JOSHUA!"

His *great shout* vibrated mighty sound waves that proceeded out of his mouth at such a strong force that they clipped the top part of the castle's brick ledge and caused it to crumble and fall to the ground. Without ceasing, these vibrating sound waves continued and traveled forward from the castle to the street and caused it to crack open and collapse and crush the empty parked cars on it like a junkyard car-crusher. His vibrating great shout then continued to the empty retail store buildings across the street and caused them to collapse to the ground, and then traveled all the way down to the Plaza, causing everyone their to cover their ears in pain and landed its ending powerful blast impact upon Saint Peter's Basilica, which caused it to collapse and crumble as well, burying the body of Ezra, and the spiritual prison holding the powerful demonic force, The Wretchedness. Then, everyone within the plaza, and along the streets uncovered their ears as they looked back in amazement seeing the magnificently built church now in ruins. Lauren and Jacob were still in the Plaza and looked toward the source of this great shout and could see the destruction going all the way back to the castle.

"I think we just found Joshua," said Jacob.

"Oh, my goodness, Joshua," said Lauren, softly.

Lauren took the lead and Jacob followed as they ran toward the castle. When they arrived, Joshua had already come down from the top of the castle's tower and was on the ground, stepping over the fallen broken bricks that fell from the castle's ledge from his great shout. With Lauren's eyes opened wide from her gift, she looked at Joshua and knew that he had fully acquired the Light of Life. Joshua looked back at her as if he was shy and embarrassed, not sure how to handle his new found supernatural power.

"So, that's The Great Shout, huh Joshua?" asked Lauren as she smiled.

"The Great Shout," said Joshua, as he smiled back.

"Bro! How did you do that? Did you two already know that he could do that?" asked Jacob.

"No. Not at all," said Lauren. Then she thought about it again, and asked, "Wait, did you Joshua?"

"I did not, honestly. How could I? It just happened," said Joshua, slightly timid, but proud of his gift.

"That explains why you were named Joshua," said Lauren.

Lauren's statement reminded him of Ezra's claims about his mother. "According to Ezra, I was named after somebody my mother and Bishop Hines knew here in Rome. But what happened to Mike?" he asked.

"Lauren's eyesight and vision is what happened," said Jacob. Joshua looked at them, bewildered.

Lauren responded, "I think I can see things before they happen, just like when he pulled out the gun on us and started shooting. I saw it in a vision, right before it happened."

Jacob continued to explain, energetically, "Then, when we ran, it was like she knew what was going to happen. She stopped, turned around, and just stood there as he pointed the gun to shoot her. He had to only be five feet away. He couldn't miss."

"Then what happened?" asked Joshua in anticipation.

"Peace and calm came over me, and I saw the gun jamming in backfiring into his face. So, I just stood still, and that's exactly what happened, and it killed him. I think when you healed my eyes, it unlocked my vision. I can see in the dark and can see things right before they happen. But maybe just like a few seconds into the future. Then, I had a vision of you jumping off a ledge. It was like I was you," said Lauren, but only somewhat convinced.

Joshua had a thought, and whispered, "*The Light of Life.*"

"What?" said Jacob, partially hearing Joshua.

Joshua answered, "Back in Philadelphia, Lauren's eyes were damaged by one of Ezra's servants during the church fires. The damage of them caused by evil and then the healing from God must have activated a portion of the Light of Life within her, causing her eyesight in the dark and future visions to now be part of her supernatural gifts. The negative was balanced by the positive," said Joshua.

"What do you mean, Ezra's servant in Philadelphia?" asked Lauren.

"It was Ezra the whole time," said Joshua.

"Ezra! No way! How?" asked Jacob, as he thought Ezra being behind these events was unfathomable.

"Ezra always claimed that my mother healed her from her physical condition. A condition that made her appear to be possessed. But she was really possessed, as a child and still this whole time," said Joshua.

"Both her father, Archbishop Bennett, and Bishop Hines said Denise healed her. So, how is that even possible?" asked Lauren.

Joshua attempted an explanation, "I'm not sure. The demon in Ezra said that when my mother died, it released a hold that my mother had on her. And when that happened, Ezra was in Philadelphia and the true reason behind the string of church fires. She also somehow used her demonic power to give The Circle members a false premonition about the Apocalypse, which she knew would start Protocol-11."

Jacob voiced his realization, "I knew something in her changed after your mother died, Joshua. Certain things didn't seem to affect her anymore, almost like she became emotionless…except for whenever she talked about the night of the attempted exorcism on her as a child."

"She called herself, Agares, the *dark angel* and demon of earthquakes," said Joshua.

"So, all the earthquakes we experienced were Ezra?" asked Lauren.

"Yes. She also said many things about you, Lauren," said Joshua, as he looked at her, hurtful.

"I'm so sorry, Joshua. I should've told you everything, including how Mike thought that Bishop Hines was your father. I love you and I will never hide anything again," said Lauren, genuinely apologetic.

"It's okay. We were all deceived by her. Nothing matters anymore, so long as we never deceive each other again," said Joshua.

"What happened to her?" asked Jacob.

"She's dead. I killed her," said Joshua.

"I wonder what type of hold your mother had on her. Now, we can't even ask Archbishop Bennett or Bishop Hines, anymore. I can't believe their dead too," said Jacob.

"Ezra, or Agares, whoever she said she was, said it was Marco that killed them. Mike and Marco were under her deception and control as well. Mike was the one that killed my uncle and aunt, and that's why he wanted to kill us, too. She used their anger and hatred to get them to do whatever she wanted," said Joshua.

"But it doesn't make sense. Why did she do all of this?" asked Lauren.

"According to her, Vatican City and Saint Peter's Basilica are really just one large prison for this other powerful demon that they have locked away in there underground!"

"The Vatican City is holding a powerful demon?" asked Lauren.

"Ezra called it, The Wretchedness, Satan's son. She said it's over a thousand years old and was formerly called The Great Legion, possessed by one hundred and sixty nine demons!"

"One hundred and sixty-nine!" exclaimed Jacob in disbelief.

"She said, it can't be killed or exorcised, only trapped, especially since Satan breathed into it. The only thing keeping it locked up is a bunch of spiritual warding and daily prayers of thousands each day," said Joshua.

"If true, that would make sense. I can't think of a place that gets more visitors and daily prayers than Saint Peter's Basilica," responded Jacob.

"Yes. But because of Protocol-11, no one is here and those prayers don't exist anymore," said Joshua.

Lauren countered, "Let's say I believe this story, which I don't. From the church's collapse from your great shout, that's got to be thousands and thousands of pounds of concrete, stone, and religious artifacts now buried over top of it. I say you sealed that prison for a very long time. No one is removing that rubble or rebuilding that church anytime soon," said Lauren.

"Your mother would be so proud, Bro," said Jacob.

Joshua smiled, but then became serious and said, "Before we break out the communion wine or non-alcoholic champagne, look around.

We are still dealing with the effects of Ezra, The Circle's prophecy, and Protocol-11. If we don't stop it, the world can still end."

Lauren chimed in, "Joshua's right. Every country is prepared for war, and they're not going to wait in silence for days, weeks, or months waiting for the Apocalypse to happen or to be bombed by another. One of them is going to have proactive itchy fingers for their own survival. They will launch missiles or a nuclear bomb, and others will follow."

"So, does this means Agares still wins?" asked Jacob.

"No, Jacob! We cannot let that happen. We must stick to the plan and the vision my mother had for Hands Across the World. It's the solution and stoppage of Protocol-11 and the wars," said Joshua, confident.

"It only takes two or three gathered in His name for God to be in the midst. We must contact all the country and region organizers of Hands Across the World to make sure they are still on board and let them know that we are now in control. They must communicate to everyone participating to shout, scream, and yell all at the same synchronized time, regardless of time zone and location," said Lauren, excited.

"Right. I still can't help wondering what type of hold my mother had on the demon possessing Ezra, and how all of that happened. Just like you said earlier, Jacob, we can't even ask Bishop Hines or Archbishop Bennett, anymore since they're both dead," said Joshua.

"Only two or three gathered in His name, right?" asked Jacob.

"Right. What is it Jacob?" asked Lauren.

"Lauren, you have the gift of sight and vision. Joshua, you have the gift of healing and the great shout. I think I may have a supernatural gift too. A gift that could help us find out what happened in the past.

"How?" asked Joshua.

"With the help of you two, unlocking it," said Jacob.

"Unlocking what?" asked Joshua and Lauren at the same time.

"My gifted memories," said Jacob.

24

Gifted Memories

Present Evening – Rome, Italy – The night before Hands Across the World.
When Joshua, Lauren, and Jacob got back to the house, they saw the
polizia di Roma, or police, taking Marco away in handcuffs. Witnesses
and video clearly showed that he killed Bishop Hines and Archbishop
Bennett with a bomb in the asclepieia. The moment Joshua killed Ezra,
the demon Agares, no longer had a hold of deception on Marco. It used
his feelings of love for Denise and Mike, his concern for Lauren and
Joshua, and his hatred of Bishop Hines' deception and sin against him.
All good things, just like Lauren argued during the Convocation, were
used to blind him and justify his anger and evil that he committed.
With Ezra dead and its influence over him removed, the truth released
him and set him free, but his guilt and shame put him in another mental prison. When Marco saw the group as he was being taken away, he
looked at them and tearfully said, "Mi dispiace...Mi dispiace," meaning he was sorry. They looked back at him in sorrow. The polizia ignored the group as they took Marco away. They already had too much
going on with the rampant violence and disorder from Protocol-11.

Before they entered the home, each one took a deep breath, sighed, and then walked through the door.

"Let's go in the kitchen," said Lauren, not wanting to remember Bishop Hines in any other parts of the house. Joshua and Jacob followed. As soon as Lauren got in the kitchen, the death of Bishop Hines, and even the death of her ex-fiancé, Mike, hit her. She was overcome with emotion and cried hopelessly. Joshua then grabbed her hand and held it as he wrapped his arm around her in comfort. Jacob cried as well.

"How do you do it, Joshua?" asked Lauren with failed attempts to stop crying. "How do you deal with all this death and pain?"

"I know Bishop Hines meant a lot to you, even Mike. So, it's okay to cry, Lauren," said Joshua.

"But you lost so much, more than any of us," said Lauren, with tears as she leaned on his shoulder.

"I die daily," said Joshua as he smiled and remembered Bishop Hines.

"I die daily," repeated Lauren.

"We die daily," said Jacob.

"We die daily," said Joshua and Lauren, collectively.

"So, Jacob. What's this special gift you may have?" asked Joshua.

"Yes, Jacob! Please tell us!" exclaimed Lauren, recovering with hope and wanting to hear some good news.

"When I think about someone, or more so when I touch them, I sometimes get visions of their past," said Jacob.

"What kind of visions?" asked Lauren.

"I think it's visions of an experience or event that was important to them. It could be good or bad or just something memorable like them holding their child after birth for the very first time, or at a funeral of a loved one looking into their casket." He then realized that was not a good example for the moment. "Okay, sorry about that one. Or even a sin they just committed, like stealing money from a register."

"Are you sure these aren't just thoughts?" asked Lauren. Joshua looked and listened attentively.

"At first, I did not. But now, after all that has happened, I believe a lot of them have been correct."

"A lot. Not all of them?" asked Lauren.

"Geez, Veronica Mars! I didn't know that this was a police interrogation," joked Joshua to Lauren.

"It's okay, Joshua. Sometimes, I don't know who it's about. I may see the vision from their point of view, so I don't know who it is, or other times it's hazy and fuzzy and I can't make out the entire vision."

"Interesting," said Lauren. She then looked at Joshua, and said, "Are you going to say anything? Any thoughts about this?"

He replied petty, "…for example…for instance…such as…what do you want me to say? I'm just listening."

"Just say anything, Joshua," countered Lauren.

"How do you think we can help?" asked Joshua.

"If you two are with me when I attempt to see these visions, that may help me remember more or allow me to see them more clearly. Remember, *where there are two or three gathered in his name, God is in the midst of us*, right?" *said Jacob.*

"Okay. What do we do?" asked Lauren.

Joshua took the lead and said, "Let's sit down and hold hands." Then, Joshua and Lauren sat on one side of the kitchen island counter, while Jacob sat on the other. Then they held hands.

Joshua further instructed, "Now everyone, close your eyes, take a deep breath, and exhale." So, they closed their eyes, took a deep breath, and exhaled. Then Joshua said, "Now Jacob. Repeat after me, Holy Spirit." Jacob repeated and followed his directions.

"Holy Spirit," repeated Jacob.

"Fill me and use me."

"Fill me and use me."

"This moment, bring all visions about Ezra and Protocol-11 back to my remembrance."

"This moment, bring all visions about Ezra and Protocol-11 back to my remembrance."

"In the name of Jesus, Amen."

"In the name of Jesus, A…"

Before Jacob even got to finish saying the word, Amen, the room felt like it spun around them twenty times at seventy-seven miles per hour. When it stopped, they all saw Jacob's visions and memories of Ezra and Protocol-11 simultaneously as the Holy Spirit revealed them to Jacob.

* * *

Jacob's first vision of the past – Marco – 21 years ago – Rome, Italy.

Marco, the caretaker, could not wait to meet her. For months, all Bishop Hines could talk about was his new beautiful female friend, Denise, who had the most compassion and care for those in need than anyone he'd ever met. And that she had this amazing ability to heal, unlike anyone in decades. This intrigued Marco, and the fact that she was single. His previous wife died from cancer, and she was also known for her charitable work and kindness to others, especially orphans and the homeless. He met her while they were in the military. She was a nurse taking care of wounded soldiers. He was one of them and they fell in love while he was under her care. After she died, Marco had no interest in dating or finding a new wife. He felt no one would ever measure up to the heart and love of his previous wife. Therefore, he spent all his devoted time assisting Bishop Hines with the home and taking care of guests who were obviously important to the ministry. That was until he heard of Denise. He couldn't wait to finally meet the lady that Bishop Hines could not stop talking about. And when he did, upon her arrival at the house in Rome, he thought she was even more beautiful in person. She looked like an angel, and he immediately fell in love. After he took her bags and got her settled in, he was more than excited to eventually spend time with her. He thought he could take her around and show her the sights of Rome, eat at its amazing restaurants, and hear all about her stories of healing and compassion for others. He wondered what he would wear; how he should act; how he would make the first move. He hadn't felt like that in a long time nor been on a date since his wife. He even went to a local dress shop and bought a new set of clothes that included a light brown vest and a colorful tie that wasn't necessarily his style. But the young female sales associate insisted that this new look suited him, and any lady would be impressed by it.

He patiently sat in the kitchen waiting for Denise to arrive back from her meeting with Bishop Hines and the *Concilium Iustitiae*. He heard how Denise saved Ezra and Archbishop Bennett from the priests who performed the unsanctioned exorcism and planned to kill them. This made Marco even more infatuated with Denise. During his wait, the doorbell rang. He was so excited and ran to the door to greet Denise, thinking it was her. But it was a delivery, a delivery for Denise. He was confused by it, but placed it against the wall, and then went back into the kitchen to wait for her. Then after a few moments, the door opened, and it was finally her. Denise walked through the front door and noticed the large gray box sitting up against the wall, placed there by Marco. Marco came out from the kitchen, and said, "Bishop Hines told me that he had to attend a meeting and to look out for a delivery for you." He was lying but he wanted something to say to easily break the ice.

"Yes. He told me the same," replied Denise.

As Denise continued to admire the box, Marco gazed upon her in the hope of gaining her attention. "If Bishop Hines is tied up today. I'd be more than happy to show you around, Signora Denise." He smiled waiting for her response. Unfortunately, Denise did not hear Marco as she sat on the floor in excitement and wondered what was in the box, like a kid on Christmas morning. "What is it?" asked Marco annoyed from seeing the surprise on Denise's face. Denise pulled the item out of the box. It was an elegant red dress with thick black lining, artfully decorated with embroidery and sheer accents, and definitely very expensive.

"Oh my god! This dress is gorgeous!" exclaimed Denise. Marco looked surprised. Denise looked back in the box and noticed another item. It was a matching red and black Venetian mask that would cover just the top part of her face. "What is this, a mask?" asked Denise as she turned towards Marco and finally re-acknowledged his presence.

"That type of mask is used for masquerading, such as a party or formal event where slight anonymity is encouraged. Is Bishop Hines taking you somewhere?" said Marco, seemingly disturbed.

"We are going to a carnival in Venice," said Denise, focused back on the dress and mask.

"*Carnevale di Venezia*," said Marco, surprised and disappointed.

"Yes. That thing."

"Elaborate costumes and masquerades are common attire for the Carnivale."

"I must hurry and get ready. But looks like I already know what I am wearing!"

"Indeed," said Marco in a softer tone, appearing that he'd rather be back in the kitchen.

"I'm sorry, Marco. What was your question earlier?" asked Denise, referring to when she did not hear him asking to take her out."

"Never mind. Is there anything else that you desire, Signora Denise?"

"No thank you, Marco." She then ran upstairs to try on her dress like she was in high school getting ready for the prom.

Marco fiercely watched her go up the stairs. He was furious. He thought since Bishop Hines has a wife, why is he taking Denise out to the Carnivale. He then clinched his fist tightly, walked out of the house, and slammed the door shut. As soon as he walked out the door, young Ezra was outside playing on the porch steps.

"Hello, Mister Marco. My dad is busy today. Do you have time to play with me?" asked young Ezra.

"Of course, Ezra," said Marco.

"Why do you look angry? You are too nice of a man to ever be angry," said the demon in young Ezra, as she smiled.

* * *

Jacob's second vision of the past – Denise & Young Ezra – 21 years ago – Rome, Italy.

Denise, Joshua's mother, led young Ezra from the tunnel into The Chamber. The same place where, just a few days ago, she and her father, Archbishop Bennett, were almost executed by a few priests who thought she was possessed by a demon. Denise stopped at the chains on the wall that previously held Ezra's father.

"I heard you were playing with Marco yesterday. Is that correct?" asked Denise.

"Yes. Marco likes me and I can get him to do pretty much anything I want," said young Ezra.

"You are quite resourceful. Because right after that, you hitched a ride over to Venice. Now, why would a little girl like you want to go over to Venice and hang out in Saint Mark's Basilica so badly? Would you like to answer?"

Young Ezra then looked around, concerned. "I don't like it here. What are we doing here?"

"I promised your father I'd help you. Being down here is part of your therapy," said Denise. She then pulled the keys to the chains along the wall out of her front pocket.

"Where did you get those?" asked young Ezra.

"After I saved you, I grabbed them off the ground when they released your father. Do you trust me?"

Young Ezra did not answer.

Denise then forcefully grabbed one of young Ezra's arms and placed it into the chains.

"What are you doing?"

"Don't worry, my child. This is a lesson I learned a long time ago that can help you with self-control," said Denise, convincingly.

"I don't like this," replied young Ezra, fighting back.

"It's for your own good," she replied firmly, as she secured one of Ezra's wrists locked in the chain, and then worked to secure the other.

"Stop! You're hurting me! Stop!" yelled young Ezra.

Denise got Ezra's other wrist secured and locked in the chain as well. "There. Now you can't go anywhere."

"I don't want you to help me anymore. Get me out of these chains, now!" the young Ezra yelled as she fought to escape them.

"Since you're a child, let's play a little game," said Denise, angered.

"I don't want to play any games. I want to go home! You're not nice, and I'm going to tell my father! Help! Help!" she yelled again and struggled to free herself from the chains.

"No one can hear you down here, little Ezra. And your father is far far away. The game we are going to play is called, Who Are You? I will go first. My name is Denise Williams. I'm from Philadelphia, right off the Boulevard actually; and I have the gift of healing..." She paused as Ezra stopped her resistance and listened with her eyes solely fixed on Denise's face. Denise continued, "...but when I met you and your father down here during the exorcism, I learned that I have another gift too. I had to look it up. I also have the *gift of discernment*. And as soon as I saw you on that table over there about to be killed, I knew immediately that you possessed her. I could see you…through Ezra' skin…through Ezra's bones…and even through Ezra's soul. I didn't see a helpless child screaming for safety. I saw a demon attempting to deceive all those around her. So now, it's your turn. By the power of God, I command you to tell me who you are!"

Young Ezra smiled and laughed. "Denise. Truly your God is with you. But for how long?"

"I gave you a command. Tell me who you are!" exclaimed Denise.

"I'm Agares. The Dark Angel and demon of earthquakes."

"Why are you here?"

The demon laughed, "Now that's a question that I don't have to answer. But I will. So long as you answer one for me. A question for a question…an answer for an answer. Deal?"

"What's your question?" replied Denise, agreeable but impatient, and without fear.

"If you knew I possessed this body, why didn't you say something to the priests? Why did you claim that my illness was for God to be glorified? Why did you reveal the priest's sins to them to show that God was with you and to save me and this girl's father?"

"I lied," replied Denise.

"You lied! No way!" yelled the demon, very surprised and skeptic.

Denise replied calmly, "I told you earlier I had the spirit of discernment. When I took a deep breath and exhaled, not only could I see the priests' greatest sins, but I also saw that if I confirmed to them that you were a demon, they would have immediately killed you. Well, killed Ezra. But I can still see her in that body. You may be in control, but she is still in there alone and afraid."

"So, you risked me continuing to possess her over her own life?"

"Not only would the priest have killed Ezra, but they would most likely had killed her father, Bishop Hines, and me as well just for being witnesses. So, I made the best game time decision that I could, given the circumstances. I lied to save us all. I just knew that I would have to deal with you later at some point, and that point is now." Denise paused, then continued, "I answered your question. Now answer mine. Why are you here?"

"I'm not here by choice but by chance. I was brought back into this earthly realm by Bishop Hines and Ezra's father, Archbishop Bennett."

"Bull crap! You're a liar and they would never do that!" yelled Denise in disbelief.

"It's true. But in their defense, they didn't know it. They were working on their sacred mission of obtaining the Light of Life…and oops… they let me in this world by accident." When the demon saw Denise still wasn't convinced, it continued, "They were experimenting in these water tank pods attempting to get as close to death as possible without dying. Drowning each other and saving each other, repeatedly, like two fools. Remember, thou shalt not tempt God right? Just like some people have done with Ouija boards, they thought it didn't work. But little did they know, they entered the *Sound of Silence* and because of the deception and greed within their hearts, it opened a portal to the *Spiritual Realm on my side, the evil side.* When I saw the portal door, I peeked in and liked the idea of finally getting back to this world. But I had no vessel to abide in, that was until eventually, little Ezra, God unbless her soul, walked in playing. One day, they brought her along with them and she got away playing hide and seek. But luckily for me, she walked in the tank room right before the portal door closed. So, I decided to use her body to bypass the travel-visa application process and hitched a ride in her. Those doors never stay open for long. And… Tahdah! Here I am. And while being here in Vatican City, I found out about a deep little secret of the Church. A secret about Basilica Papale di San Pietro in Citta di Vaticano. Do you want to know what that secret is Denise?" Denise did not respond. The demon in Ezra continued, "I know it's my purpose for being here, maybe even yours too, Denise. Will you help me?" said the demon.

Ignoring the words of the demon in young Ezra, Denise made multiple attempts to exorcise it and remove it from young Ezra. After many hours, she was unsuccessful and thought maybe her faith was not strong enough. The demon made claim to Denise that a demon of its strength was too powerful for Denise to exorcise alone. Denise thought that if anyone knew of this possession, the priests against Archbishop Bennett would definitely kill him, Ezra, Bishop Hines, and her. But if she did nothing, then Ezra would continue to be possessed by the demon. She then paused, took a deep breath, exhaled, and realized she could only do what she had enough faith to do.

"My faith may not be strong enough to exorcise you, but I do believe I have enough faith to lock you up," said Denise.

"Lock me up! How are you going to do that? You can't keep me in these chains forever," said the demon.

Denise then stretched out her hand toward the demon and yelled, "In the name of Jesus, a soul for a soul that this child may live freely! I cast and imprison this demon to where Ezra resides, and I bind its voice and actions completely shut within her!"

"A soul for a soul. You know what that means, right?" asked the demon in young Ezra.

Denise did not know. It just came out of her mouth without thought. She looked apprehensive.

"It means, whenever you die, I'm free and you belong to us!" exclaimed the demon as it laughed.

Not knowing what else to do, Denise replied, "So be it. If not me, somebody will figure out how to stop you. I bind you in the chains of bondage, now!"

At that moment, the demon and the young Ezra switched places within her body. Ezra immediately awakened with no memory of the demon or past events. The last thing she remembered was playing hide and seek in the asclepieia and walking into the water tank pods experimental room. The Dark Angel, demon of earthquakes, now bound, mute and actionless within Ezra, until…

* * *

Jacob's third vision of the past – Bishop Hines & Denise – 20 years ago – Philadelphia, PA.

Bishop Hines knocked on the door of Denise's hotel room. After a few seconds, she looked through the peephole and opened the door.

"Bishop," said Denise, somewhat surprised.

"Hello, Denise. Do you mind if I come in?" asked Bishop Hines.

"Not at all. Come in." Denise covered herself a little more as she only had a robe on from just getting out of the shower.

"I wanted to check on you before tomorrow's big day. Are you okay?"

"I am. It's not every day that you get to be a surrogate mother," replied Denise, cheerful.

"Sarah and I want to thank you again for this. She's truly glad you're going through with it. You're still going to go through with it, correct?"

"Only if you're having doubts about naming him, Joshua," answered Denise, serious.

"Sarah and I both agreed to the name Joshua. But what if it's a girl?"

"Then you and Sarah can name her. And don't you dare say Josheena again." They both laughed. She continued, "But I just have a good feeling that it will be a boy. Give little Mike a little brother and friend to play with, right?"

Bishop Hines was worried about the procedure. He asked, "Have you taken the vitamins and medications, faithfully? I know it's been a lot these past few weeks. But I think they will run a few tests before the actual procedure."

"Faithfully, Bishop. And I was getting checked regularly to make sure I was responding well to the medication. It's standard. They said I'm good for tomorrow."

He then sat on the bed facing her and said, "And this is the last time I'm going to ask. Are you sure you want to go through this via intra-uterine insemination?"

"You mean artificial insemination, Bishop?"

"I thought I'd impress you by remembering the proper medical term."

She chuckled. "Yes, I am sure. IVF is too new for me, maybe in a few years they will have that technology figured out way better than they do now, and they said this will likely be more successful the first time. Plus, I don't want to keep going through this again and again, and I do want to feel some type of naturality in this experience, especially with this being my first child. Does that make sense?"

"Of course it does."

"How about you, Bishop? Are you ready?"

"Oh, my part is done, they have it all there, and my little fish are ready to swim," joked Bishop Hines.

"That was not funny," said Denise, slightly offended by his joke. Bishop noticed.

"I'm so sorry. That was not appropriate, and I know this must be uneasy for you, especially with this type of process and all." Denise sat next to him on the bed and then looked up at his face, showing she was comforted by his words. He then stroked her hair slightly, and continued, "You are such a beautiful woman. Any man would be blessed to have you as the mother of their children, or even just to be with you for that to happen."

"Any man?" she asked, softly as she looked into Bishop Hines' eyes.

"Spending all this time with you, how could a man, any man, not wish to be with you?"

"Are you any man, Bishop?" asked Denise as she leaned into him, her lips almost touching his.

"I'm just a man," said Bishop Hines holding back his desire to kiss her. But that did not stop his hand from gliding down the crease of the opening of her robe, causing it to open and reveal Denise's chest, bare.

Denise was aroused. "Well, I've known you for quite a while now; spent more time with you than most. You seem more than a man to me; strong…powerful…dominant." Bishop Hines then leaned in and softly kissed her lips. She kissed him back, and said, "It's a good thing I have that appointment tomorrow," said Denise.

"Why is that?" he asked.

"Because we don't have to worry about what happens tonight," said Denise as she pulled her robe off her shoulders.

"Are you sure?"

"I think so."

"From my research, I think so too."

"Is that why you showed up here tonight?"

"Great minds think alike."

"Bishop Hines then got up and turned off the lights and took off his clothes. Denise, fully unclothed, helped. They got in the hotel's bed and passionately kissed each other. Bishop Hines got on top of Denise and looked at her and said, "My God. You look like an angel."

* * *

The early sun rose brightly through the hotel window and woke up Bishop Hines and caused him to grab his cell phone and look at the time. He had numerous missed calls from his wife Sarah and Archbishop Bennett. When he went to look at the text messages, three of them stood out more than the others. They were from his wife Sarah. He read the last three in disbelief.

[Sarah]: Hello? The news said another bomb hit a medical complex early this morning. I think it's where Denise is supposed to go today for the procedure or close to it. God I hope she didn't get there yet.

[Sarah]: Yes it's the same medical complex! She's going to have to reschedule for her next period.

[Sarah]: Where are you I'm worried. Call me now, please!

Bishop Hines grabbed the remote off the nightstand and turned on the television. The Breaking News on every local channel confirmed Sarah's text messages. Denise would have to reschedule her appointment as a bomb had gone off at the same medical complex where she was supposed to get her intrauterine insemination procedure. However, what Bishop Hines and Denise did together could not and would not be undone.

* * *

Jacob's fourth vision of the past – Mike – One year ago – Rome, Italy.

Mike walked back to the control panel and noticed the controls for the video. He hit the *Stop Recording* button and then *Rewind* and then *Play*. He heard the voice of the technician say:

"...Oh, and in addition to that, for centuries, The Circle has been searching for a man and woman that share a oneness to reverse the consequences of The Fall bestowed upon us by Adam and Eve. And if they agree to almost die, once or a few times, the Light of Life will awaken within them, save the world and bring us back to our true relationship with God. Oh, and by the way, the last time we tried this was with Bishop Hines and Denise Williams and that didn't work out too well either. It put so much strain on Denise's body and heart; it may be the very cause of her heart attack. Yeah, let's see how that works...Oh, and Bishop Hines, did you ever tell Mike that you're Denise's son's father? What's his name? Joshua. You both are playing with fire, and I'm not going to be the one that gets burned when it blows up in your face..."

Mike stopped the video and then clinched his fist as he felt unimaginable anger and rage. His own father, the well-known and respected Bishop Hines, had another son, Joshua. Joshua "Josh" Williams. His best friend growing up; and he had no idea. Mike thought, *How could this happen? Who else knows? Does Josh know? Does mom know?* He then walked over to the door to exit the room, grabbed the doorknob and with such anger and rage flung the door back so hard that it crashed against the wall with a loud bang.

* * *

Another memory started to show for Jacob, possibly another vision about Ezra. But this time with The Circle members, the underground of Vatican City, and Joshua. But the vision became very hazy and distorted and then stopped. It was too much for Jacob at this time. He came out of these visions sweating and gasping for air.

"Quick! Get him some water," said Lauren to Joshua with urgency.

Joshua ran to the cabinet, grabbed a glass out of it, and filled it up with fresh cold water from the front of the refrigerator. When Joshua gave it to him, Jacob drank it up so fast, like he was drinking directly from a keg at a college frat party.

"Are you okay, Jacob?" asked Joshua.

He nodded his head yes, as he caught his breath from drinking the water too fast. Then he said, "I'm good. Could you both see those memories with me simultaneously?"

"Yes," said Joshua and Lauren at the same time.

"I thought you could, but I wasn't sure," said Jacob.

"That was a wild memory trip," said Joshua.

"That's an understatement," said Lauren.

"Now we know how Bishop Hines became my father," said Joshua.

"And why it was kept a secret," said Lauren.

"It looks like Marco was in love with your mother as well, Joshua.

And Ezra, or the demon part of her, was at work fueling his hatred for Bishop Hines even at a young age," said Jacob.

"And my mother knew she was possessed. And hid it to protect everyone,"

"If not, they would have killed Ezra, Bennett, Bishop Hines, and your mother, Joshua!" exclaimed Lauren.

"She was a smart lady," said Jacob.

"But not enough power," countered Joshua. "So, she had the power to heal but not the power to cast out demons?" asked Joshua.

"It was about her faith, Joshua. It is possible to have lots of faith in one area and lack faith in another. Did you guys pick up the demon's statement that she found a secret within Vatican City?" asked Jacob.

"It was why it took me underneath Saint Peter's Basilica," said Joshua.

"I think I was getting another memory about Ezra, and this secret, and also you, Joshua, but it stopped," said Jacob.

Lauren interjected, "Well, let's not worry about that now. We have all the answers we need, and we have something more important to worry about…Hands Across the World. We must get ready for this event tomorrow and prepare everyone for The Great Shout. Protocol-11 is still in effect, and we are certain the world will go to war if we don't end all this soon," said Lauren.

Joshua agreed. "Okay. Let's get to work and give this world something that they have never seen or experienced, all in the name of God!" exclaimed Joshua.

25

Hands Across the World

Hands Across the World.

Joshua, Lauren, and Jacob woke up early to get ready for Hands Across the World. Lauren was walking around the house making calls to the events' region leaders and discussing last minute effort, which included the synchronization of their clocks, watches, and measured count down to the UTC or Coordinated Universal Time for The Great Shout. Joshua was in the kitchen on repeated virtual calls with over a hundred people at a time, from various nations, praying for today's event. Jacob sat on the stairs with his laptop as he leaned against the Roma statue, and posted on every possible social media site, popular blogs, and sending emails to any public figure or organization he could find in hopes of convincing those who were not previously going to participate to join. Before Denise and Archbishop Bennett died, they put together a thorough and organized structure for the event. Each country had a prominent and well known senior leader responsible for numerous lower level county or province event leaders, and those lower level leaders were responsible for numerous city event leaders, and those city leaders were the ones in contact with political officials, churches, non-profit organizations, and ground workers that all worked together, from designating territories or area markers where groups would gather and join hands to creating theme songs and colors for the event. Denise also came up with the idea for each region to have a boundary official to coordinate the holding of hands between different areas or boundary lines. This was imperative to keep the link connected with as few breaks as possible. A Mexican Christian aid group came up with the idea of using long lengths of rope with gloves stapled to it, representing hands, to connect groups that were separated by barriers such as streams, valleys, or walls. Even though Protocol-11 was still in effect, the Royal Australian Navy came up with the idea to situate their naval force in a line across the Tasman Sea to represent a connection to New Zealand; and then they placed another set of ships in a line on the opposite side of the continent towards Indonesia to represent a connection to South East Asia and its surrounding areas. And at 15:33, they were going to blow their foghorns, as loud and as long as possible, in support of Hands Across the World and The Great Shout. They felt, if the world was going to end, they would rather die representing and participating in the greatest world charity event ever, or be in position to fight, than hiding underground waiting to die. Other countries like, Brazil, Greenland, and parts of Africa prepared to do similar actions. There were a lot of countries that decided to focus on military and defense. But even in those countries, residents and officials still did everything they could to communicate with other regions, even enemies, to organize the event for their areas in land disputes. They heard about The Great Shout that was to occur and had hope. There was no other time in history where there were so many people from different nations, different religions, different races, different ages, working together for one collective purpose and goal.

When Lauren got off the phone, she yelled to Joshua in the kitchen and said, "How in the world did your mother and Archbishop Bennett put all this together? I can't believe how organized all of this is and how much they'd done already. From the dial-in and communication channels, the coordination between country and province borders, and even temporary lighting in time zones where it will be dark, the leaders all the way down to the local and street level have everything in check. We are ready for this event guys!"

Jacob got off the stairs, walked over to Lauren and answered, "Denise and Archbishop Bennett had been working on this for years; and they worked so well together. Both had such persuasive ways of communicating to world leaders and officials to participate in this great charity event or at least put someone in charge of handling it. Things always get done right when you start from the top and then go down."

Joshua walked into the room from the kitchen. He just got off another international virtual call. "Oh, my goodness. Hearing hundreds of people praying in their own language is one of the most beautiful things you will ever hear," said Joshua.

"I bet," said Lauren.

"I heard you two talking. I agree. But I can't believe how this didn't get much press and news while it was being organized," said Joshua.

Jacob answered again, "Remember, for everyone else, this started off as a charity event to raise money for child poverty and starvation. Also, you know eighty percent of the news only report the bad things going on in the world."

"The other twenty percent is the weather," Lauren added.

"Ain't that the truth," chuckled Joshua.

"Plus, you two have been dealing with so many other issues during the past two years. I'm certain you wouldn't have noticed anything referring to this. Your mother was a great woman, Joshua," said Jacob.

In the middle of Jacob sentence, the front door opened.

"Yes, she was! The best!" exclaimed Shary Fullerton, Pastor Williams' next-door neighbor as she walked into the house with her husband Franklin. Then, followed in the door Monty, Joshua's best friend.

"Josh!" yelled Monty, as he ran up to him and gave him a big hug. Everyone hugged each other in warm embraces.

"How? How did you all get here?" asked Joshua.

"After the bomb exploded at the Church's regional house in Bala Cynwyd, Franklin and I knew you were dealing with something bigger than any of us could have ever imagined. So, we immediately came here to help."

"Well, not immediately. We've been working on getting here for a few days, and our connections here finally came through. Right in time for The Great Shout," said Franklin, smiling.

"You have connections, here in Rome?" asked Joshua.

"Boy. Franklin and I have been coming here with Bishop Hines, way before your mother Denise," replied Shary.

"You and your mother are not the only one with supernatural gifts," said Franklin, as he smiled again.

"Lauren and I have them too!" exclaimed Jacob.

"Wait. Am I the only one that doesn't have supernatural abilities?" asked Monty as he looked around at the group.

"Joshua. So many people are already outside gathering and lining up for Denise's event," said Shary.

"You can even see them gathering down on the ground from the plane. It looked amazing," said Monty.

Lauren then gave direction and said, "It is 12:02 [PM]. We have approximately six hours before all governments initiate Protocol-11's global martial law. That means curfews, arrests, and I'm sure more violence will immediately follow. In addition, we have three hours until Hands Across the World officially begins, and we need to make sure it goes on without a hitch. We cannot delay," said Lauren.

"It's good to know the local leaders had everyone mobilize and gathered super early," said Jacob.

"And then on the turn of time of exactly 15:33 Central European Standard Time, all nations across the world will shout, yell, and scream at the top of their lungs!" exclaimed Lauren.

Joshua added, "Oh, yeah, I almost forgot. On the calls this morning, it was relayed that people are acknowledging that, if they are not in a Hands Across the World line at the time of The Great Shout, they will blow their horns, bang pots and pans, set off fireworks, or do anything to make noise during that time."

"Awesome!" exclaimed Monty.

"That means we have approximately three hours to finalize anything left. How can we help?" asked Shary.

The group continued to talk. However, Jacob was focused on his attempt to recollect that last memory vision that was unclear and got cut off. He had a gut feeling that it was the most important memory of them all.

* * *

The group of Joshua, Lauren, Jacob, Shary, Franklin, and Monty made it to the highest point of *Collis Aventinus or* Aventine Hill, one of the seven hills of Rome. They felt that was the best place in Rome for them to connect with others for Hands Across the World and for Joshua to use his great shout. They greeted the hundreds of people already on the hill with hugs and handshakes all in hope of change. Despite Protocol-11 and the smell of smoke from all the fires persistent in the air, the world appeared peaceful, at least for the moment. They linked hands with everyone, and everyone participating in the event around the world did the same. Tens of millions of people of different nationalities, races, languages, and hometowns, all holding hands with one another at exactly 15:00 Central European Standard Time. Expressways and streets filled with people getting out of their cars holding hands, malls filled with links unbroken from level to escalators to other levels, dark neighborhoods with six to twelve hour differences from Central European Standard Time with individuals, families, and children holding flashlights and lit candles, now all praying for the entire salvation of the world. Some who prayed daily, others who never prayed a day in their life, now praying together with faith having expectations of a better life, a better world. Like Joshua said, the sound of millions of people crying, and praying at the same time in their own language, and even in their own way, or the only way they knew how, was the best song that could have ever been recorded in time. It was such a divine event, all of heaven, God, the seven spirits of God, the heavenly hosts, angels in the light, demons and evil spirits in darkness and in the shadows all looked on at the earthly realm silent and still waiting to see what was about to happen, which side would triumph and the other mourn.

* * *

Then, right before the main event, Joshua, holding Lauren's hand had an epiphany. He looked at her and smiled. She looked back at him and smiled back. Joshua then broke the chain and got in front of Lauren.

She looked at him confused and said, "What are you doing? It's almost 15:33!"

Joshua looked at his watch and said, "It's 15:28. So we have five minutes to pull this off!"

"Five minutes to pull what off?" exclaimed Lauren, as everyone near them looked on.

Joshua then walked up to Lauren, bent down on one knee, and said, "Lauren. My soul loves your soul. Will you marry me…right now?"

"Right now!"

"Yes. Right now."

Shary then looked at Franklin, then looked at her watch, and said, "I knew we were here for more than one reason. You can perform a quick ceremony in three minutes, right Franklin?"

Franklin concurred, "Of course, I can. Will you help, my lovely lady?"

Shary replied, "Of course!"

Joshua then had a thought. "Wait. I need a ring! Do you have anything?" he asked, as he looked at Monty and Jacob. But they both looked at each other, helpless.

Then Lauren got even more excited. "Joshua! I have a ring! I think it belonged to your mother. I found it in the room back at the house and have been holding on to it ever since. Is that okay?" She asked with the hope that Joshua was not upset, as she pulled it out of her pocket still wrapped in cloth. She unwrapped it and then showed it to Joshua.

"Oh, my goodness. That is my mother's ring! I haven't seen it in years. It's perfect," said Joshua.

"Honey, let's do this. We have two minutes left. I will do the ceremony introductions in one minute, and you handle the vows and the seal within the last minute, okay?" said Shary.

"We have a wedding!" yelled Franklin. Everyone around them cheered in joy.

Shary and Franklin performed the expeditious wedding ceremony. Monty was crying more than anyone. Once Joshua and Lauren said, "I do!" and kissed, the alarms on everyone's watches and cell phones went off, all synchronized for the moment and time of The Great Shout. Joshua and Lauren got back in line, and as instructed by Denise, hundreds of millions of people paused, took a deep breath, and shouted with a great shout! The entire world screamed and yelled at the top of their lungs as loud as they could. Others blew their car and truck horns like trumpets. Ships pushed out the sounds of their foghorns as loud as possible. Little children screamed with all their might. Those deaf and mute stomped their feet into the ground. Those that were handicapped and unable to full speak clapped their hands. Those that were paralyzed screamed as loud as they could within their heart and soul.

Joshua intentionally waited a few seconds to join in, remembering his mother's words in his dream. Then the earth began to shake, and the sky let out a rolling thunder greater than ever heard. At that moment, Joshua knew it was time. Everyone was lined up soldier-course style, side by side, on one accord with God in the midst of them. Joshua then took a deep breath, exhaled, and yelled with his Great Shout, joining in with the rest of the world. His shout, combined with everyone else's, vibrated the land in front of them for miles, then vibrated towards the river and for miles to their backs, and then traveled in both directions, to his left and to his right, through the people's arms and hands causing them to shout even louder with a great and powerful vibration as well, and throughout the world.

In the heavens, Archangels Gabriel and Rapheal were each ready to blow their trumpets. But God told them to yield and remain silent, as it was not yet the appointed time.

Then suddenly, from The Great Shout, the Vatican City's walls crumbled to the ground. And other walls like it, all around the world, broke apart and crumbled to the ground as well. The Great Wall of China… The Walls of Constantinople in Turkey…The Great Wall of Gorgan in Iran…The Mexico-United States border walls…The West Bank Barrier…and *continued mighty through God to the pulling down of strong holds* until all old and newly built barriers, walls and self-contained city structures either fell or crumbled to the ground. Then, the land above the secret underground cities broke apart like large fault lines revealing them from above ground, and any residents already in them either perished or praised for their survival. Violently strong winds came from the heavens and blew across the earth and the seas with great tropical force. From this violent wind storm, everyone felt the atmosphere shift. When they did, they stopped screaming and shouting and making noise, and then looked around silently, and got quiet. Fear came upon them as they did not know what was about to happen next. Then, silence covered the earth.

* * *

The Lord is in His holy temple; let all the earth be silent before him. Then the great heavens opened up, and God Almighty looked down upon them and smiled. He then paused, took a deep breath, and exhaled, and blew his Spirit upon the earth and all its people that participated in this great event. And it filled their soul and sat upon each of their tongues as fire. All of them were filled with the Holy Spirit and began to speak in other languages and tongues as the Spirit gave them utterance. Sons and daughters immediately prophesied. Old men dreamed dreams. Young men saw visions, and the wonders of heaven and earth were shown in visions to all. The sun was turned into darkness, and the moon was turned into blood, and it came to pass that whosoever called on the name of the Lord at that moment was saved. And many called out his name!

* * *

It was glorious and marvelous to witness. Then suddenly, Jacob fell into a deep daydream and vision, and had a clear and complete vision of the memory that was previously cut off last night. When he came out of his vision, he yelled, "The Prison!"

Joshua heard Jacob, and then he remembered with fear Agares' words, '*It's inevitable Joshua! You will free him. You will free my master, The Wretchedness!*'

Lauren heard Jacob's scream and felt the change in Joshua. She stopped praising God and said, "Don't tell me..."

Joshua followed up her statement, yelling amongst the wind and the praises, "...the demon in Ezra was right! When evil arises, the balance of life will always create an equal and opposite reaction force of good. When good arises, the balance of life will always create an equal and opposite reaction force of evil!"

Then the Holy Spirit took control of Shary, and she said, "Yes, Joshua! Your soul was broken, but you did not give up! And from your soul's brokenness, you found your great shout!" She then softened her tone and said, "And now, this great day must be balanced as well. It is the balance of Evil and the Light of Life. A balanced equation that will remain until God ends this earthly world. But fear not! The Word of the Lord says, *'And I saw a new heaven and a new earth: for the first heaven and the first earth were passed away…every knee should bow… every tongue should confess that Jesus Christ is Lord'* and that is when our God will win forever," she said, referencing the various scriptures of the end of the world mentioned in the Bible.

"What does that mean?" asked Monty.

"It means, other than the death and resurrection of Jesus Christ, there was no other greater event of good than today," said Lauren.

"It also means that we're about to face an evil that is just as great," said Joshua, as they all looked down to the ground and noticed a large fault line that cracked open the earth, leading all the way from Joshua's feet to the ruins of the former Saint Peter's Basilica.

Suddenly, there was a loud high-pitched piercing sound. This piercing noise was so loud that it caused everyone to cover their ears and scream in pain. After a few moments, it abruptly stopped; but with it, all sound had been removed from the earth and the atmosphere. People tried to talk, yell, and scream, but no sound came out of their mouths. People stomped and struck objects against each other, but no sound could be heard. Then, large fiery meteor balls scorched the sky and fell hard to the ground causing great impacts, but again with no sound. The meteors set fires to the land, buildings, and everything near them, yet made no noise. Then, thousands of birds fell from the sky across the world. Everyone ran screaming in fear, but no screams could be heard. Joshua tried yelling at Lauren, but nothing came out of his mouth. Lauren tried to speak as well but could not be heard. Jacob put his fingers in and out of his ears in attempt to hear something, anything, but it did not work. *Jacob then remembered that the exact same thing would happen to him when he had a nightmare and nothing would come out of his mouth when he tried to scream.* The world was completely silent; sound no longer existed. The *Silence of Sound* had covered the earth.

Then, Joshua grabbed Lauren's hand and pulled her with him as he ran following the fault line crack from his Great Shout towards the ruins of the former Saint Peter's Basilica church. Once they arrived, Joshua and Lauren could see a massive crater at least seventy-five feet deep where the church once stood. The spiritual prison and tomb had been broken, broken by Joshua's Great Shout. Agares, the demon in Ezra, was right. *The Wretchedness* had been set free.

26

Late Mourning

Six months after Hands Across the World.

Law and order no longer prevailed as it had been months since The Great Shout, and sound had been removed from the earth. Some believers felt God took sound completely away as punishment for mankind's sins, deception, and selfish desires. But most people, including scientists, logically believed that everyone had become deaf and lost their hearing from some unknown phenomenon that occurred in space, like a supernova, a massive star collapsing and turning into a black hole. But for that to happen, it had to occur over a billion years ago and light years away and with its gravitational waves coming in contact with earth's atmosphere at the same time as the Hands Across the World event that caused the high-pitched, eardrum crushing piercing sound. However, it would explain the meteor showers and dead birds falling from the sky. It would not explain why audio frequency machines could not read or perceive any sound waves. Others, such as faith believers, those who received salvation during the great shout, and monster-believing or supernatural conspiracists, believed it was the scream of The Wretchedness, as it escaped from its spiritual prison underneath Saint Peter's Basilica after almost a thousand years in captivity. Whether true or not, the world knew sound no more and was forced to learn sign language, communicate by writing via phone and other devices, including artificial intelligence brain to writing prototype display devices.

At this moment, nation leaders, military officials, and research scientists were on a global video call with an attempt to recover from the horrific events of the past few months that had occurred after Hands Across the World and The Great Shout. Writing teleprompter displays and sign language were the only two communication streams. The President of The World Restoration Council, a newly created organization to handle the recovery and isolation of disaster areas all over the world, was in the middle of his pre-written displayed presentation that in part displayed, "…with that, all prominent astronomers, scientists, geologists, physicists from MIT all the way down to Buckey's Bible Community College, have confirmed that the unexplainable natural disasters that occurred during the infamous Hands Across the World charity event and great shout, had such an impact and vibrating occurrence to the earth's axis, that the earth has deviated from our universe's *inverse squared gravitational law*, and is now on a different and dangerous trajectory path closer towards the sun, maybe even to it. I must have missed a bunch of physics classes; because before last week, I was unaware that if our universe was on any other gravitational law than its current, then all the planets in our solar system would collide. Needless to write, it is an improbability that our planetary system has existed for millions of years, and earth has sustained life. Now I know some of you use this as a claim as proof to the existence of God and the recent events as Biblical. Frankly, I still side with the experts who don't believe in this great shout nonsense and believe we experienced a supernova and a large meteor beyond the size of a mid-sized state that hit earth, most likely in one of the great oceans, causing this catastrophic situation. Either way, we are now traveling off our revolutionary course by a slow and minor deviation. So, here's the bad news, the good news, and the horrible news. The bad news is that at some point we will be travelling deathly and destructively close to the sun, maybe even directly towards it. We also may collide with a few planets along the way. The good news is that we calculate no immediate danger, at least not for another three years…give or take six to eight months. The horrible news is that the earth's daily rotation is slowing down as well. We currently estimate that the earth's rotation could slow down to at least one second per day, or approximately one second every twenty-four hours. Lucky for us, any faster than that and we would fly off the earth from millions of years of its inertia. Unlucky for us, within a few months, our days and nights will become longer and could eventually come to a complete rotational stop within forty years or much sooner. If you're still not getting any of this, let me add color and paint a picture for you. We are headed towards the sun; and in a matter of months to a few years, one side of our planet will be completely uninhabitable from very long to endless nights and freezing cold temperatures, while the other side of our planet will be experiencing very long to endless days and extremely hot temperatures. The game show, *The Floor is Lava* is about to become our new reality, and so much for those stupid college research papers and political debates about global warming. Now, I'm going to turn it over to a few people that are a lot smarter than me to give you the research data, analysis models, and rates of change, that I like to call, a bunch of guesses that ain't worth a pile of cow dung!" He then punched the monitor in front of him that displayed his last written words, knocking it to the ground. The scientists took over the connected monitor displays with their prepared statements and to answer questions.

* * *

Back in Philadelphia, Joshua and the group, finally had time to mourn and conduct proper memorial services for all those that died before the great shout. Pastor and Angela Williams; Bishop Hines, Mike Hines, Officer Reese and other police officers; ATF members; and the assistances of The Church. Before they left Rome, they put together a memorial service for Archbishop Bennett, Marco, and even Ezra, as well as the few staff workers that were killed from the explosion in the asclepieia. But before all of that, along with some Roman Catholic clergy members, they retrieved Ezra's dead body and confirmed that The Wretchedness' gated prison was cracked wide open from The Great Shout, and its tomb was empty. Some of the priests conducted written and sign language council session meetings and made claimed that The Wretchedness was real and spawned from the numerous demon possessions of one of the great giants mentioned in the book of Genesis or other books not included in the Bible for this very such discrepancy or lack of hard and verifiable confirmation. Other priests denied the existence of this demonic entity. They laughed and said that the tomb was always empty; and the story about The Great Legion locked under Vatican City and eventually turning into The Wretchedness was only something used for centuries by the Roman Catholic Church to scare world leaders and dignitaries into conceding its authority, including donating its most treasured religious artifacts. So, who again is being deceived? Either way, Joshua, Lauren, and the rest of the group knew that The Wretchedness was real and on the loose and was about to cause havoc and terror upon the earth, and they had no idea how to stop it. But planet earth had its own set of problems. It traveled toward the sun with the possibility of slowing down and ceasing its rotation, thus changing the definition of day and night, and even the whole concept of time. Some argued, and others wondered, is this what was meant biblically by hell being cast into the lake of fire? Would finding a new planet to inhabit as the only means of mankind's salvation confirm a misinterpretation of the scriptural prophecy found in Revelation 21:1, where it states that God will set up and create a new heaven and new earth? If so, does this mean that the prophets of the Bible, over thousands of years ago, could only interpret their visions, including the end of the world, just like The Circle, based on the limitations of their time's knowledge and science? Like seizures possibly being interpreted as a person being possessed by a demon, or a cave filled with radiation being interpreted as evil or cursed to all those who entered, or even thinking the sun was a godly being or a lake of fire that the hellish world would be cast and thrown into, instead of it just being a ball of continuous gases and fire with other stars just like it millions of light years away? Maybe, maybe not. What they wrote was true for them, based on what they knew. We should not be deceived or incorrectly judge their writings based on the biases of our own time and knowledge. If we do, we could be making the same mistakes as some unbelievers. But within this story, a few things are for certain. The gifts of God are real and are fully activated within Joshua and Lauren, just like Jesus spoke believers would be able to do, even greater works than himself. The Great Shout happened and The Wretchedness has been set free! More people believe in God now than ever before and evil has equaled its threat, thus confirming the balance of Evil and the Light of Life. The world is about to experience the most dangerous and destructive events, and no one can communicate with sound or even hear it. If there were any two led by the power and Spirit of God and could figure it out or stop it all, it was Joshua and Lauren, with the help of Jacob,

Shary, Franklin, and even Monty.

The End…almost.

* * *

It was chaos. Violence, evil, hunger, sickness, extreme temperatures, and silence covered the earth. As the earth's rotation continued to slow down and on a trajectory path towards the sun, populations scrambled to figure out what side of the earth to be on and how to get there…

…amongst the crowd, a little girl tugged on the stitch of Joshua's jean pants. When he looked down at her, she used sign language to ask him, "Have you seen my dad?"

Joshua used his hands to sign back, "Who is your father, little girl?"

She then signed, "Father Bennett. My name is Ezra."

Joshua and Lauren woke up…

◊◊◊

"And the devil that deceived them was cast into the lake of fire…and death and hell were cast into the lake of fire…and whosoever was not found written in the book of life was cast into the lake of fire."
– Revelation 20:10;14-15

www.ingramcontent.com/pod-product-compliance
Lightning Source LLC
Chambersburg PA
CBHW031322210726
48287CB00005B/1652